The Widow's Son

The Widow's Son

Lies and Consequences Book 3

Daniel Kemp

Copyright (C) 2018 Daniel Kemp
Layout design and Copyright (C) 2018 Creativia
Published 2018 by Creativia
Cover art by http://www.thecovercollection.com/
This book is a work of fiction. Names, characters, places, and incidents are the product of the author's imagination or are used fictitiously. Any resemblance to actual events, locales, or persons, living or dead, is purely coincidental.

All rights reserved. No part of this book may be reproduced or transmitted in any form or by any means, electronic or mechanical, including photocopying, recording, or by any information storage and retrieval system, without the author's permission.

Other Work By This Author

The Desolate Garden
Percy Crow
What Happened In Vienna, Jack?
Once I Was A Soldier

Novellas
   The Story That Had No Beginning
   A Shudder From Heaven
   Why? A Complicated Love

Three Children's Stories
   Teddy And Tilly's Travels

Never read the words as they first appear,
Seldom in life are words honest and clear.
I could take you to a place where all words are true,
But only if love has touched the heart of you.
Parables are recitals with a story inside.
Ingenuous exposition but how many are lies?
The understanding of secrets is not only what you need.
Belief in the truth is the only way you'll be freed.
Daniel Kemp

The Widower's Son
We speak unto you by parables, but would willingly bring you to the right, simple, easy and ingenuous exposition, understanding, declaration, and knowledge of all secrets.

Chapter One

Part One

The Fourth Day of December 2002
Henry Mayler's Opening Story

"Let's get one thing out the way before I go any further, Mr Elijah man." Henry took a sip of whisky from the glass on the table in front of him and the service stenographer noted the pause in Mayler's account by adding a single blank space as he stopped speaking. Her normal way of dealing with such things was a single blank for brief, with a double-blank meaning a pause of some length. Before she could contemplate the occasions she had used a triple blank space, Henry Mayler had continued.

"It was me who was effing shot at Al Hasakeh on your behalf. I'm here as the injured victim of an operation that went wrong. Anyway, now that's said I'll get back to the story. After what happened in the bazaar I was acutely aware of the danger I had put myself in, but if there was to be any reaction I was expecting it inside the market, not outside. In my haste to get away I tripped over something just before getting to the car. My knee hurt badly and the fall shook me up but I managed to stand quickly and open the car door. That was when the glass in the door shattered. I had no idea what had caused it as I had heard no sound. For a split second all I could do was stare at what was once a normal car door, thinking it was something I'd done that broke it. Other than the normal loud noises of a packed Arab market I'd heard nothing that would indicate someone would be after us so soon. When I eventually got my head into gear the first reaction was to partially turn my head towards the back of the car, that's when it hit me. The only way I can describe it is that it was like having a cricket ball bowled very hard into my upper thigh. It hurt like hell. A similar thing happened to me when I'd played in a varsity cricket game in the Parks one year against a really quick bowler. I know this will sound stupid and melodramatic, but time seemed to stand still for me. Everything was moving in slow motion to the point of stopping.

"The bazaar went silent to my ears. I have no idea why I looked to the rear of the Mercedes and not the front, but that's where I looked. I was lucky in some ways as the bullet had hit hard muscles and was imbedded in them. I was thankful to have done lots of walking and standing in my job as a photographer. There was very little blood coming from the wound and just a small hole in my shorts and my upper leg. It was as I was looking at my wound that he pushed me into the car. I was completely dazed and out of it all. He was the opposite. He just stood there in the open, firing off round after noisy round in the direction from where the bullet in my leg must have come. He was shouting, but I haven't a clue what he said. All I could see was his mouth opening and closing very quickly. My ears were hurting from his gunshots as much as my leg from the bullet. The firing stopped and I had a peep through the back window. I saw one of them. He was black, but not an Arabian black. Perhaps a European black going by his modern, stylish clothes. He was on the ground and not moving, but there was another man running away in a zig-zag fashion.

"That man was tall, thin and had blonde hair. Hadad, that was my driver, was also on the ground by the rear door of the car.

He was lucky, having taken only a grazing shot to the shoulder, and was meekly seeking cover. I helped him to stand and opened the door for him to get in. He lay across the backseat holding his shoulder. Then the Russian drove the car as though possessed with its tyres screaming under clouds of dust.

"It was I who noticed the car that was chasing us. Razin, the Russian, had his eyes notched up five times their normal size and fixed like glue on the road ahead, for that I was thankful; the car was travelling as if there was a rocket under the bonnet. I told him we were being followed and he pulled a gun from under the thawb that he wore. There was another gun, I presumed that to be the one he'd used outside the bazaar, tucked under his left leg as he drove. I remember thinking that I hoped the safety was on. Very calmly he told me that as soon as he had a chance he would pull our car off the road and ambush the one behind. That wasn't the exact language he used, but that's what it amounted to. He spoke in Russian but I can understand the language. He gave me the gun from under his leg and a new clip from the trousers he wore under the robe. He asked if I'd fired a weapon; I lied and said I had.

"We rounded a sharp bend, passed some low, sandy hills and then the road turned abruptly right in the opposite direction we wanted to go. Razin slung the car behind one of those sandy hills off the road and shouted at me to get out. Clutching his gun to my chest I did. He ran across the dusty road and hid. From across there he had the clearer shot than me and hit the driver before the car had fully rounded the bend. It veered violently towards me before it overturned once, then righted itself and came to a halt. I shot the passenger from where I'd been hiding, but Razin got to the car before I had and I saw him take something from the driver. I have given thought since then about what it could have been, but honestly I have no idea what it was other than it was small and flat like a phone. But I can't swear it was a phone.

It could equally have been a letter. In fact, I think it was a letter. After he put two more bullets in them both he set the car on fire and we drove off, not speaking again until we reached Aleppo. I had the shell in my leg removed when I was taken to the British Embassy in Damascus. The stitches are due out tomorrow and my limp isn't so noticeable anymore. Is that enough for you?"

"Right, yes, thank you, Henry. We were both enthralled," Elijah announced as he left the room holding the door ajar for the stenographer who followed, leaving Henry Mayler alone with his thoughts and his whisky.

* * *

If one leaves a single word on a blank sheet of paper seldom will it convey much in the way of meaning. This was how the in-house service stenographer had begun the typed recording of Mayler's story. One word at a time, until they started to make sense. The meaning they conveyed became a sentence that could stand on its own much the same way as a writer of fiction would construct a sentence.

Gradually the sentences she typed became paragraphs resembling the opening chapter of a work of prose. The collection of words that made those paragraphs were never enough to form a cluster of chapters, nevertheless, in more ways than one, the fantasy had begun and the writer of fiction had a story to tell.

This book is simply a collection of single words that left alone would have survived without a meaning.

Daniel Kemp

Part Two

Friday Six Days Later

Have you ever noticed that no matter how much the sea changes from mountainous stormy waves to the friendly calmness that could bore a conch shell into silence, it always returns to that monotonous hollowing sound of a wind through a tunnel. However, on some occasions that hollowing sound seems to represent the chanting of an echoing death that's waiting for me below. That's how it is in my way of life. Up and down and down and up without any indication of how it will all end.

I was at home, on the sofa, watching recorded rugby games when the telephone rang. The career I had chased after like a demented dog had descended from four years of stormy hell, where bells were ringing both inside and outside of my head every day, to almost six solid months of solidified boredom in my apartment doing nothing and hating every moment of nothing. But I didn't want the change he offered over that telephone line. I was in what was politely called the latter stages of convalescence, due to a bomb going off in a pub in Ireland I'd had the misfortune to be sitting in. The prospect of going back on the front line, so to speak, was what I was waiting for, not what Geoffrey Harwood held aloft as his incentive. The repeating referee's whistle on the television was hammering my brain to death as I tuned in to Harwood's idea of normality.

"Ezra, how goes it, old man? Fit, well and healthy I hope?" Without waiting for the answer he already knew, Harwood ploughed on.

"Ready to dirty your hands again, are you? Good." Again, I had no chance to reply, not even to comment on the dawn-shattering timing of his call. After the friendship I and a man named Job had shared, I wondered if all ex-military men were cursed with an inbuilt early morning alarm clock.

"I've been holding your medical report back for about a month now, Ezra. It says you are fitter than an average Tour de France cyclist, but I thought you deserved a bit of extra leave, dear boy. Your stint as commanding officer in Northern Ireland has not gone unnoticed. You ran things extremely efficiently over there. How do you feel about taking control at *Group*, old chap? Big enough job to suit those talents of yours, do you think? There's bags of prestige to be had being in charge of one of the top four intelligence agencies, enough even for your inflated ego. A much more favourable stipend than you are receiving now and far better stability than at field control in a hotspot like Northern Ireland, albeit that it has quietened down a lot over there. At Group there's the worldwide intrigues to keep you interested. And then there's the Home Office parties to mingle amongst if you're unlucky to be invited. No, dear boy, I jest. I've had some wonderful evenings at those parties."

"I can't think of anything I'd rather not do, Geoffrey. Right at this moment I'm watching a tedious game of rugby, but even that's better than what you propose. I told them at the debrief I would not welcome a sedentary job. That was in the report they produced. I saw it. You must have read it. So what are not saying and what do you really want me for?"

"Ah, you can speak. Thought you'd died of shock. Right, got you, old man. First I want you to drive to a public phone box and call Adam. How's that for a daily bout of exercise? Adam will direct you elsewhere for you and me to meet. Please make sure nobody is following you to the place Adam points. Of course, I shouldn't have to tell you that, but you have been lazing around for some time and may have forgotten what you are supposed to do in circumstances such as these. We are off somewhere far from grand, dear boy, so wear something more suitable than a dinner jacket. I don't want you attracting unnecessary attention."

Despite the usual ludicrous pomp and ceremony that Mr Geoffrey Harwood employed as the present head of Group, I did not accept the reason he gave for such a needless warning.

"Jack Price once told me, Geoffrey, that if the person doing the following was any good at their job then they'd be practically impossible to spot. In the last six months the only trips I've made have been back and forth to a posh clinic that's looking after my medical welfare, and to the local pub that looks after my mental side. I doubt very much that I rate a 'very good' or clumsy idiot come to that, to shadow me. But what is bothering me is why the need for so much secrecy? This line has been cleared as secure. The engineers were here two days ago, on Wednesday, working their little machines over the whole place finding nothing. I'm a recovering invalid, nobody is interested in me. Can't you stop being so long-winded and tell me what you want, old chap?" I threw in the 'old chap' bit as my way of being sarcastic. It worked!

"No, I can't. Why can you not do as I've ask without comment, Ezra? You are so predictable." He stopped and I could sense his eyes staring at me through the phone for daring to use his snobbish means of address. "Your intransigence can be so dull after a while. I know how much you have missed us, and I also know how much you needed that break, but I'm serious about you taking on the responsibility of Group. Your performance over in Ireland was spoken of in high places and in my opinion your retirement was pencilled in far too soon, old chap. I'd positively hate to wave you goodbye. I think we can squeeze a good few more years out of you in a home based office not risking your nuts being shot away out on the street. We can leave that sort of thing to the young at our stage of life, I think you'd agree. It's your experience they need, Ezra, no good seeing it wasted and you ending up watching the piss-up at your own wake. I'm pleased you mentioned dear old Jack Price. We're in desperate need of his sort, but as he's dead, we'll have to put up with you as second choice." I thought I heard a faint snigger of a laugh, but never having heard him laugh I thought he must have brushed his stubble against the handset.

"You're all heart, Geoffrey, and so eloquent and persuasive."

"Good, that's that then! Go find a phone box, Ezra, and call Adam, dear boy."

"I'll go and wind the crankshaft of the old jalopy in a jiffy, just got to find my goggles and scarf. Both she, the car that is, and I hate the cold weather," I replied caustically.

"Phone box, dear chap. Take some coinage with you and leave the sarcasm in your flat," and with that the line went dead.

* * *

A few months on from my birth I was christened Patrick West by my parents, but over the thirty plus years I have been engaged in covert operations for Her Majesty's intelligence service I have used a few other names: Shaun Redden, Paddy O'Donnell, Frank Douglas and Terry Jeffries or, on the one that finished six months and a few days ago; Jack Webb. On that last tour in Ireland I was in charge of all operations against the Irish Republican Army and its spin-offs; by now, however, I'm a self-taught expert on daytime television. My operational name has been changed so many times by the hierarchy in charge of Group that it was becoming more and more difficult to remember the script and the role I was meant to be playing, whilst dodging the enemies' radar for the benefit of Kipling's Great Game for our great nation. During this last period of enforced leave I've been on the sick list but it's called a different name in the corridors of power that the likes of Geoffrey walk up and down. It's known as the surgeon's list. This is the second time in my career that my name has graced that assembly. Not bad I suppose, but nobody counts the negatives and gives away gold stars for not being sick, that's taken for granted.

In my case the surgeon has never been a surgeon, but he at first, and then she for the second time, had no need to explain the lack of scalpels. They tried coaxing the screaming voices from my head by sweet talking me, not cutting me open. They called it cognitive therapy. I called it meddling in memories that were never mine to give. On my last visits to the clinic the cognitive therapy was supposed to quieten the repetitive yelling that belonged to the girl of seventeen who had her eyes gouged out for the simple reason of dating a British soldier serving with the catering corps in Derry. A month after that attack I attended her funeral. Her constant screams of pain were permanently terminated by the serenity found in the blister strips of painkillers she was prescribed, only she emptied the whole packet of fifty pills in one go washed down by a cheap bottle of gin. For me, however, her screams will never die.

After a few days of sitting beside that girl, questioning her whilst she fiercely battled against the acceptance of her blindness, I went to see a man who told me of the whereabouts of an IRA bomber of a Belfast pub. That bomb killed three and maimed five fellow Irishmen and two women in the name of freedom from Protestant choice. By the time I got to him he had entertained some members of the Ulster Volunteer Force who had nailed his feet to the floor and his hands to a wooden beam above his head then set about removing his reproduction organs by savagely hacking them from his body and as that was not enough for their shared pleasure, they slowly peeled away his facial skin. I wonder how murder and mutilation can be justified in using such terms as freedom for the oppressed while suppressing those who disagree with the philosophy of force. I would have gladly asked the hierarchy of the IRA, if I had been given permission to go and find them. But I'm a man after all and none of what I've told you should have affected me, should it? That's what I'm supposed to do, isn't it? Be the hero that

Geoffrey Harwood reveres. Bite the bullet and sing 'God Save the Queen'. After all people like me should be the first through the doors to count the bits of bodies hanging from the ceilings so that the reports in the daily newspapers get the sums right. That's what we're paid for, right? But there were times during that last tour that left me thinking I was getting slower through the door and laying the blame for that on having only half of one foot. The other half had been shot away, but I do try to keep swinging on door handles, after all, who would appreciating reading there were fifty-one dead when someone had missed a body or two?

The foot thing was one of the reasons for my first visit to the surgeon's rooms in the clinic in Harley Street. I lost three toes to a bullet when on the very first mission I undertook on behalf of the SIS, Secret Intelligence Service. It was meant for my head but in the wrestle for his gun the shot took my toes off. It was when I was recruited for that mission I met Jack Price and the ex-soldier I've mentioned by the given Biblical name of Job for the first time. That adventure, and all subsequent ones were of my choosing, losing toes was not. Another reason for my first visit to the clinic was because I killed the man who had shot my fictional twin; the girl who had become very dear to me. I watched her die from a bullet that took most of her head with it when she was sitting in the passenger seat of the car I was driving in New York. When all that happened I was a baby of twenty-three years of age. Time moved on and others died for other causes, three more at my hand, but any feelings I had for the death of others were depleted from any remorseful side I may have been born with. I watched death and destruction from the distance I constructed to keep myself safe, unconnected to anyone.

But not this last time. Not on the *Green* for my fourth tour— *No one does four tours in that shit hole of Ireland, Webby. So nobody will be looking for you.*

Over the Irish Sea I went, not looking for anyone except the bastards who bomb the innocent for their version of freedom. But Ireland being Ireland, something beautiful will always emerge. Kerry found my weakness after I'd been there for less than a month. Hers were the latest and hopefully last screams the surgeon wanted to pull from my head. I played the man of courage, saying there were none, tucking them away in a place to find sleep, but everywhere was overcrowded. I awake to pictures of Kerry with her agony of both knees and hands shattered by hammers before being raped and the word TART slashed across her breasts. So what's a little drive to a phone box compared to running from IRA cell to English cell, ducking the inquisitions at both ends by the grace of my two-toed right foot? Metaphorically speaking of course, because I never ran. All I was supposed to do was gather the intelligence, collate and make sense of it then decide what others could do in response. Nothing safer, eh! How about lying on the floor of a pub amongst the carnage of desolation after the detonation of a nail bomb that kills the man I was speaking to only four foot away and leaves me with one kidney less to siphon the evil whisky through?

During that six months' idleness of mine I had managed to keep physically fit and in shape using the apparatus Job and I had added to a room in my apartment when he'd stayed for a few days. It had become part of my daily routine, but it wasn't my physical side that bothered me as I grabbed a hat and coat and waited for the lift from my top-floor apartment. It was that mental fight against the crashing waves of memories that flooded my head at times with no escape other than forming their own scream. But men aren't supposed to find bitterness in heartache, are they? I did though. When the lift door opened I shut the screams away and went in search of a new life-conquering telephone box.

* * *

The brief conversation I held with the normally gregarious and chummy Adam, who I hadn't spoken to since returning from Ireland, was concise and cold. The opposite to what I'd expected—"67 Lavington Street, Ezra. I know you know where that is. Jacob said to be as quick as you can," and then silence apart from the sound of a replaced receiver. He could have just been having a bad hair day, he was that way inclined, although I thought I detected a hint of bitterness in his voice as though he resented my call for some reason.

Adam was the connection operatives such as I used for the verification of orders plus those things beyond the reach of ordinary soldiers. Ezra was my assigned Biblical label, while Jacob was the soubriquet of whoever sat in the chair overseeing Group. I never had enough of an interest to enquire into the motives or calculations for everyone who worked directly inside that secret organisation to have a biblical name. The 'point' of any decision is for others to justify and find a cause. It was not mine. There were a host of similarly constructed names; Job being one. Jack Price worked outside of Group for a separate party who held the shared interests of putting the British Isles above all else. I could, as a man on the spy as it was known, appreciated the need for covert arrangements, but asking me to visit an established, well-known company location would put a face to a name and was tantamount to declaring my decision to leave the service. Had I refused Geoffrey's 'invitation' my dissent would have brought about the same end result; resignation. Whereas by going to the appointment, I turned the word resignation into the phrase of retirement from street work, with one hand holding on just in case it hadn't completely disappeared as the yearly manure added to St Stephen's *Green*, in Dublin, Ireland no doubt had.

Chapter Two
The Borough

Number 67 was halfway along Lavington Street notable by its boarded up windows and general dilapidation to the upper two floors. The sign on the plain black-painted door was broken; reading 'undry Supplies' which I presumed meant Sundry, rather than something wet. I could identify two distinct company cars with four indeterminable men inside, amongst the parked vehicles along the street, making my prognosis of retirement all the more probable. But why two, I wondered? One would obviously be Harwood's car, but I was at a loss to explain the other one.

This part of London, known as the Borough, was undergoing a huge redevelopment agenda giving rise to many properties left to decay in outward appearance but appreciate in value. I wondered if that was the decision behind its continued government use. The lack of a bell push came as no surprise, which along with a dreary sense of melancholia rekindled my dislike of every government that had reached the power they sought since my coming of age and how little had been spent on improvements anywhere. I knocked loudly, using the hooked end of the walking stick that in the cold of winter I found more and more obligatory owing to the pain in my foot. A light shone from the camera lens, beside the door, and a distorted voice addressed me asking who I was and to show some identification. I did, and as all was considered to be in order, a buzzer sounded and I was instructed to pull open the heavy door. It closed decidedly quicker than it opened.

I was standing in front of a thick glass transparent screen which crossed the whole width of the passageway. Beyond the screen stood five armed Ministry of Defence guards. To gain entry into this secure area, and subsequently the whole of the building, one had to pass through an electronic scanning machine. The place had changed!

I was in charge of an operation from here some eight or nine years earlier when Geoffrey Harwood was Director General at Group and when a Scotsman named Fraser Ughert was Chairman of The Joint Intelligence Committee, or JIC. I was working alongside one of the men I previously mentioned; Job. Being used to shortened names, Job and I christened what was a hovel in those days, The Hole. That was when the walls were covered in graffiti, bare bulbs were dangling from single wires giving off a cold dim light that cast murky shadows wherever its impalpable glare failed to reach, and rats could be heard scurrying around on the two floors above where we worked. That was then, when devices to examine what's under clothes did not exist, well not in places like The Hole. Now with its battleship grey painted walls and downlighters sunk into smooth plastered ceilings with the ornate coving restored to its Victorian beauty, I was waved through the twenty-first-century contraption into the guarded winding corridor. As I was thinking how wrong I was about quintessential government stinginess, I was addressed by another one of the guards.

"Good morning, Mr West, sir! They are waiting for you in the basement." *Who told this man my name? Does everyone I've passed by in here know it?*

Totally confused by my recollections of the past and unable to focus on any actuality, my disjointed thoughts took hold.

Was I still out on the 'spy' trapped by some shit-arsed official Irish Republican Army terrorist group who were fishing for a name and threatening me with a gun? *What to do next? Training, man! Training. If it's there, use it.*

Reeling from the shock that my body and mind was in, I stepped backwards as though making room to swing a punch into his throat to disarm him, use his weapon first then my own and shoot my way out the front door. That's what I was taught. If caught, shoot them all and get away, half a foot or not. I felt for my holstered, service issued handgun, but it wasn't there.

Why am I unarmed? Was Adam so unusually matter-of-fact because he and Harwood were working together and I was in a trap of their making?

Perhaps it was remembering Geoffrey's name that switched my mind into logical thought. My gun was left the other side of the glass screen. Of course I had left it there, *I'm on service premises, you fool.* If the sentry thought I was insane his manner never reflected it. He carried on as usual as this garbled mind of mine speculated as to the *they* whom the guard referred to. Were they beer swilling Group disciples waiting to condemn me to an office on the back of a sausage roll party? Or a party of Group's finest interrogators wanting to know the names of my agents to pass on to the Irish desk at MI5's prestigious property on Millbank?

That's why I'm here without a sidearm. It's clocking-off time and playing the clown in appreciation of a ring-fenced, inflation-proof, armoured-lined pension. I couldn't be bothered to ask who the *they*, who waited for me, actually were.

I headed off along the well-worn stone floor in the direction of an under–the-staircase door which Job and I never opened but always smelled of damp when walking past it towards the noxious toilet. The staircase had gone. There was no door!

"I'm sorry, but there's nothing in that direction apart from the boiler and service areas. The lift that will take you to the basement is over here, sir," my personable guard politely told me.

Feeling rather conspicuous by both the awkwardness of my movement and the raw naivety of my surroundings, I turned to see a door that simply blended into the side of a painted wall. The guard pushed it and as though anaesthetised I entered and pressed the *Down* marked button. Quite a few seconds later the door opened onto a far more spacious open area than where I'd left. What appeared to be bank after bank of droning electronic television screens greeted me. In front of these flickering machines sat lines of motionless headset-wearing figures. Some were quietly speaking into their microphones, others were staring straight ahead. On the furthest brick wall was yet another screen but unlike the others. This one took up the space of the whole wall, made up of smaller screens mounted together with the pictures alternating between seemingly unrelated sites then switching to one enormous location I'd seen on the smaller screens.

The place smelled of artificially warmed air with a whisper of the standard authorised civil-service disinfectant. It was neither pleasant nor unpleasant. It was just another impediment of an office job. From this huge central surveillance area I could see six opaque glass-door-protected corridors leading off in opposing directions. On the walls in between each spoke of this imaginary wheel were more television screens that kept switching from one scene to another. The two middle screens on each of the walls were showing overhead shots of a barren, sandy terrain devoid of movement other than a few birds on some expanse of water in the far distance, and the second, the inside of what appeared to be a fairly busy airport departure and arrivals lounge

17

with people going to and fro carrying, or pulling, suitcases of various colours and sizes. I was gazing around, open-mouthed, when one of the glass doors opened with Geoffrey Harwood standing in the opening.

"West, how splendid and on the same day as invited! Welcome to the Hub, come through." He turned and I followed like his pet dog waiting to be patted on the head and shown where to sit and beg. I didn't have long to wait. After a short walk along the softly lit passageway he turned left and entered a spartanly equipped large office that had a fresh appeal to it I had not experienced elsewhere.

"Take a seat," he instructed as he walked behind the centrally positioned white marble topped desk supported either end by two matching rounded white pillars. In front of this monument to power were four soft white upholstered, wingback chairs. His seat, the *Joseph* seat, was a red and yellow leather wrap-around, tilting chair that he delighted in showing me how it effortlessly rolled across the floor.

"Better than the last time you were down here in the basement, eh?" he asked, spreading his arms wide to encapsulate the whole room.

"I never came down here, Geoffrey. I thought there were only rats living down here." As I sat I thought better of that childish comment. "I had better stop making stupid, derisive statements like that, hadn't I?"

"Yes, I think that would be wise. Let's get down to future business and forget the past, shall we?" I nodded my agreement, but could not resist smirking as I moved my chair closer to his throne.

* * *

Until roughly a year ago my role within the secret service had demanded being on my own or part of a small team answerable to a single master. During the last eight years or so of my covert operational usefulness of being *on the spy*, Geoffrey was that master, but I hadn't always obeyed his instructions. Geoffrey was one of those who cared passionately about the correctness of, and suitability of a person to an assignment and the willingness to agree to his uniformity of thought. I didn't always do that. My regard centred on how the operation could be accomplished without my, or any other, unnecessary death.

He explained how the position I was being offered became vacant because of his promotion to the chair of permanent secretary to the Her Majesty's Minister for Home Affairs, becoming the one that the Director General of Group would have to ask before dropping a bomb on someone or the need to replace civil service toilet rolls. Not only does the Minister rarely know about those sort of things that I and my like do during his or her five years of elected tenure, he or she is dissolvable. Whereas Director Generals of intelligence departments are not. They are immutable, unless the lure of retirement beckons too strongly. Up until now it has been the order of things that Harwood, and those who went before him, and those who will follow, are the ones I must listen to and comply with, albeit in my own way. He removed his heavy framed spectacles, picked the sleep from the corner of each eye then gently massaged the bridge of his nose. He began as he replaced his glasses.

"A package arrived at the Russian Consulate in Notting Hill Gate last Monday. The Russians have him listed as an under assistant trade attaché, but unless Hampshire has fallen into the English Channel he's anything but. He certainly is not here to underwrite trade agreements. I want you in charge of finding out what he's up to and why, that is, Patrick."

Instead of directing his gaze at the screens on the wall, he paused to look at me as if he was expecting me to say something. The lines of age were drawing their patterns across his tanned forehead and around his mouth and eyes, which were of a cloudy iris with dull hazel pupils. Despite the amount of time he spent in the gym the skin of his neck had creased as had his once taut but now heavy jowls. His voice and alert manner may have belied the truth of his years but his features could not deny the severity of it.

"We have him registered as a spook and an important one at that. Fyodor Nazarov Razin, a full lieutenant general with rows of medals of honour to his name. He is an old school Moscow Centre trained hood. His relatively narrow file records him under that name with the appendage of Raynor as his working code. As I said, he arrived at the consulate last Monday and has visited the Russian Trade Delegation on Highgate West Hill each day since. He goes nowhere else, Patrick. Which is strange to say the least. The Delegation premises have been on statutory watch for donkey's years and the Russians have known of the house opposite since the day we unloaded our camera equipment. There was no point in trying to keep it secret. It's now an automated site, permanently staffed by two lamp-burners from this department who spend all day drinking tea and eating my budget out of biscuits. The Russian General's travelling arrangements have not altered one iota. Tube to Charing Cross, an unhurried stroll to the Savoy for a late breakfast, then on to the Silver Vaults in Chancery Lane and when finished in there, a number 191 bus from High Holborn to the Swains Lane bus stop at Highgate. He then walks sedately up the hill to the Delegation. Likes a walk, does our Mr Raynor hyphen Razin, but not as far as the Karl Marx family's tomb in the cemetery. Strange race of people, the Russians."

The 'wall' along the passageway to this office had appeared to be solid as we walked along the corridor but from where I was now seated I could make out the shadowy silhouettes of those I had seen in the Hub moving about their business; however, I could discern no sound. There was no obvious means to deaden the noise, no acoustics tiles lining the ceiling, walls or floor, nevertheless Harwood's usual gravel voice was softened and slightly faint. Normally, after this amount of time spent listening to him, I would have the start of a headache. I wasn't fearful of one just yet.

"We see him walk out of the Consulate and then in at the Delegation at Highgate, with not much in between. We know where he goes, but he caught us flat-footed on that first day. We had British Transport cameras in Notting Hill Station and Charing Cross to review, but neither were of any use. Crap stuff really. There was nobody on watch or notified at the Savoy in the Strand and no eyes inside the Silver Vaults at Chancery Lane. Apparently, he had the full English at the Savoy including that disgusting black pudding thing they serve. He washed it down with a pot of English breakfast tea. Not a drop of vodka to be seen. I have assigned cover to each of the locations now, but …" His voice died away and was replaced by a languid sigh. I said nothing, waiting whilst he gathered himself until at last he could continue.

"Even though this Raynor file dates back almost twenty years there's not a lot in it. Our first sighting is logged as being in Istanbul in 1983. Incidentally, before I get too far ahead of myself I have arranged for the Home Secretary to telephone us here to officially appoint you as Director General of Group." He checked his ostentatious gold watch. "Any time in the next thirty minutes Oliver Nathan will declare you in charge of this place and the offices at Craig Court, Westminster, but not the offices at Greenwich. I have set something up there that I'm taking as the outside source to my new role. I'm unsure of its practicality to me and I may offload it in your direction at some point in the future. That's of course if it doesn't go with the new me, old chap."

Another groan, followed by the removal of his spectacles, holding them up to the light this time to check the clarity. He waited until satisfied before going on.

"After you have accepted Oliver's gracious offer I will require you to move into the rooms on the two newly furnished floors above the entrance to this building." He stopped speaking and glared me, daring me to argue. I didn't, thinking that my overused sofa at home might recover from the indentation in my absence.

"Your current apartment at Canary Wharf cannot be sufficiently secured for what your new status will require. Unless that is, the government buys the whole block," he laughed. I didn't. "That's not going to happen, Patrick, no matter how long a face you pull." At first I thought that remark was aimed at my lack of appreciation of his 'buying the whole block' comment, but I was wrong.

"No, in fact you may come out this considerably richer. I can recommend a man in the Acquisitions and Disposals sections of the Audit Office who knows absolutely everyone when it comes to buying and selling property." *Why am I not surprised at that, Geoffrey?* I thought.

"That's for the future of course, for now upstairs is secure and the available rooms are perfectly habitable for a short period of time. A long way from the shabby mess they were in your day, I can positively assure you of that." I swear those thick grey eyebrows rose a full inch as he emphasised his importance and his renowned faultless memory.

"Did you ever stay in those upstairs rooms, Geoffrey?" I asked scornfully.

"I did not, no. There has been no need for me to stay, but you do have a need, Ezra, so we will dispense with any implied disadvantages of the working-class boy that may be developing in that contemptuous mind of yours. From this day on you are one of us, old man; a giver of orders as you were in Ireland, only now on a far grander scale. You now have a size twelve shoe-print on the upper floors of HM management, got it?" He didn't wait for an answer, he was not used to people disagreeing. Onwards he ploughed.

"I will give you a cursory introduction to the facilities and staff on duty today. However, we are on the starting line so to speak, so you will have to familiarise yourself at a later date. As you've no doubt noticed, this is a state-of-the-art establishment. I instigated and designed it all and had it overhauled and updated in the spring. Your personal assistant will be the one to fully brief you on the toys and gadgets I've installed, but for now let me show you one. In here," he was leaning over towards the lower drawer of the desk, "there is a push button. Dig around a bit and you'll find it. If I were to press it, like so, up pops a high-security safe from the floor. How's that!" Abracadabra, up popped a tall, grey polished safe beside his chair.

"It is unlocked by fingerprint identification and a key." He threw it across the desk. "Your prints have been uploaded to system. Don't lose the key. It's the only one in the building. Copies are kept somewhere, but it would take a decade to find them. In the security operations room, the SOR, you passed it when you entered the building, there is another safe, a combination one. All documents, both into Group and away from Group, will be held in that safe, not the one here. This one is for the in-house, top security, Director General eyes only. Once a day, at varying times chosen by you, a courier will attend and papers being forwarded on will be handed over to him or her, and incoming mail distributed from that operations room safe by your duty officer. Your PA, along with the station and duty officers are cleared to A Grade classified level of documentation. All communication above classified and addressed directly to you as Director General Group will be in cipher and can only be read in the Pink Room." My eyes lit up in surprise, expecting some flamingo-dressed girls as waitresses in there. I asked the question.

"Are the drinks served by scantily dressed maidens waiting to see to my every need in that room, Geoffrey?"

"Don't be silly and try not to think about sex every second of the day, dear boy. The room is not pink and in fact it's not a room. It's a secured cubicle behind a door off your dayroom beyond this office. Where was I?"

"Talking about paperwork, Geoffrey; as always—old boy." A narrow-eyed stare was my punishment for that remark.

"All paperwork will be locked away when finished with in either your safe here, your PA's safe or the combination one in the security operations room. No casual behaviour with my precious files will be permitted." He paused for breath. As his chest expanded he clasped his hands together behind his neck, rolling his eyes towards the ceiling as his head was pressed firmly backwards into his grip. It was from that position he next spoke.

"If you remember nothing else remember this, Patrick; I remain your boss. As permanent secretary to the Minister for Home Affairs it's my role to keep the wheels turning without disturbing the minister from his political duties. You report to me and only me. I will not tolerate the peddling of trivia. I am not one of the pettifogging civil servants that no doubt you will come across. Got it?"

A light was flashing on a multi-coloured console sunk into the surface of the desk. As I hadn't a clue as to the meaning of the word pettifogging, I was pleased for the interruption.

"Press it, dear boy. It will be Oliver. We are on speaker but nobody outside this office can hear." I followed his instructions and as I listened to the Home Secretary I was subjected to the hostile Harwood stare. He was waiting to pounce as my final, "Thank you, sir," left my lips.

"Both inside this address and controlled from this address, you have a variety of expensive equipment at your disposal,

Patrick." He looked concerned, as the furrows on his forehead grew deeper.

"Perhaps I should call you Joseph now, dear boy. Let's see how we go, shall we. Solomon, your station officer, can fill you in on the subtleties and capabilities of that equipment along with the open loop to GCHQ. Please, use it all prudently and whilst you're finding your feet ask either Solomon, or the duty officer Abraham if you're unsure about anything. Do not antagonise the Americans." I interrupted him at this point.

"Was all the expensive gear made in America and leased from them, Geoffrey?" I tried to appear disdainful in dismissing my own country as the place of manufacture. It worked.

"Most certainly it was not. Made within the shores of GB and stamped with the Queen's monogram. English technology mixed with a bit of Scottish innovation, as I understand."

"Fraser Ughert must be pleased then." All I got was a wearisome *hmm* as a reply to my introduction of Fraser's name.

"Look after the personnel here and do not encourage them into your questionable habits. Your old name of Ezra has been returned to the database awaiting reassignment sometime in the future. That incidentally is now one of your duties." Did I detect a slight tone of regret there and if so what for? I tried to prise him open.

"Strange day to pick for an appointment of this kind, Geoffrey; a Friday. I would have thought Monday would have been far more suitable. Perhaps an introduction to the place today with some walk-throughs by the station officer or his deputy over the weekend, and then I'd have more time to absorb all of it. Is there an urgency that you're not willing to divulge?"

"No, no urgency at all, dear boy. The truth is today's perfect for me. I'm not in town over the weekend and those plans of my appointment are set in concrete. There is no possibility of anything of mine being rearranged." I had always found that if there was a need to repeat something then something else was being covered up.

"I am to sit at my new desk on Monday, so it was today or put it off until I had my feet well and truly under the table in the realms of Whitehall. It would be impossible for me to run both departments in tandem for the time it would take to be settled into my ministerial work."

"Jolly hockey sticks for you then, and sod me, is that about the strength of it? You have certainly dropped me into the mire with this one. The whole of this place to assimilate with staff to get to know and a top-ranking Russian spy on the prowl. That's a lot to deal with first up. Anything else to unload on me, like the Russian fleet about to drop anchor in Portsmouth?" He smiled broadly and simply shook his head.

I had not had enough face-to-face meetings with Harwood to appreciate any change to his nature, but I did know that he hadn't always occupied a desk inside the security services of this country, in fact, my closing route into Group had not been dissimilar to his own.

* * *

In November 1989 Geoffrey Harwood, then aged forty-nine, was outside of a small town named Belcoo, near a crossing between the north and south of Ireland waiting for a car carrying the two members of the provisional IRA responsible for killing eleven Marine musicians at the Deal Army Barracks, in Kent on the mainland of Britain the previous month. He'd had a tip-off. They had been in hiding in the south, but unfortunately for them their brigade commander wanted them back to inflict more bloodshed upon the Protestants of the north. They were warily taking the circuitous route favoured by Irish terrorists returning from atrocities to the relative safety of Belfast. In those days, Geoffrey was in the same role as I had been; blending in with all around, *on the spy* and operating on his own.

The grey coloured Ford car was on time crossing the unguarded border and was carefully approaching Harwood's parked, battered Land Rover on the Sligo Road at a little after three o'clock on the autumn morning. As nobody could be seen inside the suspect vehicle, the driver of the Ford increased his speed with renewed confidence. Nevertheless, time spent in murdering others had taught them to keep their Uzi machine pistols close at hand.

Geoffrey was three hundred yards further on from his Land Rover, well hidden in a shallow trench he had prepared behind the stone pillar of a gateway leading into a field used by grazing cattle. When the car was almost on top of him he powerfully threw a newly designed tyre shredder across the carriageway, causing all four tyres of the Ford to burst and the car to slam heavily into a ditch twenty yards on. On reaching the vehicle Harwood withdrew the two syringes of the toxic Botulinum poison from the small bag he carried. It was the standard service issue toxin in that day and age. Both syringes were emptied into the IRA murderers whose heads were embedded into the broken windscreen. Next, he carefully unscrewed the caps of two metallic tubes that remained in his holdall until they made an audible click. These he laid side by side inside his bag on the rear seat of Ford. He sprinted back to his Land Rover before the pale greenish-yellow liquid slowly emerged from one. As he drove hastily away from the scene towards Belcoo, another car approached on the same side of the road as the crashed Ford. The colourless gas from his second phial mixed with the coloured liquid at the precise time that extra car stopped beside the crashed Ford. There was nothing left of either vehicle and nothing recognisable left of the bodies inside the Ford, but parts of the two bodies from the other car were identifiable. One was a woman of twenty-four years and the other, a child of five.

The number of times Harwood visited the *surgeons'* clinic was not recorded in his personal file nor was there any medical prognosis, but Adam, in one of his 'need to gossip moments', had declared that the incident had led Geoffrey to be obsessed with detail.

'Before all that happened he was never interested in the specifics of how an operation was to be undertaken. He just wanted the who and the where and leave the rest up to him, but not now he's been shunted home to Group and placed in charge. When he was out on the streets he was good. But now it's all numbers to him. Even the number of paperclips needed before Branch has finished with a folder is itemised. He's a pain in the arse, Ezra. They have a name for it. Obsessive compulsory personality disorder, OCPD. His is the obsession with perfection.'

If Adam had my security clearance, and read of the circumstances of Harwood's experience in Ireland, he might have looked at Geoffrey's subsequent behaviour less critically, but, then again, I never came across a side of Adam's nature anything but confrontational and at the end of the day does any assassin give a toss about what a psychiatrist called a surgeon thinks of them, because I certainly didn't.

* * *

My attempt to extract more from Geoffrey on the timing of this appointment had not worked; his renowned reputation for stubbornness was well earned.

"As you are Group's official Biblical Joseph, Patrick, I think it's time to change seats." With that royal pronouncement he rose from behind the multi-functional desk and with another melodramatic sweeping gesture offered the chair to me. I remained where I was.

"Why so much interest in this Russian going between two points that are well known to us, Geoffrey? Surely if there was anything of interest he would be going somewhere we do not know of? Can't a detail out of *Faction*, at MI5 do their job and simply follow and report on him?" He stared at me as would a father at his dull-witted child.

"No, I think not and I wonder about your powers of assimilation, dear boy. This one is a big fish swimming in our pool, Joseph. Note the word—our. He would spot a follower and what's more, expect one. He's fresh out of Syria with a hands-off sign plastered on him by the Yanks. Oliver doesn't like that, nor do I. Oliver wants it treated by Group before other departments become too deeply involved, i.e. we do not want 5 and their guns looking at our Raynor. Okay?"

His fingers started tapping the top of the desk where he stood with his eyes flashing towards that watch of his. He seemed to be in a hurry, but as I only had old rugby games to watch I didn't move.

"If you're not feeling in a symbolic take-over mode, Joseph, let's involve your man Solomon and have a quick breakdown on what's going on around the world." Another theatrical wave directed towards the door. I still wasn't budging.

"At this stage, Geoffrey, I have no wish to know who Solomon may be, and I'm not moving anywhere until I know why this Razin, or Raynor, is so special that he warrants me giving up my sofa and my televised sport."

"It is simple, dear boy, look upon it as one more job for Queen and country that requires your deft hand of experience. Nothing more than that, I can assure you. You are the exact man for the work. After it's finished you can triumphantly pat yourself on the back for your outstanding efforts in Ireland and if you wish go home." He had moved towards the office door and opened it ajar, letting in the sounds from the Hub. His voice became more distinct and louder as his fidgeting increased.

"Originally, I was instructed by those above to invite you to a slap-up meal to celebrate the highly complimentary remarks coming their way from the Home Office after the Sinn Féin member Donald Donaldson opened up fully to the Northern Ireland enquiry. Using him in the way you did was a pure work of genius. He will be suitably taken care of when he's finished delivering all that's been siphoned away. The talks in Belfast are going well, with the concessions coming along just fine. I'll tell you the truth, Joseph." He held on to the long chrome door handle, still keeping it ajar.

"When your name was first put forward I was against promoting you to Controlling Officer, Ireland, but I must give credit where it is due. I had you marked down as nothing more than a meat and potato street plod. A good plod I grant you, but only as good as the next Irish bullet. Despite my misgivings I have to bow to your commendable action in the CO Ireland seat." Another pause. His silence coincided with some sort of isometric exercise pushing clenched fists into alternating hands, thereby leaving the door to softly close, accompanied by an electronic clicking of the lock to the safe before it retracted into the floor. He passed no comment on his toys.

"Partial retirement packages had been settled upon, dear boy. Withdrawal from the line with a peaceful few years ahead overseeing some NATO dispatches, or a seat at the American desk at Vauxhall and then it goes pear-shaped as they say. Up pops one of old Fraser Ughert's pet poodles. A certain Armenian German chappie by the name of Henry Mayler. Who else other than you could I appoint as Director General at Group at this point in time to look after him?" He looked at me for an answer, or perhaps some sign of gratitude. When only a quizzical look was forthcoming, he carried on.

"The arrival of the Russian package is a pain in the backside I'll grant you, but he comes second to Fraser's operative. Mayler is a German with strong Armenian roots. Top drawer material and once again exclusively ours, or more to the point—Ughert's. Mayler is who we are off to see when we can finish with the formalities here."

I butted in. "Henry, Geoffrey? Sounds more English or French than German. And he's a long way from Armenia. Did he lose his way?"

"Complicated situation and I'm only too pleased to confess to my incomprehension of it all. You, being Ughert's pseudo son, or at least close relative can put his mind to it and unlock the secrets. Case notes are in your floor safe. Most of the documentation on Razin is in here." He went to open the top drawer of the shiny chrome filing cabinet that stood alone against the wall by the doorway opposite the desk. The drawer wouldn't open.

"Ah, yes! I should explain. When your office door closes the whole cabinet will lock until opened from the console built into your desktop. Incidentally, this door," he held the long chrome handle once more, "is opened from the corridor by your palm print, an ingenious device fitted to the wall. I had absolute control over all the gizmos installed and the interior design of the whole Hub. In the dayroom, adjacent to here," he pointed to his right, "that you will have to see some other time, I installed a lot more ultra-modern equipment, all in keeping with the rigours of the job you understand, dear boy. Nothing beyond the necessary parameters. At a push you could use the dayroom on a permanent basis, but it wasn't designed for that. It was intended as a place to think and ponder."

That was Geoffrey Harwood's world. The one where methodical systems were the key to success; pigeon-holes filled, but never overflowing. Rooms for a lie down and rooms for sleeping. Safes popping silently in and out of hideaway locations and press button A for a shave and B for the tissue paper to stem the blood. I almost burst into laughter before I successfully managed to push away images of him locking and unlocking doors to test whatever technological devices were on the other side. Happily I managed to focus on business rather than upset him.

"I've got this Russian Razin in one corner of my mind and the English named Armenian German in the other, but I've got nothing to connect them, Geoffrey. Why are we going to see this Henry Mayler chap and not knocking on the Russian Consulate's front door?"

"There was a bit of trouble involving the two of them about a week ago in Northern Syria. Ughert dealt with it by extracting Mayler. Razin hyphen Raynor, please don't forget the file name, made his own way here. When we're all finished with Mayler we're posting him off to Canada with all the relevant legend materiel and a fistful of gratitude. It's being finalised as we speak. What you need to find out is what led to that trouble in Syria. Why, is another question we should be asking. Hopefully you can find it in Berkshire and in Uncle Fraser's notes which are neatly filed for your later pleasure in here, dear boy." With theatrical aplomb he opened the drawer smiling as he did so, which I never knew he was capable of doing.

"You can read them when you finally use Joseph's chair or, if bored, stretched out on the heated spa bed in the dayroom of which I am completely ignorant."

Bored by standing, he returned to what was to become my chair. As he sat he inadvertently allowed it to swivel, slightly causing his mouth to gape open and the mousey eyes behind his glasses to open wide in surprise. Settling into a more balanced position he continued in his appraisal of the situation.

"The wheel needs to spin, Joseph." At precisely that moment the blue light on the inset console started to flash.

"I think it would be best if you take it sitting here, dear boy, and that way the game can begin in earnest."

Chapter Three
The Farm

A modulated female voice informed me that the cars were waiting and I confirmed that Geoffrey and I were on our way out. No more than five minutes later I had shaken hands with everyone Harwood introduced on our rapid tour of the operational floors and, surprisingly, the domestic ones. Geoffrey had his high-speed skates on. Two very important people were missed out: my station officer and my personal assistant, both of whom I was told were importantly engaged. We then left the building and went to meet Henry Mayler housed on the farm outside Brightwalton, in freezing cold Berkshire.

"Why the need of two cars, Geoffrey?" I asked as we drove over Blackfriars Bridge in single file with four police outriders as escorts waving us through red lights. I wondered if this was the way Geoffrey would travel all the time when he'd moved into the powerhouse of politics or only when he wanted to impress some minion.

"I'm heading straight for home after Berkshire. I wouldn't want to leave our new Director at Group floundering in a pigsty waiting for a local cab, would I. Your position comes with certain privileges such as a car and protection." He nodded towards the partitioned off front end of the vehicle where the driver and another man sat. I had taken notice of them and of course knew what they were, but what I did not know was that the two in the car behind were to be my protection. I chose not to acknowledge any of them, instead asking about our destination.

"I've heard of the place where you are housing Mayler, but I've never had cause to inquire about it before. Is it a working farm, Geoffrey?"

"Very much so it is, hence the usage of the Ministry of Agriculture and Fisheries in Whitehall as Group's cover for Craig Court, your other office. Sadly that government department has now lost its name, becoming part of the Department for the Environment, but our connection continues to be the same as it was. For all intents and purposes the farm is an experimental place implementing government policies verbatim. Everyone there has signed the Official Secrets Act and although not within our direct supervision they are in-house-trained coming under the Department for Defence, the new name for the War Office." He reached into the leather-covered divide between the rear seats of the car and withdrew two plastic wallets, but his attention was diverted elsewhere.

"I have to be home by a specific time this evening so the police escort is to ensure that I am. Oliver Nathan and his wife and a few other influential people are due for dinner." As the distraction of an early summons home left him, he wearily passed one of the slim wallets to me.

"Here, you should keep this on you at all time now you have the Joseph chair." It was a Department for the Environment ministerial pass in the name of George Warren.

"Do they live in Kent, Geoffrey?" I asked as I pocketed my pass.

"Do who live in Kent?" he replied quizzically.

"The Home Secretary, Oliver Nathan and his wife," I responded, equally bemused.

"No. They live near me, outside of Guildford. What's with the Kent bit?"

"You summoned me to your home in Farnborough, in Kent, at some ungodly early hour in the morning a good few years back. You said you'd give me a lift into town after we finished speaking then kicked me out of the car in the middle of Blackheath in the pouring rain."

"Yes, I do remember that," he replied vacantly. "You had that big lump of a chap named Job following us if I recall correctly. You were once again sticking your nose out too far, too fast." His impassive face turned away from me to stare at the floor of the car in thought.

"Know anything about Freemasonry, Joseph?" suddenly he asked.

"Not much other than I've heard it is a secret society with funny handshakes and even stranger symbols. I think they're pro-royals, but I'm not certain of that. What's the reason for your question, Geoffrey?"

"Hmm, no matter," he announced, shaking his head. "You will find out soon enough, probably from Ughert. But now, if you'll excuse me, I have some reading to do for the new job on Monday. Step lightly with the chap we're on the way to see. Ughert told me he's fragile material is our 'Enry, and suffice it to say Ughert is the only one to know how fragile that may be." With an affected pronunciation to the 'E' of Enry, he closed our conversation and open his document case.

* * *

I left him to his files and assorted reading material as I dreamingly gazed out of the windows at the fast moving darkened background of London, oblivious to the sound of the escorting police sirens. The grey slate painted sky threatened either rain or snow from which the identically, coloured pedestrians hurried away to lunch appointments or simply to grab a quick bite to eat alone or with friends. I had lived the life of a cloistered monk since I'd returned from Ireland and it wasn't until now that it bothered me. Perhaps it was the thought of four people around a dinner table exchanging unimportant conversation and sharing moments of pleasure that had shaken my solitude, or perhaps it was the responsibility I had accepted so readily moments before. The nigh-instant assessment Jack Price made of me almost thirty odd years back, was spot on: I was not only after the adventure being offered, I was chasing the power to construct my own excitement. But my experience of life had taught me that often the pursuit of power exceeds the excitement to be found in its capture. Optimism for anything other than that would be stupid. Maybe that sour thought only applied to women other than Kerry, she had been different. Then again they were all different, but not the disappointment; that was always the same.

One person who wasn't a disappointment was waiting somewhere over the horizon to meet once more. The first time since our disagreement in his office at Whitehall, with Geoffrey Harwood sitting one side of him and a man I later found out to be the Prime Minister's special advisor on all things American on the other. Fraser Ughert and I nearly came to blows that day before my naivety over a woman was exposed to the undeniable truth outside of his London club in the back of his plush ministerial motor car with other large men in the front. Had I changed from those days? Had anything changed from those days? Was Ireland my moment of full comprehension of what I'd become through choice?

Perhaps I should have taken a bite from the carrot Fraser dangled in front of my gaping mouth that day and never set foot on the *Green* of Ireland again! Maybe Sleeping Hollow, near New York, and the sexually deprived rich women that were being offered as my income was really my vocational calling. The acceptance of Francesca Clark-Bartlett's suggestion to supply exotic sex to her wealthy friends who would use my body for their own gratification would now be nearing its closure, but I'd be a rich man with only the screams of delight to remember not, those of pain, but what of her? What of Job? The man who would walk through walls for Jack Price and later for me. Three of the closest people I'd known had gone leaving enormous holes in my life that I had never filled and never looked to fill.

For the passing of Job I blamed the man sitting beside me. I gave Harwood an earful as soon as I heard, which was three weeks after they buried the man. Adam too came into my line of fire. Both of them had valid excuses: *How could we tell you? We had no way of knowing where you were for a start.*

But in my mind Job's death was Geoffrey's fault. He wanted Job to remain on the books and Job was too loyal to decline. I paid my meagre respects to my friend one cold and damp winter's morning similar to this one, where he lay beside Jack Price, both beneath headstones, in graves at Plumstead cemetery, a long way from Jack's detested Guildford. I had briefly wondered who had arranged that, but then remembered a conversation Job and I'd shared where he'd told me of his plans. I was named Terry Jeffries at the time.

When I'm through with this life, young Terrance, I have made arrangements to be buried in a plot next to Jack's. Call it what you will but that's where I want to lay. We can make plans to blow up Guildford and wipe out the top floor brass of the intelligence lot. Jack will become C of everything and Woolwich will be the new exclusive suburbia for you and me and our concubines. Jack will have too much to do to care.

I was not sorrowful so much for their death, that's an inevitability we all face even those who shroud themselves with respectability in decent Guilford, but Job and I had killed together without ever knowing each other's birth name. A strange life, a strange meeting, one where I had asked him if I was to become anonymous—

Like the department you work for, Job?

Anonymity means that there's no name,—he replied, then added—*You will be given a name to suit the circumstances you're needed for. People like me have no need of a name.*

A sad life in which honourable people are hidden from public view in order to help the dishonourable achieve their wish of staining the world in the red, white, and blue of the Union flag in order to deserve the label as the finest intelligence service in the world.

At that moment of pointless retrospection my foot sent a sharp stinging pain through my knee into the top of my thigh, causing me to crumple in my car seat and Geoffrey to look away from his reading. He was annoyed as he asked if I was okay, to which I replied that I was, then we fell back into what we were occupied with. He, his readiness for Oliver Nathan and me more memories. The muzzle end of a gun pointed at my head. A brass knuckleduster catching the rays of sunlight bursting into my pristine New York apartment before the blow on my face. Amputated toes, a busted jaw and eye socket. Fianna, my make-believe Irish twin sister first tenderly nursing me and then what happened? The road to Damascus lined with lesbian feelings on one side and me on the other? Choices, options, a decision? A love expressed? A densely packed street in New York with two crashed cars, one with my Fianna Redden with half a head. Two gunshots, two deaths. The other dead? Did it matter who he was? Best to forget the name of Alain whoever he was. Sagacious advice from Fraser Ughert whilst Jack Price gave up his remaining stock of cancer lessening, pain relieving morphine for me during the rushed flight home to escape the consequences of a killing on American soil.

Then my meeting with Dickie Blythe-Smith at the Travellers Club after the prescribed period of convalescence in a nursing home on the sunny South Coast near Brighton, with a private medical team to soothe my honour and pain, but no help for the half a head propped against a passenger seat in a car next to me as I killed her killer. Screams, what of them? Take a life, lose a life. It all comes out in the screams.

I had been softened up for the London meeting without any need. I offered as little resistance to Dickie's bribe of a pathway to power then, as I had just done down in The Hole. A tortuous route perhaps, but nonetheless, here I was on the back seat of a luxury ministerial car and soon I would be on the back seat of my own with guards to watch over me. Would there have been any room for a twin sister, real or not, on my journey? What would Jack and Job have to say about my lofty position? Would Jack forgive my desire for the grandeur? Or would his reply be along the lines of—*in order to forgive there must be something to forgive and the quest for ceremonial pomp and glory is an unfaithful quest and therefore deserves no recognition.*

I smiled as the thought stayed with me. But my equable thoughts altered as I recalled the empty space which I'd allowed Kerry to fill. All grace, legs and everything else that boiled the blood inside a male more akin to shotguns against knees than what she had to offer. A brief encounter? Yes, it was. Satisfying? No. Dangerous? Of course it was. Memorable? Oh, yes, she was that. But I wish she hadn't been. And I wish there were no graves, no headstones, or plaques in remembrance to those I had loved and felt a need to cling on to.

* * *

On our arrival at the Brightwalton Farm, Geoffrey left me alone to sign several sheets of officially stamped, important looking documents, whilst he paid what he said would be his last visit to the farm's guest. There was an edge of genuine sadness in his voice as he said that. On his return I was introduced to more who needed to know who I was. It was then that Henry Mayler was officially released into my responsibility whilst I remained on the premises. I said my goodbyes to Harwood when he declined to introduce me to Mayler, preferring to deal with the paperwork he was required to sign off on. So, I made my cumbersome way alongside one of the two men from the car that had followed Geoffrey's, across a rutted farmyard then through a cluster of small unmarked, green corrugated buildings until I found two armed Ministry of Defence guards on duty outside the one I was looking for. Thankfully the clouds had not opened and the place was reasonably dry.

* * *

It was a slightly built man who welcomed me from his perch in a comfortable looking chair in an austere but warm and light lounge with three closed doors leading off of it. On the coffee table in front of where he sat was a bottle of Scotch and two glasses, one unused. I poured a large measure into the unused glass and from the cabinet hiding the ice-making machine topped the tall straight glass up with ice cubes. Harwood's description of Mayler's confinement had been exceptional. He had been concise—*the ice machine is in the roll-top wood-effect cabinet.*

According to the file I had speed-read in the car, my drinking partner was thirty-two, born on the third of January 1970, but age had not been kind to him. His thick, dark, rusty coloured hair failed to cover the two inches of hairline that bore a hideous scar caused by an explosion in Iraq ten months before it all kicked off for him in Syria. The furrowed lines below the scar travelled as far down his forehead to his sad, sunken brown eyes, above which he had no discernible eyebrows. The rest of his face, although unmarked by the violence of his abnormal life, was creased with sharp edges to it around his cheekbones and to his jawline. When I went to sit on the long sofa opposite where he sat and had not moved from, he smiled, exposing heavily nicotine stained teeth. The smile widened as he lit one of his cigarettes and offered me one; a Tekel. Turkish. I took it, drawing wantonly on it, then I began.

"I understand you have been handled by Elijah up to now and all of what I'm about to ask has been covered by him. No matter. I want to go through every trivial detail again. I would like to start at where and how you met Fyodor Nazarov Razin for the first time, please. You might include why you were in the same part of the world as he was, Henry."

"I see! The new Joseph man is an impatient man. Similar to the one I have just said goodbye to. Let it not be me that delays you from your vital appointments, sir." There was no sigh, no sign of resentment before he began. The file said he was a stoic and pensive man. The analysis was correct.

"I first came across Razin in an American military camp at Khost, Afghanistan in December last year. It was a year ago yesterday, on the ninth. All the press corps were huddled together for calls to announcements from their propaganda bureau, or so the Americans said. I thought perhaps it was for the convenience of an enemy mortar shell or friendly fire. What is it they say—truth is the first casualty of war—well, if those who expose the truth are all blown up then there would be no truth to kill would there?"

His sunken eyes travelled across mine looking for a response, but I had no answer to that, in fact, I didn't understand it. We exchanged exhaled cigarette smoke and sipped our whisky until he spoke again.

"How is Elijah since I saw him? I would like to see him before I leave." His deviation annoyed me.

"He's fine. Back to Khost and those details, if you would be so kind, Henry."

"You're not interested in me, are you? Your interest lies with Razin the Russian and him alone. But what of it? Same with the old Joseph as it is now with the younger one. At least Elijah cared. Okay, I give you what I got." A long draw on his scented cigarette and a single gulp to empty his Scotch preceded his rebuke.

"My cover was the same as always, international freelance journalist. I am, or was, a war correspondent who carried his own camera. My cover was good, it was authentic and what's more I was an ace cameraman. But no, don't lose yourself in that drink before your own ears hear the truth of how good my cover was, it's burnt to the file, Mr Joseph. It's been on there for nearly forever. Razin was billeted with us all, in the bed next to mine in the roughed out, tented press quarters. Before you ask, Control had not sent me there for him, or at least that's what I believed."

I watched as he slowly refilled his glass using his left hand, on the back of which was a tattoo of an eight-pointed red opened rose above which was a traditional four-pointed cardinal cross in gold, and a four-pointed ordinal cross in silver. I saved any questions about that for a later date.

"No one knew of Razin until I told Control of a suspicious Russian bear pretending to be a Finnish tree-hugger. He told me to snap away then send him the pictures. I took a few and a copy of his press pass. That was signed by the same General who had signed mine, but if the Yankee General had known that Oban Raikkonen from somewhere in Finland was really Fyodor Nazarov Razin from Moscow Centre, he would have torn it up, I'm sure he would. Why was I there? I was there to save the world from American expansionist plans and substitute them with British ones. What else would I be there for? I bet you're wondering how I knew he was a hood if Control hadn't told me? I'm not a Russian spy hunter, but equally I'm no fool. He wasn't there for his health, but he might have wanted the opium. That's why I was there. Looking after HMG interests. I wasn't going to stand by and allow the poppies to be processed in Arkansas instead of Kandaha. That was just too long a flight for flowers. Processing plants were being built in the valley of the Hari River, near Herat in eastern Afghanistan. And so Control told me that the Brits wanted to stop the greedy Yanks, but he never told me what the Brits wanted to put in its place and I never found out. Everything went back to London including America's plan to run thousands of miles of gas and fuel carrying pipes from the Caspian into the Arabian Sea. All the information is safely locked away in MI6 safes, Mr Joseph sir."

His glass was full and as he added more to mine I offered no objection. I asked how he knew Razin was not who he was supposed to be.

"He was speaking Russian into his phone. The dialect he used sounded Finnish to others I guess, but not me. I learned all the nuances of the Russian language from a very early age at the hands of a Russian tutor, but I'd had the chance to practise some of them when I was freelancing in Istanbul, Turkey for an American magazine. I was there for over a year. Armenians are adopted Russians, you know. We are hated by the Turks and we hate them back. You will know that when eventually you read my file. Anyway, I was mostly educated privately until I attended Oxford University when I was nineteen. I am digressing, I apologise. Razin, or Oban as I knew him then, never spoke to anyone in the camp for the first few days. On the phone, yes, but not verbally to any of us. When he wasn't using a phone all he did was sit on his camp bed holding a thin silver stiletto bladed knife, a vicious but beautiful looking thing held over and stabbing into the dancing flame of a candle. All day he sat there. Only once did he attend a press conference which I found suspicious but the Americans never did. He would never fell asleep before me and was always awake before me. I thought he was a demon who never needed sleep. It was because of all those things that I noticed him, plus his size. He is large, Mr Joseph, like yourself."

Henry's file read that he never tried to hide his sexual orientation. If it had not said he was attracted to men I would not have guessed he was anything but heterosexual until the way he spoke that last sentence. I thought the pitch of his voice carried overtures of a sexual nature.

"I was on my way out one evening when Razin called me over—'*Hey, Rosco, come here.*' I went. I had nothing else of importance to do." He shook his head and went slightly pale at this point. When he leant across the table to extinguish his cigarette I could smell the starch on his clothes.

"Why did he call you Rosco? I asked. "Was that the name on your press pass?"

"No, I am always who I am; Henry Mayler. I asked him the same question—why Rosco? as he stabbed at the flame of one of his candles and he just smiled before he started into his introduction speech.

'Do you know where this flame goes when I blow it out?' he asked, before supplying his own answer.

'No, you don't know, do you. This flame is the only thing that's consistent in life. You light it. You play with it, you blow it out. But where is it when it's not alight? Ah, your face. I bet you think I'm mad. A flame is a flame after all, isn't it. You're probably right, I am mad, but aren't all of us that come wanting to photograph bodies after being blown apart by land mines or tank shells mad? No? Not you? Is that what your face is telling me? You want to capture the look on American faces in defeat or victory? You think

you will sell those images to a magazine editor? Is that your game, little Rosco?'

"He stood and asked if I knew what happened to a human soul if it had no time to grieve when dead. I thought it was stupid and another of his rhetorical questions, offering no answer as he turned from me and made his way towards the open flap of the double canvas tent. He was almost there, thirty foot away from me when he suddenly stopped and walked all the way back."

'The soul is the opposite to my flame. The flame forgets what the soul cannot. The flame will always forget as it never stays long enough in a single place for any memory to remain. A flame is trickery, my little Rosco friend. It is mercurial. That's why it flickers when there is a painful memory that needs to be thrown away. It shakes and shakes until the memory is gone. The soul cannot be like that. The soul holds memories which must be forgotten in grief before it can be guided to the afterlife. And there we have the irony; in order to grieve we must have time, but the longer we spend reminiscing the more chance of the memory being stolen by time and vanishing as my flame vanishes when extinguished. If you believe what I have just said proves I'm insane, then think of the flame being a woman who plays games on us. When the flame isn't alight, we can't see her in her game. When she comes to life in the flickering flame she plays another game as you look on. You know the sort I mean, don't you?'

"By the way he was standing there looking away from me, and the length of the pause, I thought this time he had definitely decided that he'd finished, but he hadn't and this was the bit that Elijah really loved. The big Russian was two paces from me, but he closed that gap and bent so close that his face was almost touching mine. The garlic on his breath was suffocating me and his body odour was nauseating. I still smell that face in my nightmares, Mr Joseph, but the odd thing is I can't remember him walking away. All I see in those nightmares is a ghost beside me whispering the Elijah words in my ear,

'If it is mere curiosity that has brought you here, leave now. If you are afraid of the places you find yourself in, withdraw from them. Look within yourself for the truth because you will not find it in me or anyone else. I am the earthly depiction of destruction and death'."

"Did any of that mean anything to you, Henry? I asked.

"Yes, I've heard words like that before." There was a slight hesitation to his reply. "None of what he said worried me, Mr Joseph. What did was the spectral glaze that covered his eyes, and as he fell silent it left him with a deathly scowl on his face the like of which I'd never seen. He scared me then and that look still does. He and I have met again of course but that first memory will not leave my mind, no matter what side he's supposed to be on."

"You have a remarkable memory to be able to recall exactly what he said and recite it to Elijah, and then to me, Henry."

"Is that merely an observation of yours, or a question, Mr, sir, man? But of course I do. That's why you Brits fell in love with me. If you'd read the files you would know that I also have a photographic memory, and I'm able to read lips. I do passable voice impersonation as well. Boris Yeltsin is a favourite when I'm drunk. That's when I can juggle twelve oranges at the same time. I'm a good all round circus act when on form, Mr English. Stop commending me on my attributes because of your failure to acquaint yourself with them. That either proves your own incompetence or you have not found sufficient time to read about me; in other words I'm unimportant to you."

Ignoring the annoyance hiding inside his clouds of cigarette smoke, I pressed him to answer more fully. "Was there nothing else he said on that first occasion?"

"Elijah had someone typing it all up whilst I was being recorded on a machine he had running. He was old-fashioned and thorough."

"So am I. I have both those records, but I'm from the old-school way of doing things, so there's a bit of a conflict going on inside me. One side wants to rely on the files, but my old-school training wants first-hand knowledge. Indulge me a little, Henry, please. The whisky is nice and smooth and I'm in no rush. We can natter a while longer, unless you have somewhere to be?"

He sighed regretfully but seemed to mellow as he accepted another of my proffered cigarettes and the refreshed glass I pushed towards him. He drank from the glass but didn't light the cigarette. I changed tack with the questions, but I hadn't forgotten what he obviously wanted to forget.

"I understand you met Razin earlier this month just before you arrived in this country, but you also met last month in November. Can you enlighten me on those meetings? We'll make a start with the first one in November, please." My question had allowed a genie to escape.

"Did that knowledge come by word of mouth, or am I wrong and you have read some page of my history? I know what it is," he said as his dejected body slumped in the chair before he continued. "You only had time to thumb through the pages and speed read, didn't you? You are brand new and if I was a betting man, which thankfully I'm not, I'd say you were like me—living on your wits for most of your life. If that were so it would explain how you're having trouble trusting what you're told and certainly why you won't depend on what's written down. You trust what you see and hear only. How am I doing, mister spy catcher? Is there a Greek siren calling you back to where it's hot and the bullets fly? Please, don't let your frustrations become my problem, will you." After the display of petulance he carried on.

"Yes, it was a Friday. The sixth of November to be precise. I was in Kabul, but not on business directed from Control. I was in that part of Afghanistan freelancing for a magazine I do a lot of work for. I was in a café when the news on a radio said an

Iraqi suicide bomber had been arrested. As the report went on it said that the bomber's target was the Afghan Defence Minister. I was about to leave for my appointment with that government minister, Mohammed Fahim, just as that report was broadcast. At first I put it down to coincidence, after all he was a target for the Taliban and I just happened to be going to the Defence Ministry. What else could it be? But a couple of hours later, after finishing my report, I was in a bar watching the recorded arrest on the huge television set, when in walks Razin and plants himself down next to me. You would know all this if you'd read the files." His voice was rising as his anger grew. I had been wrong to assume he had settled down.

"Go on, please," I asked fruitlessly. His eyes fixed firmly on me then through clenched teeth he offered his indignant explanation of why he was so irritable.

"I have been kept in this country for six days. Every new day you spend questioning me delays my flight to Canada. If you were going to keep me locked up on a smelly farm in freezing cold England why bloody mention Canada? Everything about today has been a waste of time. Sod your old-school preferences. I was promised a new name, a solid background, money and a safe place in bloody Canada to live. Now Russian Razin turns up in London and old Joseph has me dragged out of a nice London hotel room wearing a hood over my head and driven here. If the Russian wants me dead don't you think he would have shot me by now? And if you think he's looking around for where I've gone then you're making it rather easy for him to find me. I heard those police horns way before I heard your elaborate cavalcade pull into the yard."

I went for more ice as he stood and wandered towards a window overlooking the farm grounds and the copse of trees standing on the hill beyond. His right hand was tapping at his leg as he walked. The grey coloured clouds hovered low across the frosty fields, threatening a difficult drive home. I briefly wondered how close Geoffrey Harwood was to home before the pain in my toes shot into the back of my leg and I thought of making things more difficult for Henry and seeing where it led.

"None of that has been my doing, Henry. Up until now your safety has been our prime concern, and I can categorically assure you that every effort is being made to place you in Canada with a legend guaranteeing your well-being and safety. Transfers between countries of this kind are not always a straightforward thing to arrange. The red tape involved in crossing international borders for stateless immigrants, which you would have to become, can be endless, but believe me I'm doing as much as I can to hasten things along. However, I'm the one now in charge of your future." I sat and watched him. "Nothing is set in stone in this game. You should know that by now. Work with me and I'll work your ticket, if you don't—" I never finished that warning.

It was the wretched figure of a man who turned from the window twirling his cigarette dextrously between the fingers of both hands. He was shorter than I thought. Probably no more than five foot six or seven. Weighed in at around nine stone nothing, and I worried about his choice of location as he looked as though a strong Canadian wind would blow him clean away. He lit the cigarette, leaving it between his lips with his hands thrust deep into his pockets as he stood there resembling a stand-up comedian whose joke had just failed. I hadn't finished with him.

"When I ask a question I expect an answer not a trip down memory lane and then back again. A little while ago I asked if Razin said anything else to you in December last year when you were both in Khost playing with candle flames. I then asked about the meeting last month. You have yet to completely address that first question and if I were you I'd think long and hard about your answer."

"I apologise, Mr Joseph. I wrongly judged you to be in a hurry as I thought we'd covered all that. You must have all day, the same as I do. Okay, what did Oban Raikkonen from Finland say? He told me a fictional life story that evening over some beers while we watched the ISAF troops play pool and have a laugh."

When Henry finished relating the story that Razin had spun him, I asked what else had happened when Razin sat next to him in that bar in Kabul.

"He leant heavily against my shoulder and spoke in his Russian. He had never spoken to me before in his native language. He said that he knew of my meeting and he knew the Iraqi bomber was going to the same place. Told me the bomber's middle name, which had not been reported by the authorities. I checked it out and he was right. Said that the minister presented a useful target—'Он убьет две цели за один раз,' which roughly translates as killing two targets in one go.

'You found out too much too soon, little Rosco and now you are beginning to get noticed, you son of Dietmar of Magdeburg. You have avoided being killed today as did your ancestors in centuries before at the hands of the byword for sadism and the dark side of Catholicism; Konrad von Marburg. I might not know of the next Farsi Ahmadulia Pasclli, and he or she might get all the way and blow you up. You must stop picking at people's toes, Rosco'."

"Was that all he said, Henry? Nothing definite about him stopping this terrorist on your behalf?"

"Wasn't that enough, did he have to shout from the minaret at the mosque to satisfy you? Well, he didn't. He smiled and left immediately after the toes thing. I contacted Control."

"So you contacted Control directly? Is that how it played?"

"Not direct, no. My call was not taken. I dialled my get-out-of-jail number and left the message."

"You didn't actually speak to anyone?"

"I've just said that. No, I didn't speak to a person."

"And what time was it you recorded that message?"

"Three-ten in the afternoon, but why? Did the automatic clock stop?" I did not answer.

"How long did you have to wait for Control to reply?" I asked.

"Two hours and five minutes."

"I'm all ears. Why did Control say it took that long, Henry?"

There was a noticeable tremble in his voice throughout this reminder of the past and I foolishly thought it was because of my veiled threat. At that time I knew nothing more.

"What did you do whilst you waited for London to call, Henry?"

Chapter Four
Early Friday Evening

After a rummage around the two domestic floors of Lavington Street that was to become my new home, as Harwood had articulated, and hastily dismissing the sentimental thoughts of a rapidly approaching Christmas, I settled into two chicken sandwiches, my first food of the day washed down by part of an adequate bottle of single malt and set about reading more about Mayler and then, if possible, Comrade Fyodor Nazarov Razin.

Henry Mayler officially signed on with us whilst at Oxford University. His father was a practising doctor in of all places; Harley Street, approximately fifty yards from the surgeons' clinic I had attended. The family had a house in Montagu Square, a pleasant ten-minute stroll away. The Maylers had moved into the six-storeyed spacious London home in 1954, arriving that year from the state of Washington in America carrying fictional isotopes in their hand luggage. Henry's grandfather, Arek Mayler, one part of the Armenian family link, came with his eight-year-old son, Dietmar, but not his wife. Frau Maddalen Mayler had died giving birth to their son in Germany in 1946. Dietmar changed his name to Christopher when eighteen, shortly after Arek had passed away. Christopher followed his father into the medical profession but not practising in Harley Street. When aged twenty-three and at St Bart's medical college he met and married Elizabeth Simms, a fellow St Bart's student. Henry was born to the proud young couple the following year; seven months before Christopher was killed in a road traffic accident. Elizabeth Mayler took up private medical practice in the Harley Street premises in 1976. Today the Mayler Clinic is a world famous establishment dealing in cosmetic surgery and where Elizabeth acted as a consultant until Henry was nineteen years of age when she too died suddenly. Although a healthy woman with no family history of heart disease she died of heart failure whilst asleep in her bed in Montagu Square. On the death of his mother the freehold of the Harley Street and Montagu Square properties passed to Henry, who had not only shown an interest but expressed a passion for photography after studying the sketches and photographs of his mother's reconstruction surgery.

The imposing home in the square had been purchased a week before Arek Mayler's arrival by an insurance consultant from Richmond in Surrey named Oswald Raynor, who paid close on fifty thousand pounds for the property which was immediately leased to Arek. All this had been investigated before Henry's signature was allowed on the Official Secrets Act form on the first Sunday of June 1991 and so it said, found to be in order. The serendipitous fact of Henry being raised a stone's throw away from the psychiatrists I'd seen twice was not lost on me and nor was the name of Raynor. I needed a walk to clear my head. I was surprised to find the security office fully staffed, thinking that most would be at home by now at nine-thirty at night.

"Going out, sir?" the young smiling face of a uniformed sergeant asked me.

"Yes, I am, officer. I thought the hat and coat might give the game away," I replied with the least amount of sarcasm I could manage.

"It's just that we would expect to be given notice whenever you required an escort. I wasn't being funny, sir," he replied, straight-faced, adding, "It is in standing orders, Mr West."

"In that case I will have to rewrite them. I'll have that looked at first thing in the morning. I'm perfectly capable of walking down to the local pub and back. I won't be long." I made to go past him but he stepped across my path to prevent me.

"Sir, I must advise against it. But if you are determined to leave without one of us I insist you sign out to that effect and you will have to use one of the rear exits from the building. The front entrance is secured by a time lock. It cannot be opened."

"What happens if someone is taken ill or has to go somewhere in an emergency, sergeant?"

"We have three secure tunnels that emerge in a series of side alleys off either Blackfriars Road, Hopton Street or Stamford Street, sir. If any of those occasions arise we use one of those exits, but we try steering clear of the Stamford Street one, it is the longest. It's quite a walk." His face had taken on that serious look that parents adopt just after they have reprimanded their child, daring them to repeat the offence.

"Okay, I'll take that one. Point me in the right direction and I'll get out of your way," I replied, somewhat ruffled. He smiled back, but it wasn't a warm smile.

"Walk with me as far as the security gate, which I presume I'll have to sign out of, sergeant. You can tell me about this place as we walk."

* * *

We were in the basement via the lift walking towards one of those corridors I'd seen earlier in the day. The buzzing of the television screens seemed noisier than they had been, but the amount of people had not altered. I stopped at the centre console behind a man who smelled of a scented liniment.

"What's on television?" I asked flippantly.

"This is a satellite picture of northern Syria, sir, just outside a place called Resafa. It's on the strategic route into Homs. At 10:16 yesterday morning GCHQ notified us that they expected something big to kick off near there, or on the banks of Lake Assad, a few miles away within the next week or so. The window of accuracy was not specific, sir." He nodded towards one of the other screens on the mention of Lake Assad and the operator of that visual display raised a hand in recognition.

"On our centre screens," his tuition continued in the same cadence as it had before. "We have eyes inside and out of Aleppo International airport, monitoring all incoming and outgoing flights along with a link to the cameras in the arrival and departure lounges and in the meet and greet hall. With the technology at the Doughnut, sir, all passengers on the boarding list can be accurately accounted for coming into or leaving the airport. If any slip away before customs, we would be alerted. We are looped to GCHQ and AIS, the new installation of Mr Harwood's at Greenwich, but if and when the balloon goes up we monitor and have ringside seats here waiting to forward on your orders. Those at the Doughnut simply gauge and follow, as do the eyes at AIS."

How nice of you to tell me, Geoffrey, I silently thought, guessing that somewhere there would be a mention of it locked away and recorded by my orderly predecessor.

"Tell me something if you would," I asked of my teacher. "I'm not familiar with that AIS thing you mentioned. What is it?"

"Its full name, sir, is Auxiliary Intelligence Supplement. It was established by Mr Harwood about four months ago. I'm not privy to knowing all its capabilities, sir, but it complements what we get from GCHQ and can implement telecommunications tap-ins which they can't. Greenwich has developed very clever practical technology, sir, but very secret. From what I understand they're years ahead of anything the Americans have in that department."

He had allowed the secrecy of his blessed machinery to take precedence over telling me of a live operation that required my assessment and my full-time attendance at The Hole. That was either utter incompetence on Geoffrey's part or deliberate. Neither were worth thinking about at this stage. I turned back to the young sergeant who was going to show me the Stamford Street exit, and changed the destination.

"I know my office is down the corridor to the right, but I do not know what's down the others. I think it would be an opportune time to become acquainted with what's around me. I wanted the walk to clear my head of something unrelated to what's going on. However, that will have to take second place. Now it would be more prudent to get to know this place. Consider yourself my guide, sergeant.

By no measure of anyone's imagination had I been sufficiently briefed, but it was no point telling my uniformed friend of that, or my instructor on the capabilities of communication, and there was certainly nobody to complain to.

"As you will, sir," he replied in the practised resigned manner of non-commissioned officers worldwide. "The first one to our right is where the loos and showers are. I don't know offhand how many there are but there are quite a lot. I understand your facilities are en-suite, sir. The staffing lamp-burners and my security lot have our own facilities on the ground floor."

I met this information with the same blank stare that met all of his unambiguous descriptions of the rest of the tunnels. I was bored. The display screens were still and I needed more than just my office chair.

"Let's go further afield, shall we," I suggested.

In silence he took me to where the longest tunnel emerged at a shuttered outside entrance between two buildings off Stamford Street. The two other tunnels emerged in a similar concealed fashion. Back inside The Hole I explored the back rooms of the building all the way up from the ground floor to the very top, discovering why it was that the accommodation on the two floors where I was to live was so narrow. In those adjacent rooms to my own were enough workstations for roughly ten people, but I doubted it was a comfortable place to work, as all the windows were boarded up and like my own place, the air-conditioning provided the only air. I hoped horse liniment and disinfectant were not often needed. According to Sergeant Cooper a total of eight women were employed; three in the upstairs offices and three in the basement. He never mentioned where the other two worked and neither did he comment on their appearance. I did not ask. My advanced looking dayroom was more than ample. Not only was there an impressive walk-in shower, but there was a thermal steam and spa room as well! A separate area had a television and an adjustable armchair to watch it from, or fall asleep in. There was a small gym with a rowing-machine to keep me awake if I needed to. After finding out that Geoffrey had preferred to alternate between Craig Court and Greenwich, rather than use these facilities to unwind, it became even more inviting.

* * *

My office seemed to have enough modern technological 'toys' to be a development area for a James Bond film. The concealed floor safe paled into insignificance against the remote controlled wall which, on depressing the button marked *Command* on my desk console, revolved one hundred and eighty degrees revealing a wide three-way-split screen monitoring the images displayed in the central Hub. As I peered at the lifeless images, one changed from the barren sandy deserted landscape and fairly busy airport terminal to one of moving traffic and pedestrians on visible street lighted pavements. I recognised the area. Cooper was at the door looking at the same scene as I.

"That's the Russian Consulate at Notting Hill, is it not?" I looked at him as I asked but he had a deeply vacuous expression on his face. I lifted the telephone that Geoffrey had declared as the connection to the Hub.

"Who am I speaking to, please?" I felt like an idiot having to ask and more so having remembered that I originally wanted a walk in the fresh air. Silently I vowed to rectify my stupidity and self-indulgence as quickly as possible.

"I'm Hannah, sir, your personal assistant." One of the three women basement workers Cooper had mentioned, I correctly assumed. "I was waiting to formally introduce myself earlier but our departing Mr Harwood was in a hurry. The images are as you say, Notting Hill. The monitors were alerted that our subject was on the move so the intel in your office changed automatically as all of ours did. Yes! There's our level one now, sir. See?" I couldn't see her, but already I had formed an image from her pleasant sounding voice and my resolve at curbing my egotism was starting to crumble immediately.

It was him. Mr Fyodor Nazarov Razin, alias Raynor. Tall at six foot three inches, broad shouldered and strongly built by the look of him. He was wearing a long snake-ish green trench coat that finished inches above his brown weatherproof shoes. It wasn't only the colour and length of the coat that struck me at first, it was also the three huge pockets down each side covering the whole length. All appeared empty but having a sizeable capacity. On his head was not the traditional Papakha Cossack fur, but a flat cap more at home on the streets of Leeds, in God's own county of Yorkshire.

"Are you hiding in some secret hiding place, Hannah?" I asked, bemused.

"No, sir, I'm behind the wall opposite the display screens you're watching. The wall can't be moved from my side, sir, only you can do that. It slides out of sight when you require me and is replaced if you want more privacy. The button is one of those on the console. Middle-end-left, I believe."

My image was about to be tested. Would Hannah be the ultra-efficient civil service female employee with the same thick black-rimmed spectacles as Geoffrey Harwood and who looked more like a man than a woman, or would she resemble the goddess Fraser Ughert had as his personal assistant back in his day as Chairman of the Joint Intelligence Committee? There was a button to find before all could be revealed. I couldn't find it. I'd switched on a hidden hi-fi system, turned on the shower in the adjacent dayroom as well as the BBC news on the television. Middle-end-left was obviously not precise enough for me. The next thing I knew was that a beautiful, graceful woman who must be Hannah had entered my office and was standing beside me.

"I think I had better find it for you, Mr West. Don't worry about all these gadgets, it won't take you long to get used to things, I'm sure." Her very shapely legs had carried her pleasant voice into my domain, and I wasn't disappointed at all as she reached over and pushed the required button. Early thirties in age, tall, curvy in all the right places, elegantly dressed with straight long black hair above the porcelain white skin of a sculpted face with a small upturned nose and high cheekbones. There were no wedding ring or glasses to distract me from her cold, but huge, remote hazel-coloured, eyes as they pierced into me. I'm not sure if the look I returned carried the same remoteness of hers, but at least I tried to assuage my egotism. It's not always the clothes people wear, or the way they speak that marks them out as coming from a different way of life than most. But skin cannot lie. Smooth, unblemished, flawless skin comes from the preserve of the wealthy where nothing is allowed to contaminate it. I looked forward to investigating my assumption later.

* * *

With most thoughts of Hannah's obvious sexuality removed from my mind I returned to the Hub where my previous informer of AIS secrets and the inside of Aleppo airport now became my invited educator into satellite pictures. He, Peter, wanted to explain the intricacies of space cameras, but all was falling on stony ground. I was watching Razin, not caring how that came about. He was standing outside the gate of the Consulate in Bayswater Road smoking a cigarette and appearing perfectly happy to just to stand there in the evening chill. Why would he want to do that, I wondered?

"How often has he come out of the front door for a smoke, Peter?" I asked.

"As far as my knowledge goes it's the first time, sir. Every day since he arrived he comes out of the building at eleven am on the dot. A very punctual, and up to now a systematic man is our Russian gentleman. There is nothing in the log book about him coming out the building at any other time, sir."

"When did he arrive again, please?"

"He was waiting on our camera screen Monday morning at eleven, Mr West," Peter replied.

"I understand he has never varied his routine. Never a bus instead of the tube? A cab thrown in perhaps?"

"No, sir, always a walk to the station, exits at Charing Cross on the correct side of the Strand for the Savoy then after breakfast, it's a brisk walk to Chancery Lane. From there he…"

"Yes I get it. He takes a bus to Highgate and walks up the hill to number 177." I'd interrupted his summary and successfully stopped him somewhere between the intricacies of fixed satellite services compared to the reconnaissance ones we were apparently 'hooked into'. I apologised for my rudeness. He seemed surprised by my apology.

"Why is he outside now? And why's he not moving?" I asked of nobody in particular. It was Hannah who replied, standing beside me again.

"I think that is for you to determine, sir."

I took a deep breath and thought back to Ireland. Things there were more straightforward. One target for both sides. They hated us and we hated them. The secret was to get to them before they could do much damage to us. Here, it was far more complicated. First the enemy sometimes turns out to be your friend and the opposite applies when it comes to a friend. Then there were the Americans. Being kept out of this one for reasons unexplained to me. Or, was it that they wanted us to stay out the way, and we were only too willing to play?

"How many have we had on the street working this guy up till now?" I asked.

"We started on his journey to and from Highgate on the day of arrival, Mr West. One of our static watchers at the Consulate followed his outward journey as best he could. After his destination was known, Mr Harwood arranged cover at Highgate West Hill and had the lamp-burners in a car in Robin Grove, a street forty yards from the Delegation." The voice came from behind me and sounded calm and resolute.

"And who are you?" politely I asked of a fresh-faced man no more than twenty-five-years of age, of the same height of me but a fraction of my build.

"Mathew, sir, deputy duty officer."

"Very well, Mathew, and where's your number one?"

"He has a bit of a belly problem, sir. Probably in one of the loos; again."

"I see. And what is his name?"

"Abraham, sir!"

"Okay, Mathew, how many more from lamp-burners did we then assign to him?"

"In total we have seven, sir, but that number does not included the two on stationary watch opposite the Delegation."

My head was swimming with names, facts and dates but at least with this biblical naming structure the faces of the heads of departments might change, but their names did not. It was useful with less to remember, I told myself, then quietly laughed at my forgetfulness.

"Remind me again who's station officer, Hannah?"

"Solomon, sir. He'll be with his staffers in the two rooms they have at the back of the building on the ground floor. He and they will be watching the same scenes as us."

"Sergeant Cooper, please ask him to attend my office at his earliest you know what. I'll need you, Mathew, and of course you, Hannah. I think we'll leave Abraham to the latrines. If he should emerge tell him there's a shout on, but to keep well away, Peter. No, a change of mind on that. Send him home with orders to report back here only when he's fit for duty."

"I'm sorry, sir, but there's a blue flag alert from 6. The expected incoming has arrived at Aleppo airport." It was a voice I had not heard before from somewhere along the line of flashing screens.

"Okay, I'm going have to rely on you, Hannah, for most of this while I catch up. I want your normal in-house procedures adhered to and open any auxiliary communications access to GCHQ and AIG that you may have. We can't afford to have any main lines crash with no back-up on occasions such as this. I want the duty officer on the second floor at Millbank and his counterpart on the Syrian desk at Vauxhall on line as soon as possible, Mathew, and you smooth talking them. There is no need for anyone to be alarmed or any notifications to top-floor personnel flying around just yet. As you're fully aware I'm a long way off knowing what's what around here. As soon as Solomon shows, someone point him in my direction, please. I will need him."

As I flopped into the waiting chair in my office wishing there was a game of rugby to watch instead of two immensely serious developments that would require me to comment and act upon at some time soon, I could no longer contain my pent-up irritation at being unprepared. The two shouted words of 'fucking hell' summed up how I felt. Then, much quieter, I added, "All I want now is the effing Russian army to march into Estonia and I might as well go up on the roof and play with the fairies."

"The soundproofing doesn't work until the door is fully closed, sir. I think everyone now knows that you're a human and not a robot like some I won't mention." It was an all-smiling Hannah holding the door open. I returned her smile.

"Well, I'll count that as a plus on a day when there are so many minuses. That centre screen, is it the waiting lounge at Aleppo airport?" I asked, thinking only Hannah was in the room.

"It is, sir, yes," answered a man who I had not seen before and I had not seen arrive.

"And you are?" I asked.

"Solomon, sir, your station officer."

"Right, good, you're just in time to tell me if that fair-haired chap being greeted by the Arab with the red sash across his shoulders is the target of this exercise?"

"Yes, that is him, sir. We had the shout with the photograph moments ago. I have the photograph and profile story here."

"I need neither, Solomon, but thank you. I want you to set up a three-way depressed radio link to GCHQ, and Geoffrey Harwood, whom I presume will be at home. This will now have to go higher than Mathew's link to duty officers. We need the deputy directors at Millbank and at Vauxhall both at the end of a telephone before I've finished with GCHQ and Mr Harwood.

Make sure that when you call both services, Solomon, you first ask the receptionists for Sir Elliot Zerby and Sir John Scarlett. I have no wish to rub anyone up the wrong way on my first day by forgetting their bosses' knighthoods. However, at this stage I do not want the two Director Generals. I want their deputy heads only. Have we anyone on Razin, Hannah?"

"Two in a car and one on foot. Shall I muster more, sir?"

"I think it's too late for them to make a difference, but please do."

"Please make sure that door is firmly closed when you leave, Hannah." Her wide appealing lips wore a soft smile as she and Solomon turned and left.

If I was required to be honest then I admit to suspecting that I was being outmanoeuvred as soon as Harwood replaced the telephone after the morning's invitation to a callbox, but it had never crossed my mind that I'd be left to sink so quickly and drowned by what I was watching. As the scene in the airport lounge played out I realised that I really had been done over and perhaps not just by the other side.

Chapter Five
Uncle Fraser

A pitiless jumble of snow and rain carried on a brutish, swirling wind greeted me as I walked the short distance from the warmth of my official car to Fraser Ughert's open door of his palatial home in the wilds of Chearsley, in Buckinghamshire, about twenty miles from Oxford. It was past midnight that Friday when I arrived.

"Why did you make such a fuss by turning this visit into an official one, Patrick, you know you're more than welcome at any time? I was expecting the next telephone call to be from the PM asking if I was up to seeing the new head of Group. Hardballs was punching particularly low. Said he wasn't surprised that you wanted to see me, but was surprised that I had agreed."

"I know I'm welcome and so does everyone connected to the Service including Harwood, or Hardballs as you prefer, Fraser. I don't think I can afford to even try to dodge their interest. The cameras they're using nowadays can be a pain in the arse as well as an instrument for good. I've been set up and I'm buggered if I know why. Sir John Scarlett at 6 has a one-time Irish operative of mine being filmed walking into Syria on a surveillance camera everyone knows I'm monitoring. Whilst a Russian, I don't know what, acts as a diversion. I saw my operative, Liam Catlin, lying in a pool of his own blood ten foot away from me when a bomb exploded in the Erin Arms pub, in Derry, almost nine months ago. What's more, whilst I was laid up in an army hospital plugged into too many machines to count I spoke to Peter Levy, the Home Office chief pathologist, and he confirmed Liam's death. Now why would he do that if he wasn't dead? And why does this Russian lieutenant general emerge at the same time Catlin appears three thousand miles away? I never buy into coincidences. I'm inclined to believe he was telling me that he knew what was happening but was not part of it. Somebody is playing a long game here and I'm happy enough to play as well, but I'm not being the sacrificial pawn at the start of any game."

"I see, Patrick, but I'm sure there's a rational reason for all of it. Let's start at the beginning, shall we? Why was there the need for you to speak to a pathologist about the incident in Ireland? Straightforward case, I would have thought."

We were entering the drawing room from the hallway and taking our positions seated each side of his inglenook fireplace with a roaring log fire to warm my aching bones. I managed to stretch out my legs and ease the pain in my foot after that two-hour atrocious drive from London.

"Political! I was told the Irish Office in Whitehall were sweating over possible future legal action coming from relatives of the civilians that were killed or wounded in the pub. Beyond me, but there you have it. I was checking on the numbers."

"So you never attended the post-mortem?" he asked as he pushed the three-quarter-full decanter across the small table between our chairs towards me.

"No, didn't have time. You know how it is."

"And I know the tricks top floor can pull. I think you'd better grab your glass and follow me, laddie." With his index finger across his lips he led the way to what he called his bunker; his office on the front corner of the house. The room was full of filing cabinets and furniture but nothing could subdue the smell of pipe tobacco. With the door firmly closed behind us I took up the conversation.

"Never thought of opening a window and letting in fresh air, Fraser? This smoky atmosphere can't be good for your health."

"If I open a window any Tom, Dick or Harry can aim a directional microphone in through the gap and the same could apply to an extractor fan. The tobacco smoke is part of me, laddie. In any case this room must be kept airtight. You see I don't think it's you that they're after, Patrick, it's me and what I know. This place is as secure as anything there is in this country. The glass is specially made to obstruct any speech monitors aimed inside and as I value my privacy, it also jumbles up the camera shots. We can make some remarkable equipment in this country. The books that stack the shelves are fake. They are an anti-bugging device invented by a Scottish friend of mine. Let's get on with business though. I'm pleased you've met Henry Mayler as I believe he is the key to it all. If he had not been who he is I would never have taken him on and become his case officer. There were a lot quizzical faces turned my way when that happened. Have you seen that tattoo of his?"

"Yes, I have but I didn't see any comments on it from you in his file."

"You won't. That tattoo is the clue to what he is. Look, I'm not going to mess you around with pretty stories or tales of spin. It's my opinion that although Henry's tattoo must have been seen by many in our business before me, none were either unaware of its sensitive background, or could not find the connection to his birth. When I discovered it all I hid it. I hid it from every intelligence department in this country. It would have stayed hidden if Fyodor Nazarov Razin had not emerged from his hole."

"Were you successful in concealing it from the American services?" I asked before he could continue.

"Of course I was. I certainly don't want them spooked."

"Then I don't know why there's an American 'hands off' notice plastered on my Russian. Care to get down to some of the graphics of this, Fraser?"

"I will but I can only give you so much tonight. I'm afraid there are not enough hours to tell you it all. I need my sleep nowadays. Mrs Ughert's domineering nature has trapped its quarry since I became a septuagenarian three weeks ago."

"Do you think you were forced to retire, Fraser?" I asked without much compassion in my voice.

"Force as in power or strength then no, seventy was always going to be the official cut-off age for me, but I was hoping to continue my influence into next year because of Henry, and I'm still hoping I'll be able to manage that, but time is running short for what I believe is about to happen. There's nothing sinister to my retirement, but I can't allow Mayler to be handled by anyone other than me at the moment. I don't know the whole story yet, laddie, and I want to. Perhaps your Russian, Mr Raynor, may have the answers." He gave me that avuncular look of his that so annoyed Geoffrey Harwood. He lit his old meerschaum pipe and I added to the smoky haze by lighting one of my cigarettes. He filled our glasses up before continuing.

"I believe the tattoo to be the sign of a mystical order, thought to have vanished some six hundred years ago, called the Rosicrucian Fraternity. Mayler's tattoo was said to be the symbol of that organisation and was referred to as the Rosey Cross."

"That ties a loose end up for me and as you know who Fyodor Nazarov Razin is, it makes it even better. Henry Mayler told me of his meetings with Razin where he was called Rosco, short for Rosicrucian perhaps. He had no answer for it and I believed him. Was I wrong, Fraser?"

"Not at all wrong. Let me explain some things. When Geoffrey Hardballs had your chair at Group and Sir Gerald Butler was Director General at 6, Butler called me one day and invited me to lunch. That in itself was suspicious as it was the only invitation

I'd ever had from him. He never even asked me out to lunch when I took over as chair of joint intelligence.

"He told me that Arthur Drefus, a dean at Oxford and a long-term talent scout for the security services, that I knew very well, had signed up an Armenian German with what looked like some sort of secret order tattoo on his hand. Drefus was very unhappy about a couple of things though; one being the tattoo. Despite those reservations he said the boy had huge potential if he vetted well, so he passed his papers on to 6, eventually landing on Butler's desk. Butler said he firmly believed nobody had picked up on the importance the recruit represented, not Drefus or any in vetting. Nearing the end of that lunch he passed me a slim file with no heading or classification, and he told me of his retirement plans.

'I'll be off within three months, Ughert, I have my retirement planned, but before I leave you and I are going to create a false cover to handle this Henry Mayler chap Drefus has recommended. I know you're on the square and I also know of your extensive knowledge of the history of masonic rituals and the parallelisms to hieratic customs. Mayler is a Rosicrucian and not just an ordinary one at that. Look at his birth date—03/01/1970. The numbers, when added, equal twenty-one, divisible by three. By the time 2003 is here Mayler will be thirty-three on 03/01/2003, the date adds up to nine and if divided by three we get three, with Mayler having two more threes in his age. You and I both know the significance of the number three to the whole of the Masonic order in all of their diversities. You and I are also aware of the list of Masonic degrees. You will be seventy, I believe, a few months before Mayler reaches that pinnacle of time and I'm hoping you will still be around to handle him or at least guide someone else in his handling. Perhaps by then you will know what he's up to and stop or help him, depending on what it is. At this moment in time I can supply no

reason to suspect anything harmful to this country, but I'm a suspicious old fart and I think you are too'."

When Fraser finished recalling that conversation he looked ill at ease, fiddling with his pipe and rubbing his blue-veined nose. There was something he was hiding.

"Geoffrey Harwood asked me if I knew anything of Freemasonry on the drive to the farm, Fraser. When I told him I didn't, he implied that I would be hearing more."

"Yes, Hardballs has mentioned it more than once recently to me." His face took on a grave expression as he tried to fashion a smile. My mind was in third gear racing into a corner where I didn't want to turn over.

"Did Razin dig up the significance Henry represented to us and now he's haunting you with it, do you think?"

"I am thinking along those lines, Patrick. Yes, that could well be the reason he's here." He knocked out his pipe and stared at the wall opposite.

* * *

Fraser Ughert and I had known each other for some thirty years, in which time we'd worked together on a couple of assignments, including the one with Jack Price and Job where I'd lost my toes. In that time a shared respect had developed between us and a deep trust, but he had divulged a secret that was not his to tell and I could see it worried him. He had always been a painfully thin man, accentuated by his predilection of wearing clothes at least two sizes too big, but as he rose and moved towards a hitherto unopened bottle of malt whisky I noticed how unsteady he was on his feet, rocking from foot to foot.

"I changed the antecedents of all members in Mayler's family, Patrick. Had I not I'm not sure what would have happened. I'm not sure anything would have, but I was not going to chance it."

At least his smile had return to normal by the time he regained his seat.

"All I do know is that Henry Mayler is a big fish in someone's pond. Henry's grandfather was never a doctor, in truth he was a rocket scientist for the Nazis who, in 1946 with his wife, walked from the Soviet sector of Germany into the American part using a crossing point at Helmstedt-Marienborn. At that time in history there was not the physical barrier that Churchill described as the Iron Curtain. Germany was a mess at the end of the war that the Soviet army gave itself little chance to clear up, being more interested in what it could take from the German people than what the German people could do for them. There was one Russian not so badly focused; Marshal General Georgy Malenkov, who Stalin had appointed in charge of missile technology. Sorry, this where the lesson gets a little boring but it's necessary.

"Under the leadership of Lavrentiy Beria, head of the MGB, Ministry for State Security, Malenkov helped to organise the takeover of Central and Eastern Europe with specific instructions to recruit ex-Nazi rocket engineers into the blossoming Soviet missile programme. Magdeburg, Henry's grandfather's home town, was a central location for Hitler's rocket manufacture, and one of the top scientists of the facility was Arek Mayler. Malenkov appointed a Colonel General Sergei Kruglov in charge of the Magdeburg region, who unknown to Malenkov was a member of the Rosicrucians and the Freemasons. Can you see where this is going, Patrick?"

"It's a bit blurred but I'm willing to learn," I replied, suppressing a real yawn."

"Okay, I'll move it along at a pace to keep you awake, young man. Arek Mayler's passage across the divided Germany was made easier by Kruglov for two reasons: one, they shared the same order of Rosicrucians, and two, Kruglov had Mayler in his pocket because there were remaining members of the extended Mayler family still alive and living in Magdeburg. Arek worked as a spy for the Russians, stealing anything of worth from the Americans for whom he worked at the Los Alamos laboratory until it closed a year after he arrived in 1947. He then went to work for the Atomic Energy Commission at their Hanford site, working on weapon grade uranium until he was ordered by his Russian handler to take up residence in London in 1954, and to practise as a doctor, which at one time he was but that was a long time ago."

"But you wrote him up as a fully functioning doctor, Fraser, with printed certificates and qualifications?"

"Yes, I did."

"Are you telling me that you covered Arik's back and you're doing the same for his grandson Henry Mayler, while he too works for the other side? Because if he does work for the Russians then why are we relocating him and what on earth is going on?"

"Let me go back a fraction to Colonel General Sergei Kruglov. That seemingly insignificant man became minister for internal affairs of the whole of the Russian Federation. He was fluent in several foreign languages, including English and was awarded the Legion of Merit and created an Honorary Knight Commander of the Order of the British Empire for organising the security of the Yalta Conference and the Potsdam Conference during World War II. But he and us didn't finish there. When the two branches of Russian national security were merged, he became head of the new MVD, the precursor of the KGB. That was when Mayler came to London, in March 1954. It wasn't a coincidence, nor was the name of Raynor being used as his cover name. Are you following where the Rosicrucian connection comes in now?"

"No," I replied.

I didn't expect his silence. I was gazing at those fake books whilst attempting to concentrate on the story, but when he stopped speaking I thought he might have taken offence at my apparent lack of respect and be about to rebuke me in his customary Scottish manner. But as I gazed towards him I saw a contorted mess of a man half sitting, half standing with his head falling to one side with a look of sheer terror plastered on wide eyes as his spectacles fell from a hand which clutched at his chest in panic. I watched as they bounced on the carpet without breaking, only for him to tread on them as I reached out and stopped him from falling.

"Top drawer, this desk. Small bottle of a red spray. Hurry, laddie!" he spurted out, gasping for air, with both his arms around my neck as I lowered him to the floor.

Chapter Six
Saturday AM

To my surprise, but fortunately not to my humiliation, Razin was outside the Russian Consulate at the same time on Saturday morning as he had been on every morning for the last five, only this time he turned right instead of left towards the underground station. He wore the same unmistakable coat with the fur collar turned up and as a further precaution against the bitter north wind, a beige woollen beanie hat. I had covered my back by having as many operatives as I could on the street if he did show, but as the Silver Vaults in Chancery Lane were closed I had concentrated what I had nearer Notting Hill Gate. The only intelligence we had from the vaults was the name of the man Razin always contacted, and the fact that he always carried away four unfolded envelopes in those huge pockets of his on the journey to Highgate where he unloaded them. We had no idea what was in those envelopes. The named trader was an American with an FBI and police record from here. The FBI one was for an armed assault some thirty years back and here he had flagged up as 'a person of interest' on a recent bullion robbery. Without his marriage to an English woman, who had since passed away, he would never have gained British citizenship. We had nothing on him, and could not guarantee that his name would not light up any interested American monitor if we paid an uninvited visit. We couldn't lift him and risk alerting Razin.

The total weekend staff at The Hole was the same as Friday's, however, my weekend Hannah was more the image of what I had expected; efficiency with no frills. The duty officer, Abraham, looked younger than the deputy I'd seen yesterday but I was pleasantly pleased to see the same Solomon who had been on duty the day before. Despite the fact that I had no tangible explanation I felt more in control this morning than I had done the previous day.

At the Consulate I had two lamp-burners with an additional two in two cars, then there were three others, in the two remaining cars I had available. I was confident that with the static satellite cover providing an overhead view I had enough. My eyes were glued to the visual display unit in front of me whilst I listened to the tape recording of my meeting with Fraser the night before. He'd had an attack of angina, but thankfully he was well equipped to deal with it having, so he told me, suffered from them for a good many years. After the self-administered mouth spray, he found his breath and he was able to add one additional comment before his wife, Molly, led him away, confused over who deserved her cutting glare the more. He said,

"Gerald Butler arranged for the Maylers to move to England, Patrick, knowing exactly what Henry's grandfather was. Search for Meredith Paine. He and Sir Gerald ran the whole operation from 1954 onwards, but Kruglov was ours well before then. Look up who Oswald Raynor was. It might become clearer if you find what he did and begin to understand why Butler had no choice but cover everything up."

That's what I must do, I told myself, observing the screens as the coffee I'd ordered arrived; but I said it out loud. "I must find Paine." My two heads of departments and my personal assistant looked startled, but the girl who had brought the coffee went ashen-faced and hurried off towards the kitchens before I had time to request a spoon. I thought it best to drink the coffee without sugar rather than risk more anxious examination of my word—Paine. As the warming, but bitter drink hit the back of my throat I watched Razin make his way briskly along Bayswater Road towards Marble Arch. Along with Solomon I retreated to my office to watch not only him, but for any more signs of Liam Catlin around Aleppo airport.

* * *

I had read the compact files on all of my station officers, but the one who was here on Friday and again today stood out above the rest. Real name Michael Simmons, aged thirty-six years, rank of station officer for three of them. He walked with shoulders back and swinging arms in a military fashion, practised no doubt whilst serving in the Life Guards, the senior regiment in the British Army and having a nickname that reminded me of Geoffrey Harwood—The Piccadilly Cowboys. Simmons' file read as though it should have been him promoted to my chair instead bringing in a street man like myself from outside the club. The short exchange of pleasantries I'd shared with the man only served to increase my inquisitiveness as his accentuated r's and elongated s's were of the same manner as Harwood who had served with The Sherwood Foresters before they were amalgamated with another regiment. If the two of them did share similarities then I could not imagine Geoffrey scurrying around in the same fashion as this Solomon seemed to have done on Friday.

* * *

My three lamp-burners were doing the job of keeping in touch with Razin by staying close enough to see if he spoke to anyone, but hopefully not being noticed by him. Solomon had moved the three in the two cars ahead of all this, waiting in side streets out of sight. Razin turned left from Bayswater Road into Edgware Road, and he entered the first café he came to. Within seconds a woman in her forties and a man in his thirties appeared on the two streets corners flanking where he sat. They were both wearing bright yellow tabards with the word of the charity for the homeless—*Shelter* emblazoned on them. They were ours! Each carried an equally bright yellow collecting bucket which they shook whilst trying not to watch Razin selecting a hubble-bubble pipe to puff on. Hannah could not find anything recorded on agency databanks about the Lebanese café to cause suspicion, but Solomon pointed at the waiter who took Razin's order and then delivered his coffee.

"I'm sure that's Oman Rezach, a known Iraqi member of Al-Qaeda who's wanted in connection with the Nairobi Embassy truck bombing four years ago. I'll post it through recognition then get in touch with the Africa desk at Vauxhall if it comes back positive."

"If you're right, hold on to the information for a while, Solomon. I want to see what else he wants to show us because I believe that's exactly what he's doing. If he wants to give this one over to us I wonder if there are any more he'd like to unload."

It seemed to me that my first inclination to believe Razin was stringing us along for some reason was right, as he'd made no attempt to conceal his presence in this country nor had he tried to hide this morning's walk. I was trying to fathom out why that was and why he gave us a known terrorist so easily, when he rose from his table making a show of leaving what appeared to be a tip and walked to where one of the Shelter collectors was. He chose the female operative. She played the role to perfection, pushing her 'bucket' towards him and rattling whatever loose change there was inside practically under his nose. He reached inside a pocket of that coat of his and put something in the bucket. Then after a bow that Geoffrey would have been proud of he turned away from our 'collector' and waved at my other collector on the opposite corner. Was that right? Perhaps he'd stumbled? Yes, that must be it, stumbled and shot his hand out to protect himself. No, that wasn't it.

"Did he just wave at the sky, Solomon?"

"Worse than that, sir. Ruth, the girl holding the bucket, saw the address on the envelope he pushed into her bucket. It was addressed for the attention of Mr P West, 67 Lavington Street."

* * *

I telephoned Geoffrey Harwood at his home which being a weekend was tantamount to treason; despite knowing that, I compounded the issue by swearing at him and calling him a wide variety of indecorous names. Finally I shouted, "Who knew I was fronting this operation, Geoffrey? Who effing knew?"

Two hours later, and still as agitated, I sat opposite Harwood in his new office at No 1 Millbank, overlooking the Thames, the Box and the Houses of Parliament. I could smell his pride and taste the superiority in his answers. I could also tell how much he hated his weekend being disturbed.

"I would have appreciated something in the way of an apology for disturbing last night's evening with Oliver, but as it appears you have a tendency of wanting to disarrange my affairs I will put a stop to it once and for all. I've absolutely no idea as to the breadth of knowledge of your appointment, Joseph, but if you're thinking there are senior officers plotting your downfall and you need a shoulder to cry on, old boy, then I'm certainly not going to massage your enormous ego. I take it that was the thought you carried on last night's flight into Uncle Fraser's arms?" He was as angry as I had been, but his self-control was better than mine.

"No! I needed some clarification, Geoffrey. It wasn't my fault that I needed to disturb you and Oliver. You should have briefed me better."

"Is that what you think, is it? Why so much fuss? Why not simply ask me or just slide over to Chearsley instead of telling the whole intelligence community of your intentions? Why was that necessary?"

"Because I don't trust half of those who make up the intelligence community and I wanted the other half to know where to look for the bodies. Why was I never told that Liam Catlin was not killed in the Derry bombing? Who deemed it necessary for it to be covered up and what the hell is he doing in Syria?"

The customary Harwood sneer greeted that attack, the very one that had earned the label of Hardballs from more than only Fraser Ughert. It preceded his sarcastic reply.

"Why were you never told, dear boy? Because you were being transported on horseback or, at best, a helicopter while the rest of us were floating through the universe on clouds of cotton wool taking little or no interest in the inconsequential things in life such as yourself. You were nothing more than a soldier with a soldier's responsibilities and a soldier's need to know. In other words you never needed to know. That was then, now is now. Why was it covered up? By that I think you mean why was Catlin not covered up in a body bag. Ha, ha. There's a joke there, Joseph. Oh do try not to look so glum, dear boy. Back in those dark days of unmitigated fun and violence in Ireland, you were not told about the bigger picture because you didn't know there was a bigger picture.

"Now you are in charge at Group you're told what's hiding behind the first coat of paint the same as I was. One day the whole bloody painting will be hanging on my wall with my paintbrushes underneath and there will be no mention of you in the margins. Now, if you'll be so good as to allow me I'll get to your third ridiculous question and call an end to this farce. What the hell is Catlin doing in Syria? He's working for us within a group of Kurdish Sunnis, bestowing Her Majesty's love on their camels and horses as well. Can you see beyond that first coat of paint? Razin knows Mayler, Mayler knows Razin. Mayler has contacts within the Kurds, Bashar al-Assad of Syrian notoriety has Russia as an ally. Razin's Russian. Catlin is balancing things up by looking after our interests. The Americans want us to have no view on the situation that will develop between the Kurds and Assad and we, dear Joseph, old chap, say, well, you know what we say when told to keep our hands off.

"You should have come straight to me before throwing a tantrum and disturbing our elder former colleagues. You will not dispose of your layers of fragility that you're trying desperately to hide any quicker by running to outside help than staying within the camp. The first thing you must consider is that we are all on the same side as you. I hope you won't be making that mistake again, dear boy. That would be a mistake too far." The sneer had turn venomous by the look of his tightened lips and narrowed eyes.

"I'm still waiting for you to answer my first question, Geoffrey. How did Razin know?" I was up for the fight if he wanted one.

"Now you are becoming more than tiresome. Are you accusing me, Patrick, because if you are then—" He screwed his lips tighter, biting hard onto his bottom jaw, never allowing the threat to materialise into anything concrete. It was left floating in the air, slowly mixing with my cigarette smoke.

Chapter Seven
Saturday PM

It had been snowing during the day and more was falling as we drove further away from the centre of London, transforming the beauty of the English countryside from its normal alternating shades of lustrous green into a kaleidoscopic pattern of white shapes beyond a road of wet, grisly grey. I thought I'd left Mayler with the impression that I'd finished with him, and to be honest, normally what we'd spoken of and gone over would have been adequate, but none of what I'd since learned fitted any description of normality.

Henry was huddled up alongside one of the electric heaters in his accommodation wearing a big army issue overcoat, woollen gloves and a fur hat with earmuffs. I guessed he was too cold to register any surprise.

"Are you trying on the everyday clothing for Canada, Henry? Good to see you're getting into the spirit of it all. Acclimatising yourself with the temperature as well are we? Very good, but would you mind if I had it turned up a wee bit whilst I'm here, then you can have turned down again when I leave." I hoped my sarcasm would not be missed by the guard who stood holding the door open.

"Would I mind? Are you joking, Mr Funnyman? I'm freezing my balls off in here! If it gets any colder I shall be a eunuch by the time I leave. I've asked for the heating to be turned up, but who am I to request such a thing. I showed one of guys who are supposed be looking after me the ice hanging from the toilet cistern, and he laughed and asked if I was a man or a mouse."

"I'll have the heating turned up right away, sir," the guard at the doorway replied before I'd asked.

"I shall give our guest my duty officer's telephone number and if he gets cold again he will call that number. The word will climb the chain to me and when it does I will descend on you and your commander with all the considerable power I enjoy and the two of you will be spending the rest of your careers freezing at the weather station we have in the Arctic. Tell him, please, that I will make sure you both spend as much time as possible patrolling outside." The door was closed quietly on the guard's departure, but I didn't wait until the tin hut warmed up before I re-questioned Henry.

* * *

We sat beside each other in the back of my ministerial car with two mugs of steaming coffee and the heater turned on full with Jimmy, my driver, and Frank, my whatever you want to call him, standing in the farmhouse doorway about ten yards away incessantly looking in the car's direction, but I was at a loss to understand why. I wondered if it was in standing orders or just an intuitive gesture of theirs specifically for me owing to the fact that Henry had a psychopathic side to his nature I had yet to read of. Perhaps it was simply because I was looking feeble in these aged years of mine, decrepit and in need of someone's muscles or eyesight to survive a chat with one of ours? Or was he one of ours?

"I want to go over the last meeting you had with Razin. The one that took place in Syria a week ago." He went to speak but I stopped him. "Before you tell me that you've already told Elijah and you are sick of repeating yourself, I'm afraid I must insist,

Henry. I cannot grant you a passport to a brighter future until we have covered it all."

He drank greedily from the mug of coffee, the steam coating the window that he sat next to. The distorted outside lights from the farmhouse transformed his sharp-cornered face into a cadaverous figure of gaunt bones and shrivelled skin. He wiped the condensation away from the window, peering aimlessly into the clear night's sky before he began.

"I don't often see this side of the buildings," he announced with a tone of regret in his voice. "They have, on a few occasions, allowed me to walk through the yard where I'm told the modernistic milking sheds are, but walking there is kept to a minimum. I was told the cows choose when they want to be milked and wouldn't want to see me before that happened. I might spook them, they said. I thought that was funny. Me, a city boy, spooking a wild animal instead of the other way around, madness!" A look of sadness descended upon him which his next observation did nothing to remove.

"The milking is all done by an automated system, apparently. When I was told, it made me wonder how long it will be before there will be no jobs for humans? But I guess there will always be one for us, Mr Joseph, men on the ground as it were." I didn't answer nor did I think he wanted one. He did want to talk.

"Do you know what my first job for the service was, Mr Joseph? Have you got that far yet in my memoirs?"

"Tell me, Henry. You will always find a listening ear with me." He laughed at my reply.

"One day you'll read them I'm sure of it. London sent me into Chechnya, via Armenia, with a Russian passport about this time of year in 1994 to photograph the Soviet weaponry and whatever I could get on their military. I was raped there, Mr Joseph. I bet that's something you never knew."

Wow! He was right I had not read that, but apart from feeling sickened by it, what could I say. I left any response to him, as, thankfully, he never lingered on the event. I guess the screams inside his head were mostly his own, but from somewhere came the solace that allowed him to continue.

"I want to become as impersonal as that milking machine yet hold on to my personality. I don't want to become a robot which I feel I'm being groomed for here. Same questions, same answers, only repetition of what's led to our introduction. Can we not move on from that and speak of my future in Canada? Will I still have a role to play, be of use; that kind of thing? I don't expect you to be specific, but just an idea of where you see me being of service."

My raised voice of frustrated protest rebounded inside the car, causing Jimmy and Frank to run towards us and before I could say or do anything both rear doors were slung open and two HP-35 pistols were pointing at Henry's head.

"As I just said, Henry, I think we should concentrate more on what I want from you rather than what these two men might do to you if I raise my voice again. Ask yourself who would pine over you? Who would ask where you are? Is there anyone? No, there's not, and we both know that. I'm not blessed with as much patience as Elijah. My question was about Razin. Please address that."

"Razin, yes. The Russian."

As he spoke the guns were holstered and we were left alone with the promise of more coffee to come, away from the exactitude of rape.

"Okay, I start again at the beginning for you, because you know who can make good coffee and where the heating valve is, not because you threaten me. I had been in Damascus for a matter of days. I arrived at 10:28 on Saturday morning and it was late on the Wednesday that I met with Razin. That's as precise as

I can get. My wristwatch broke the day I arrived and the thing which ferried me from place to place had a broken clock. I'm sorry." I interrupted.

"Ferried you say. I have a Mercedes mentioned in the file and a driver by the name of Hadad as your guide. Is that correct?"

"It is, yes, Mr Joseph. I used the wrong word. I apologise for my lack of understanding of your English idioms, but really it was a wreck on four wheels. Hadad met me at the international airport in that Mercedes. From there we followed the trail of Alaz Karabakh, the man London had sent me to trace and report on."

"What did London tell you of this Karabakh and what was he up to exactly?"

"Control said that Karabakh was a Syrian-Armenian who was stirring the Sunni Kurds up along the M4 corridor of Northern Syria to rebel against the government led by Bashar al-Assad. He was, according to what I was told, instrumental in forcing the Damascus Spring uprising upon Assad after President Hafiz al-Asad died." He stopped and lit another cigarette and when satisfied all was well with it added, "Karabakh was killed in a place called Al Hasakeh."

"That's not written down anywhere! Why have you never said that, Henry?"

"I did! I told Elijah because he was the first person I saw when I came to England." His tired, brown eyes fell on me and without blinking held that apologetic gaze for longer than I liked. His confession had decimated me and he knew it.

"I think we could both do with that other coffee, Mr Joseph. My throat is dry and I reckon you could do with the distraction."

If I was distracted it didn't last long. Henry Mayler was into his stride before any thoughts of mine could drown out his dialogue.

"Hadad, my driver, was given to me by London but I never trusted him. After following this Karabakh character for four and a bit days and getting names and photos for Control, Hadad comes to me with a story he'd heard from someone inside Assad's holy of holies. Karabakh is to secretly meet a high official from the Arab Socialist Ba'ath Party, the same party where Assad is the God, to discuss a union between an Islamic State of Iraq, an umbrella grouping of a number of Iraqi insurgency groups and Osama bin Laden's Al-Qaeda. Those were the exact words he said. He then told me that the Al-Qaeda man was from ISI, the Pakistani Inter-Services Intelligence. This meeting was to convene at a place called Al Hasaketh, in the north-east corner of Syria.

"In my initial briefing London told me that Karabakh was one of the people who made massive amounts of legitimate money by something called 'put-options' placed on two airlines before bin Laden's attack on the Twin Towers. I wanted into this operation so much. I wanted those photographs. This was the holy chalice, the stone of the sacred philosopher. Pure uranium for Henry, to power many more operations."

"Were you under the impression that your cover, and therefore your value to us, was coming to an end, Henry, only you made that last statement sound rather sombre and despondent?"

Our coffee arrived via Jimmy, and I took the opportunity to have a smoke outside the car. Henry joined me with his sweet smelling Turkish cigarette that he had still to finish. Before I had left what Harwood called 67, and I referred to as The Hole, I had directed the morning security chief officer to thoroughly sweep my car, my office and my upstairs living area. Nothing had been found, but I still had that uneasy feeling of being intrusively spied upon, if not that then at least evaluated.

"I did think my usefulness was ending, Mr Joseph. This operation was my first since the one in Afghanistan that I told you about. Over a year doing kosher freelance photography was making me question if I'd ever be used again."

"You hadn't spoken to Control for almost a year, is that true? Was this strange, or had you had breaks of that length before?"

"Yes, it was very strange. Before Afghanistan we would message each other on the phone if I was out of reach for any length of time. Sometimes we would meet and chat if nothing was on and we were near each other. Not often, that's true, but sometimes. Once when everything was warm and friendly we went to a party together. But after Afghanistan ..." He shrugged his shoulders with his eyes visibly moist.

"Was there anything different about how Control contacted you with the information about Alaz Karabakh, and were you told at the same time that Hadad was to be your driver, or did that come at a different time? It's important that you're accurate and precise, Henry."

"I am always accurate and precise, Mr Joseph. Control's instructions came the usual way with a series of numbers in an SMS. The numbers translated into a designated street somewhere close to where I was. On a wall along that street would be a chalked written message in code again. That would direct me to an address somewhere close by. At the address I would be given yet another number coded message. Once I had deciphered that final message I was aware of Hadad and Karabakh."

"Okay," I quietly replied before setting off towards the yard and those milking sheds he previously referred to under the clear sky with a full moon to guide our steps. When we out of sight of the main house we started where the file had finished; Karabakh in Al Hasaketh with a political leader and a Pakistani hood, presumably to oversee the proceedings.

"The meeting was in a grocery shop in a bazaar in the town. A difficult if not impossible place for me to get close for photographs of London's target meeting Assad's man, and the ISI agent, but I had what I thought was a piece of luck. Hadad knew the owner and while they exchanged hugs and greetings by the thousands I got my look into the backroom. I was wearing a wireless pin-hole camera that shot the video into a remote receiver I'd left in the car. It was on record for a regular ten-second burst and although I figured I had enough from the first take, the element of uncertainty was too strong to ignore. It then went-tits up, as you English say.

"I pretended I'd tripped over some crates beside the closed curtain beyond which was the meeting. By the time I'd dusted myself down the camera had run for a full cycle again and I was certain I had the three of them on film. That's when Razin and I saw each other. He must have been there as the Pakistani ISI. He slit both Karabakh and the Arab Socialist man's throats in a single movement. He used the same knife that I'd seen in Khost. 'Follow me,' he said in a cold, calm voice and I did. 'Grab your driver,' he said and I did. If he had said cut your driver's head off and here's the knife to do it, I would have done it. How do you kill two men and act as if it's a normal day, Mr Joseph?" Although I had an answer to his question I decided not to offer it. Instead I asked a question of my own.

"I need an opinion now, Henry. A core feeling you may have had. Would you say Razin butchered the other two to protect you, or do you think he would have killed them had you not tripped?"

"Oh, I believe strongly that he murdered them for me, Mr Joseph. Of that I have no doubt. I wish it were different or I could fool myself into believing your second theory, but that would not be the truth. Have you an answer as to how I can go on knowing that my stupidity cost two lives, or should I carry on ignoring it do you think?"

It was Henry's act of stupidity that cost those two lives as Razin would not risk being exposed without a good reason. He wasn't there to murder anyone, he was there to listen and direct. I had no words that could have cured Henry's debility, his sickness was irreparable.

"Why was it that you needed London to extract you from a situation that Razin seemingly had under control, Henry? I mean it wasn't as though your life was under threat, was it?"

"Yes, it was and it still it is. I told all of this to Elijah when I reached London. My Control had vanished. Don't ask me how I knew, I just did, but Elijah never mention it. He had a typist type my report as I was telling him, although I can't be positive he recorded it on his machine—

"After what had just happened I was acutely aware of the danger I had put myself in, but if there was to be any reaction I was expecting it inside the market, not outside. In my haste to get away I tripped over something just before getting to the car. My knee hurt badly and the fall shook me up but I managed to stand quickly and open the car door, that was when the glass in the door shattered. I had no idea what had caused that as I had heard no other sound. For a split second all I could do was stare at what was once a normal car door, thinking that somehow I had broken it. Other than the normal loud noises of a packed street market I'd heard nothing that would indicate someone would be after us so soon. When I eventually got my head into gear the first reaction was to partially turn my head towards the back of the car, that's when it hit me. The only way I can describe it is that it was like having a cricket ball bowled very hard into my upper thigh. It hurt like hell. A similar thing happened to me when I'd played in a varsity cricket game in the Parks one year against a really quick bowler. I know this will sound stupid and melodramatic, but time seemed to stand still for me. Everything was moving in slow motion to the point of stopping. The bazaar went silent to my ears. I have no idea why I looked to the rear of the Mercedes and not the front, but that's where I looked. I was lucky in some ways as the bullet had hit hard muscles and was imbedded in them. I was thankful to have done lots of walking and standing in my job as a photographer. There was very little blood coming from the wound and just a small hole in my shorts and my upper leg. It was as I was looking

at my wound that he pulled me inside the car. I was completely dazed and out of it all. He was the opposite. He just stood there in the open, firing off round after noise round in the direction from where the bullet in my leg must have come. He was shouting, but I haven't a clue what he said. All I could see was his mouth opening and closing very quickly. My ears were hurting from his gunshots as much as my leg from the bullet. The firing stopped and I had a peep through the back window. I saw one of them. He was black, but not an Arabian black. Perhaps a European black going by his modern, stylish clothes. He was on the ground and not moving, but there was another man running away in a zig-zag fashion. That man was tall, thin and had blonde hair. Hadad, that was my driver, was also on the ground by the rear door of the car. He was lucky having taken only a grazing shot to the shoulder and was meekly seeking cover. I gave him my hand to help him into the back of the car. Then the Russian drove the car as though possessed with its tyres screaming under clouds of dust.

It was I who noticed the car that was chasing us. Razin, the Russian, had his eyes notched up five times their normal size and fixed like glue on the road ahead, for that I was thankful; the car was travelling as if there was a rocket under the bonnet. I told him about the car that was following and he pulled a gun from under the thawb that he wore. There was another gun, I presumed that to be the one he'd used outside the bazaar, tucked under his left leg as he drove. I remember thinking that I hoped the safety was on. Very calmly he told me that as soon as he had a chance he would pull our car off the road and ambush the one behind. That wasn't the exact language he used, but that's what it amounted to. He spoke in Russian but I can understand the language. He gave me the gun from under his leg and a new clip from the pants he wore under that robe. He asked if I'd fired a weapon; I lied and said I had.

We rounded a sharp bend past some low, sandy hills and then the road turned abruptly right in the opposite direction we wanted to go. Razin slung the car behind one of those hills off the road and shouted at me to get out. Clutching his gun to my chest, I did. He ran across the dusty road and hid. From across there he had the clearer shot than me and hit the driver before the car had fully rounded the bend. It veered violently towards me before it overturned and came to a halt. I shot the passenger from where I'd been hiding, but Razin got to the car before I had and I saw him take something from the driver. I have given thought since then about what it could have been but honestly I have no idea what it was other than it was small and flat like a phone. But I can't swear it was a phone. It could equally have been a letter. In fact, I think it was a letter. After he put two more bullets in them both then setting the car on fire, we drove off, not speaking again until we reached Aleppo.

"I left Razin in Aleppo with Hadad. He had spread some sort of gel on Hadad's wound after we'd dealt with the pursuing car. Razin said he would take him to a safe address and get him help. I took the car, which was covered in dried blood on the back seat, and made it to the British Embassy in Damascus without incident. There I had the bullet removed from my leg. My leg ached like mad but on the Saturday morning after arriving I carried everything I needed in my rucksack and had my passport ready in my hand as I headed towards the Turkish Airlines check-in desk at Damascus airport, when Razin appeared like the ghost he is and grabbed my arm, spinning me around to face him.

'We will meet again, my little Rosco and it will be then that I decide if you live or die. In the meantime play the game that you do, but do not antagonise me again.'

"So perhaps now you can see why I am worried, Mr Joseph, and not only about a big Russian bear. It seems obvious to me that Elijah has not told you all of my escape from Al Hasaketh. That is either because he does not trust you or he works against you and for someone else. Neither of those scripts are written in my favour. I'm grateful for any changes you can make for my present welfare, but I want to know if I have a future and if not it would be nice to know why I am to die?" I did not answer his question.

"Did you ever think to ask Razin what it was he took from the driver of the pursuing car, Henry?"

"No, Razin is not the type of man who someone like me ask questions of."

"Why did you say you thought it was a letter after you said it was a phone?"

"Oh, I don't know. I think I was dreaming of a letter. I had one once from a lover, but, yes, you're right. I don't know if it was a letter or a phone. I think I thought of a letter because the driver was dead and hopefully my lover is not. It may have been the sight of so much blood in one day had turned my mind inwards on itself, Mr Joseph. I think you are a man who is used to seeing blood."

Memories can be killers in themselves so much so that no matter how many times or how many ways one tries to eradicate them, they never diminish or leave the mind. Some stay at the front of the queue whilst others hover in dark places and attack when the rest of the body is sleeping. I have a moderate memory, no better or worse than most people, but Henry was so different, he was cursed with a unique memory.

"When did you contact Razin and tell him that I was to take control at Group, Henry?"

"The second day I was kept in the lovely hotel that overlooked Lord's cricket ground. It was the medical man who attended to my leg who left instructions to call him. I followed the instructions, leaving a message at their embassy in plain English. 'A Mr Patrick West will be in charge at Group from the tenth of this month'. Plain and simple he'd said and I kept it that way."

"And did you go through Elijah to sanction that call, or did you call without asking permission?"

"No, I'm not a Russian spy, Mr Joseph, as you well know. The request went through Elijah. He was the man I was taken to after arriving at Heathrow airport in the rain. He said he was to be my Control until they could place me in Canada."

"Was this man Scottish, Henry?"

"You really are wandering around in the dark, aren't you? Yes, he was, and it was he who first told me your name." He stopped speaking to stamp on his cigarette, grinding it into the concrete before he began again in a sombre voice.

"You know London sent me back to Chechnya in 1999, this time to photograph the slaughter in the capital of Grozny. London had no regard for me being raped. Maybe they are all like you and never read of it. If they did read it, they could not have cared less. I was not raped again although I feared it every day I was there and I was there too long to let go of that fear. After the devastation of Chechnya they ordered me into Dagestan to watch more killing. I was cold there, Mr Joseph, like I'd never been cold before. At least I will be warm back in the hut before one of the guards comes to shoot me, eh?"

I noticed the noise of the wind had died away along with the solitary cow that had been mooing somewhere in the distance. All was quiet and it was the silence that hurt. It wasn't Henry's answer I couldn't handle, it was the answers hiding in the same silence hovering around a different place. I knew Razin's knowledge would have come from nowhere else.

Chapter Eight
Big-Wigs On Sundays

The warming memory of a shared love will stay forever if undisturbed by hatred or envy. Loving relationships that have finished can burn through the entire body causing misery and pain if they are allowed to, but how can they be stopped and never reignited? It seems that the flimsy kind, those of a few nighttime distractions or the kind that temporarily interfere with the clarity of rational thought will stay hidden if not played with or dragged into the present. However, the question remains; what is to be done to remove entanglements that hurt when broken and every now and again we are unable to stop reminiscing about? I was being driven across country away from the farm with its undisclosed secrets towards Fraser Ughert and the conundrum to be faced, when Fianna's memory dominated me as it had done so many times in the eternity since her murder. Once again I was considering how to permanently remove her and the memories from my mind without finding any answers.

Please don't think I'm being frivolous by asking what must appear to be both an irreverent and an irrelevant question about the dead, as I do realise that dear ones that have passed never leave us. However, in order for me to move away from a feeling of responsibility for Fianna's death and Kerry's, I must bury their memories deeper than the bodies. I have tried distractions with married women thereby side-stepping the issues of love, devotion and family. I have even had the interference of a pseudo marriage thrust upon me by the intelligence service, offering vapid sex with a female equivalent of myself suffering the same neurotic illness. Neuroticism was a symptom of greatness according to the long lamented Jack Price.

'The bigwigs who play at being spies at the weekends down Guilford way will not like you, Patrick. Your abnormal obsession with our work frightens them. The devout in this job have that effect on the mentally ill-adjusted, and believe me when I say there are plenty of mentally deranged bigwigs down Guildford way.'

Not a person over impressed by authority was our Jack, and nor am I. It was Molly Ughert who opened the door.

"Oh, sorry, I was expecting Fraser to open the door, Molly. I had telephoned ahead making sure my visit wouldn't interfere with your Sunday lunch and I was trying to save my blushes after last night," I tried to defend myself in a clumsy way. It wasn't necessary.

"You're always welcome here, Patrick, and there's a place set for you at lunch. Last night's attack was nothing new for him and sadly nor I. If he's not working himself into an early grave over you and his beloved secrets, it will be something else no doubt. Come in out of the cold. Go through, he's in his office. He is in there every day now. He seems busier at home than he ever did, despite him telling me he's retired from the service." She pulled a face that resembled a painted clown wearing a wide grin. She must have been born smiling, must have Molly.

"I'll invite your men into the kitchen through the back door so as not to disturb you two. I doubt anyone's fed them. Incidentally, you are coming Friday week, aren't you?" she asked as she turned to go.

"Friday week, Molly? Why, what's on Friday week?"

"It's Christmas Eve, Patrick," she announced, then in admonishment said, "Oh dear, I shouldn't have said your name, should I? I'm so sorry, but I'm sure the house is clean. Fraser has it swept every week."

"Is it, Christmas Eve I mean? Never mind about the name. It doesn't matter nowadays, Molly. I'm so sorry about my surprise, I didn't know I was invited."

"Of course you're invited. It's a standing invitation. Are you coming or not?" she asked, hands on hips resembling my judo instructor just before he knocked me out for calling him a bastard without adding any sir to my accusation.

"I would hardly say no to your fine cooking, Molly, would I! Count me in," I replied with little confidence of being able to come.

"Good! My youngest sister is coming. I'm sure you remember her I hope. She was delighted with your company the year before last. She missed you terribly last year."

"Geraldine, yes I remember her. How could I forget?"

A very elegant, seductive woman aged about the same as myself and of the same height with a captivating character. I wished she was not my type nor was I hers. We had noiseless sex on Christmas Eve and during the following two days. We were discreet, but I was dubious over how long our affair would have lasted before Molly and Fraser became aware of it. Something I would not like nor, I suspect, would she.

"Right! I'll expect you sometime on Christmas Eve before midnight, that's if the ghosts in London don't need you."

Molly closed our conversation with that surprising remark and turned and walked away, leaving me to guess whether *ghosts* was a term Fraser had used, or something she had thought up. I gave her the best smile I could given the circumstances of not fully trusting her husband and walked solemnly towards his office. Fraser was bent over his desk in the bay window surrounded by filing boxes and old-fashioned ledgers, one of which was opened at the letter M. All the lights were on and the heavy duty curtains drawn even though it was only a little after twelve noon.

"Your cigarette brand is in the box, Patrick. Prepare yourself for a long initiation, laddie. I take it you have interviewed Henry Mayler at the farm again?"

"That would be right, Fraser. Henry managed to surprise me with a couple of things."

"You, surprised? No, I don't believe that. I knew you would work it out. All Henry did was hasten the outcome and dot a few I's. Have you had time on the drive to work it all the way through?" he asked as he poured a very large Scotch for himself and an equal measure for me.

He wore that soft derisive smile of his, the one that said, *I know more than you know and if you're good I'll let you in on the secret.* I smiled, not only because of the whisky but because I was right, there was more to come.

"Henry told you about his Control going missing and me stepping into the breach, did he?"

"Not in those words, no. He thought he had vanished, but was not certain. What he did say was that his Control did not speak to him for about a year and nobody answered his plea for help for over two hours when he was in Kabul after the attempted suicide bombing incident. Another thing he said was that Karabakh, the man he was instructed to follow was a Syrian-Armenian who was stirring up the Kurds. You omitted that fact from Mayler's file, Fraser. He also added that you wanted Razin to know that you were now Mayler's Control and I was taking over at Group. Shall we open up with why that was necessary?" At that moment one of the telephones on the desktop rang.

"You're a busy man," I remarked.

"I wish! Did Molly ask how hungry you were? If not that's what she's about to do. Always rings before entering."

Seconds after he had replaced the receiver she had her head around his door asking me if I wanted something now or would wait for lunch in an hour or so. I said I'd wait. To which Fraser seemed relieved, asking the same question as his wife had done about Christmas.

"Thank goodness for that," he said when I replied that I was coming. "There was a time when being surrounded by so many family members would have sent my heart racing, but nowadays the thought of being with Molly's two sisters, our two daughters, plus our two brothers and entourage slows every cell of my body to a crawl. I shall dust off the chess set in readiness." He retrieved the Mayler file from the opened folder.

"Have you had time to find much out about Oswald Raynor, Patrick?"

"No, other than what you told me of his payment for the London home of the Maylers in 1954."

"Yes, so the story would have us believe. But his real claim to eternal fame is that he killed a Russian mystic named Rasputin, of whom you have most probably heard." I jumped at the chance of displaying my intellect.

"Called the Mad Monk by some." I sat back pleased with my memory of Rasputin's more common name.

"We in this county had many names for the man," he expeditiously dismissed my remark.

"Rasputin's story goes back a long way, Patrick, way before the Maylers were settled in this country and way before Sergei Kruglov was a colonel general. Back as far as when the Tsar and Tsarina of Russia were being advised by him. We in this country were well aware that the advice this, as you called him, mad monk, was giving the Tsar would dramatically change the then

First World War raging in Europe. If Russia withdrew from the fight in 1916, and sued for peace with Germany, as Rasputin was advising, all the Kaiser's troops and munitions would be brought to bear on the Western Front and there's no doubt that would have changed the outcome of the war. However, we also used Rasputin, but we played him in another way to the Tsar. Our Royals and the Romanovs were related of course, as were many minor Russian nobles to our own nobility. We suggested that if, as we predicted, there was a rising against the monarchy then Rasputin, with our money lining his pockets and the promise of more to come, would be ideally placed to barter with the leaders of that revolt, the Bolsheviks, and save the Romanovs with the aim of keeping the Tsar as ceremonial head of Russia. As early as 1905 we had penetrated the Bolshevik party but the information from our assets close to Lenin and Bogdanov indicated that Rasputin was having more of an effect on the Tsar than we had given him credit for. Our money had not changed his convictions. The counselling to pull out of the war was gaining favour with Nicholas. Ways were therefore sought to remove this Rasputin and his damaging advice without provoking the royal family.

"In 1916 there was no military intelligence or security groups like we have now, but there was a group within the War Office designated as an intelligence gathering service and it had its own Director General of sorts; our very first C, Captain John Scale. Oswald Raynor was one of the men available to Scale. Contact was made with sympathetic Russian noblemen and a trap was set for Rasputin. Oswald Raynor killed Rasputin. Move the time on thirty-eight years to 1954 and Raynor, now sixty-four years of age, had known of Arek Mayler since 1945 when he and Colonel General Sergei Kruglov met at the conference at Yalta and again met five months later at the one at Potsdam. Oliver Raynor turned Kruglov's head our way with the usual promises of wealth and prestige along with twinkling badges of rank. The Honorary Knight Commander of the Order of the British Empire was one example of what Raynor and Scale provided and the other honour, the Legion of Merit, he arranged with the Americans which Butler told me gave Kruglov a great laugh."

"Did we know that Arek Mayler was passing secrets to the Russians when he was working at the Hanford and Los Alamos sites?"

"Yes, we did. However, our hands were tied so to speak as regards that. We could not expose Arek Mayler as a high level Russian asset because that would have exposed Kruglov, and the intelligence that came from him was considered to be of greater value. This went on for years, but most of what Arek leaked was retrievable by Kruglov, which we in turn played out to other countries' intelligence services so that not all that went back to the Americans came directly from us. It was when Raynor knew Kruglov was about to be discovered that Arek Mayler and family were moved into Montagu Square and Meredith Paine used the company budget to hide the purchase of that and the Harley Street address by using Raynor's name, and in so doing notified Kruglov that his asset was safe. Arek was told that his life as a Russian spy was over and his role as a British one was about to begin. That was the price we exacted for his rescue from the imminent arrest for treason. Meredith acted as his direct handler and things ticked along just dandy. He gave us what he had on the various stages of atomic research the Americans had reached, and cheekily we sent him back occasionally to meet with old colleagues and discuss any progress they were making in the same research fields as well as in missile development.

"When Arek died we left his son, Dietmar stroke Christopher, alone. First to grieve and then to finish his medical exams. Tragically he would not play the game we wanted him to play. Said he wanted out for himself, Elizabeth, and the child she was expecting. We could not allow that as he was aware of what his father had achieved for us and the Russians. Pressure was applied, but he was obstinate, completely unmanageable. Threatened to go to the Russian Embassy and then the America one to expose his dead father as a traitor and in consequence us as his ultimate handlers. Meredith Paine ordered his death. It was signed off in-house and everyone hid their heads in shame apart from Henry of course, as he knew nothing of it. He became the widow's son by default.

"The feeling doing the rounds at that time was that Elizabeth Mayler knew the score and to some extent that was true, because when the proposition was put to her about taking over in the Harley Street address and running it with us paying for and overseeing her son's upbringing, she agreed. We assisted her progression in every financial way possible, Patrick, but Henry Mayler's connection to the Rosicrucian fellowship was our paramount consideration. Christopher's noncompliance was unfortunate, but Henry's birth date added to his father's growing intractability at the time of that birth, changed our perspective considerably. However, Meredith Paine could only see the possibility of a double asset in the newly born male child, he was not conscious of the vital Rosicrucian connection. Sir Gerald Butler was, and with him came his words of warning."

'This is a timeless commitment, Ughert. It passes from me to you seamlessly, understood?'

"When Henry's mother started to make demands about her son's nurturing, we were not about to be indulgent with her as we had been in the beginning towards her husband. She was unhappy with him going to a male only college at Oxford. She wanted us to place him some where he would be able to mix with more females and perhaps disguise his idiosyncratic preferences. She was aware of his sexuality and wished it to be discouraged. We didn't allow the disagreement to fester as we had done with Christopher. Rather luckily Elisabeth's heart failed shortly after Henry moved to Oxford. After a few weeks of being there Arthur Drefus noted the boy's sexual orientation and that was the other concern he expressed when advising Henry's recruitment. On leaving university the casual approach he was adopting in pursuit of like-minded companions was becoming an acute embarrassment to me personally and needed channelling into something less public.

"I was made aware of a young Communist Party card holder who was of the same inclination as Henry working in a branch of the Department for Works in Marsham Street, Westminster. It was not a classified job in any sense, so nobody had fully checked his background and he never flaunted his Communist association. As you are now aware there have been very few people who have handled the Maylers. Kruglov at first, then Meredith Paine, Gerald Butler, followed by me. You are the next in line, laddie. The details of how this minor clerk in the Department for Works was recruited and subsequently how Henry Mayler and he met are unimportant. Suffice it to say that he did as I asked, and for several years was very good at deception. His name was Bernard Higgins. It was essential that I managed our prime asset myself, not only because of what Butler had told me, but also what I knew of the Rosicrucian order. I gauged that the hands-on management of Henry Mayler away from the centre, using an unknown controller, could work if I handled it correctly. I'm pleased to say it did work, maybe better than I thought it would, because now I have regrets which I would not have had if I'd not participated so closely. Let me now tell you of Bernard Higgins and more of my mortification.

"I rented a bedsit in Baker Street near the station, a few steps from the photography college where Mayler was studying, for Bernard. Henry was a creature of habit. He would purchase a coffee in Baker Street prior to arriving at his studies. It was easy to get Bernard and Henry to meet. Henry was hooked from his first sighting, alternating his sleeping accommodation from Montagu Square to the bedsit within days of that meeting. I was required to grease the rather austere landlady's palm more than once."

"And what on earth is the regret for?"

"I am getting to that, Patrick. I wanted everything that Henry Mayler reported graded as ancillary information, not upper level, top-drawer, top-floor stuff. In fact I needed Henry well out of the limelight and in that way I could find the precious time needed to handle the information and keeping him close whilst moulding the reports Bernard sent to his Communists friends. The regret is twofold, one for Bernard's death. His body was found by an American army motorised patrol out of Khost, in Afghanistan, in the week following that foiled assassination attempt in Kabul in November this year. He had been beheaded. I'm not ruling out the beheading being done to look as though the mujahideen were responsible. Among other things your friend Liam Catlin is in that part of the world to find out what he can about Bernard's sudden death."

"And the second regret?"

"I'm unable to tell you all of that story yet. Some things need to unfold before I can."

"Why did Bernard Higgins wait a year to contact Mayler? Henry was visibly upset by that."

"There I think, lies the secret. I ordered Bernard to start a relationship with a CIA officer stationed in London."

"Do you want to share the name with me, Fraser?"

"It's all in what is happening now. You must be patient for a little while and then it will be up to you to tie the pieces together."

I frowned, poured two more glasses of whisky, lit a cigarette and passed on making further inquiries down that avenue.

"So who ordered Henry Mayler into Syria if Higgins was dead?" I asked.

"I did, Patrick. All was done by machine. We never spoke."

"How did you get his instructions chalked up on the wall he told me of?"

"Sorry, more of that later."

"How about Liam Catlin? Who sent him in?"

"Yes, that was me too."

"Who's playing who here? Catlin's a killer, not a tracker, as you and I well know. Henry is the type to go out and find people, then upstairs call in people like me and Liam Catlin to kill them or decommission them at our commander's behest. I'm becoming very worried at the way this is unfolding. First I'm told there's a 'hands off' notice on Razin pasted there by the Americans, and then along comes Mayler with a tale of a firefight leaving a body who in Mayler's words could have been American. Somewhere in that mess Bernard Higgins and a CIA agent have a knees-up leaving heartbroken Henry Mayler alone and forgotten about. Perhaps Catlin is going to kill at least one American and put some indigenous agitators in the frame. Are you running the whole operation from here, Fraser, and telling those up high sitting on Mount Olympus absolutely nothing?"

"No, not nothing, Patrick, I tell them as much as they need to know. Bernard being dead is not what they need right now, nor is the real reason for Catlin's visit. As for Henry, there is no need for me to inform anyone."

"Why did Geoffrey Harwood refer to Mayler as one of your pets, Fraser? You've intimated that he knows nothing of Henry Mayler."

"Hardballs knows nothing of Henry's real interest to me. All he knows is that he's an asset who I ran personally for a time and he's now in need of a babysitter. That's where his knowledge ends and his resentment begins. He was of some logistical use to me. Now he's fretting around hiding any reference to him being aware of Henry. He has no idea what Henry has done for us and if he looked he would only find trivia. What was it he called you when he was selling the head of Group to you; a meat and potato agent, was it?"

"Yes, something pretty close to that. Is Lavington Street wired to your office here, Fraser?"

"If you can remember that far back Lavington Street was my department's property once. It was I who let you and Job use it. A few years ago it was being redeveloped, so of course I had it soft-wired. Geoffrey's people found most, but not them all. But you don't have me to worry about. When Geoffrey moved from Lavington Street he made sure that his AIS at Greenwich had eyes and ears on your domain at Group. He has two cameras and three listening devices. I have noted the positions on this paper. Take it and do what you want with it."

I took it and briefly looked at it. The listening devices were of little importance, but one of the cameras was overlooking the lounge of the upstairs flat. I reflected on why that would be and what I could do with it. My deliberation was cut short by Fraser's perseverance.

"The tunnel that leads to the exit at Stamford Street is the only place where you have complete freedom from any outside interference. There are two lengths of the tunnel where all piping and cables are sunk into impervious tubing so any bugs would have to be mounted on the surface, and easily visible as would the work installing them. Although you cannot be intruded upon along those stretches you can transmit from them. You have my word on that."

I looked at him and worried why I would have need of a safe place to speak with anyone. Just how important was this Henry Mayler and what did he know?

"How deep are the Americans in this?" I asked.

"It's not just the Americans, laddie. I wish it were. It would make things a whole lot easier. No, not just them, it's a world within our own world and I don't mean our intelligence world. I mean the whole world."

"How long have you known Fyodor Nazarov Razin, Fraser? And precisely why is there a 'hands off' from the Americans?"

Chapter Eight
The Savoy

Straight after lunch with the Ugherts, I was bombarded with facts about how we had interfered in other countries' affairs to the advancement of what Fraser called the British State. Next came how European countries had tried but failed to curtail that advancement, and how the world was not only divided by ideology and religion that ended at defined borders, but by states within states; secret corporations existing for their own solitary benefit. Of course the obligatory mention of various American intelligence services allied to their Russian equivalent were introduced to the one-sided discussion. Then finally we came to Liam.

"I hid Liam, Patrick. That was my decision alone. Part of the plan was thought up by the Irish Office thinking of Catlin's welfare. They, and his section leader at special forces, were mindful of the operations he'd undertaken on this country's behalf, twice as many as you incidentally, and proposed an enforced leave from frontline duties. They knew he would refuse, hence that's where I came in. I hooked my plan onto the aftermath of the pub bombing and hey presto Liam Catlin, as Liam Catlin, was no more. But it never ended there. The final say on all matters rested at the Joint Intelligence Committee and I saw to it that the thick blotting paper in that office absorbed it all. Catlin was moved sideways to sit in the waiting room biding his time. It was as easy for me to maintain Catlin's cover as it was to hide Henry. There was nobody for me to answer to other than the parliamentary head of the Home Office and his counterpart at the Foreign Office and Commonwealth Office, neither of whom would have any interest in an assassin able to run to the national press at any given moment provided I kept him below their sights."

"Was my appointment timed for Liam's scheduled arrival in Syria or for Razin's appearance in London?"

"For Catlin's re-emergence, laddie. As I've previously said I want you to supervise Mayler's departure and settlement out of the game. Razin's untimely arrival is, I think, to announce that he's not finished with Henry."

"You do realise I'll go to Syria if needs be don't you, Fraser?"

"Yes, I know you'll probably try. But I don't want you somewhere you will be wasted in both senses of that word. There is a colossal amount of footage to unfold on that arena within the next few years for which the foundations are only just being laid. You can't just jump in and play the spy whenever the fancy takes you, Patrick. There's no point our Director General of Group being out there doing a collection job when I have Catlin with a Kurdish Syrian we trained at Hereford already in situ. The two of them have history together in that part of Arabia. Some of it highly unusual." He refilled the glasses, then on lighting his pipe he began to recall one moment of unusual excitement.

"They were on a British Airways flight that landed in Kuwait the day Saddam Hussein sent his army to invade in 1990. We had prior knowledge of that invasion but not the date. As soon as the pilot of the aircraft in which Liam and Narak Vanlian were travelling heard the news he thought about turning around and flying back. His request went through British Airways to Number Ten. The Prime Minister asked me for my advice. I told him I wanted Catlin and Narak Vanlian to land. The decision was made and transmitted to the pilot to allow flight to continue. As you can imagine the chaos and confusion on the ground aided the two to slip away into the country. Over a period exceeding a year, they cultivated several friendly groups of Kurds that might be useful at some future date, through Iraq and into Syria. Catlin uses Aleppo to travel home from and arrive at. It's his local. He's returned to Syria to meet up again with Vanlian who stays there preaching the gospel. I have need of you on home shores, Patrick, because it will be here where the lasting tomorrows will be constructed. There's one last thing before I must leave you and have my afternoon nap. I want your help in flying someone into Afghanistan without Geoffrey or any other service branch knowing. This AIS department he's put together is a bastard to circumnavigate if entering the country, but I'm hoping it's not so clever looking into departures.

"Hang on a minute, Fraser, let's backtrack a bit. What will those 'friendlies' that Liam's meeting be used for?"

"Whatever benefits civilisation, Patrick, for the good of the majority."

"And who decides what civilisation wants; you, or a committee chaired by Geoffrey and his ilk from Guildford?"

"No, it's not as cold-blooded as that. And I'm not about to tell you any more on the subject. Just ask yourself this—if the intelligence we are getting is correct and there is going to be a huge upheaval in the Middle East in the next few months and years, who would you want making those decisions—the governments of the West or the thugs of the Politburo with power-mad zealots sitting beside them?"

"Given the choice, and having the ability to enforce that choice, then neither option would I choose, but sitting on the fence wouldn't solve any crisis would it? I haven't an argument of a third choice to put forward. I'll shut up and leave you to carry on installing the good guys." He made no effort to reply to my lack of decision. He simply grinned and carried on.

"There's a flight leaving RAF Northolt at 06:23 tomorrow bound for Cyprus. I want you to register this person," he passed me a business card with what appeared to be Egyptian hieroglyphics written at the top of it, "as a captain in the Engineering Corps and get him on board. Use the name on the card. You will have to conceal his passage out from RAF Akrotiri, Cyprus on another military flight into Basra. But I want him in Basra by the early hours of Tuesday morning at the latest. Incidentally, while I'm still awake, at both the coalition bases in Khost and Kabul there is an active CIA attachment on station. I have to consider that Bernard Higgins discovered a connection between that agency and the invisible state that I've mentioned. Let's hope I'm wrong."

"And there was I thinking that Catlin had gone to shake native Bedouin by the hand and exchange gifts. Just as long as I'm not treated like a meat and potato street plod by you as well, Fraser," I laughed but was not fully convinced by his answer.

"Never, laddie, not my style."

* * *

I spent most part of Monday going over what Fraser had said, the files that I had and searching for things Fraser had not told me. I put my day shift Solomon, Michael Simmons, in charge of arranging and setting up a meeting with Razin for the following day. Simmons had served three years on attachment to the Queen's Own Gurkha Logistic Regiment during one of the few peaceful periods in British military history, being stationed overseas in Poland and Estonia as well as doing another three years in the intelligence service in America before being called home with the expectation of the top position at Group on his mind no doubt. His record was impeccable, but more importantly he'd done the boring legwork in all of those overseas places. I needed his experience, plus I wanted to smooth away any rough edges that might be left after he had been passed over in favour of my own promotion. What I asked of him was not impossible, however it did need a surreptitious hand.

As far as anyone was aware Fyodor Nazarov Razin had not been followed since his arrival by any agency, nor had anyone suspicious been seen approaching or being approached by him; but Simmons knew the drill—

'Always suspect there is someone watching, but never look too hard in case you scare them off. Keep them interested in the sting so they miss the trick!'

As a professional he was aware of the precautions to take. As was I. Razin called me on Tuesday morning using the one-time-use phone number from the mobile telephone Simmons had managed to slip into his pocket at Notting Hill Gate station. It was then that I changed the rendezvous point from the Silver Vaults to the Savoy Hotel, not telling a soul until it was all was in place.

When Michael Simmons passed the phone to Razin he included a sealed note of mine. Simmons reported that the Russian had surprised everyone on the platform that morning by reading the note without taking any precautions. He then nodded his compliance in Simmons' direction adding a nonchalant, 'okay' as if an additional spoken word was necessary to confirm his agreement. That casualness was in conflict with all my training in tradecraft experience on the street while out on the spy. I could think of only two reasons why he would be so carefree: one, he was so important that nobody dared to follow him, and two, he wanted to be seen speaking to British intelligence. Whatever it was, I was taking no chances, hence the change of venue.

Since time began, and England had any semblance of a security service in need of information about other countries, the

Savoy Hotel close to the geographical centre of London acted as a source of intelligence gathering. When Group was inaugurated during the War to end all Wars those in charge took advantage of the plethora of loyalists to the Queen and flag one could rely on being employed there. It was there in the early 1930s that the late Jack Price worked as a young pageboy passing on gossip to the intelligence gathers of the day. A fledgling MI5 security service used him as a listening post in the days of Mosley's fascists and some intelligentsia in favour of Nazism. There was nobody in London more accustomed to home-grown spies using the Savoy than the doormen and front desk of that prestigious hotel.

At the rear of the highly polished, imposing, mahogany front desk, where the concierges stand and survey the sumptuous lounge floor with its scores of tapestry-covered chairs spreading out before them, there is an innocuous door blended in the panelling that leads to where extra diaries are kept along with catalogues of regular guests and their wants and needs. It is also used as the place for a sneaky cigarette with a cup of tea whilst resting weary feet. If one does not know of it, then its coordinated exterior has worked, and its function kept secret. My sealed note explained how Razin should ask at the concierge desk for Mr Jones of Seaworld Corporation and then he would be shown the door. We met as the kettle was boiling and my cigarette was alight in a freshly emptied ashtray.

"I read that you're not a Freemason," he declared as he let go of my welcoming handshake.

"Wow! That's some opening you have there. Shall I pop out and buy the necessary regalia while you wait here for me?" I asked sarcastically.

"No, Mr West. I prefer it that way," he replied with no semblance of a smile. "You will not be burdened by the rituals of the Freemason lessons and degrees. They can be overbearing at the best of times. To know nothing of visits to the entrails of the earth or how to rectify your soul in order to find the hidden stone of the true philosophers is really no disadvantage in our present trade. Or is it?" Like Geoffrey Harwood he didn't overburden himself waiting for an answer.

"But no, I am all good as you say in the West. Fantasy is an unknown world to me, unless you count Russian politics as fantasy. I'll have a tea, Mr West, and smoke a cigarette like you."

The file never lied about Razin's age. He was every inch as old as the file said, but at fifty-seven years, only five ahead of me, he looked wrinkled and ancient. His skin was ravaged by wind and rain, motley, blotched and red-veined. The lines across his forehead were of agricultural proportions being deeply cut trenches with the corrugations around his mouth almost as deep. There was a blanched three-inch-long scar on his left cheek and an inch long one under his right eye that appeared younger in age. The whites of his eyes were a washy-grey and the iris, a much faded brown. His small hooked nose was in disproportion to rest of his oblong, hollowed out face where his thin lips rested halfway between a permanent smile and a permanent grimace, giving him an enigmatic expression impossible to read. He had brown hair, parted on the left side and worn at a cropped military length. A pair of spectacles were removed from the inside of that distinctive coat of his which sounded heavy as he laid it across a chair tucked against the wall by the door. Under the coat he wore no jacket against the cold of a London December, just a sleeveless grey sweater, white shirt, and black trousers with highly polished, matching leather shoes.

"I guess you must find London mild at this time of year compared to Moscow, Lieutenant General?" I asked as I offered a light for his cigarette. "The last time I was in Moscow it was very warm. Two years ago at Easter time, stiflingly hot in fact. My daughter Stefanie is the principal ballet master with The

Vaganova Academy in St Petersburg. She was in Moscow with three eleven-year-old students from the academy who were undergoing some training with your own Royal Ballet company who were visiting Russia."

"Couldn't our lot go to St. Petersburg? That would have saved your daughter the trip," I said, not knowing why, but it elicited a curt reply that I wasn't expecting.

"No. If they could they didn't." He exhaled some smoke in my direction. With a distinct display of annoyance I wafted it away.

"Was it at the State University in Moscow that you learned to speak my language as well as you do, General Razin?" I had no reason at that stage to show any disrespect but my politeness escaped my guest.

"I'm not here to waste time chatting amicably over cups of tea, Mr West, as pleasant as that may be. My government does not know of my close connection to yours, so to save some time I'm going to cut through all the bullshit and get right into why I am here in England which I imagine is what you would dearly love to know? Approximately two years ago, I informed British Intelligence that the Pakistani ISI was taking an active role in several Al-Qaeda training camps. The ISI helped with the construction of camps for both the Taliban and Al-Qaeda. From 1996 until this time last year the Al-Qaeda of Osama Bin Laden and Ayman al-Zawahiri became a separate state within the Taliban organisation. Bin Laden sent Arab and Central Asian Al-Qaeda militants to join the fight against the Arab Socialist Ba'ath Party. Among them was Bin Laden's elitist fighting force; the 55th Brigade. The aim behind the intervention was to create a global Islamist revolution. Remember those words, Mr West—global Islamist revolution, as they might haunt you very soon.

"According to the American Joint Task Force counter-terrorism analysts' report I have read, the 55th Arab Brigade was integrated into the Taliban's military where an Abdul Hadi al-Iraqi was asserted to be in direct operational control. Mustafa Mohamed Fadhil was his second-in-command. Don't worry about the names as I've written them all down for you. The Americans are making huge noises saying they have Abdul Hadi al-Iraqi in Guantanamo and they're saying Mustafa Mohamed Fadhil was killed in Afghanistan, but I know that all to be a bag of shit they are trying to sell to the Western press to make themselves look better than the fools and liars they are. I am swiftly getting to the point and no, I cannot supply the evidence at this moment in time, you will just have to accept what I'm saying as the truth. More tea, Mr West, and shall I be mother?" I accepted his offer, smiling at the memory of his not so long ago retort of not staying for tea.

"Two days before the attack on the World Trade Centre in New York, on September 9, 2001, a man by the name of Ahmad Bassriud, but more commonly known as the Lion of Talik, was the target of a suicide attack by two Arabs posing as engineers at Khatuja, in the Sahar Province of Afghanistan. Bassriud died in the helicopter taking him to hospital. The funeral, although in a sparsely populated rural area, was attended by hundreds of thousands of mourning people. He was a hero to them, defending their villages against the might of my country's army and the Taliban. The assassination was not the first attempt on his life. Al-Qaeda, the Taliban, the Pakistani ISI, and before them the Soviet KGB, and the Afghan Communist KHAD had all tried to assassinate Bassriud. He survived those attempts with the help of his followers; let's for the moment call them, friends.

"When the American-led war in Afghanistan began, its stated aim was to capture or kill Osama bin Laden and his Al-Qaeda militants as well as replace the Taliban with an American-friendly government. Bassriud was to become the link between President Bush and the next government of Afghanistan. He was precisely what Bush needed; a forward thinking patriot who would relish the challenge of realising Afghanistan's potential. However, someone, or perhaps more to the point, some organisation, didn't want that and that's why he was killed. I can see I have your attention, Mr West, that is good, but I will need it for some more time, so do not use it all up too quickly.

"There is an American woman who was contracted two months ago to work as a translator for the CIA at a place that was referred to by those who contacted her, as the Posideium. She is my asset, not my government's, but mine. I am disclosing this in confidence, as I have been told my trust in you will not be misplaced." I just sat, listened and watched his gnarled hands illustrate his tale in calm motioning movements.

"I hope that is true," he added chillingly as I withdrew a cigarette and pushed my pack of Dunhills towards him.

"She is telling me compelling stories of regular meetings between senior members of a US intelligence corps and current leaders of Al-Qaeda. All are rostered, numbered, dated and filed openly. It's also attributed to serving officers, but some, not all, of that information is deliberately constructed to mislead. These meetings are not new. A few have flagged up in Moscow Centre in the past. They have been taking place since 1997 under the operational and file name of Gladio B. That name is also written down. Originally Gladio B was a 'stay-behind forces' directive aimed at a possible Soviet invasion of Europe. My superiors were aware of it under that title and designed for that purpose. They dismissed the whole programme as an absurdity and an imaginative myth. But they are unaware what it has developed into.

"According to my asset, some of those named senior CIA agents, note senior please, have met with Ayman al-Zawahiri, a man who is the second in command of Al-Qaeda and senior official of a variety of Islamist organisations which have orchestrated and carried out attacks in North America, Asia, Africa, and the Middle East. They met with him at the American Embassy in Baku, Azerbaijan on numerous occasions between 1997 and 2001. Al-Zawahiri and other leading mujahideen have been transported by American aircraft to Central Asia and the Balkans to participate in Pentagon-backed destabilisation operations. She, my agent, found a 1997 communique emanating from NATO, in Brussels. It requested Egyptian President Hosni Mubarak to release from prison Islamist militants affiliated with Ayman al-Zawahiri. This he did. Those militants were flown under unrecorded CIA intelligence orders to Turkey for training and use in operations by the Pentagon. Those former prisoners are now in Syria.

"In this same file there is evidence of how part of an Al-Qaeda leadership had been training some of the 9-11 hijackers at a base in Turkey in full acknowledgement by persons within this CIA roster. The file is genuine, Mr West, and my operative is the best there is. It is my estimation that Gladio B has transmuted into a cover operation for projecting American power in many of the former Soviet spheres of influence. What I'm not sure about is where the authorisation for such things is coming from. What also worries me and should worry you too, is does this conspiracy extend as far as their Armed Services Committee and the Joint Chiefs of Staff?"

His stony glare gave nothing away in sentiment. His voice was a mechanical recount of facts and figures, name and places with no feelings to the words he chose to use. This was a front line artisan, not an office decoder in a silent room with headphones on and radio dials to stare at all day long whilst jotting down unusual transmissions.

"Intelligence derived from intercepted, deciphered signal traffic in Lubyanka Square, Moscow's Centre of the Federal Security Service, leads me to believe there's some secret foreign policy driven by forces beyond normal constraints to increase covert action and spread disruption through certain parts of Africa, around the Caspian Sea and most importantly in Afghanistan's near neighbours of Turkmenistan and Pakistan."

He stopped speaking to remove a packet of cigarettes from a trouser pocket. He pushed my packet away but offered me one of his. It was a Tekal cigarette. The same brand as Henry Mayler smoked. 'I smoke too much,' he said on taking one. As I lit mine he began my tuition again.

"In a part of Turkmenistan, on the shore of what remains of the Aral Sea, there is a top secret Soviet Union biological establishment with weaponised smallpox, sarin, cyanide and other pathogenic weapons which had not been decommissioned. But when it was last inspected there was an inconsistency. Not all that should have been there was there when the inspectors called. I was included in the select few who saw the report to that effect. Significant spores of anthrax encephalitis were no longer held in its secured state, they were gone. Four cases containing six rounds each of 95-pound M107 artillery shells in which the phials would be loaded, along with 10 cases containing the same number of shells of phosphorous 97-pound M549 shells are unaccountable, Mr West. This particular stock was never intended to be fired from Russian weaponry. It was calibrated to be fired from American guns in someone else's hands, not ours. Ours were to be whiter than white in this conspiracy. We now find ourselves embarrassed as we will not know who fires them and at whom.

"The other senior officers on that inspection committee who read the report, then interviewed several high ranking army and naval intelligence commanders leaving them convinced that someone high up sold them to terrorists, but they have no answer to why other pathogens were not sold. I don't know why either, but I think I do know who was responsible."

"Are we to know who was responsible, General, and if that theft represents a threat to the West?"

"Yes, I will tell you who the culprit is and if I could I would tell you the target, but not yet, my friend, there is work to do first. I have to refer you back to the file again. Everything revolves around that. The original file of Gladio B, with the logistical additions including the digital signatures and my connection to your intelligence service has now been encrypted, and would you like to guess where the code to unlock that encryption is?"

"With you?" I volunteered.

"No," he laughed, "If only it was. I believe your Mr Ughert holds that key, and I'm sure he knows where the encrypted file is, but would you like me to tell you and save you the wait?"

"I'm guessing you might just be on the verge of enlightening me, General. I would certainly appreciate if you could tell me that, yes."

"It is with the head of the people I intimated who shielded Ahmad Bassriud before he was assassinated. They are the friends of his that I spoke of. All are Armenians and perhaps you have heard of their fraternity. I used a shortened version when I spoke to our young friend Henry Mayler that I'm sure you are now aware of; Rosco, but to be more precise, they are known as Rosicrucians. Bassriud was assassinated by a drone strike, Mr West, and the only ones I know who have drones in Afghanistan are the Americans. If you are ever presented with an opportunity to erase my name from any file that falls into your lap, you will remember our conversation of today and how much I have assisted you, I hope."

Chapter Nine
Djibouti

The pulsating beat of reggae music cannoned through the sparse vegetation closely followed by the thundering roar of approaching motor vehicles; however, no music or diesel engine noise could eclipse the rhythmical *rat-tat-tat* of machine guns as they were fired into the air by the columns of mercenaries announcing their arrival at the settlement at Sagi, deep into the desert of Ethiopia. By the time the guns were put away and the band of some thirty or so heavily armed individuals had satisfied their individual carnal requirements, seven men and three women were loaded into two of the open trunks and driven to the port city of Djibouti, the capital of the strategically important country of the same name on the tip of the Horn of Africa, at the entrance to the Suez Canal. From there the hostages were taken to Karachi in Pakistan by boat, where they were divided up.

After a variety of transport methods the seven men were coerced to train as mujahideen soldiers at a place called Faryab, on the border of Afghanistan and Turkmenistan. Several months later and by a sheer stroke of luck three of these seven along with two other mujahideen, were captured by a British special forces patrol after a short fire-fight in the mountains near Pakistan. Of the twelve combatants the British engaged, those five were the only survivors.

On interrogation by the British chief intelligence officer stationed in Kabul, using the translation services of trusted, indigenous Afghans, all three identified two vehicles in the Kabul coalition military compound as being the same models and colours their capturers used when entering their village at Sagi and being transferred into the same before departing from the harbour at Djibouti. They were personnel carriers used by the American Army. What's more, all three positively connected the accents of their abductors to that of Americans troops they encountered on five or more occasions whilst fighting in Afghanistan. That was one of the reports locked away in the floor safe in my office at The Hole. Another one carried the same markings; Top Secret. Level One. Eyes Director General Group:

Dated 23 September 2002
From Strategic Studies Group
Copies To:
Her Majesty's Prime Minister of the United Kingdom
Secretary Of State for Foreign and Commonwealth Affairs
Chair Joint Intelligence Committee
Director General Internal Security
Director General Intelligence Service
Director General Group

Intercepted signals at GCHQ strongly suggest negotiations to lease an area south of the port of Djibouti, where the construction of an American naval base is proposed, are nearing completion. The Americans have already named the base as Camp Lemmonier after a French General who served in the country of Djibouti.

Taking this now certain installation into account, along with the previous communiques forwarded on and attached to this one, it is our estimation to anticipate the following:

1. When fully operational (estimate 2005, if negotiations are concluded this month) Camp Lemmonier will become the centre for a network of any number of US military drones and surveillance bases stretching from the Horn of Africa to The Caspian Sea.

2. The smaller air bases, or remote control drone stations, will have few requirements to become fully operational. They can be situated within local military bases or civilian airports and adequately screened.

3. Due to its tactical location Camp Lemmonier will serve as the axis for aerial operations reaching from the Red Sea as far north as Kazakhstan, including all Pakistan airspace.

4. Drones that will be capable of flying into Saudi airspace, as well as across Pakistan, will not be able to unless permission is granted by home countries. Doubtful in both cases. Therefore we conclude that no permission will be requested. Their radar signature can be impossible to trace without state-of-the-art equipment which neither country has at present. Their probable source for this equipment would be Russia or China.
We have no further information on the above at this time.

5. Long Term Prognosis

We have examined the available intelligence and it is our opinion that the Americans plan to execute further interventions in the immediate area of the Gulf as far east as Pakistan and, if conditions favour it, into the oil rich country of Kazakhstan. It is our combined belief that the concluding end of the chess game for the any American administration is Kazakhstan, and in particular an area known as the Kazakhstan Block, a geological paradise roughly centred on Lake Balkhash. We have intercepted three geological reports addressed to Rosneft, a Russian oil exploration, extraction, and production company, which when analysed detailed huge deposits of gas and oil exceeding known amounts anywhere else in the world, but not only that. There is as much as a quarter of the world's proven uranium reserves in the immediate region.

We ordered a special analysis of financial undertakings in the area and uncovered an English company, registered in the Netherlands, called Barrow & Martin Investment Group. They have been tendering for several sectors of land near Lake Balkhash and its shoreline for industrial development. The company's portfolio did not elaborate further. However, after much digging we found this investment company to be merely a subsidiary company of a far more important group; N M Rothschild & Sons Limited or Rothschild Group, headquartered in London.

There are two obvious routes for gas and oil exports from the Caspian region: one would be through Iran to the Persian Gulf, and a second would be through Uzbekistan, Afghanistan and then either Iran or Pakistan, into the Gulf of Oman. However, a more readily immediate route would be to utilise Western allies of Turkey, Armenia and Azerbaijan and then a conquered Iraq. The port facilities in Kuwait would prove to be ideal. The Americans could re-garrison Saudi Arabia which would facility a two-pronged attack on Iraq. Those troops would have to be stationed for a defined short period of time and then withdrawn. It is our opinion not all will be withdrawn.

At some point the seaport of Ras Al-Bassit, (historically referred to as Posideium) at Latakia, in Syria, becomes pivotal to one party or the other for the overall success in the area. Israel will be encouraged to engage Syria in a military confrontation which the American would then feel an obligation to support on the side of the Israelis. We assume the Russians would side with both the Iranians and Syrians. The escalation of the hostilities will be engineered by one large indigenous terrorist grouping to act on several fronts. We are to be asked to facilitate this. It is not part of our remit to advise on that participation, however, if asked we would add this warning. We must be aware of the general feeling of subjugation in the whole of the Arabian Peninsula. To be seen assisting in arousing unnecessary hostilities in the area on behalf of an aggressor could lead to a global Islamic backlash against this country. The intelligence services would be well advised to tread carefully.

Signed,
General Sir Ralph Warrington
Strategic Studies Group
Ministry of Defence
Whitehall

Those last two sentences kept whirling away in my mind, as did the whereabouts of Liam Catlin. Liam had studied languages at Oxford, often bragging about his knowledge of the different dialects of Arabic and Russian. He was also good at insinuating himself into local Irish Republican army cells. I had no doubt that he would be a founding member of any terrorist army in Syria.

* * *

The ping of Geoffrey Harwood's message announced its arrival on my computer screen. He needed to see me. I knew the reason and decided to ignore him for a couple of hours just to piece things together and to chat with a London-based guy who worked under the CIA umbrella who I'd run across in the past. I was hoping he could shed some light on certain things. We met in the restaurant in the centre of Regent's Park. The wet snow that was falling forced my attention on Geraldine Darkley, Molly Ughert's younger sister, and the Christmas I would be spending in Buckinghamshire. I'd heard that she'd divorced her husband about a year back, on the grounds of his adultery. That was either an act of extreme chivalry on his behalf, or he had walked around with his eyes firmly closed to where his wife's infidelity must have far exceeded his own. She had a partiality for certain men: single, attractive, and well built. I wondered if that divorce had made her more discriminating when it came to sexual partners and now she concentrated on the desirable rather than the merely available. Shamelessly I hoped Fraser and Molly were still fond of afternoon naps as well as early nights. Christmas loomed large on my horizon.

Spencer Morrell, my American friend, and I had very few similarities, in fact I could only think of one: we earned our money in the same trade. He was loud, brash and tawdry whereas I was quiet, modest and refined. I also lied better than him. He told silly jokes and I had no room in my memory to store them. We had known each other for some twenty odd years, first meeting five days after an attempted assassination of the Israeli ambassador to the United Kingdom outside the Dorchester Hotel in London in 1982, and then five days later during the heightened security measures taken for the visiting President Ronald Reagan to address the Houses of Parliament. Our paths intertwined several times over the intervening years and could have ended when Liam Catlin and I were victims of the IRA bomb. Spencer was five minutes away from the Erin Arms on his way to meet with me when the bomb exploded. He was the American unofficial Irish desk in Ireland, trading names of Irish Republican supporters back in the good old US of A for names of left-wing agitators wanting to visit American shores. If anyone knew the real reason for Liam Catlin being in Syria I suspected he would. I was not looking forward to his annoying habit of nosily clearing his throat before speaking. That hadn't altered.

"Ahem—I can't tell you a dime about Syria. In fact that goes for the whole of the Middle East. It's not that I won't, it's just that I don't know. Ahem—whatever's about to kick off in that neck of the woods is hidden from my pay grade. But I can tell you this much; it's going to be something big. I've been fed so many stories over the past couple of months that whoever is in charge of the misinformation has forgotten the stories already broadcast. The first ones are starting to do the rounds again. According to that one, we, that's the US, are going to take over Saudi Arabia while the Israelis invade Syria then the two of us, with your lot and the Canucks of course, will take Iran. UK troops will parachute into Egypt and at long last get your hands on the Canal, all to yourselves this time. Ahem, no Frenchies to be included. Too much bad water between us and the French over Bosnia to swap handshakes with them again. As for any Russians in the area, they will pick their skirts up and run for home." He laughed, which infuriated me, but I did manage a polite smile.

"Heard anything of Liam Catlin, Spencer?" I asked.

"Nothing since he was pronounced dead back in the summer. Unless I start hearing voices from the grave then I don't expect to either." He gave me a long quizzical stare.

"No, I didn't mean from him, I meant about him. Awards or mentions. That kind of thing? Only I've heard that he might be getting some sort of recognition in the New Year's Honours list. Wondered if you'd seen a copy floating around Downing Street last time you were invited there."

"Ahem—I haven't been close to Number 10 for some time. The nearest I've been to any of your politicians was when I was a guest at Shepherds the other day for lunch, but not the restaurant frequented by Westminster Parliamentarians. An Italian sandwich place in Soho Square."

A raucous Texan laugh had some diners turning their heads towards us. As he said—pay grades make a defining barrier to the downward passage of secrets. Spencer knew nothing, which in itself was surprising as he was Director General of the CIA desk in their satellite building situated beneath Admiralty Arch in

Spring Garden, Trafalgar Square and a regular caller at Number 10 as well as the Foreign and Commonwealth Office, both via the St James' Park entrance.

* * *

It was gone 6pm by the time I reached Greenwich, partially due to the never-ending traffic, but also because I was hoping that by arriving late Geoffrey would be in a hurry to get off. That wasn't the case, which did not help to focus my full concentration on what he was saying all the time.

"I have no paperwork regarding the meeting you had with Raynor aka Fyodor Nazarov Razin, Patrick. I'm sure that's only a hiccup as you're relatively new to procedure, but I would like a full report; very soon, old boy. And oh, before I forget, in all your future references to said Russian you will use the cover name of Raynor not Razin as you are so fond of, please."

Suitably reprimanded, I lowered my head in acknowledgement of the instructions, determined to forget it as soon as the opportunity presented itself.

"That's why I'm here, Geoffrey. I thought I'd tell you what happened face to face rather than send an impersonal message over in computer jargon. In essence nothing happened. He's here for two weeks. Goes home to St Petersburg this coming Friday to spend Christmas with his daughter. It's all innocent stuff. He has a cousin working in the Silver Vaults who buys Russian icons on Razin's behalf, sorry, Raynor's behalf. He makes himself as visible as possible so we won't get our knickers in a twist and scale up our activity and rattle the cages of his bosses back in Moscow. Not that he has many, but even so. He said that despite having permission he'd rather keep it on the QT than not.

"We had quite a chat about how the Soviets had originally stripped the country bare of precious icons then leaked them onto the black market making shedloads of money. Those who sold them off are the ones holding all the roubles and wanting to buy them back. Razin, oops, Raynor is their go-to man. He makes a bit on the side which again is known, but he upsets nobody and wants to keep it that way."

"Is that all you got? You were with him for over an hour, Patrick. Did you sit staring at each other holding hands for most of that time?"

"No, Geoffrey, I took notice of everything he said but I can assure you there was positively nothing to be excited about."

My physical presence was opposite Geoffrey Harwood in his lavishly appointed office suite under the old Royal Palace in Greenwich, but my mind was churning over what was said by Razin at the Savoy.

"There is a copy of part of the Gladio B file, Mr West, held by a section of the CIA that has no mailing address nor an office in a listed building. There is nothing significant in that file on operations conducted under its banner, but what it does hold is absolutely crucial to its safety. An open reference to the three members of the Armenian Rosicrucians who have the whole second file between them. I knew of that. The Americans know of it now, and I have mentioned it you that they have possession of the more detailed and valuable file. Notwithstanding all of that, I'm left disturbed and puzzled. I'm told that the security measures taken by the Pentagon, and other American security institutions that retain secret documents are of the highest quality matched only by ourselves and perhaps the British, so why is the location of the sharp end of the Gladio B file in the hands of three Armenians? If the American Senate committee on governmental affairs had knowledge of that breach I wonder if they would allow it to remain that way. It is somewhat odd even for those at Langley."

Razin and I were off the tea and into the hip flask I was in the habit of carrying, whisky having the same effect on him as me; it increased the craving for cigarettes. I had lost count of the combined number we had smoked.

"On the day before the World Trade Centre attack by Bin Laden and his terrorists, Donald Rumsfeld gave a speech where he announced that $2.3 trillion in Pentagon spending cannot be accounted for. $2.3 trillion! He identified the military and the intelligence bureaucracy as the biggest threat to a peacetime America. Powerful words from a former Secretary for Defence as he was then—*biggest threat to peacetime America.* Why would that be, I wonder? Of course, more newsworthy events overtook that story the following day, conveniently some would say, pushing it into oblivion that has found little mention in the aftermath of the Twin Towers attack. That figure is astronomical by any standard, matched, I believe, by only five countries who have anywhere near that figure as an annual gross domestic product. Despite a leakage of such magnitude, we have monitored no unusual rise in military spending. We concluded it was invested elsewhere; possibly into a covert private army. Perhaps, that's Donald Rumsfeld's threat to peacetime America? You and I have survived the Cold War and the dangerous military manoeuvres named Ryan and Able Archer's of the 1980s when Reagan and Thatcher were not only threatening my country, they almost obliterated the world. Since that time Russia and the West have become almost brothers. So why the evocative words of a peacetime threat if no enemies can be identified? The political arm of America evidently doesn't trust the military, but why do you suppose the good guys don't rat on the bad guys, Patrick?"

As Razin's question faded into the walls he rose from his chair and did the thing I least expected. He emptied our ashtray, filled the kettle and prepared to make more tea.

"My flask not to your taste, Comrade General? I thought you said you hadn't come to drink cup after cup of tea, and here you are being mother and doing the housework as you brew. What changed your mind?"

"Filthy ashtrays and your habit of avoiding questions, Mr West? Are you playing for a suitable amount time to concoct an answer?"

"No, I'm not. It's simply I have no definitive answer to give. A stab in the dark would be that it's probably because the good guys don't know who the bad guys are and don't trust a soul to ask."

"Your stab in the dark has struck at precisely the correct target. None of what I've told you is known to this serving President, and apart from one before him, unknown to all the presidents dating back to the CIA's inception in 1947. I won't be silly and ask if you would like the name of that President. It was Richard Nixon who devised the plan whilst serving as Vice President to Dwight D. Eisenhower. In 1954 he first set about constructing this deceitful policy aided and driven by the many generals who wanted to wage war against Mother Russia, and never forgave Eisenhower for not agreeing to their expansionist plans. Some of those plans were even pointed at an invasion of this country, Mr West. Just imagine London's Savoy being in crude American hands.

"But you and I were saved from the deceptive Americans and the serpent is no longer controlled by the military. By various means not known to me, the original designs of generals and admirals for world domination has been altered in style to accommodate the financial ambitions of eight concealed families with histories dating back several centuries. Those eight business leaders with only the most viable commercial formats in their minds want complete control of this world, not just whatever percentage it is they have now. Please save your curiosity as to how I know that fact, as I don't know you well enough to disclose it. I also cannot give you a comprehensive list of their names as I don't have one. I don't believe anyone outside their circle has one. However, I can visualise a day when you and I will have knowledge of some of them.

"Let me swiftly move on to Henry Mayler and Fraser Ughert. I was present when Henry had the Rosey Cross tattoo put on his hand. It was the 6th of April 1970. When written in numerical form—6/4/1970, the numbers add up to twenty-seven, a number divisible by three leaving nine, and then divisible by three again leaving three. If you were to add Henry's birth date of 03/01/1970 it comes to twenty-one, a number also divisible by three. Is a picture forming in your mind, Mr West?"

These were of course the same numbers Fraser had thrown at me and obviously were of importance to him and Razin, but I didn't want Razin to know of my prior knowledge so it was with my best mystified expression that I greeted this disclosure.

"No, you look bewildered. Let me give you another number to work with. On the third of January next year, Henry will be thirty-three years of age. Got it yet? 03/01/2003 equals nine. Divide that number by three again and you get three. Rosey Cross time once more. As I said, Henry will be two threes at thirty-three. Any hairs on your neck standing up? Has Fraser Ughert ever mentioned the third-third degree in Freemasonry to you?" I shook my head at his question.

"Has he told you that he was Henry's Control?" To that I answered that he had, and that's when all the walls came tumbling down.

"Ughert has told me that you are different from any British agent I may have heard of or come across, and certainly different from the normal civil servants that work in your establishments. I'm hoping what I've heard is correct and you turn out to be the tempest that destroys the temple. But be careful to step away from any whirlwind's path in good time. I've been told of a tempest that regularly blows through Djibouti and the surrounding poor countries of Africa, sweeping many men and women up into its arms. Nobody has an interest in who is enslaved to die alongside terrorists or sold into the European sex trade for the money to buy weapons. Numbers on paper are only numbers on paper after all. And the truth is only the truth when it doesn't disturb our sleep. Be careful you do not wake too many sleepy liars, Mr West."

"As we're discussing truth, General, Henry told me the story of your escape from Al Hasakeh, and how you ambushed the chasing car. That was bloody smart thinking on your part. He added that you removed something from the driver's pocket after you shot him. Care to tell me what and why that was?" It was self-evident by his screwed-up facial features that I'd rattled him, but I hadn't anticipated his reaction.

"It that what the Armenian said, was it? I shot the driver and I took something from his pocket? No, that is not what happened. My shot wounded the driver and caused the car to leave the tarmac and overturn, but Mayler shot him dead and took a mobile phone from his pocket. He crushed it under his foot saying that it probably carried a directional finder. Why would he get that mixed up?"

* * *

"Am I boring you, Patrick, or are you distracted by the bulging Christmas present list you must be thinking of?" Geoffrey shouted at me as my mind was orbiting around what Razin had told me about him knowing Fraser Ughert. That, along with what he told me of Henry Mayler, was exhilarating of course, but it was more than I had bargained for. Whichever way I looked the question of why he had chosen me to tell was all the more disturbing. Yes, Head of Group was a prestigious role within the joint intelligence community, but I was well down the chain of overall command. Who above me could I trust? Geoffrey had stopped his rambling cross-examination in favour of a more personal insulting assault.

"Are you spending Christmas with the Ugherts? Ah, of course, now I know who it is who has your concentration. Your fantasy goes by the name of Geraldine if I'm not mistaken and provides more creature comforts than I can possibly do. I doubt you will be absorbed by much else, will you?"

In days past his acerbic remark would have got under my skin, so much so that it wouldn't have taken much more for me to punch him until he was unconscious. As that would have led to an inquiry in the New Year where I would at least be reprimanded, I chose propriety over reprisal, but tinged with enough indictments of blame to bruise.

"No, my mind was far from Christmas, Mr Harwood. I was lost inside the grandeur of this office of yours. Must be right up your street worshipping the paintings of past grandees and favourite sons of these shores. But, Geoffrey, tell me, will you ever get your portrait on a wall beside any of them? You will have to do something of great magnitude and merit to achieve that, I fancy. Maybe if I was to mention a file I came across relating to the abduction of seven men and four women from a country I find hard to pronounce, then that might possibly lead us both to something meritorious?"

"Djibouti. It's perfectly simple, Joseph. The deployment of the muscles at the rear of the mouth are useful. I very much doubt what you've read could develop into much," he remarked, as though human trafficking was an everyday occurrence he had to deal with and dismiss from his conscience.

"I've read the attached statements from those that were rescued; three men with some remarkably detailed knowledge of caches of Taliban weapons, distribution routes and some ins and outs of Pakistan, but there's another thing in there that appears not to have been followed up. They all say that in the camp where they were kept, there were many others who had also been forced to join the Taliban after being caught by traffickers. Was anything done about that, Geoffrey? Did I miss something?"

"Am I to be entertained by your working-class sarcasm, Joseph? If so, then it is very tiresome, but I'll indulge you. I passed that report over to the Americans, the Pakistani, and the security service in Djibouti. We have no diplomatic contact with Ethiopia. From memory three villages in Pakistan were named, but I'm unaware of what happened after it was handed over. Did you read that report from General Sir Ralph Warrington at the Strategic Studies Group? Complete rubbish I thought, but some up the food chain gave it the nod. Fraser Ughert was one of those. Although he is officially retired his opinion is sought after on all things American and pertaining to the Middle East. Come to that, not much escapes his observation or his unrequested comment falling into fertile minds. He's had a state-of-the-art security system installed in that office of his, paid for from the public purse. It's as though he's never left and nobody has the balls to tell him to go."

I ignored the begrudging remark and offered no comment on his speculation.

"Anything done about the report of American involvement in the abduction of the Ethiopians?"

"As I understand things it was marked down as pure conjecture. Not much to go on really is it; shouted voices in a noisy hostile situation? Standing orders required me to keep the report on file but had it been left to me I would have tossed in the shredder."

"And those 'others' the Africans spoke of as being forced to become soldiers for the mujahideen to throw at the enemy. Nothing done about that report, Mr Harwood?"

"That taunting of yours has passed over the invisible line of respectability. Cut it out right now or resign right now. You were not at the meeting discussing those reports and therefore you're not entitled to pass judgment on those that were. We bat for the same team, Joseph, at least I hope you do."

That statement carried a reprimanding stare of biblical proportions, and instead of being turned into a pillar of salt I sat in silence for a short while thinking of the words Razin had employed in his recounting of the abductions, and the manner he had delivered them. I could have told Geoffrey why nobody wanted the report followed up, but I didn't. Harwood was the type who needed no disentanglement of words used by the defeated to find the truth, he coloured history in the colours of the conquering victors. I kept my lips firmly closed about that side of my morning conversation at the Savoy, leaving Razin's words swimming around in my brain as I waited for the anger to dissipate from Geoffrey's face before attempting another question. At last he calmed down.

"The word is that the Americans are unaware of Liam Catlin's arrival in Syria, Geoffrey. Would that be correct?"

"I think it is safe to assume that, but although they have nothing directly from us, their ignorance cannot be taken for granted. However, if your follow-up question is, do I know which country Catlin is in right now? I can honestly announce I'm unfamiliar with the whereabouts of field agents since my upwards movement from Group," he answered with a forced smile. Then, when the smile could be held no longer, he added, "But the honest answer to your question is no, Joseph. I've no idea at all, old boy."

Honesty in the world where Razin, Harwood, Mayler, Fraser Ughert and I live does not prevail in great quantity. More often than not frankness depended on whose bed one got out of that morning. Nobody opened their hearts to integrity or honesty, neither did many give a truthful answer to a straightforward question. To hear truth being declared twice as an answer to one question could only mean two lies were exposed. My time here had run out. I had more important things to do than bandy words with an unconcerned mandarin.

"Who is to be chair of the Joint Intelligence Committee now Fraser's stood down, Geoffrey?" He almost exploded as he stood to deliver another admonishment.

"You know damn well there's nobody been appointed to that position. If there was he would not tell you either. Catlin is not your concern anymore, Patrick, and I'm ordering you to stay out of the case. If not, you could well lose your Joseph role and find yourself out of a job looking for a Christmas manger to hang your hat in. Have you got that?"

I had a fair reason to pick a fight with Geoffrey and I would have landed at least one blow, but that was all I had at the moment; one suspicious minor detail nagging away at me. Maybe there were no more uncertainties to uncover in which case I would have looked extremely silly mentioning what I had, or perhaps there were, and I would have shown my hand too soon. By reacting to Harwood's provocation I would have allowed the impression of defying convention to remain a characteristic permanently implanted into my file. Whereas Henry Mayler's file had no mention of any impropriety within our industry. Instead his service record was decorated with acts of tact and decorum, on a few occasions just one level short of heroism, but Bernard Higgins, God rest his soul, might have testified differently had he not so cruelly died.

Henry was good, but being good at one's trade does not quantify one as being dependable as Bernard may also have testified. Mayler was the epitome of the average Russian's opinion of Armenians; clever, but subversive. He visited his clever and rebellious nature every available time he was able, finding it in any decent bottle of whisky and then, having found it, he would make love to Bernard before messaging his contact in Springfield, Missouri, and telling him of the next target for unconventional terror attacks. Bernard Higgins knew nothing of that contact. Henry, on the other hand, had everyone jumping through hoops or dying at his bequest; as at Tel Shnan, on the outskirts of Homs, in Syria one Tuesday night in September 2002.

* * *

The drab thin window coverings were ineffectual against the garish light from the crescent moon but caused no distress to the sleeping Kurds; however, every lock on every door proved inept for its purpose to the people who wanted those doors flung open. The two adults inside the dwelling, a man and a woman, the two children, a boy and a girl, were murdered without a sound, along with thirty-nine other pairings, most not as silent, in the township of Tel Shnan, but the explosions set off by those who committed the atrocities were heard all the way to the United Nations building in New York. Unfortunately, there was no international outcry as it had become a routine occurrence for the government in Damascus to deal with, and no matter how incompetent and corrupt they were the UN had no power to dissolve them. The powerful 'They' of the ruling Arab Socialist Ba'ath Party, led by Bashar al-Assad, blamed and pointed the accusing finger at the Turkish mafia who had, so the rest of the world were told, connections to several Kurds living in the township who had in the past helped the mafia to ship drugs to Europe.

'This is no more than a revenge attack like so many others. My security officers tell me that the Turkish Mafia mean to control the whole distribution and cease sharing arrangements with the Kurds.' So said the Syrian foreign minister to the members of the UN council who bothered to attend and listen. The already beleaguered Kurdish population did not believe a word coming

from the government. They simply carried on waiting for the day they could exact revenge.

Chapter Ten
Wednesday With Fraser

"Henry Mayler had a Russian handler from the day he was born, laddie. Lieutenant General Fyodor Nazarov Razin is on our side. He's a double, Patrick. His real name is Alexander Sergalovich Kruglov, son of Colonel General Sergei Kruglov, whom I've mentioned as instrumental in the Maylers' escape. Now you and I are the only two living souls within any intelligence service who know that."

"Wow, Fraser, that's the scoop of the century, but you must have given both Razin and Henry a long lead. Was nothing compromised?"

"No, nothing until Henry blows a gasket about being shot at outside the market in Al Hasaketh. As I previously told you, he was followed there. All we could get from Hadad, his driver, was that he phoned a number he had previously used and told whoever it was at the other end where Henry wanted to go. He was paid in American dollars left in a dead-letter box, but the dollars are not the only interrelationship he had with our friends in America. Hadad's told his interrogators that his call was answered by a man with a strong southern American drawl. He said he knows the different dialects used in the States because he watches a lot of American films and television programmes. Not much to go on is it, but one never knows.

"Let me give you some background information on Lieutenant General Fyodor Nazarov Razin. Years ago I was heading up a 'burn operation' aimed a Czech who worked at the Czechoslovakian Republic Embassy which backed on to the Russian Consulate at Notting Hill Gate. Small world, eh, Patrick? She had been comprised when trying to offload some delicate information from an asset of ours she'd intercepted onto a Frenchman who was also working for us in a sordid Bayswater hotel room, thinking he would reward her with a wedding ring and a ticket to Paris. She was in an elevated position in the Czech radio room and I had her marked as a long-term prospect. However, that wasn't to be. She and our Frenchman were routinely photographed in the hotel room, catalogued and registered, but no approach was made to the woman that night. We can't be certain what spooked her but something did.

"Her body was discovered in the early hours of the following morning in a car which had crashed into a tree in Holland Park Avenue, a mile or so from Notting Hill Gate. There was a man in the car with her. He was, according to Fyodor Nazarov Razin who at that time was an attaché at the Russian Ministry for Trade, her Russian Control and the other man she had shared her information with. Fyodor stopped a *crash signal* being sent to Moscow Centre that would have signified a top-level breach to Soviet Security. That breach originated from our man on permanent watch over the Barents Sea, backyard of the mighty Russian Northern Fleet, who the Russians were completely unaware of. The information he passed concerned a spy trawler—an AGI in NATO parlance, meaning Auxiliary General Intelligence. They were thought to be crammed with submarine interception and detection equipment. They were a ubiquitous presence during the Cold War, shadowing NATO exercises or loitering off naval bases. This one was special. Polish-flagged, she was pulling a device long coveted by the British and Americans, a two-mile string of hydrophones known as a towed-array sonar. It was the latest thing in Soviet submarine-detection technology.

"Because of Razin's intervention the operation mounted to capture this device was successfully completed by HMS Conqueror, the submarine that had sunk the Argentine Cruiser Belgrano in the Falklands War. Her bow was fitted with electronically controlled pincers that cut through the three-inch-thick steel cable connecting the towed sonar to the trawler. The name of this audacious exercise in piracy was Operation Barmaid. Fyodor killed the girl and her handler in the car. Quoted diplomatic privilege to remove the bodies and the car before the Met Police could investigate, then cleaned away any connection to himself."

His eyebrows rose as his face beamed a smile as wide as the bow of a submarine and his laugh resonated around the room.

"Not much in the way of conscience, has our Razin. It was he who extended my education on the Mayler family with all its nuances. You see, Razin is not only a Mason but a Rosicrucian to boot. He knows the importance Henry Mayler's birth represents to the fraternity."

A pipe was filled and lit in a way of celebrating a significant moment, one where intelligence had been shared between equals with no chance of subversion. This time I smiled back at him. I never told him of my suspicions. I never thought it necessary to display my foolishness so easily. As I poured two more glasses of Scotch he picked up the story.

"One night I was walking towards Baker Street to get a cab when I was stopped by a man who came out of a doorway of a bank on the corner. It was Fyodor. He hasn't changed, he was brusque with words that far back. He's mellowed a little but still goes straight to the point.

'I know who you are and I think I know what you want. If I'm wrong then at some time in the near future I will be right.'

"From that opening he quoted the right words to me and off we went for a drink in pub nearby. That's when I learned of Bernard and why I recruited him. Before you ask about where Razin's interests lay in all of this I'll tell you; he looks to himself first no matter who that affects. Four months after Bernard and Henry had fallen in love, a Russian by the name of Oleg Dievsky was caught at the Leipzig–Altenburg Airport taking pictures inside a restricted hangar of a top secret Russian fighter jet. He was one of ours. Within five days of his imprisonment, Razin had used data Henry had supplied Bernard on an American airbase in Northamptonshire where he been invited to take post-Cold War photographs. The photographs were low grade, but he used them to organise Dievsky's escape through Finland and back to the UK. Why would he do that? He did it because Dievsky knew some of Razin's set-up in Germany and Poland. He arranged it because it suited him. Ever since those days I managed to keep Razin's involvement removed from what was shown at ministerial level. His name was never known to heads of security departments until last week when he played his hand to meet with you. The collaboration I've told you of must be kept open, Patrick, no matter where it leads. He's played his hand and must bear the consequences. But nobody needs to know of his previous collaboration."

"I'm still struggling to understand what happened in Al Hasaketh. If Razin wanted to save Henry then why does he mean to harm him now? He had him to himself on the drive to Aleppo. Why not kill him then? Why did Razin run the risk of exposing himself to the outside world when he must have suspected that you would have reached out to Henry?"

"I think there were several reasons. The main one was that he had been found out. Henry was followed to that meeting by those who shot at them both. Hadad, the driver, had sold

Henry out to them. We can't be one hundred percent sure, but it's our belief it was a renegade unit inside the CIA who Razin and Henry killed." Fraser wasn't ready to stop there until I forced him.

"By 'we' can I assume that's you and Razin, Fraser, and is there anyone at Joint Intelligence Committee level who agrees?"

"That's why I stood down, Patrick. I believe the pot is reaching boiling point in Iraq and the surrounding area. I need to focus solely on Mayler and that Gladio B file held in Armenia. We will find out where Iran, Iraq, and Syria come into White House planning inside that file."

"What about this significance of the number three Razin and you have spoken of? What's that all about?"

"It's a very significant number, Patrick. To start with The Holy Trinity is one: Father, Son and Holy Spirit. Another would be the three degrees in the basic lodge of Freemasonry and just to finish on a third: there were three original masons working on Solomon's Temple. There are many more examples but the numbers 7, 9, 11, 13, 33, 39 are also important, none more so than the number 13. When the Seal Of America was designed the country consisted of 13 colonies. If you have a chance take a look at that Seal front and back, add up what's on the symbols, like the 13 olive leaves on the branch with the 13 berries. How about the Great Seal of the United States, where a bald eagle is holding 13 olive branches in one talon and 13 arrows in the other, and there are 13 levels of stones from bottom to top in the pyramid. There has never been a President of modern day America who has not been *On The Square* or *The Widow's Son*, but being a Freemason is not spoken about openly, nor admitted to.

"The codes are hidden, Patrick, but not from the initiated. The greatest power of all is created by the symbols if the uninitiated never discover that the symbol exists. When Razin said these words to Henry on their first meeting—*We speak unto you by parables, but would willingly bring you to the right, simple, easy, and ingenuous exposition, understanding, declaration, and knowledge of all secrets*, he was quoting from the Rosicrucian exposition and confirming to Henry that he also was a Rosicrucian. I bet Mayler never told you of his response, Patrick, because he never told me. His reply to Razin was—

I do declare that the golden age of Zep Tipi will return. The waters of the abyss will recede. The primordial darkness will be banished, and the 33rd degree of the human vessel will emerge into the light.

"That response was believed to have died in 1403 when the Rosicrucian were said to have disappeared. In the Masonic order the 33rd degree Masons are the receivers. Henry's Zep Tepi could be looked upon as the age of receiving incarnate demons which the Egyptian mysterious religion represented. It is an ancient, violent and immoral world which Razin and I believe Henry is seeking to re-establish. In Chapter 13 of the book of Revelations of the Bible are these words—*one who understands can calculate the number of the beast, for it is a number that stands for a person. His number is six hundred and sixty-six.*

"I have seen a mathematical equation that converts the date at the base of the pyramid on the Seal of America, of 1776 into that number by dividing the nine Roman numerals—MDCCLXXVI into three equal groups. Don't ask me how it was done but believe me, when it was explained I did understand." This was getting way beyond my comprehension. I interrupted him.

"Don't you think you're making symbolic letters fit a number that you want them to fit in order to invent a conspiracy? You'll be telling me next that Martians invented Scotch when they landed in Scotland." My discourteous remark had no effect on any bushy eyebrow.

"As I said—the codes are hidden in Masonic symbols and if they are only known to the few, then the esoteric nature of the concealment has functioned successfully."

"So are you saying that America represents the devil?"

"I'm saying that there could be a few acolytes of the Rosicrucian fraternity in America that possibly do, Patrick, yes! Allow me to try and explain. The political power in America is split into different orders representing differing beliefs of what is right and wrong. Freemasonry is much the same. For example all Masons believe in a Supreme Being no matter what religious faith is held. But there are several other beliefs in Freemasonry. Apply that to America and everyone there, either in government or in a government service, believes in democracy and freedom from tyranny, only as I've indicated, there may be a section broken away from direct government who see the achievement of that aim differently."

"So in what order of Freemasonry are you and Razin, Fraser? I was going to say in what order of masonry are you, but that sounds as though you're part of a building. I stopped myself otherwise we both might be laughing."

"But we are part of a building, Patrick. As Freemasons we are part of King Solomon's Temple, but to answer your question directly, Fyodor Nazarov Razin and I are part of the order of Knights Templar and although our order has connections to the Crusades we are foremost a fraternal order of Freemasons who believe not only in a Supreme Being but also profess in our belief in Christianity. Only Christians can belong to The Knights Templar. One of the obligations of entrants to our order is to declare to protect and defend the Christian faith. The Knights of The Red Cross, the Rosicrucians, were once included in the system alongside Knights Templar, The Knights of Malta and The Knights of St Paul but they could not agree to certain rites, sometimes called degrees of Freemasonry, so they went their own way but not into oblivion as was believed.

"It is the opinion of this intelligence service, and our counterparts across the Atlantic, that there is a group of people who in various ways directly control events in this world to their own advantage. Those people have been until now impossible to penetrate to either confirm or deny this possibility. They are known as the Twenty Club. Recently we have gained some useful information on the circumference of a smaller, more select inner circle, but more of that later. It would appear that the club's aim is to create a single world-state over which their interests would preside. This is not new. In 1878, the former British Prime Minister Benjamin Disraeli said;

'Governments do not govern but merely control the machinery of government, being themselves controlled by a hidden hand.'

In the early 1900s, Theodore Roosevelt also spoke on the matter. He said;

'Behind the ostensible government sits enthroned an invisible government owing no allegiance and acknowledging no responsibility to the people. To destroy this invisible government, to befoul the unholy alliance between corrupt business and corrupt politics, is the first task of the statesmanship of today. This invisible government has to be destroyed.'

"I believe an imperceptible empire has been set up above and beyond all forms of democracy."

"Why twenty, Fraser? Razin told me he believed there were only eight people behind it all, not twenty. Has he got his numbers mixed up?"

"The Russian agrees there is an invisible regime. However, he wants to circumvent the body of administration and go straight at its head. The club of eight he spoke of are not simply concealed, they are shrouded in a dissimulated series of separate codes. There is at least one Russian in that inner circle that Razin says he knows nothing of. The others in my circle of twenty are protected by statutes and laws, regulations and charters and the ability of modern technology to mask identities. If it were possible to penetrate that outer circle the probability is that no one would name the central eight because of fear of reprisals. We have to find them ourselves then deal with any problem they represent."

"Call me slow, Fraser, but I'm still unclear about whose side Henry Mayler is on and why is that file in Armenia?"

"Why Armenia? Okay, I'm going to start with how we know it's there and again I'm going to summarise somewhat. A signal from the CIA desk in the embassy in Sofia, Bulgaria was intercepted and deciphered at GCHQ in October this year giving details about a Russian named Dmitry Sklyarov. That report came straight to me. As a result of what I read I sent Henry Mayler to meet with this man. That meeting took place at an internet convention in Las Vegas. Sklyarov was an expert internet technician who was born on the banks of Lake Sevan in Armenia. Henry had heard stories from his father of the road that runs along the lake's shoreline in an elongated circle to and from that city. He had visualised it many times but never been there. As a consolation he could combine his secretive work of intelligence garnering with perhaps illumination on those passed-down memories when he met Sklyarov.

"Sklyarov was a conversationalist and not only did he elucidate on Henry's childhood stories, he told Henry that he had hacked into the Pentagon's computers and what's more he showed him the evidence; the actual signal that the American operative I know as Robert Zaehner, or the Doctor, intercepted. It was intended for a person called Arnold who I can't find. The signal told Arnold the names of the Americans who had access to the original Gladio B file, also where it was hidden and instructions how to download and then erase it. I contacted Harwood's set-up at Greenwich, this AIS of his, gave them some of that signal and they then worked it backwards and found the IT address of the recipient. Geoffrey was happy to preen his feathers whilst he looked on, sitting on his hands. Two further signals emanated from that discovered address. Not only were they successfully deciphered, one of the recipients was known to us. The file was moved on my instructions. I not only know where the first Gladio B file is, Patrick, I now know where the reconstructed one is and its contents. Razin knows nothing of that. Harwood gained another medal by notifying the FBI about the leak and they arrested Sklyarov. I have the key that opens that highly controversial file without any other agency knowing.

"This country has a strong relationship with Armenian Freemasonry which dates back as far as the beginning of the Ottoman Empire, but the Turks hated all Armenians. In 1915 they murdered more than a million simply because of their race. In 1922 the independent country of Armenia was swallowed up into the Soviet Union. We used that situation in our favour. When it became free of Russian dominance it did not find complete peace. Its borders with Turkey and Azerbaijan were under severe blockade and as the situation could not be resolved the Armenian government renewed its ties to Russia and invited them to maintain a military base within Armenia. We sat back rubbing our hands in delight. The information our Armenian friends passed our way was top-drawer stuff and we managed to get more classified material from within Russia when our contacts moved into more lucrative positions. It was through one of these contacts that I got a look at the second Gladio B file."

"What are you going to do now you've seen it, Fraser?"

"That's for another day, laddie, and trust me, not your business. Let's tackle that first question of yours. Whose side is Henry Mayler on? The simple answer would be that he is like Razin in that respect; he's on his own side. He has been playing us and Russia against each other since he began working with Bernard. He fed Bernard, then he in turn fed Razin and Razin informed me. The roundabout churned merrily away in the playground and all was fine until Henry stepped away from the straightforward gathering of intelligence into the real dangerous game of front line spying. Your game, yours and Catlin's.

"A couple of years back, when Henry was building his own association of dissident Kurds on our behalf, we supervised two shipments of weapons into a place north of Latakia, on the Syrian coast, by boat. Everything went smoothly for the first landing. The lorries were loaded and safely driven away, but on the second occasion when almost all had been unloaded the Kurds came under fire from a detachment of troops loyal to President Assad. According my report the troops were being 'advised' by Russian special forces from a Spetsnaz company. That's when Henry got that scar of his. He was trying to be too clever with the hearts and minds of his rebels and had overstayed his mission. A lorry he was hiding behind was hit and exploded. He was like you; lucky. I have, shall I say misgivings, when it comes to his affiliations to the Rosicrucian movement. The asset of mine in Armenia met Robert Zaehner, the NSA man who intercepted the message AIS tracked. Zaehner, the Doctor, says he managed to run some communications on this Arnold character. At one stage he thought he had him hooked. He threw some low-ish grade intercepted Italian intelligence, held by the CIA, on Israel's military strength on the Golan Heights into Arnold's path. Arnold bit on it. Arranged a drop-off point inside a recently established American Medical Mission in the capital of Armenia. The Doctor left what he called a thumb-drive, and I would call a memory stick. He hung around to get a sighting of this elusive Arnold, but no definite show. The intel remained where Robert Zaehner had left it.

"We have weak footage from a newly installed camera showing a shadowy figure near the dead-letter box, but, quite honestly, we cannot be positive if it's a man or a woman. This could be purely coincidental but Mayler was in Armenia at the same time as that drop-off. Be that as it may, there is no evidence to suggest that Henry Mayler was anywhere near the Medical Mission. Razin is more superstitious than I, hence all his interest in the numbers. He is right to worry though. Next year we are both expecting an event where Henry will be at the centre, but we are unsure of exactly when that will be."

"Could this event be planned to happen in Canada, and is that why he wants to go there, Fraser?"

"That is a question that has no answer. I gave him the standard choices then added the countries where he speaks the language and we are capable of relocating him. He wanted an English speaking destination and chose Canada."

"He gave no reason for that then?" Fraser shook his head.

"If he's decided on that side of the Atlantic, why ignore America? Surely there would a better chance of blending into the background there than the sparsely populated Canada?"

"I never attempted to persuade him either way. That was not what I wanted to do."

"Ah, so we have a purpose to his relocation. What was it you wanted him to do?"

"A short story, laddie, to cover a point that we haven't broached. After Razin left Henry with that veiled threat of 'killing two targets in one go,' in Kabul in November, Henry travelled west. Quite a far distance in fact, further than two hours five minutes would take him. Would you care to know where he resurfaced?" I laughed and gave a short chuckle before adding the obvious reply,

"That would be nice of you, Fraser, if it's no trouble."

My sarcasm was not wasted nor was my smile, as he imitated mine in the amused expression he returned.

"JFK International Airport, in New York! Came off a direct flight from Damascus. Our Russian friend had him followed from Kabul to Damascus, and then followed again once in New York, but he has not told me where Henry went in New York."

"Why not?" My question was treated the same as many Fraser managed to parry away throughout his career; ignored, instead he introduced a facet hitherto unknown by anyone other than himself.

"I have arranged for you to meet with my Armenian asset. Our old friend Jack Price recruited her and had an extended influence over her mother. Yes, my operative is a woman and an extremely good looking one. It will be a hands in your pocket approach, Patrick. I hope you understand that."

He stopped speaking, peering at me over the top of his spectacles, waiting for the standard sexist remark from me. There was none for me to make other than smile at the thought of not only having Geraldine's company to look forward and Hannah back at The Hole, now I was to meet another beautiful female. I could hear voices inside that imaginary conch shell of mine. They were quickly drowned out by Fraser's dialogue.

"Jack was ace at spotting talent, where he fell down was on his ability to pick the truth from what he was told, but dear old Jack was confused by many things in life. That must have been evident to you when you two worked together. It's of no importance now, of course. When Jack ran across Suzanna's mother in 1956 she was a university student who worked in a brothel in Budapest to supplement her income. Suzanna was born nine years later when her mother was twenty-six and not in good health. With help from this country Taline and her daughter were resettled with family members living very close to the Russian border, in a place named Akhtala. The family had money to which we surreptitiously added more, helping to pay for Suzanna's education.

"Curse me and mine if you wish, but the head of the department who you met after your convalescence from the gunshot

152

wound you incurred, Dickie Blythe-Smith, played the long game in Akhtala by using Jack, his name and Taline's past. Details of that will serve no purpose. Suffice it to say Suzanna was tutored to achieve success in every walk of life, working exclusively for me after Jack passed on."

Chapter Eleven
Nusaybin

Liam Catlin meet Narak Vanlian, code name Fade, a Syrian by birth but British by persuasion, in the car park outside the arrivals gate at Aleppo airport just as the outside cameras were temporally shut down by technology available to GCHQ through Geoffrey Harwood's AIS at Greenwich. The Syrian security offices were not in slightest bit interested in the British passport holding Catlin, who was a regular visitor to Syria having stayed in the country for various amounts of time. After a brief exchange of pleasantries Vanlian drove the Syrian registered Land Rover towards the Turkish border crossing at Nusaybin. Liam had been sent to accomplish two missions, one to work with Narak and reinforce the friendship with the Sunni Kurds and second to retrieve the data inside the first Gladio B file. That night they were welcomed by a group of Kurds they both knew well. When terms and tactics were settled with the Kurdish emissaries, Catlin and Vanlian immediately set about their assignment, travelling for two days and nights through the arid countryside of Turkey meeting the Kurdish leaders they were cultivating. Each leader wanted one thing, weapons, and conveniently Catlin knew of a British company who could supply all what they wanted. Venery Munitions Ltd; an airline and shipping company registered in Weybridge, Surrey, England.

The first of many consignments from the company arrived from Egypt at Gaziantep Airport in Turkey the day after Fraser's fictitious captain in the Logistical Corps had landed at Aleppo airport on a flight from Afghanistan. The three did not met, they had no need. By the time Fraser's mythical army man crossed the Turkish border he had become Simon Ratcliffe, Middle East executive officer for Venery Munitions Ltd. Once inside Turkey Ratcliffe set about the distribution of his cargo from the company's offices in the centre of Gaziantep, a few miles from the airport.

Later the same night as Liam Catlin's arrival, Ratcliffe moved back into his company residence, alongside the cool clear stream on the periphery of the scenic Yıl Atatürk Kültür Park. His 'wife' had missed him. At least that was the impression she gave on the doorstep of their home as he alighted from the taxi. Kiss, kiss, hug, hug—*oh how I've missed you, darling!* Inside the home that reflected his notable position in life, their relationship was far from normal. They had what Fraser called an *engaged audience* who paid handsomely for the information Mr Ratcliffe could deliver via the wives of the government officials Venery had to deal with, and for the information the beautiful Mrs Ratcliffe gathered from the embassy boys that caught her eye when accompanying her husband to dinners or soirées. As always sex was the pecuniary consideration above all other when it came to persuade a *rabbit* to disclose that which they should not, and of course the supplied information was first seen by those that maned the Turkish desk on the fifth floor at the Box, Vauxhall, London.

* * *

Taking turns to sleep Catlin and Vanlian made their way northwards towards the Black Sea resort of Sarpi, where they crossed the border into Georgia and settled into a hotel in Batumi for their first decent night's sleep. The following day they set off on the hazardous drive across snow-covered Georgia to Armenia. They were met at the border by Christopher Irons, an MI6 operative who had recently been posted to the United Kingdom Embassy in Yerevan, under the guise of a UK Government official visiting the First World War graves sites with authorisation to interact with local commissions on any renovation work required. However, Irons had spent the last two months in Basra, training special forces in the capturing of specific targets. On the night of Tuesday, December 14th, Catlin and Vanlian stayed at the British Embassy in Yerevan as Christopher Irons' guests.

* * *

In the early hours of the following morning, December 15th, Solomon notified me of the fact that GCHQ had alerted Group of substantially heavier than normal radio traffic issuing from our embassy in Yerevan. There were three coded signals and four in open text. AIS followed the signals and found that the three coded messages were to a mobile phone number registered to a name that didn't exist at a New York address that similarly was non-existent. When Solomon asked his opposite number at GCHQ for the deciphered messages he was told he could decipher them himself using standard coding books. He tried but found they were in a code that was not logged in his security safe. He checked the duty officers' safe, along with the front security office's safe. As a last resort he brought the three indecipherable signals to me. I had no code books. I followed protocol to the letter and reported this breach upwards to Sir John Scarlett at the Box in Vauxhall and Sir Elliot Zerby at Millbank. Within seconds of my scrambled phone-receiver being replaced, Hannah had a call on hold from Geoffrey Harwood at Millbank, a few buildings closer to Parliament than Sir Elliot's office.

"You don't need to know what those signals refer to or to whom they were sent, Joseph. Just log them as communiques from outstation YA and leave it there. You are standing on people's fingers as you tread heavy-footed through the maze. We appreciate your candour, dear boy, but confine yourself to being a good soldier and do what I say, please. That is the end of this conversation." For him it evidently was, but I couldn't leave it there.

* * *

Wearing my overcoat and my distinctive cap I sent the duty officer to quickly exit the building and jump into the waiting official car with Jimmy at the wheel and Frank holding the rear door open for him. Meanwhile I travelled under and beside the various pipes of all dimensions and some minutes later left The Hole by the tunnel that emerged in Paris Garden, a side street off Stamford Street. Hannah was waiting in her inconspicuous grey Ford Focus. It had worked as nobody was tailing us. She drove sedately with me flat across the rear seat, arriving at the corner of Knightsbridge and Old Barrack Yard early that Wednesday evening. I walked from there to the Grenadier public house in Wilton Row where I met with Razin. He was beaming from ear to ear.

"If only my name was East then East meets West in a backstreet pub to raise the steel curtain, Mr West," he laughed, and I smiled back.

"Churchill called it an Iron Curtain, Fyodor, and in any case I thought you lot had preached perestroika to the peasants who lapped it up, glasnost and all. Do they still queue outside McDonald's in Moscow? Cheers," I added as I took the glass of whisky he held out to me.

"I went there when it first opened. It was party policy to attend. Big Macs were a novelty in those days. As is your request, my English friend. First, what makes you think that your coded message is Russian?"

"A hunch, that's all."

"So it could be one of yours that you can't read and no one's telling you what it says. You're taking a risk."

"I would be if it contained our firing codes. That would be treason on my part, but as this is not I'm fine with giving you a peep at it."

A table became vacant so we sat at the side of the window almost on top of the radiator, a comforting change from the cold easterly wind that was howling outside and had blasted through my leg. Razin looked at my copies of the two signals from the British Embassy from which I had removed the recipient's address.

"Yes, I can decode this, Mr West, it's a standard Russian encrypted message. When was it sent?"

"Today," I answered, almost choking as I swallowed my Scotch.

"If you have some spare paper I'll do it now for you."

From one of those huge outside pockets on the front of his greenish coloured trench coat he removed a paperback copy of *The Lady with the Dog*, a short story by Anton Chekhov.

"This week we have Chekhov, next week who knows, and the procedure changes each week as well. Page number, line number, word number along that line from the right, the following week perhaps count the word number from the left margin. Sometimes when it is addressed for me only, there is a fourth number that refers to the letters in certain lines that make a separate word. We also change the edition. There was a time when Great Britain had a ghost walking unnoticed through our corridors in Moscow Centre and climbing ladders to the top floor for more than a peek at what was happening. That ghost gave your country a code one day that filled your feeding bowl for years. When that was discovered we changed things, but just our choice of literature, not the method of sending or decoding the signals. This week it a simple short story with no complications at all. Let me begin while you replenish our glasses, Mr Director General."

When I returned to our brass-topped window table overlooking the shadowy mews with its dampening cobbles and tiny cottages where more was garaged behind the differently painted double-doors than a horse and carriage, Razin had deciphered the first communication and was about to complete the second. I watched his gnarled fingers with manicured nails turn pages of Chekhov's novel then scroll down the paragraphs and along lines, silently mouthing the count as he did so, eventually adding a word to the other side of the finished message.

"Today is an unlucky day for the East, but I can't say that it's anything else for the West. I have lost an asset in New York but you have confirmation of a traitor in Armenia. The first message was from Martin Lennox who signs himself as communications director South Caucasus region of Eurasia. Before we go any further I must request your phone, Mr West. For mere seconds, I assure you, and then I'll return it. I'm going to give you an American FBI officer on the express understanding that what I'm doing is solely because of our mutual interest in Henry Mayler's Rosicrucians. Understood?" When I had nodded my agreement he continued.

"For what I am providing you will give me the courtesy of allowing a call to Lennox and give him a head start from the three British agents in your embassy where he is." He went to the other end of the bar and made his call to the communications director South Caucasus region of Eurasia. On returning, he asked, "Did someone at Joint Intelligence tell you that Lennox was one of mine?" Before I could answer with a lie he answered his own question.

"Of course not, how could they have known?" With another smile plastered on his face he continued, only this time reading from the deciphered messages: "Although you have redacted the address where the message was sent I know Lennox is signalling the New York City District FBI office as his message is to Field Agent Robert Hanssen. The message reads:

From Moscow Communications Station: 7 Ilyinka Gates Square One/Two 1) Liam Catlin, English/Number 231457J CN/Antelope, and 2) Narak Vanlian CN/Fade. primary Syrian/File Central Committee Number AG142 AG 59012478T with affiliations to JIC Brit, crossed border Syria/Turkey then Turkey/Georgia and entered Armenia at Ninotsminda Tuesday, December 14 in company of station resident Yerevan at 6pm local time. Reason Unknown.

"The second signal is more ambiguous and needs to be as it refers to eliminating both your Catlin and Vanlian. Lennox did not know that his signals would be intercepted of course, but took precautions just in case. There are no specific instructions regarding places and times, all it says is, quote:

Two/Two. C/V not to progress further than centre YA. Please arrange via Arnold.

"Do you know this Arnold, Mr West?"
   "No, I don't, but by the tone of your voice I guess I can count you amongst those who wished they did."

Chapter Twelve
Wednesday Evening

Fraser was sitting well back in his chair staring at the computer screen with his glasses lying on his colourful blotter in front. He did not hear me enter his office. Molly had opened the door before I'd rung the bell and on seeing Hannah sitting at the steering wheel of her little car her facial expression changed from an appeasing, smug grin to one of coquettish astonishment. Unlike her husband's face, I could read Molly's facial expressions easily.

"New flame, Patrick? Shall I be laying an extra place for Christmas lunch and warn Geraldine? If I know anything about my sister I know how much she was looking forward to your exclusive company."

"No," I laughed, "that's my PA, Hannah, Molly. Nothing going on there I can assure you. Far too busy for that sort of thing. But I am shocked you knew about Geraldine and me. I thought we'd kept all that secret." Her returned snigger was acerbic and mocking.

"Probably from Fraser you did. Away from his secret life he only sees what's straight ahead. I have age and experience on my side, young man. Plus I expect you are no different from most men and I know my sister. Go and get your Hannah and point her towards the kitchen. Fraser's at his desk, been there since before dawn. He needs to slow down, Patrick." Her caution was not lost on me.

* * *

"Anything wrong, Fraser? You look worried," I asked as I lugged a heavy chair towards his desk and sat in it.

"Yes, radically with my hearing! I never heard you arrive. Despite that I think you're right, laddie, there is something wrong. Something seriously wrong." He replaced his glasses before continuing.

"This second Gladio B file has another file hidden inside, but I can't get through the firewall that's inserted on it. It's in a code that I've never seen."

"You told me you'd seen inside both Gladio B files. Read it all."

"Well, I have, but this one was hiding under some encryption that appeared when I clicked on an 'insert tab' I hadn't looked into."

"That's more than likely the encryption key Razin mentioned when we were at the Savoy. But if we bring him in on it he'll have to see the whole file. We can't allow that, can we?"

"No, Patrick, we can't. Perhaps the only man who could get us in would be Arnold, but we have catch him first. A chicken and egg scenario."

"Not necessarily, there could be another way. Razin gave me a heads-up on a coding system the Russians have as operational when I met him this afternoon. He said they're using a system that once was broken but the principle was sound. All that's changed is the method of deciphering. If that method could be broken, then your box of tricks can be opened. Razin called a Martin Lennox, the signals officer in our embassy in Yerevan, from my phone. He's Razin's man! I had my station officer send a direct signal to our ambassador, bypassing Lennox and his communication staff. The essence of it all is that approximately five minutes after Razin called, Lennox left the consulate for Zvartnots Airport, our time 16:25. Both Catlin and Vanlian are watching him wait for his flight to Moscow as we speak. We can't physically lift him from there without causing a diplomatic incident, but I'm reckoning that if you spoke to him directly you could offer him an incentive to switch flights and return to England. Use my phone and he might think that Razin is behind it, if not he'll wonder what the hell is going on. In the unlikely event of him refusing your offer, we can order Liam to take him somewhere and get the pad-code another way. You said yourself that there could be a Russian inside your circle and perhaps he could have had a hand in the coding." Our eyes met, but there was no emotion showing from either of us. I carried on explaining my plan.

"Lennox has no close family as such, but he does have an elderly mother in a nursing home in Gloucestershire. There are ninety minutes remaining before he boards the Moscow flight and three hours later the knowledge we need will be beyond our grasp. It's a seven-hour flight to London from Zvartnots with one change. We can put Christopher Irons on the seat next to Lennox and let them work up the formula between them."

Twenty minutes later, after being offered immunity along with various other niceties, Martin Lennox had changed his destination to London and thirty minutes after that Solomon received confirmation that he had boarded the flight with Christopher Irons. Harwood was fuming when Fraser answered his landline telephone and passed the receiver to me.

"Why is your mobile phone not on, Joseph? You have a major position inside Joint Intelligence yet I'm beginning to doubt if you have an ounce of common sense. How can any of your staff at Group get hold of you if something kicks off if they don't have my insight and do not know where you are? You had strict instructions not to interfere with Catlin's role, but you couldn't resist, could you! You're not in charge just yet, and you can't run to uncle Ughert and hide behind his kilt forever. That won't work any longer. Sir John Scarlett is threatening to close down my department at Greenwich because he believes they screwed up with one of his overseas assets. Ordering him off station without explicit permission. I want you in my office at 8am sharp tomorrow morning. I have pencilled in a meeting with the Home Secretary for 8.30. You are to be replaced."

"Would you rather I'd let our Armenian communications officer, Martin Lennox, fly to Moscow where he could tell the Russian newspapers just how easy it was to cipher off our diplomatic signals and divert them to Moscow Centre, Geoffrey, because that's what would have happened had I not ordered Liam Catlin to keep hold of Lennox's hand until Christopher Irons could bring him home to Heathrow. You could have told me where Catlin was when I gave you a chance and that may have hastened things along. Would you prefer I inform the Home Secretary how intransigent you are with field operations, either unwilling to adjust to the changing sequence of events, or downright unable to? You should carefully consider what I have said before you ask for any resignations, as it could be your signature on the form. Whatever your job is, Geoffrey, you will perform it so much better by staying out of my way, and I'm sure you don't want me to obstruct your passage up the political ladder. Leave me alone and I won't drop any of your psychiatrist's reports in your way. And yes, I do have copies. Lennox is my department's source now. Keep your hands off or my next call goes to CIA headquarters, Langley, with a faxed copy of those trick cyclist's reports." The line went dead.

"That was particularly cruel, Patrick. How long have you known about Geoffrey?" Fraser asked, with a sly smile on his otherwise screwed up cherub face.

"One of my faults is that I pore over document after document on people I work alongside. I like to know who I can rely on when the walls are crashing down or when someone has a machete hovering over my head. Both situations would require contrasting abilities. I would never use any information to further my career, but it's a different matter if someone wants to stop me from doing my job properly and don't tell me you wouldn't have done the same, Fraser."

He never replied using a spoken word. Instead his usual inscrutable expression changed to one that acknowledged my singularity just as Molly pushed open the door holding a mug of tea in each hand.
"Why are you looking so satisfied, Fraser?" she asked.

* * *

It was raining hard when Hannah pulled away from the Ugherts' home in the winter's dark and we headed back towards London. As I opened the front passenger door and sat beside her I silently questioned why I'd done that. Why not the back seat where for the most part I had travelled comfortably on the journey here? Then I wondered why it seemed so wrong to sit in the front. I looked for disapproving glances from Fraser or Molly, but we had passed through their gates and onto the main road by the time I'd thought to look. Before we had driven a hundred yards I was a fidgeting wreck, strumming my fingers on my outstretched knees or using them as a set of drums accompanied by a far from melodic hummed tune. I had tossed my briefcase into the rear and in order to get it I needed to lean close to her, reaching to retrieve it from the seat behind hers. In the end my agitation was too much to control without something to grasp onto and nullify my chaotic behaviour. Realising I was going to be embarrassed either way, I gave in and reached for that briefcase. With the feel of a folder I had read a thousand times and could recite backwards occupying my hands and fingers, my physical composure slowly returned, pushing her femininity into the corners of my mind. Our strained conversation alternated from how impressed she was with Molly Ughert's hospitality to Fraser's once exalted position as head of joint intelligence.

'Before working for you, sir, the highest position I held was personal assistant to the deputy head of the Russian desk at The Box. I was in that role for two and half years. But I've never been that close to any of the top floor men in my life before today. I understand you're to spend the holidays with them, Mr West.'

Whether it was her reminder of the forthcoming reunion with Geraldine, that also waited in those corners of my disorientated mind or the impending meeting of the 'good-looking' Suzanna, or maybe something totally away from the female form, but there was something that I couldn't explain restraining me from having a normal conversation and would not let go; perhaps it was the price of six months of chastity.

I resigned myself to concentration on work and it was whilst I was in one of those moments of revision that my thoughts were suddenly broken by a question from Hannah regarding firearms.

"Are you armed, sir? Only there's been a car on our tail for a couple of miles. Pulled out from a lay-by a few hundred yards from the Ugherts' drive. I've tried slowing and then put a bit of a move on but the car stays the same distance behind. As far as I can see there is only one occupant."

"It could just be a coincidence, Hannah, maybe it just doesn't want to pass?" I replied, trying to spot the offending car in the nearside door mirror.

"Here, sir! Use the main one. I can shift it back afterwards." Her hand moved towards the driving mirror, and I stopped her before she reached it. But it was not Hannah's hand I grasped, it was Kerry's that I held and Kerry's face I addressed. "Leave it, Kerry! If they see you moving it they'll know they've been seen. Leave it, but pull over at the next opportunity. I will dive out the door making it look as though I need a pee. If it passes us then clock the make and number. As to whether I'm armed or not then yes I am, and I hope you are too. Let's both hope it doesn't come to that."

"Who's Kerry, sir?" Hannah asked with a coy smile and for a split second I wondered where she had got that name from.

"Someone I knew once. Sorry, I was lost in what I was reading and the name was included in it," I lied.

"Look there's a roadside café in front. I know it's closed but no matter. I'll jump out at the side of it then you park a little way on towards the exit. If the other car passes you just clock the make and number as I said and we'll run a check, but if it pulls in I'll try for a closer look from my end. Stay in the car, please. No heroics on this shift."

The car stopped outside the café building, headlights shining at the corner behind which I sheltered. As I un-holstered my pistol I saw the vague outline of Hannah getting out of the car, but in my mind's eye it was Kerry as she approached the George Hotel, in Limerick, seconds before she was grabbed and bundled into a van with me sitting helpless and unaware at the hotel bar.

"Get back," I shouted towards Hannah's car.

"There's no need for anyone here to get excited. I am un-armed, Mr and Mrs West. Please, put the guns away."

It was a disembodied women's voice with a heavy foreign intonation coming from sultry lips painted with a contagious smile that was framed by a perfect face. What followed was not so perfect.

"Then the seventh angel blew his trumpet, and there were loud voices in heaven, saying—vitriol. But they didn't say that, did they, Mr West? No, of course not. Mr Ughert used the word vitriol. Except he gave the full definition using just the letters—*visit the interior of the earth, and by rectifying what you find there, you will discover the hidden stone.* My name is Suzanna Kandarian, and I'm given to understand that I'm expected."

* * *

There was only one other thing Fraser told me about Suzanna Kandarian apart from being good-looking and that was she was unorthodox, which I guess driving the car she had stolen from the airport where she'd just arrived proved the point. However, the fact she had no place to stay, as she told us, presented problems that demanded anything but a maverick response to deal with, as did the warning from Fraser for the need for complete secrecy regarding her existence. In one of the scarce moments of shared conversation on the drive to the Ugherts' I had learned that Hannah was living with her elderly invalid aunt in a house in Bermondsey, South London and when a chance arose to speak discreetly to her I suggested housing Suzanna with her as her aunt's home help. She jumped at the chance, more, I think, because of the adventure this might produce than the conformity of a live-in helper, and to her question "can I keep the gun, sir?" I answered "yes," more for persuasion than for any obvious need.

As we drove on towards London, I called the communications centre at Lavington Street to arrange for an anonymous phone call to the local police alerting them of the abandoned stolen vehicle and heard how Solomon had been followed on his detouring trip to the carpark at the rear of the Home Office, returning safely but unable to identify the two passengers in the car that had followed.

"I got the number okay and traced it to the Russian Embassy motor pool, but in spite of getting reasonable photographs from the rear-facing camera in the car, sir, I could not match their faces to our databanks."

The Chapter After Number Twelve
Suzanna Kandarian

Jack Price was working the Soviet outpost of Hungary from 1955 looking for weaknesses he and MI6 could exploit, when he stumbled upon a radical movement inside the Hungarian Working People's party who were plotting to overthrow the Marxist-Leninist government. He met and moved in with a journalist at the *Szabad Föld*, a weekly newspaper based in Budapest. By June that year not only did Jack have his journalist flat-mate, Emma Nagy, trolling her newspaper leads for his overlords in London but she had introduced him to the brothel where Taline Kandarian plied her trade. He used Taline in many nefarious ways to obtain information from a specific target; the Minister for Internal Affairs. Nearing the second half of October 1956 the political climate that prevailed inside Hungary was changing, encouraged by the United States' covert economic and psychological inducements to break away from the Eastern Bloc. The CIA, although boasting to have operatives and outstations in many Soviet areas of interests, in fact had none and no reliable local sources. Allen Dullas, the director to the CIA, depended entirely on his British *cousins*.

London's Russian Satellite desk logged a message from Jack Price on the 22nd October 1956 informing them that over twenty thousand students were to convene in central Budapest and demand independence from Russia. A signal the following day told of over two hundred thousand demonstrators having gathered outside parliament, demolishing part of a monument dedicated to Josef Stalin and raising the Hungarian Independent flag from his boots! London ordered Jack to intensify and widen his efforts at gathering information. Emma Nagy's uncle was the Hungarian Working Party's secretary and when shots were fired, his organisation seized guns from military depots and distributed them to the protestors who went on to vandalise symbols of the Communist regime. He told his niece that he had heard that a Soviet military intervention had been requested by parliament. By 0200hours on 24 October, acting in accordance with orders of Georgy Zhukov, the Soviet defence minister, Soviet tanks entered Budapest. Although Jack had put a stop to his love affair with Emma Nagy, she still held affection for him. A little before midnight she telephoned him in advance of the Russian occupation.

Jack used that call to protect his long-term asset, Taline Kandarian, and in order to do that he had to sacrifice Emma to the State Police. By November 1956, Jack had played Taline into becoming the mistress of János Kádár, the new Prime Minister of Hungary. She stayed in that role for the remaining years of her life during which time London apportioned some of the material she smuggled out to Allen Dullas's Central Intelligence Agency, much to Jack's undying disgust. Taline's involvement in the Hungarian Revolution, including her connection to London, was obliterated from all records by Dickie Blyth-Smith and kept secret by him, Jack Price and then Fraser Ughert.

In 1966 Kádár helped in the arrangements for his dying lover to return to Armenia, knowing precisely what she and Jack Price had done with the intelligence he passed on to her. He died with that knowledge, never divulging it to a soul. Suzanna was born three months before her mother died in the city of Akhtala. She was raised by close members of Taline's family, learning to speak Armenian, Russian, Turkish, Azerbaijani, Kurdish and English. She also learned how to steal and how to kill. To the secure files of the Russian desk was added a folder titled *Sarah Mariah*. On the opening A4 sheet of paper were written only these six words in longhand—Look Within Yourself To Find The Truth.

* * *

The original concept of the 'leaving sleeping agents behind advancing Soviet Bloc lines' policy which was the first Gladio B file, was forever corrupted by the Vice President of America, Richard Nixon, in conjunction with Allan Dullas. It was concealed inside the parameters assigned to the Office of Technical Services, or the OTS as it's referred to. From the offset, government finance intended for national security and the military was siphoned off into prearranged holding banks owned by private individuals, who over time augmented those accounts with money of their own, until eventually it was the privately held money that became the controlling influence in the direction of both Gladio B files policy. Through the 60s until late 1980, that influence was directed at predominately South American and African countries' infrastructure and economy, but it then developed into something far more sinister and deadly.

In 1982 the file began to be transfigured in such a way as to obscure not only the names of the eight families now in complete control, but alarmingly their ambitions. It was those objectives that were to be addressed. Financial funds from one banking group in Panama found their way into the hands of the Palestine Liberation Organisation capitalising the assassination attempt of Israel's London ambassador that led to the Lebanese war in June of that year. This was the first recorded excursion into the foreign affairs of a Middle East nation by those families. Over the years that followed that area of the world became a lucrative experience for the arms manufacturing industries, pharmaceuticals, and construction companies. All the commercial enterprises who profited from this war, and subsequent unrest in the Lebanon and her neighbours, were parts of huge international conglomerates whose owners are impossible to trace. Of the outer circle who were said to be accessible, three are dead and were murdered professionally. Within a few minutes of opening the *Sarah Mariah* file I was reading of the people who had died at the hands of Suzanna Kandarian over a period of eleven years. Or more precisely from when Operation Desert Storm was in its combat stage.

On the 28th of January 1991 Suzanna was in the Black Sea resort of Odessa as was a native Ukrainian, Sergey Malovich, the Chief Executive Officer of Moxon Oil. Sergey had a passion for women of a particular nature and his 'facilitators' knew his tastes by heart. Dark-haired, wheat-ish-coloured skin, tall, slim but sensuously beautiful, in fact the usual physical attractions of a hot, sexy woman but having another quality as well; intelligence and personally. In essence, enough to keep him amused whilst away from his wife and three children staying at their winter home in Bermuda. Suzanna arrived on his first evening in his hotel suite and stayed until morning. It was then she disappeared through the service entrance wearing a blonde wig, blue contact lenses and the yellow and white overalls of a cleaner, leaving Sergey lying on the bloodied, disturbed bed with what remained of a body after massive dismemberment. Although her description was circulated by international police agencies and by the various minders and facilitators of that outer circle of the twelve, no trace of her was ever found.

In the same year, Suzanna was in Beirut when an official from the French national bank met the Lebanese finance minister purportedly to discuss France funding a dam project in the Western Beqaa District of Lebanon, but the real motive behind the meeting held at the Loravva Hotel was to move vast sums of money through the Lebanese financial mechanism into France. The money was from a Chinese pharmaceutical company exploiting families in the outlying regions of China by testing a birth restriction drug on unsuspecting mothers. Suzanna found the Frenchman on his own the second night of his stay. This time she used a drug called Devil's Breath, or scopolamine. He was laughing as she slowly cut off his penis. He told her the name of the source of the money after being tortured for over three hours during which time most of his extremities were removed. The name was in the *Sarah Mariah* file under—Pending.

Two years later, in a tunnel leading from a recent borehole of a South African coal mining company, the mutilated body of Arjun Laghari, the amalgamation and procurement Chief Executive Officer of the Indian Rawalpindi Chemical Company, was discovered by returning miners after a three-day break caused by the collapse of an underground connecting shaft. Beside his shredded body was an empty 500 mg phial of methanol. He had, according to police reports, been tortured for the best part of two days. Methanol was the same poison used on Sergey Malovich before various parts of his body had been systematically removed. In both toxicology reports there was mention of two unknown chemicals in their blood stream, related to but not containing, Fentanyl, an opioid used as a pain medication. The following two recorded deaths were just as brutal using the same method to sedate and torture, then a lethal dose of methanol injected to finish the victims, but it was the last murder that interested me the most, set out in a separate narrow folder within the file marked—EnQ

According to the file the victim, a tall, medium-built man with blonde hair, aged between twenty-six and twenty-eight took ages to determine, but eventually was identified as William B.

Guerny II of Florida, America. The confusion over his identity was twofold; one, his hands, feet, teeth, and face, but not head, were missing and two; William B. Guerny II had died on a service operation executed by American Special Operations Command during the Gulf War in the Saudi Arabian city of Khafji, on 30 January 1991. He was one part of a three-man Navy SEAL team referred to as Task Force Blue.

His crudely disfigured body was found in an abandoned car left at Mosul Airport, Iraq, on the day of my appointment as Director General of Group. There were no notes inside the file to account for the American Embassy seal being at the top of the completely redacted document, but his body was identified by two bullet wounds in his left calf and by his unusual blood type, and he too had been tortured over a period of days. The following inscription to the EnQ folder was added to the brief biography and signed by Fraser Ughert.

William B. Guerny II was shot dead by agent Sarah Mariah on orders originating from my office.

The letters IAR, meaning Incinerate After Reading, were in the margin after his signature.

Chapter Fourteen
A Death

At eleven minutes past three on Thursday morning I was awoken by the buzzing of the telephone on the occasional table next to where I slept in the dayroom. It was the Duty Officer who broke the news to me.

It took Jimmy, with Frank beside him, fourteen minutes to arrive at The Hole, but less than thirty minutes to drive the forty odd miles to Chearsley in Buckinghamshire with three police outriders as our escort. Molly was waiting in Fraser's office, staring lovingly at his vacant office chair. I had never enquired into how long they had been married, that was not in my nature, but for some reason only known to her, now she decided to tell me.

"It would have been forty-three years in January, Patrick, since we pledge our vows on one freezing cold day in the Kirk of St Nicholas, Aberdeen. I was two years younger than Fraser and according to his mother making the biggest mistake of my life. No woman has ever made a better choice of a husband." She did not cry, I think her innermost sorrow overwhelmed that show of emotion.

"You must all be wanting some breakfast. The best I can do for so many would be to offer toast and marmalade, I'm afraid," she declared apologetically and then needlessly asked, "Would that be okay, Patrick?" I told her that we could send out for something to eat and drink but she was adamant with her offer which I hadn't the heart to refuse.

When we arrived the Ugherts' sprawling home was surrounded by uniformed police officers of varying ranks with the compulsory blue tape around the entire perimeter. Inside the house it was overrun by forensic analysts with their white sterile uniforms, their cameras, and their tripod-mounted lighting. In the still dark morning the place was mystically quiet and ineffable. Even in death it seemed as though Fraser's spirit was monumental. I was acquainted with Chief Superintendent Maxwell of the Ministry of Defence police who was in charge of the scene, having had several dealings where our paths had crossed over in Northern Ireland. During my time in Ireland it seemed to me the Irish desk employed more within its authority who were concerned with bureaucratic issues and less personnel for the capture and prosecution of terrorists. He was another Geoffrey Harwood in that regard, being especially interested in routine documentation and administrative tasks. Needless to say we did not share a respectful relationship. He was talking to the Home Office pathologist who I'd met once before. As I approached them my burner phone rang; it was Razin. He was angry and worried. I didn't bother to ask how he knew because as soon as I'd said hello, Geoffrey Harwood and entourage arrived in an emergency response flashing convoy. I turned off the phone without explaining why. Hannah was in the lead vehicle with Geoffrey and after I greeted them both, the three of us entered Fraser's office.

The weapon, a Russian Nagant M1895 revolver with the suppressor attached, was in a numbered plastic evidence bag with its cylinder separated and beside it. The detachable cylinder was empty with the one fired distinctive round lying beside it. There was no 'live' ammunition in the bag. I had been told Fraser had been shot once in his heart. Either this weapon was carried by a supremely confident and accurate assassin or one who was extremely sloppy. Hannah saw what had registered in my mind and read my thoughts.

"I'll run it through our systems, sir. Although I don't see how I can keep the search from other agencies if we're serious about finding whoever's done this." I could feel her anger in the words she chose. I nodded at her request, then sent her off to console Molly as only a woman could do.

As was looking around the scene Maxwell had his notebook open and was approaching. Frank, my protection officer, was standing beside me. A glance from Maxwell in his direction was met by a steely, wide eyed stare in return.

"An expert kill. According to the pathologist the shot went into the centre of the heart," he said without any acknowledgement in my direction. However, I managed to get past his surprise of seeing me at the scene without having to raise my voice despite his incredulous disposition which he did not try to hide. When, with a sarcastic tone to his voice he asked who to make his report to, me or Harwood, I loved every micro-second it took me to tell him that it was I who he reported to.

Apparently Maxwell had arrived approximately ten minutes before us and some five minutes after Fraser's body had been removed by the pathology team on the instructions of the police officer who was first on the scene. He judged it more important to the integrity of the site that Molly Ughert was not subjected to a sight of her dead husband and his removal made no difference to the investigations. When Chief Superintendent Maxwell read this from his notes I praised that decision, asking him to pass that on to the officer.

From his notes I learned that entry to the house had been made through a fairly small pantry window that although barred, the cement was old and too soft to hold the steel. It was possible for a slim person to get through. The silent alarm was triggered and flashed up on the Home Desk special operations screen at MI5 headquarters on Millbank. The duty officer paged Special Branch at Barnes, the SO15 department at Scotland Yard, number Four Regional Crime Squad and Thames Valley Divisional Headquarters at Kidlington, who instantly assigned two ARVs, armed response vehicles, patrolling nearby, along with despatching their helicopter stationed at RAF Abingdon. They arrived almost simultaneously at the Ugherts' residence, blue light rebounding from the low black clouds, sirens bouncing off buildings half a mile away and the helicopter's search lights illuminating the thick woodland that encircled the property as far south as the River Thame. Fraser had an aversion to cameras inside the house which he never switched on, fearing interference with his and Molly's privacy, but although those outside were working, none had captured any image of any intruder.

Although the shock of Fraser's death made it difficult for me to focus, two things were obvious: Fraser's computer was shut down and where I had last seen it, and his prized red-leather desk blotter was missing one vital object. Molly had presented him with the prestigious blotter last Christmas and whenever I visited there was always a ringed notepad lying open across it waiting for his scribbled pencil additions. I looked further in case he had shifted it in any struggle, but no—no sign of a struggle and no notepad. There was a glass holding a small amount of whisky beside his pipe which was extinguished but not cleaned out as was his habit, had he finished whatever it was he was doing and retiring for the night. As I scanned the desk more thoroughly I noticed the computer screen was not central to where he would have been sitting. It had been moved. Maxwell was droning on in my ear about the lack of footprints outside on the hard frosty ground and the amount of smudge marks on the kitchen door as well as Fraser's office door. "The killer wore gloves," he announced as though that would be the damming evidence to solve the case. I tried to look interested in the boring details of nothingness but within this structured chaos my mind would not function.

Hannah appeared with two welcome mugs of tea for Frank and me, along with news that Molly was keeping herself busy and intent on holding Christmas despite what had happened. According to Hannah, Fraser's brother and wife were flying in from Canada and due to arrive this coming Sunday, and Molly's older sister with her husband, daughter and the two grandchildren were arriving from Scotland this weekend as well. Geraldine's plans could not be altered at this late stage, Hannah added with what appeared to me a suggestive smile on her face. It was not the smile that intrigued me as much as what she said Molly had told her.

"Molly said that Fraser had been burrowing, her word not mine, away at something he'd found in a file on his computer a little while back. He had moaned all day about it and told Molly that he wouldn't give in until he'd sorted it out. Seems strange that the computer is turned off, don't you think, sir. Unless of course, he'd found whatever it was and was on his way to bed." Frank, not one to usually comment, made a gruff *hmm* sound and then pretended to cough.

Hannah's suggestion had merit but the fact that his reading glasses were in another evidence bag alongside the one holding the murder weapon, meant that he was either wearing them, or had them around his neck, when shot. That detail, with the displacement of the computer screen and unfinished-with pipe, nagged away at me arguing that he must have been working when the intruder broke in. Then I saw it! A thick, heavy book lying vertically on top of the upright others on the shelf. The title was *Great American Feats*, Fraser's pet after-dinner subject.

He argued there were no great American feats but there were many great Scottish American feats and even some great English American feats, but until America had more than three hundred and eighty odd years of history there could not be a true American feat yet other than a Native American's great feat. The 'feat' thing was the bit of the joke. Frank followed my line of sight, and from the almost imperceptible nod of my head invited Harwood and Maxwell to follow him towards Molly Ughert's appetising tea and toast. Inside the hollowed out book was a remote controlled, wireless tape recorder that was switched on and running. I removed it, placing it in my pocket then followed my nose. I was confident I had covered everything.

* * *

I was quietly admiring Molly, who was keeping thoughts ofer dead husband to the back of her mind by concentrating on providing everyone with at least a hot drink and her mental preparations for Christmas. She was in conversation with her elder brother, who had just arrived from Aylesbury, a few miles away. Both looked in my direction as I entered the packed dining room.

"You are still coming for the holidays, Patrick?" she asked and by the look in her brother's eye he too needed an answer. I said that I wasn't sure but would obviously try my best, at which point Molly burst into tears which has always been too much for me to deal with. Her brother recognised my discomfort and took over consoling her, presenting me with the opportunity I required. Within five minutes Frank, Hannah and I, with Jimmy driving, were on our way back to Lavington Street.

* * *

"We have our usual tail, sir." It was Frank who alerted me. "It's a White Opal this time, approximately one hundred yards behind and keeping a steady distance. I registered the number with

Solomon at Group and he confirms it's Russian. There are no diplomatic markings on the plates. It started following as soon as we left Mr and Mrs Ugherts'. I was wondering if you wanted to give them something else to think about this time, sir?" he inquired.

Frank's official in-house label was my PPO, my principal protection officer. He did not work inside Group, he worked for Group. That meant he did not regularly fraternise with members of Group other than myself and those I chose to introduce. He had been recruited from the Marine Corps, the same regiment as the two pals of Job's who had helped me ten years or so previously. In that episode of my life they had assisted in two executions which although illegal were justifiable to both myself and Fraser and JIC protocol. I judged Frank to be as reliable as they had been when I'd read the files on all my in-house resources.

"Yes, Frank, I think we should. Let's get that chopper overhead and then block the road, Jimmy. Make a big play without pulling weapons. You up for it, Hannah?"

Within in a mile we had the road closed behind the now stationary Opal and all four of us surrounding the occupants threatening to un-holster our handguns. Diplomatic passes were waved in our faces as we lined the three passengers up lying face down on the damp tarmac with their hands behind their heads. They were all unarmed. I had a dog unit arrive and then a police transport vehicle that carted them off for a firearm discharge examination before anyone was allowed any contact with the Russian Embassy. I was expecting Geoffrey Harwood to call me, but he didn't. Instead, we made Lavington without any interruptions. Once there Hannah and I were undisturbed listening to Fraser's remote tape recording of his intruder and then his murder in my office after all the latest technology had been applied and the sounds made much crisper and more audible. The replay machines were operated by a technician named Saul.

* * *

Fraser must have heard a footstep and realised the silent alarm would have pinged up in Millbank. Knowing that whatever help was on its way would probably arrive too late, he set about his final preparations. His narrative was steady and clear:

"There's a noise from somewhere near the kitchen. I'm praying that it's you that finds the tape, Patrick. I haven't got much time, but all that I had I've shoved into the *Sarah Mariah* file sometime back as insurance. It doesn't explain everything but I hope it helps. The computer password is the date you met Dickie Blythe-Smith at the Travellers Club. Shake the cages and gets results, laddie."

His voice fell silent and was followed by the sharp click of a door catch. Next came Fraser's raised voice questioning whoever was there along with Saul's interpretation of what was occurring:

'Who are you?'

'Move your hands away from that computer,' a voice demanded.

"We believe this to be a simulated voice, sir," the technician informed us both. I asked Saul why he thought the voice was not real. My question was brushed aside with a scornful smile similar to Geoffrey Harwood's plastered on his face—

"We have ways of knowing, sir."

'Why did you shut it down, you stupid old git?' This time the voice was not synthetic. It was shaky, harsh and erratic.

'I didn't plan to shoot you. All I wanted was information from that computer, but now I've got no choice.'

From the tape came the suppressed shot from the Russian handgun, a faint click of metal and the almost silent sonic boom. The weapon was not the make-believe silenced variety in movies and TV shows that in reality do very little to suppress a firing noise. The plastic sliding sound of the computer screen being turned came next, closely followed by a muffled rustling noise that I attributed to the killer thumbing through Fraser's missing notepad. Then the noise of a zip being undone and the identifiable sound of paper being stuffed into a pocket of a coat.

In the distance came the sirens of the police responders and the faint leaden helicopter blades beating its path towards the house. As the piercing decibels increased, the metallic slipping of heavy bolts and the thud of a key releasing the lock of a door could be clearly heard. Nowhere had we heard any footfall. Within seconds of the assassin making his escape came the metal clattering of the helicopter hovering nearby, then cars sliding to a halt and feet running across the gravel towards the house. A heavy knock on the Ugherts' front door was followed by the crash of glass as the whole triple-glazed window in Fraser's office was smashed down by sledgehammer blows.

"There's a man's body slumped behind a desk with no sign of movement, guv. Shall I go in?" It was the voice of the police constable who first saw Fraser's dead body.

A forceful, 'no, do not enter the building,' came the reply, quickly followed by Molly Ughert's discordant voice joining the outside mayhem of more arriving police responders. Although it was indistinct it was possible to hear her ask incredulously, 'what's going on?' To which the police officer replied that he needed her to leave the property. Sadly I never heard any paramedic ask where the injured person was.

The only sounds left on the tape were those of the pathologist's call to the mortuary asking for transport, and the first faint sounds of the forensic photographers with the evidence recorders going about their business. The outside pandemonium was heightened by barking dogs being added to the theatre just before the final curtain was pulled across the performance with no raised voice calling 'bravo' or 'encore'.

* * *

Despite an extensive search by the dogs, aided by the lights from the helicopter, nothing relating to the killer was found during the night, however in the daylight hours of Friday morning motorcycle tracks were discovered in the woods behind the house. The consensus of opinion was that the escaping murderer must have worn night vision glasses as the helicopter would have seen any headlights. There were no traffic cameras on the sideroads and nothing unusual was reported from any motorway cameras.

* * *

By the time I had arrived at Lavington Street the Home Office had been busy as had the Russian ambassador. The permanent secretary to the Minister of State for Foreign and Commonwealth Affairs wanted to know why I had impeded the free passage of three Russians with diplomatic papers. I told him that I had legitimate reasons to believe they could have been involved in Fraser's murder. I told him the fact that no residue of a discharged firearm was found on any of them was immaterial, the fact that a Russian firearm had been used was not. It was relevant. When alone I eventually found time to return Fyodor Nazarov Razin's call. I did not tell him that Fraser had been murdered. I told him that he had died of a heart attack. He offered sympathy and assistance. The offer of help I appreciated, the sympathy I found awkward to accept. We had much to discuss, ideally after Fraser's killer had been found.

In my world Sir Elliot Zerby at MI5 was my boss, but in practice Group was beyond both his and Sir John Scarlett's jurisdiction. My organisation was answerable directly to the Home Office and to the Chairman of the Joint Intelligence Committee, a position which since Fraser had relinquished it, no one occupied.

By accepting the Whitehall job offer, Geoffrey Harwood had removed himself from the hierarchy of the intelligence service, moving sideways into politics. Nevertheless, in the pecking order that was represented by the mandarins of the civil service he was one step above me on the slippery ladder. Whilst he and I were alone together at the Ugherts' home he had asked if I thought Raynor, he persisted in using Fyodor Nazarov Razin's file name, was behind the murder. I answered no to that question, adding that regardless of what I thought everyone who knew of Fraser must be a suspect. There was a peculiar look on his face when I said that.

* * *

By 4:30am I had contacted every departmental head of all the external and internal desks of both intelligence communities, and I had securely transferred every file my security clearance could access that Fraser had worked on in the last eight years over to Group. I passed the files that I could on to Hannah and both the station officer and duty officer, who started looking for clues straight away. I was about to start on the *Sarah Mariah* file which I'd left on Fraser's PC for my eyes only when my solitude was disturbed by Michael Simmons, my mister dependable day station officer who had arrived early for work that Friday morning.

"Mr Harwood is on his way over, sir. He asked if you were free, but if not he said he would wait. He's due to arrive in fifteen minutes."

Ordinarily it should have been me requesting an audience with him, but this was a far from an ordinary time. I was wondering if it had anything to do with the tense look he had on his face when we had last spoken.

"Look, Patrick, I want to be completely open with you. Incidentally, is it okay if I drop the 'Joseph' bit? All a bit pompous between friends, I think. I'm a little out of my depth now that Fraser Ughert's gone. I do realise he'd stepped down, but he was still there if you get my meaning. It wasn't as though we got on well, the opposite was true as you know. You and he were so close that if I'm honest, it made me sick with envy. But he was the buffer where I could fall back on for help in any crisis that was above my head. And I'm sinking here, Patrick. I really have no idea in the slightest what is going on, dear boy." Up until the 'dear boy' point, I was actually believing him but it stopped at that condescending remark.

"Get to the point, Geoffrey, as you may have noticed I have my hands full."

"That is the point. You're now the one in charge. Oliver Nathan sends his condolences and his congratulations on your temporary elevation to Chair of the Joint Intelligence Committee. I'm only the messenger boy, of course, but you have my support, dear boy. One hundred percent behind you, Patrick. You have increased levels of not only security clearance but you now have the extra authority. In theory at least, you outrank me, being only answerable to Parliament and even then, only the most senior ministers thereof."

"Do you mean I have the power to order toilets rolls without asking your department?" He sighed at my scoffing remark without offering any comment. My foolishness was unnecessary and irresponsible in the circumstances. I put it behind me.

"Does temporarily in charge mean until Fraser's killer is found, Geoffrey?"

"Not necessarily, no! It could be permanent depending on results of course."

"And who's judging the results?" I asked suspiciously.

"Well, no one person. So don't get on that socialist platform of yours and start quoting that slogan you are so fond of—'of each to their own,' and what have you. It makes operational sense for you to take control. You shared Fraser's confidence. You are currently in contact with the Russian in this country and you must know that Liam Catlin is where he is because Ughert put him there. GCHQ and my Greenwich AIS department can configure any signal traffic to and from him if you're in doubt as to his location. I was never privy to the mechanism of Fraser's Machiavellian mind and I very much doubt I would have made sense of it had I have been so. You, on the other hand, think along parallel lines. Oliver and I are in agreement that it's early days for you to do the job, however, someone has to and you're the Charlie, dear boy. Soak it up and I'm being sincere when I say I hope the position becomes permanently yours."

Geoffrey Harwood was covering his back and hoping for a dismal performance by yours truly and then a plea from up high for the sacrifice of his political career, accompanied by a multitude of incentives to take the JIC position. He had nothing to lose, but on the other hand, nor did I. The belief in coincidence had never held a high position in my psyche, and the arrival of a trained killer in the shape of Fraser's mysterious Armenian contact, seemed too advantageous to fit the killer's profile. Although there was nothing in the *Sarah Mariah* file to point the finger of accusation at Suzanna Kandarian, she was I deemed the next person to see in this investigation. However, that was something for the daylight hours, a time after dealing with the ensuing melee of inquiring voices on the secure telephone lines, unlike the throbbing of the burner phone in my pocket. Fyodor was incessant, but I could do nothing to ease his worries.

* * *

Before speaking to Razin I needed to put Suzanna some place other than Hannah's aunt's address. I could not interview her there whilst the aunt was in the same house and according to Hannah, she seldom went out. I needed somewhere private. Fraser had what he'd called a bolt hole in Peckham. It was not a safe house in the service accepted sense of the word. It was not conspicuously safe in any sense of the word safe. A third floor, end of balcony flat in a tenement block on a council estate near the high street with constantly changing nearby residents. Fraser's use of it had been clouded in mystery with speculation varying between the fanciful and the bizarre, but it suited my purposes, no matter what its history. Suzanna was waiting at the flat as I'd requested, but she was not alone and I had not anticipated that.

* * *

Seven-fifteen that same Friday morning, Christopher Irons, the MI6 operative who had escorted Martin Lennox, the Russian spy, home from our embassy in Armenia two days earlier, was waiting in Schiphol airport, Amsterdam for the incoming flight from Odessa, Ukraine. At the predetermined spot in the arrivals lounge he ordered a coffee and sat patiently for his contact. The flight carrying Exxon Mobil chief negotiator Josh Polish was punctual. Polish left the twenty-three-page document detailing the proposed Black Sea and Arctic venture with the Russian oil giant Rosneft lying on the chair next to Irons, who promptly put it inside his document case and headed off to the taxi rank and the rush-hour ride into central London.

* * *

Once again it was the Stamford Street exit I used to meet Jimmy, this time driving a previously unused car from the motor pool. Even allowing for its fresh use we doubled across our route several times before we both were satisfied that we hadn't a tail then drove off to meet with Suzanna in Fraser's bolt-hole. When I met Frank on the communal balcony outside number 37 Tiptree House, Church Road, Peckham, the first words out of his mouth were to apologise.

"Sorry, sir, there was nothing I could do. He was here when I got here. I couldn't call you as he took my phone. You'd better go in then you'll understand."

Suzanna was in what passed as a kitchen and Christopher Irons, whom I'd met once at the elite training centre at the Royal Marines Base, Poole, was seated on a sofa looking straight at the front door.

"Come on in, laddie, we're all waiting for you." The hair on the back of my neck stood bolt upright.

Chapter Fifteen
The Resurrection

Only five people at Chearsley were aware of Fraser's orchestrated death: Molly Ughert, who with her performance should appear at the Old Vic on a regular basis, the Home Office pathologist who was Fraser's fishing partner, the two men who placed his body in the private ambulance and the senior police officer who arrived first on the scene; all three were members of his Masonic lodge. When Fraser was first appointed Chairman of the Joint Intelligence Committee, Christopher Irons played the same role as Frank was now doing for me; he was his *consociate* and not only that, he became a close friend. Suzanna Kandarian also knew of the deception; she had choreographed it.

"I needed her for her expertise and knowledge. Was it the Russian handgun that had you convinced, laddie?"

His taunting only served to irritate me further as he skirted around my question of how he came by that Russian handgun with a mere look towards the ceiling as if I should already know. Eventually, after highlighting my ineptitude as a detective as many times as he thought necessary, he came to the point of his trickery.

"It was crucial that you were appointed as Chair of the Joint Intelligence. Absolutely crucial, laddie! It means that you can draw the sensitive files that could have been denied to you at

Group. No matter how I disguised it, had I requested a sight of the old material, bells may have rung in the wrong ears. Molly and Graham, my fishing buddy, will hold up on my funeral arrangements until after Christmas if necessary so you and I, Patrick, have only a splattering of days to find the meaning in those Gladio B files or we will be searching for a spare cadaver to fill a coffin. Suzanna's here to keep the locals from breaking down the door, which jokes apart could happen if any become suspicious. She will play the part of a prostitute and Christopher is elevated to her pimp. You and Frank will be her regular punters. As I said, she did the spadework for my little pretence. Pretty convincing, eh?

"I need you to start with some solid information. Three years ago Exxon and Mobil oil merged to become the world's largest 'Big Oil' company and will become the largest trading company ranked by capitalisation in a few years to come. The man who owns that company is in line to become yet another Presidential nominee of America that you will come up against. His family is not only extremely powerful in their own right, they have many influential friends scattered around the world. We believe they are one of the inner eight that the two of us have spoken of. We have a jump on Fyodor with this information. He knows nothing of the association, laddie, but I suspect he will and I'm sure he can add the numbers up as good as I can." There was a pause as he locked eyes with me.

"ExxonMobil is due to open offices in Yerevan and to formalise their plans with a Russian State oil company for oil and gas pipelines crisscrossing that part of the world which will be, we believe, divided up between the States and Russia. Martin Lennox, the Russian spy who should know these things, described *that part of the world* as an area from the Ukraine and the Black Sea, across to the Caspian Sea then down to the Persian Gulf, obviously encompassing Afghanistan. It is my belief, although Lennox denies knowledge of this, that Iraq, Iran, Israel, and Saudi Arabia are compromised somewhere in the game plan. Can you imagine the power a company that controlled almost all the world's fuel resources would have over the rest of us? And please, don't quote the other OPEC producing countries, they will be swallowed up by a conglomerate with that amount of political persuasion. And yes, before you ask, Henry Mayler fits somewhere into that picture. I'm a little unclear where, but that birthdate of his is the only key I have at present."

A lengthy uncontrolled sigh left his lips as he sat and reflected on his inadequate knowledge. I had nothing to add in the way of comfort, but comfort of a sort was on hand. Suzanna sauntered into the room carrying two sparkling glasses and an unopened bottle of his favourite oak cask, single malt whisky.

"I bought three bottles," she declared smilingly as a watery sun fought through the smoke from his pipe to assist the unshaded ceiling lamp.

"I've read about you," I said, pouring the golden whisky into both glasses. "While you're here, Suzanna, can I put something to bed, Fraser?" I asked and he nodded his acquiescence whilst she remained standing.

"I know what you said about Henry travelling to New York after that meeting with Razin in Kabul, but you haven't covered why it took two hours five minutes to answer Henry Mayler's cry for help. Would it have anything to do with Suzanna cutting off Bernard Higgins' head over in Khost? And if so why the fuck have you been lying to me all the time? Here's another question while you're thinking of ducking out of that one," I was angry and it showed. "Why did you need Mayler to tell Razin I was to be appointed head of Group? Why not just tell him yourself?" I finished my Scotch in one gulp and reached out for the bottle, but the black-haired beautiful gipsy towering above me had it in her hand and was beginning to fill my glass while I stared straight into her soulless eyes.

"Suzanna did not sever Bernard's head, Patrick. That was done because of his affiliation with the CIA officer I told you of. But yes, that was the reason for the delay in answering Henry. I needed confirmation of Bernard's death. I have not been lying to you. This subterfuge was necessary for the reasons I've already said and to convince Hardballs. For not one moment am I suggesting the Geoffrey Harwood would be in league with any outside agency, nevertheless his chosen circle contains politicians with whom he habitually associates. I have never trusted those of a political nature. Fortunately we don't have to worry about popularity. Do we, Suzanna?"

That last statement was sternly directed at the thirty-seven-year-old woman who would not take her wide, direct and chilling eyes off me. She left the room and silently I was relieved. She scared me to hell and back. I ignored her exit.

"Have you any thoughts you would like to share on who Henry Mayler met in New York after rushing off there in November, Fraser? I won't ask him in case something compromising turns up." My pride was hurt.

"He didn't say, laddie, but ask away if you wish."

"How about William B. Guerny II? How does he fit in?" A puff on a pipe preceded his reply.

"Suzanna cleaned up after Razin and Henry left Al Hasaketh. The body on the ground was dead as Henry suspected. Suzanna and I had reasonable suspicion who the second man was. Guerny was found and I wanted information that only he would know. I deemed it necessary to keep him alive until we had no further use for him. Does that shock you, laddie?"

"No, but I am beginning to get doubts about this operation. How did you know where Henry was going and where to send Suzanna?"

"Hadad, Patrick. He was rotten and we knew it. That's how Razin was at the rendezvous and not a Pakistan security man."

I sat and thought about that for a few moments, during which time I could hear Frank speaking to Christopher Irons about the training at Poole. It had never crossed my mind that Frank had undergone the same courses as we had.

"I can't see any relevance to the security of this country if it's only big business you're after, Fraser. What role has the Joint Intelligence Committee in all of this?"

"Ever heard of fracking, Patrick, or to give it its full name Hydraulic Fracturing? If not, I suggest you cram up on it. Also look up antidotes to methanol poisoning, it could come in handy. The long term aspiration of the company I've spoken of, ExxonMobil, is to start hydraulic blasting in the Arctic Circle to find gas and oil. Methanol is one of the propellants used. It's a poison that you've read of recently. Suzanna leaves some evidence of its use to remind those in charge of the toxicity of their poison. She hopes they might take notice. You and I are too cynical to believe that they would, aren't we? Do you honestly think that an uncontrolled operator will pay much attention to safety in the Arctic or in the Middle East? These types of people have no regard for life other than the life their profits buy. It is our business."

"Okay, I take your point, but where did you hide your magnanimity when it came to Alaz Karabakh and old Hadad, Mayler's rabbit and driver? You were Henry's Control for the year Bernard Higgins was unavailable, were you not? So where was Bernard Higgins for the year between Henry meeting Razin in Khost and then meeting again in Kabul? Why was Henry Mayler sent to Khost if not to find Razin?"

"I'll try to tackle one at a time, laddie. Let's do Bernard Higgins. The straight answer is I have no answer. The little I do know is that he and Henry attended a press party held at what was to become the site of the American Embassy in Kabul in December 2001. While at that impromptu party Bernard met a NSA operative named Franklin Dubass. Born in Cape Town, South Africa but a nationalised American due to his mother being one of theirs. Dubass was lost to any signal intelligence the day after that party. Completely vanished. Strange to think nobody wiped his past clean, but there we have it. Henry remembers Bernard talking to an American who was distinctive in a couple of ways; he was completely bald with an ugly scar running from the top of head to his collar line at the back of his head. Henry asked around and found the name.

"That night Bernard made an excuse to Henry, said he had the chance to get useful intel from Dubass and pass it on up, so be a good boy and don't shout too loud if he wasn't seen for a few days. Henry waited patiently for a week, but no show from Bernard. Henry's message to that effect found me, and I moved him back to standby readiness until further notice. That was easy as we have friends in journalism who are always in need of a decent freelance photographer. Notwithstanding any favours being drawn on, it was an awkward situation for me to deal with, having to keep a low profile yet run a comprehensive review of our standing. Why, for example, had Bernard never tried to contact Henry? But Henry was my main concern. My second was Razin. I did not want him getting strung out and anxious. I pulled no punches in trying to trace this Franklin Dubass, but not a sniff. Then, I think it was the tenth of November this year I heard that Bernard's body had been found. Obviously the situation regarding my involvement in the verification of that was as tense as it had been when he had first disappeared. When I had the confirmation I instructed Suzanna in the tradecraft used between Henry and Bernard and she took over the messaging. That's when I assigned him to Syria to follow Karabakh. We've gone in a circle but finally we've fallen upon my second regret I spoke of regarding Bernard Higgins. I can never be one hundred percent sure that Henry was not compromised by the affinity Higgins found with the NSA man, Dubass. If Henry was not as important as he is then I would have ordered his annihilation to cover any breach of Fyodor Nazarov Razin's cover. I can't be sure how Razin would react if he knew of this lapse in security. It's worrying, Patrick and it's a loophole I don't like."

He leant forward in his chair, placing his head in his hands, staring at the faded floral carpets as if looking for faults in the weave. From nowhere Suzanna glided into the room as if walking on air. I hadn't noticed that extra deftness before and perhaps it was the severity that had impacted upon him that focused my curiosity, but the extent of her assiduous attention to his distraught condition exceeded my expectations. She knelt beside him adding her hands to his and turned his head towards the smooth skin of her face, then she gently kissed him on the lips, pulling away with an enigmatic smile across her face. Fraser regained his collectedness, smiling reassuringly at her. They touched hands before she once again refreshed our glasses, remaining where she was.

"Is Molly aware of Suzanna?" I asked as she stood. I didn't know what reply I expected, but I had not bargained for what I got.

"Yes, Patrick, she is. Suzanna is Jack Price's daughter."

Chapter Sixteen
Jack Price and Others

"I was Jack's rookie back in 1956. I'd been destined for the service before birth as the Ugherts had served in one capacity or another since time immemorial. After the usual period of life at the family home near Edinburgh, I was boarded out at Glenalmond College, eight miles from Perth in Scotland, as was my great-grandfather and grandfather before me. In the same steps as those two I attended Corpus Christi college at Oxford University. It was in my penultimate year that I was presented to a person whom my English literature tutor simply called a government representative; it was Jack. Apparently, the two of them had served together in Italy at the end of the War. My tutor, a Mr Grace, was caught in an explosion of some kind and lost the bottom half of his leg. There's no space in my memory to recall exactly what Jack Price said, all I know is that I went straight from Oxford to preliminary school at Cranleigh in Surrey. I did the standard four weeks in Inverness on firearms, then on to Lord Montague's estate at Beaulieu in the New Forest where I think I stayed for almost a year. I guess it was all much the same in your days, Patrick. Observation and survival with as many skills as needed to fulfil those two necessities. Jack picked me up from Waterloo station when I was turfed out and thrown to the wolves. I think that was in 1955. In 1956 Jack, with me running after his shirt-tails so to speak, were in Budapest and Jack introduced me to Taline."

"So Jack stayed in a relationship with this Taline for nine years and said nothing of it to me when I was asking about his past. I felt sorry for him when he told me his two children had left him and never contacted him. Perhaps they knew and took sides with his wife when she left him. It's funny how you think you know someone but you really know so little about them."

"You didn't know Jack for long, Patrick. I knew him for thirty odd years and he was still surprising me until he died. I knew nothing of his connection to the Royal Family and that operation in New York you and he were on. The only reason behind telling me of Suzanna was his impending death. He knew I was in a good position to look after her welfare and future. After all she was only an infant when he passed away. I met with him a week before he died and he gave me his written instructions on that date. He was adamant and precise in how she was to be raised. Initially it was Jack who funded her upbringing but when Jack's capital ran out the department took over and I was placed in charge of her."

"Did they ever meet each other?" I asked, being sentimental.

"I can't say for sure, because I never took over until his death of course, but I would imagine they did even though Suzanna has no memory of it. I told her what I could of him and left it there."

There was more glasses filled with the whisky, more puffs on pipes and cigarette smoke before Jack was pushed to the backs of our minds with the present day operational affairs taking over.

"Have you forgotten to turn your phone on, Patrick? Is nobody looking for any updates on my murder?"

"My dayshift Solomon, Michael Simmons, is fielding the calls. I'm very fortunate in having him."

"Good! How's Razin shaping up?"

"He's very jumpy. It didn't help me pulling over his 'tail' on the way back from yours yesterday morning. That caused quite a diplomatic fuss. I was surprised Geoffrey didn't give my ear a bashing about it."

"What possessed you pull the car over, laddie? I wouldn't wonder if Hardballs was upset."

"It wasn't only petulance, Fraser." I was upset that he didn't know why. "Strange though it must sound I was angry that you'd been shot. I wanted to shoot someone but all I had was an Opel car with three hoods inside. It was a way of making them take notice, that's all."

"Hmm, the same weakness Jack Price suffered from."

"You hid your association with Jack bloody well, Fraser. I knew you'd met before we all did in New York, but I hadn't a clue just how well you two were acquainted. You're just full of surprises. Got any more up your sleeve?"

I sat and listened in astonishment as he narrated a tale far more complex than the one he originally told. Jack Price had been instrumental in introducing Henry Mayler to Fraser and Razin to Fraser. I recalled Jack telling me a story of how he was presented with a three-corner chair as a kind of insult to his loyalty by a Barrington Trenchard who sounded as though he was Jack's own Geoffrey Harwood, only from a personal viewpoint he turned out to be far worse. Jack had to carry that chair from Marylebone Station to his flat in Baker Street. The same flat into which Fraser moved Bernard Higgins. By that time Jack was dead of course and had no say in the matter. Despite that fact, from what I heard from Fraser he wouldn't have raised any protest.

* * *

Suzanna's mother had a large family spread throughout the Caucasus region, stretching into Iran and Afghanistan with ancestral ties to the Assyrian race. Over the years following her death and protection of Hungary's Prime Minister János Kádár, some of her secrets became known by factions who were disadvantaged by them. They took their bloody revenge on as many of her family as they could find. Some who survived were amongst the supporters of Ahmad Bassriud and more importantly one was among the three who held the secret to unlocking both Gladio B files.

* * *

At 2am on Saturday, Liam Catlin left the British Embassy opposite Lover's Park in the centre of Yerevan, Armenia and made his way to the Genocide Memorial Complex, about half a mile away by foot. He was met there by a woman who after an exchange of spoken codes gave him directions to a square-chinned, chiselled-faced, moustached man, as tall and as wide as Liam himself. The man commented on Liam's winter clothing because as cold as it was in Yerevan that early morning in December, where they were going it was considerably colder.

"Put this on. You'll need it! The heater in this old rust-bucket of a truck is not very good. We have a three-hour journey to the north ahead of us. It will be at least twice as cold as it is here." He tossed a heavy striped woollen Afghan shawl at Liam.

"It's the blood in the brain that freezes first," Marek Kandarian added, as a flat grey, peaked cap followed the shawl and the chiselled chin man fixed Liam with a stare from eyes identical and as cold as his sister's.

In almost complete silence they travelled and for the last mile or so without lights on the vehicle, being guided by the blazing stars in the clear dark sky until Liam's rattling transport pulled to a halt a few hundred yards off the main connecting road from Armenia to Turkey outside the tiny village of Ashotsk. Inside the truck it stunk of tobacco, garlic from both men's breath and the stale smell of grime. Outside it was the harsh stinging taste of unmitigated cold that Liam inhaled as his gloved fingers fumbled with yet another cigarette.

"Mr Catlin, it would be a pleasure if it wasn't so cold. Your Mr Elijah calls me the Doctor." That was how Robert Zaehner introduced himself. "I'm here as my government's representative to witness the destruction of a no longer needed record that I understand is sensitive to some. Shall we get on?"

The 'Power Book' computer was concealed beneath the floor of the crypt of a monastery carved into the side of hill in an area adjacent to where they met. On its hard drive were copies of all the original handwritten directives from Nixon and his then CIA director, together with some from the NSA director of the day and others from military commanders around the world until 1991, when this technically advanced portable computer became available. It contained the numbers and names of Panama bank accounts into which siphoned funding had been paid and from which various 'black operations' had been instigated. Central America in particular was targeted by this cache of money.

Liam connected a power line the Armenian chiselled-faced driver provided and punched in the code that he and two others had kept secret for eleven years. Robert Zaehner ran a flash drive download and when happy that all three hundred and thirty-three files were safely recovered inside the memory stick gave it with a degree of sobriety to Liam Catlin. He stood back and watched as Liam poured an accelerant on the now separated grey components of the computer, lit a taper and set fire to it. When the flames had died the ashes were raked over and set alight once more. Finally, what remained was crushed where it was and the crypt resealed before both men returned to their transport.

* * *

At 8:23 on the morning of the 18th December GCHQ, AIS, and the signals room at Lavington Street received the same two-worded message from outstation YA: *Tickled Pink*. I was made aware of the signal by Michael Simmons. From the part of the tunnel Fraser had said was secure my first call was to Razin. I held my breath and trusted Fraser's word.

* * *

Fyodor Nazarov Razin had not slept since being notified of the false reason for my hasty departure from Group's headquarters very early on Thursday morning. He was beginning to boil by the time he heard back from Moscow Centre. The man bearing the name he gave them, a dissident Russian colonel who had been banished to Dagestan where he was supposed to be held under house-arrest, could not be located. To make matters worse he had failed to register at the dedicated militsiya police station in his precinct of the city of Makhachkala for the past twelve days. He was a known member of the Shariat Jamaat Islamic Jihadist group who were also off the radar.

"The senior sergeant said he believed the colonel was in Chechnya planning an attack with those Islamic militants somewhere in the Caucuses, General Razin. He was about to report that suspicion to your department in the Federal Security Service."

"Was he?" Razin shouted at the communication equipment in the concrete underground bunker beneath the Russian Consulate at Notting Hill Gate. Whilst his voice was still rebounding from the four walls he picked up the secure satellite link to the Russian Defence Attaché's office in Highgate West Hill.

"Has there been any reports concerning the Turkmenistan militarised compound on the shore of the Aral Sea? In specific, the chemical arsenal?" he asked without any niceties.

Twenty minutes later he had the negative answer he was worried about. Once again he dialled the number of Patrick West's burner phone. There was no answer. There was more desire for urgency this Thursday morning than any other, but suspicions could not be aroused in Moscow. All must go on as before. No alterations to the schedule, no changes in the mannerisms nor destinations. At 11am Thursday he left the Consulate and the eyes began to follow. All went as normal until he entered the Silver Vaults. It was there, beyond the watchers, that he started his meltdown sequence. Inside the safe deposit box he kept, on the second underground level in Chancery Lane, he'd hidden his collection of passports and identification documents, along with bank cards, cash in dollars and the three throwaway mobile phones. He put what he needed into those giant pockets of his coat, joining his copy of the one-time code book for the coming two weeks that he had taken from his own office at the Consulate.

In total he ran twenty-one groupings of agents spying for the reasons Razin gave them. Eleven cells throughout Europe and the Middle East, a further five in North America and the same number in South America and although all were autonomous and well protected if, as he suspected, Fraser Ughert had been murdered then that cast them all into danger and more so—himself. There was no little black book containing nexus couplings related to signals of decamp—run—hide, the next stop is the firing squad. Each group was different. Made up with different numbers. Had different Numero Unos. Some were calm mannered men or women. Some were jumpy. If he sent the alert cue all would be frightened. All would scatter, never to be trusted until he found each one of them and systematically killed each one.

I could be overreacting. Maybe old Fraser's heart did finally gave out on him. The fuss they would mount would be the same as if he had been murdered. West must be busy, but—why too busy for me? I will give him the benefit of the doubt and wait till Saturday midday, he decided in silent contemplation.

*   *   *

By the time I regained my office seat that Saturday morning after speaking to Razin from the tunnel, Hannah had more calls on hold than the number of hot meals I'd eaten since being appointed head of Group. I had more pressing things to do. I next telephoned Fraser.

"What was his reaction when you told him that the original Gladio B document had been destroyed?" he asked in a severely agitated voice.

"He said he didn't care because very soon all hell was about to be launched on America and we all would probably die in the aftermath of retaliation."

That's when I told him about the weaponised anthrax and phosphorous shells Razin believed to be in the hands of a militant separatist Jihadist group who were supplied by a mad Russian colonel whose only son was killed in an American air strike on a mujahideen strike force in Afghanistan in October 2001. Fraser was silent for a while and I worried that this time he really might die of a heart attack, but he seemed to sense my concern, asking me to continue to tell what Razin had said. I obeyed him.

The colonel was discharged from the army a month after his son's death following the shooting of two American tourists near his home village of Listvyanka in the mountainous Russian region of Siberia, who were hiking along paths called the Great Baikal Trail. The American government were told that the colonel was mentally unstable and would be locked up for life. That was a lie of course. He was sent to Dagestan where he had family and it was there his son converted to Islam. Not a word of the incident was reported by the international press. The local authorities informed the parents that it had been an unfortunate accident and when asked for the bodies to be flown home, were conveniently told that as the lake was one of the deepest in the world and there would be no possibility of any recovered bodies. They had no choice but to accept that explanation.

"Where's the target, Patrick?" Fraser eventually asked.

"If Razin knows he's not telling me. All he's saying is it will be an American target. He added a rather salient specific. The Iraqis are equipped with American M114 howitzers. Those artillery pieces fire the same calibre of shells that are missing. They have a kill range of roughly twenty miles. Be that as it may, Razin's Federal Security Service has intelligence of a new Iraqi super-gun based around the original Gerald Bull's design. It was built in a factory in Italy and arrived in Beirut three weeks ago. If that information is correct, and Razin is confident that it is, then Saddam Hussein's army has the capability of firing United Nations banned toxic chemicals and incendiary munitions for hundreds if not thousands of miles."

"I'm not ignoring any of that but it's way too high for me to pass comment on. That's for Oliver Nathan and the PM to deal with. But what did he say after you told him what I asked; Henry Mayler had seen inside the first Gladio B file, laddie?"

"Nothing, Fraser. The line went dead."

Chapter Seventeen
Kirkuk

Frank had been backwards and forth to Peckham using all three exit tunnels from The Hole and hopping from bus to bus on his Friday journeys to Fraser. The files and signals I'd successfully drawn from the Deferrals department for Fraser had been, so Frank told me, useful. High praise indeed from Mr Ughert. When I spoke to Molly on the telephone she had carried on with her role in the duplicity brilliantly and had I been a critic at a West End show I would have given her a best actress award for the performance. Somehow or other I had managed the impossible in keeping Fraser's feigned death and location a complete secret from the investigating Ministry of Defence and Special Branch agents as well as the heads of the various intelligence departments who had asked. As a bonus, no overseas service had heard a whisper. But good things never last, do they? This was one that could never be kept secret for long. Michael Simmons sent three of his lamp-burners to walk the block around number 67 Lavington Street for me with four more trailing behind at set distances and working their way wider. 'Nothing suspicious' was the shared analysis of the experts. No marked cars on the route and nothing parked that looked questionable. With the foot traffic it was a different matter, but we left two of the lamp-burners at each end of Lavington Street with radios to signal if they saw anything dubious. I was oblivious to the sleeting rain on the short walk away from number 67 to the car that Saturday lunchtime, itching with nervous energy as Jimmy put the car into gear and with Frank back beside him we pulled away, driving south towards Peckham.

* * *

On the bare-wooded dining table in the Peckham flat Fraser had six phones spread out in front of himself, each with a written label stuck on it. I saw the one dedicated to Molly and the one marked Group. The other markings were just numbers that meant something to only him I guessed, but I was wrong in that assumption. Ignoring my presence, Suzanna seemed to coast into the room with another numbered marked phone, placing it on the table with the others, then announcing that the call she had just taken was from someone called Nola who was a she. Apparently Nola could confirm whatever it was Fraser had asked. I sat opposite him and without looking at Suzanna, asked for a coffee. I stared straight at Fraser and lit a Dunhill cigarette.

"Do you take anything for that?" Suzanna asked and I thought she referred to my rudeness.

"If I did would you like me to share it with you?" I replied scornfully.

"I haven't got nerve damage to my right leg as you do, Mr West. I would also add that both your knees are showing wear because of the strain your right foot is putting on them. If I had it as bad as you do I would seek medical help, especially in your position and as it's free in this country. If I was in Armenia I'd have a cure for you, or at least a remedy to ease the pain. It's more likely the cold and damp that makes the pain worse. Good morning by the way, Patrick."

I was in acute discomfort from my foot to the top of my thigh, but how did she know? I silently asked as I returned her belated greeting.

"Can we put any confrontation out of the way, please? Today is not the day." Fraser looked at us both with a stern and angry frown.

"Make it two coffees, Suzanna, please. I'll have another." Suzanna left and he addressed me in an edgy manner.

"How does Razin know that this Russian colonel acquired the anthrax and the ammunitions then passed it all on to this Islamic Jihadist group; Shariat Jamaat?"

"Are you okay, Fraser? You seem unusually irritated this morning. Suzanna and I were only establishing rank. It would appear that neither of us wants to share you. How's that angina of yours doing? You know you can't get yourself over-stressed. That will kill you for real and we'll be having Molly to deal with. Where will all of us be then?"

"Have you spoken to Molly this morning as she was saying much the same an hour ago? Suzanna's as bad! I'm not having it from you as well. Answer my damn question, laddie, before I scream and swear at you in Gaelic."

"Phew, excuse me for coming and showing concern, Mr Ughert, sir. If that's what you want then here goes. Razin said this colonel was the last commanding officer of the base. He signed the manifest when they sealed the doors and first concreted over the place. It was opened up under orders from the Kremlin because of a radio transmission that was intercepted from the Kurdish Democratic Party alleging the Iraqi nuclear power programme had restarted. The plant bombed by Israelis jets in 1980, was not being rebuilt, but a new one on a site near Kirkuk was underway. In a second part of that signal it went on to allege that an ex-Russian colonel had sold the whereabouts of a number of classified weapons to a member of the Dagestan-based Shariat Jamaat dissident group who had connections to the Kurds. The Shariat Jamaat group had insufficient means of transport for the quantity of weapons available so the information was sold on to a member of the Ba'ath Party of Iraq. The intercepted transmission was examined by Razin who passed it on to the Nuclear Registration Department within the Kremlin, who sent engineers and inspectors to the Aral Sea site to maintain the stability of the forgotten two kilograms of highly enriched uranium fuel stored twelve hundred feet underground that in theory, nobody could access. The uranium, although untouched, was airlifted to a safer site that Razin did not disclose. It was then that the manifest was checked and came up short."

Fraser sat shaking his head in disbelief. He reached for the glass of water that was on the oblong table beside his pipe and reading glasses, then withdrew two blister packets of pills from a pocket on the side of his heavy woollen sweater. He broke two tablets from each then swallowed them with a mouthful of water.

"That's Russia for you, Patrick," he declared, coinciding with a coffee-transporting Suzanna. "Totally unorganised!"

"If ever they got their game together then best we all look to Heaven for our salvation as nobody will be safe," Suzanna added as she found places on the cluttered table for our cups. She hadn't finished with helpful advice.

"Here, I found some painkillers in my bag. Take two whenever you need them." She held out an unmarked packet of tablets which I hesitantly took. She mocked me with a soft deriding chuckle.

"If I wanted to harm you, Mr West, I would not be as obvious. They will kill your pain, but nothing else." Her laugh was louder as she left to join Frank in another room where I could hear a television on.

"We can't keep this information to ourselves, Fraser, but that will mean disclosing our tie-up with Razin. There's no way we can hide that."

"Then ultimately we don't, laddie! He's almost served his purpose. We have access now to the second file. I can't pull that up whilst I'm here. If I do then that will send my whereabouts to all those that want to know including Razin's Federal Security Service. Nor can you pull it up. Not just yet." He stopped speaking, rose from his chair and walked towards the window overlooking the empty, sodden park beneath.

"Grey, Patrick. The worst colour God invented and the Russian nation adopted it with Lenin and his cronies. I'm not saying the Tsar was any bloody better, because his lot were not. But eff me. A land of soulful poets and artists crushed under Communism. I honestly despair. America is no answer. They are rash, disdainful, unaware and uncaring of anything or anyone beyond their confines. Those descriptions could stand for the UN as well. So who's left? Us? The French? The Germans? No, there's only one thing that the world desires and that's oil. That's all anyone cares about. We would kill each other for it. In fact, I believe we will. It's Iraq this inner circle of eight are after first. I think they will flex their muscles with that one. Then possibly Saudi Arabia, after all they are the world's biggest producers and America are the world's biggest uses. That won't stay that way for long. You wait until India, Brazil and then the giant of China awake to democracy and want cars and industrialisation. Guess who will want to supply the oil needed for that huge market."

"Where did all that come from, Fraser? What have you found from the files Frank delivered?"

"What have I found, well that's a question and a half? Incidentally, you have two good men in Frank and your station officer, Michael Simmons you said his name was. Look after them, loyalty is a dying commodity in this screwed up world."

"You are in a bad mood. Is there something apart from Razin's news that's set you off?"

"When I was Chairman of Joint Intelligence everything that landed on Sir John Scarlett's desk at 6 came over to me. We shared an asset in Turkey that you helped reunite. The logistical officer you secreted away on a flight out from Northolt to Cyprus, is one half of that agent, the other half being his fake wife in Gaziantep, Turkey. I had shared some of her intel with Razin just enough for him to put his nose in the trough and hunt around a bit. He did, and I expect he's told you what he found out. However, if he hasn't I will. Our Mrs Ratcliffe, that's the cover name, has kept herself busy, this time with an attaché from the Israeli Embassy. To abridge that message which I saw this morning, it seems one part of a CIA special forces network, known to Mossad Intel Centre as G3, is in readiness to land at the place you mentioned as the site of Iraqis' nuclear power project—Kirkuk. Now that could be to blow the place up, but I think that's a non-starter. It could mean they want to authenticate the information, yes, possible, but unlikely, or it could and probably does mean, they want ground level intelligence to mark the site for an airdrop. This CIA special forces group G3 exists, Patrick. The intel Mrs Ratcliffe got, stands up. But it leaves a question that's unanswered at the moment, why American special forces and not Israeli? Where are they going launch this drop from? It will be highly embarrassing for any Islamic nation or Israel.

"There's one man inside American intelligence that I trust. I mentioned him sometime back; Robert Zaehner. It was he Liam Catlin met before sending the *Tickled Pink* communiqué. He was at the scene of Gladio B's destruction to make sure an accurate copy was taken. He knows full well the ramifications of us holding that recorded file. The fact that he has to trust us is neither here nor there. He could have tried to get his hands on our copy but he didn't. The only copy of the file is in the diplomatic bag winging its way here. It's addressed to Director General Group, Craig Court, Whitehall. Harwood never goes there now, Patrick, and he never checks if any bags go there. Why not, laddie? Because nobody goes there anymore. But you will go and show your face in order to collect it."

"Which reminds me, when are you going to resurface and show your face?"

"As soon as I possibly can, but that might mean you doing Christmas without any knowing winks at Molly."

* * *

"When this is all over, sir, you should write a book titled *The First Nine Days*. I know the Official Secrets Act won't allow you to do that, but you could change your name and then who would know?"

I had finished briefing Hannah on the situation regarding the Gladio B files, Fyodor Nazarov Razin and Henry Mayler when she suggested the book under a pseudonym. Solomon was smiling sitting beside her and I was picturing them together away from this life of deceit-filled misery. They looked suited to each other. I had come a long way since leaving my Canary Wharf apartment and my sedentary undisturbed life of referees' whistles. The puerile thoughts I'd had on being released into a life where an attractive woman was my almost constant companion had been replaced by a more mature approach to life. The irony of my graduation into maturity compared to Fraser Ughert's regress into something akin to senility did not escape me. How did he expect to return from the dead and what would be the excuse he gave to his peers?

Chapter Eighteen
It's a Mess

Group had a long and distinguished past, beginning its journey sometime in the middle of the years that spanned the First World War inside a building at the end of a cul-de-sac called Craig Court at the Trafalgar Square end of Whitehall. To the naked eye the building that closed off the short unremarkable street was a plain bricked one with no doorway and higher windows than street level. That was how it was meant to look to the casual eye, because on the other side of those red bricks and windows with standard issue civil service, over-sized net-curtaining was the eight inches of concrete, lined by seamless steel, secret establishment that only those who had need of its services knew how to get in. The main entrance was through another government department, now called The Department for Environment, Food and Rural Affairs. There was though another way into Group's offices; through the linked myriad of underground tunnels emanating from all the state offices along Whitehall arriving at one central security post. That post and the one dividing the Department for the Environment etc. of the UK from a shady organisation that helped the UK to have an environment both kept digitalised log books. As chairman of JIC I had every right to examine them, but the way Fraser phrased his comment about Craig Court not taking deliveries nowadays, had left me with reservations about visiting the place to acquire the memory stick of Gladio B. I requested those log books and set the staffers at Group to check on visits made by Geoffrey Harwood and Fraser Ughert from November last year.

The remark Fraser had made concerning the documents and signals that landed on Sir John Scarlett's SIS desk at Vauxhall ending up on his desk in Whitehall had aroused my interest, and as I started to look at those that had transferred across, one caught my eye. It was the date that notched up my interest—November 10th 2002. Four days after Razin and Mayler met in Khost where Bernard Higgins' body was found. It was in open text, after its interception and translation at GCHQ.

Special Collection Service F6: Signals Intelligence: Kabul: Body of F. Dubass found.

On another open text intercepted message dated the same day was the following—Accredited Finnish Journalist Oban Raikkonen re-entered Khost compound from Kabul. Both these signals had Fraser Ughert's Joint Intelligence Committee stamped receipt on them. There were no other intercepts passed to Chairman Ughert that day. Hannah broke my concentration.

"I have Mr Harwood on hold. He says it urgent and there's an unmistakable ruffle to his voice, sir." What possibly could have ruffled Geoffrey on a weekend?

"Good afternoon, Geoffrey! What brings you out to play at this time of day on a winter Saturday?"

"I have just had the Director of the CIA post in Spring Garden congratulating me on my role as case officer to a high-powered Russian spook, code-named Raynor, Patrick. He wants to know if I'll share him! That's what has brought me out to play as you so eloquently put it. What the bloody hell is going on?"

"Did you tell him that he must already be registered on their books as they stuck a 'Hands Off' notice on him, Geoffrey?"

"Do you know what, Patrick, I had just struck my golf ball into the water as he called. I clean forgot in the excitement. Be my guest and tell him your bloody self."

* * *

Sir John Scarlett left the words of *bloody good show, Patrick*, for no apparent reason ringing in my ears as he replaced the receiver at his end of the scrambled phone connection just as Michael Simmons entered my office via Hannah's with a case containing a standard issue Heckler & Koch submachine gun. The same as the Ministry of Defence security staff were armed with. There was an opened case on Hannah's desk. She was inspecting the magazine and the three others that came as standard.

"What's wrong?" I asked, half expecting to hear that Razin and the Russian army were outside trying to kick the door in.

"The security at Brightwalton Farm has been breached, sir. They have one dead and one critically wounded. Henry Mayler is missing. Both guards' weapons are missing as well, Mr West."

The look on his face as he delivered that final part of the summary exactly mirrored my innermost feelings of wretchedness and despondency. Nine days of hell had passed by, how many more were there to come?

* * *

With a blaring, flashing police escort we arrived at the farm to find yet another scene of chaos. The tiny falling snowflakes were more prominent beneath the yellowing light from the tall perimeter beacons painting the few dark clad figures moving laboriously along the fence line in a murky gloom of despair. I dispatched Frank to find the site commander of the Farm whilst I sent for the Berkshire police officer in charge of the headless armed response teams running everywhere. I had ordered our weapons to be left in the car.

The police officer in charge wore a sullen pout when acknowledging my security pass and credentials. Having established that we were not under immediate threat of an invasion that justified so many weapon-carrying police members around the yard, I suggested that they concentrate their energy in trying to find how someone got beyond the outer security line.

The tone of his voice when repositioning his men could not disguise the bitterness of rebuke, but it wasn't his failure to find Henry that depressed me. It was the continuing breakdown of security all around me. Frank found the site commander and from him I learned the injured Ministry of Defence guard had died from his wounds. Two dead bodies and two missing submachine guns. What would I give to watch a game of rugby!

"We had what we refer to as 'weekenders', Mr West. That is not unusual. On occasions other agencies than yours use our facilities. I had formal notification from Sir Elliot Zerby's Department F, that a contingency of their own security were arriving at 16:30 hours in an armoured convoy from the Atomic Energy Research Establishment at RAF Harwell with one guest to be accommodated. As per standing orders, an hour prior to arrival at 15:30 I ordered the opening of our specialised amenity and a routine sweep of the accommodation outbuildings including where your project was housed under our aegis. The first constable was found at the rear of his building dead with his throat slit. The second was twenty yards from the open door also with his throat slit, but alive and breathing. Unfortunately, there was nothing we could do to save him."

We had walked side by side across the snowy yard and the swept duckboards that had been laid as a path to Henry's hut with the site commander reading from a notebook at times, until we were outside the small building where I had interrogated Henry Mayler. Frank had followed. Hannah was in the site camera room reviewing tapes.

"Before you sent out a team to open up your amenities as you put it, Commander, what time previously was the area around my project checked?"

"It's a fifteen-minute timed sweep, sir, so 15:15 sounds right to me."

"Before I leave I want that timing confirmed. I will need the footage from that sweep as well others from elsewhere. I take it you have found nothing suspicious on any camera sweeps so far, Commander?"

"No, sir, nothing," he declared as we had arrived at Henry's hut.

"We have left the inside as it was when my officers arrived. I'm afraid it's a mess, Mr West."

"Explain something to me if you would, Commander? Who asked the county constabulary to attend?"

"It's automated, sir. Your predecessor as Director General Group, Mr Harwood, put it in place when your project was placed in our care. We had catered for other assignments but after assessing our safeguards he deemed it necessary. There were some Home Office cutbacks at the time that he said he was worried about."

"How many officers from Defence have you at any given moment, Commander?"

"We have three staggered shifts of eighteen personnel."

"And there was only the one person in one hut being protected by those eighteen?"

"That's correct, sir. Two static guards at all times with six patrolling the perimeter. Those eight would be changed every two hours, with one of the two commissioned officers of each contingent overseeing the duties changes. We would also have one officer inside the camera room. Unfortunate we were three officers short on this shift through illness. We had nobody on the cameras, Mr West. However, they were all fully functional."

Frank went inside the hut whilst I waited beside the dejected site commander who kept apologising profusely, but no amount of apologies would resolve the situation nor would a search across the fields. I didn't wait for Hannah's confirmation. To me it carried the Razinesque hallmark of slit throats. Mayler was long gone and I suspected Razin knew exactly where he would be taking him. As I was running things through in my mind the site commander's radio burst into action. One of the perimeter patrols had found a hole in the wire fence and tyre tracks that the weak snow flurries had not completely obscured. There were no cameras that covered that part of the fencing and the satellites operated from Lavington Street provided no clues. Apparently nobody had yet invented satellite cameras that could penetrate clouds.

Although the hut was sparsely furnished every piece of furniture in the first room was overturned, or smashed and lying on its back. Henry's open packet of cigarettes lay where a boot had crushed it alongside a broken glass and a practically empty bottle of whisky on its side. The door had been on a latch that only operated from the inside, and this had come away from the doorframe when the door had been kicked in. A struggle had taken place and by the look of things Henry had put up quite a fight, but part of my life has been spent making others believe what I wanted them to believe. Could this be such a situation? I called Razin's number from my burner phone, but his was switched off.

The time it took to drive from Brightwalton in snowy Berkshire to the drizzle-infected part of London that was Lavington Street could, notwithstanding the maddening Christmas shoppers, be measured in hours and minutes, but the time it took to probe into the information that was stored in my memory could not be measured in such a way. In fact the stored material would take more than measured time to analyse, it would take a degree of wisdom I was unsure I possessed.

* * *

After I had grabbed a few hours' sleep, and utterly insensitive as to how time played with others' minds, I called a meeting in my office with Hannah and Michael Simmons that Saturday night to share what we knew and to make sense of it, but I had no idea what we did know for sure.

"Okay, let's start with any ideas why the American 'Hands Off' notice on Razin came as a complete surprise to the head of the CIA stationed in this country who disturbed Geoffrey Harwood's afternoon. Who do we think posted it?" I looked from one mystified face to another and had there been a mirror in the room then I would have seen a third blank expression registered on my own. Then it happened.

"Excuse me, sir, but it's urgent," my head of communications announced on entering the unlocked office.

"Command AIS notified us of unusual signal traffic emanating from the Grosvenor Square NSA station desk a minute ago. They have ears on that part of the building which GCHQ do not and they have the ability to decode."

I assumed that the somewhat crestfallen look of my communications officer was because the new boys on the block had replaced our main source of transmitted information. Although I was highly tempted to sympathise by adding *let's hope it's only temporary*, I didn't. My maturity was growing before my own ears. Geraldine flashed into my mind and was the reason for the mischievous smile that I could feel stretching across my face. Maybe that was what accounted for Hannah sweeping her long black hair away from her face. But perhaps I wasn't as mature as I thought.

"What does Command AIS quantify as unusual when it comes to signals from the NSA desk at the American Embassy?" I asked.

"The nature of them, sir." His indignant expression did not alter, forcing me to re-evaluate my opinion.

"Go on, man, tell us."

"Both signals refer to us having a Russian operative named Raynor who is subject to an American 'Red' notice. By using the word Red, whoever is working the desk is implying that Raynor is also an American source. AIS added it would be understandable to some degree if those signals were coded for ratification purposes to Fort Meade, or the Pentagon, or the CIA at Langley, but they're not, sir. AIS added that they are in a wrap around NSA coding with one addressed to the headquarters for the United States Armed Forces in Riyadh, Saudi Arabia, and the other to a relay station in Erbil, Iraq." Who wanted to blow Razin's cover, I wondered?

"What's a NSA relay station?" I asked naively.

"Interesting point, sir." As I heard that reply I visualised going through a re-education process on satellites.

"The National Security Agency have no requirement of numbers on the ground outside of the coastline of North America. To put it in plain English, the NSA is simply a monitoring and forwarding element of American security. In London for example they have only nine personnel on rotating duties. A relay station is an unmanned moving transmitter, usually mounted in a car or lorry. It looks exactly the same as a car radio which in fact it is with a slight modification. In essence, it's a short wave radio signal booster intended for local conversion. In the case of this Iraqi one it has been used before. According to AIS it was used by the NSA transmitter located at the American Embassy in Berlin fourteen days ago on the third of this month." Although my withering attention was focused on what I was being told the date slammed my concentration into top gear.

"What sort of range would a relay transmitter in Erbil have, do you think, young man?" I hesitated to ask.

"Anything up to three hundred miles give or take, sir."

"And have you a transcript of the Berlin message?"

I was trembling as sat alone recalling what I had read. The signal was sent from Berlin at 03:11 on the Tuesday morning over thirty-six hours before Mayler arrived in Al Hasakeh and was shot on leaving. It stated that a pro-Syrian Ba'ath Party Regional leader would be in Al Hasakeh, roughly two hundred and fifty miles from Erbil, the following day meeting a British long-term agent codenamed Karabakh and a high-ranking officer from the Pakistani intelligence service representing Al-Qaeda. Where did the British agent named Karabakh spring from? I never knew he was ours. Some of the information would be known to either Razin, Fraser, Hadad, Mayler's driver, or Mayler himself, but none would know all of it and none of those four could have been in Berlin.

* * *

My duty officer's inspection of the ledgers of Group at Craig Court had turned up nothing regarding visits by Fraser or Geoffrey. So it was with a lightened heart that I and Hannah went there to collect the memory stick of the destroyed Gladio B file on the way to Oliver Nathan's hastily convened COBRA meeting in a basement room at number 10 Downing Street.

Opposite me sat Oliver Nathan with Geoffrey Harwood at his side, sheets of foolscap paper, six sharpened pencils and a Home Office monogramed pen laid out in a tidy fashion in front of them both. Sir John Scarlett sat to the left of the Home Secretary with Sir Elliot Zerby to the right. They had the same writing material but no pen. In the middle of the oblong table was a miniature recording machine looking unexpectedly at home on the vast surface on which it was placed, flanked by so many empty chairs and by the sterile painted walls which resembled an Eastern Bloc interview room. I felt lonely even though I had Hannah at my side. Oliver opened the proceedings:

"I've read the report you submitted to Sir John, but for the life of me I can't get my head around it, West. You say you were aware of a strict Hands Off notice, and as much as I can sympathise with your frustration over that, you ignored it, and met with this Russian coded Raynor in the Savoy Hotel where you say he told you of weaponised anthrax being in terrorists' hands. Is that about the strength of it?"

"Yes, sir, that's how I came to know. That's also where he informed of the alleged CIA duplicity."

"Yes, I see," he replied running his fingers through the paper report Hannah had prepared, "but before we can proceed with any of this we will require cast-iron proof, or as near as damn it. Do you know where the Hands Off restriction originated?"

"That's the worrying thing, Home Secretary. The only person I can trace it to is Mr Harwood when he was at Group."

Four pairs of eyes around the table joined the eyes belonging to Geoffrey Harwood and centred on me, who too was searching for an answer.

"I could find nothing from Sir John or from Sir Elliot, nor from GCHQ, Minister. I now must assume that it came from Mr Harwood's AIS at Greenwich, but I have been unable to verify or discount that."

"And why is that, Geoffrey?" Oliver Nathan asked as all the six pairs of eyes shifted to him.

* * *

"What did Hardballs say to that one, Patrick?" Fraser asked as I recounted the meeting at the Home Office in Whitehall in the less unfriendly but as austere surroundings of his flat in Peckham later that Saturday night.

"He said everything was your fault, Fraser, and if you were alive he'd kill you."

"Is that what the Sassenach bastard had to say, was it? Excuse my use of knowledge related to your ex-boss's birth, young lady." With a smile etched on his face he addressed Hannah, then in more sombre voice he spoke to me.

"There was I thinking the man had no sense of humour. I will have to ask him about that when I return to the living, laddie."

"And when is that going to happen?" I asked.

"Soon, I hope. But first tell me about the rest of that meeting and where you are with Mayler and Razin?"

It was well past midnight by the time Hannah and I left Fraser to his thoughts. The jumbled ones that I had were quickly interrupted by Jimmy. "I don't know about you, boss, but we're all a bit hungry."

I apologised for my lack of consideration, asking for any known restaurants close by. As always Frank had an answer but it wasn't close, it was the other side of the river. As we would be going to pass near Lavington Street I asked to be let out at number 67 where I proposed to carry on working. Hannah offered to stay to help and although I attempted to dissuade her my objections were not that insistent.

I hadn't stayed in the flat above the Hub for more than one night, perhaps spending a few hours during the day simply to change clothing but it still had the attention of a housekeeper who one of my PAs had instructed to stock the cupboard with soup, eggs and cereals. There was milk in the fridge, ice in the freezer and sufficient whisky on the table to quench my thirst. I grabbed two glasses and was about to pour the whisky when she stopped me.

"You need food and then sleep, sir. You don't need that." The somewhat motherly advice took me completely by surprise and it wasn't that I didn't like it, the opposite was true. My sordid imagination was thrown into disarray.

"Call me Patrick, Hannah, and I'll stay with that beautiful name, as it suits your own natural beauty."

"I'll keep to the sir, and I'll have a bowl of soup with you, then I'm going home. Anything else would not be right." Was I that obvious, I thought, then realised I had the burden of transparency to carry in my mature years.

I flopped into the nearest armchair saddened by her rebuff and resigned to my ineptitude. As I sat I carefully watched as she heated the soup and collected two spoons and dishes, and then the abject tiredness I felt forced the closing of my eyes and I fell asleep before the soup was served. There was no superman who died in that chair and there was no woman who loved him to shed any tears of regret.

Chapter Nineteen
Sunday

Liam Catlin and Narak Vanlian separated at the Turkish border from where Liam made his way to Gaziantep and the home of the executive officer for Venery Munitions Ltd whilst Narak travelled to Antakya airport where he met the single American G3 'Black Ops' operative. It was his role to mark the target at Kirkuk so the top-secret 184th Intelligence Wing of the Kansas air national guard could launch a drone strike, then he would find a safe landing space nearby for the ground landing of US troops. The two arrived at the target on Tuesday 21st December, the same day as Geraldine arrived at Chearsley, in Buckinghamshire to be welcomed by a tearful Molly Ughert.

Simon Ratcliffe opened the door to his home in the cool shadow of the Yıl Atatürk Kültür Parki and welcomed Liam Catlin as though he really was the brother he'd told the French reporter of the *Herald Tribune* magazine who sat next to Mrs Ratcliffe enjoying her close company. As the evening wore on and the conversation edged towards the reason for the journalist's invitation to the house, Liam feigned embarrassment in continuing to divulge stories about the Kurdish nationals he said he knew so well.

"There's only one other thing I will say, Pierre, and then I must leave the subject. The Kurdish people are a peaceful race trying to accept the situation as it is. Being divided by international boundaries is not ideal for them and yes, it's true, there are some radicals who advocate for their own boundaries along with their own nation, but they are in a small minority, hardly worth a mention by your renowned publication."

When Pierre Dupont submitted his article he believed Liam was deliberately misleading him by suggesting the Kurds were not a voracious nation willing to die for their sovereignty. He was unaware that the difference between a good intelligence officer and a great one is that the great one will have you believe that the decisions you're making are your own, made without outside influence. Fraser Ughert was a great intelligence officer and Catlin was great at following orders.

* * *

The television opposite the chair in which I had fallen asleep woke me. I couldn't remember switching it on, but as I stretched awkwardly on waking I guessed I must have. Then I saw her and wondered where she had slept and if the gossiping had started. She read my mind.

"If you're wondering where I slept then you have nothing to worry about. I took some of the soup for myself then went to my office and after half an hour's work fell asleep there. I came back a minute ago to make sure you eat something before you start all over again. I must have woken you. You must look after yourself, sir. Drink less whisky and eat sensibly. Here." She passed me a breakfast dish with cornflakes and milk. I was so ravenously hungry that I almost asked for more. As I was spoon-feeding myself, watching the news channel on the television, the topic changed to a scene outside a well-appointed house in Belgrave Square, Knightsbridge, where there were several ambulances and armed police officers. I turned the volume up to hear the reporter saying that a man and a woman in their late forties, thought to be Lord and Lady Shoreham, were found dead in the house. The reporter went on to say that unfortunately two members of staff had also been found murdered. Their dead bodies were discovered, unmutilated. It was that word that shot through my body with the same amount of pain I'd felt when shot in my foot. The girl said that the Shorehams had been dead for at least two days.

"It's her," I shouted at the screen and then still unappreciative of Hannah's presence, "I bet they've found an empty 500 mg phial of methanol in that house."

"It's who?" she asked as she took hold of my tottering bowl of cornflakes.

"Ah, Hannah, yes, I meant to tell you about Suzanna. She's Fraser's lady-killer in more ways than one. Her modus operandi is to render her victims insensible enough to cut lumps off them, then when she's got all that she wants, she shoots them up with a massive dose of methanol to finish them off."

"Oh, not the sort of lady you'd want to take your eyes off then. But I doubt you've spent much time in her company with your eyes on anyone else," she remarked in a trite manner to my annoyance but I did not reply.

"Would you like me to contact the chief investigating officer in Belgrave Square and discreetly ask, sir?"

"You can do that, Hannah, yes. But I think I'll ask her keeper straight out. Where's your car?"

"Parked around the corner, sir, in the service carpark."

"Do you fancy another pick-up in Paris Garden?"

* * *

The degree of signal traffic and footfall, both in and out of the Russian Consulate in Bayswater, demanded that the alert level be raised to level two, one short of all-out war status, with double staff at Group, all signal installations and anywhere with connections to Foreign Affairs. To highlight how serious the situation was, the Russian desk/department at the box in Vauxhall was triple manned even though it was a Sunday. I was answering call after call on the drive to Peckham until in the end I had no choice but to transfer them to Abraham, the duty officer back at the Hole, with strict instructions on how to deal with the problem. Specialist Operations at Scotland Yard had no new intelligence on Fyodor Nazarov Razin nor Henry Mayler. According to all the data stored at MI5 and at Special Branch, no attempt by either had been made to leave the country by any airports or shipping ports that would generally be used. Despite the level of coverage the pair were attracting, there were more parts of this island to launch a small boat that could possibly be covered, and more fields for a small aircraft to take off from than buses in the whole of the London. I had nothing to add to the expert search, not yet anyway.

* * *

Fraser had a phone to his ear when we arrived and Suzanna was apparently having a bath. As he opened the door the phone was deposited in a trouser pocket before he said goodbye to whoever was at the other end.

"No one important, Fraser?" I asked, irritated.

"That takes us both back in time, young Patrick. Back to what Jack Price call that group of his, NOMITE wasn't it? No One is More Important Than Each. You are the most important one here, laddie, After Hannah, of course."

"Haven't you forgotten your Suzanna, Fraser?"

"You're fishing for something, Patrick, so get to the point, please."

"Lord and Lady Shoreham, plus two members of staff, were found murdered this morning at their home in Belgravia. I happen to know that Lord Gilbert Shoreham is chairman of Blake, Harplip and Klenix, the multinational pharmacy company who were the target of a hostile take-over bid awhile back by the Indian Rawalpindi Chemical Company. I did some research about that company after their chief executive was mentioned in that *Sarah Mariah* file of yours. It was Suzanna Kandarian who killed him. I'm wondering if you're instigating and condoning murder in the heart of London nowadays?"

"Your industrial knowledge does you credit, laddie. Ever heard of the Mumbai based engineering and development company named Amtamo?"

"Can't say that I have, Fraser, no."

"A Russian branch of the Shoreham family survived the revolution, prospered under Stalin, going on to have the controlling interest in that company as well as stock in Rosneft Oil. You and I know that Rosneft are in partnership with the American oil giant ExxonMobil. It would not take too much imagination to put the Shorehams into the circle of eight of whom we've spoken. I take it Hannah is aware of those people?"

"I'm not sure if we did get that far, but I'm absolutely sure we have only skirted around Suzanna's contribution to the puzzle."

"Hmm, what's the use of a PA if one does not confide in one!" He was puffing hard on his pipe as he gave me one of his stares of disgust.

"You will have to catch up in real time, Hannah. And in any case I can explain it all better than your boss. The Doctor, Robert Zaehner, have you heard of him, Hannah?"

"Yes, sir, I have," she replied.

"Good! Then at least I don't have to do your job entirely for you, Patrick. Right, onwards. Robert and I go back centuries, probably as far as the Stone Age. A slight exaggeration, but given the circumstances of euphoria then quite understandable! No, do not look so perplexed. All will be explained. Directly after you forced the husband of Francesca Clark-Bartlett to withdraw from becoming his party's presidential nomination, Robert was approached to step into the breach. I think that all occurred in '72/73, Patrick. Is that right?"

The all-knowing avuncular look from Fraser was accompanied by Hannah's look of astonishment. I was unsure whether her surprise was for his revelation or my lack of an answer.

"A story for another time perhaps, Hannah." He knocked his pipe out as Suzanna, wrapped only in a white bath towel around her body and one around her wet hair, stood frowning in the doorway at him, apparently unable to see Hannah and me.

"Good morning. Have you had a busy night, Suzanna?" I blurted out uncontrollably, ignoring everyone else in the room and trying to ignore her intrinsic sexuality.

"He should not smoke that thing at all, but if he cannot stop, then leave it alone until later in the day. His heart will give out on him if he continues to disregard his doctor's advice." She had the same annoying habit as Fraser of sidestepping a direct question.

"I shall make tea for you." Without waiting for an answer she turned away and the schoolboy inside me attempted to hide his embarrassment. Hannah cleared her throat, before adding, "Was it something I said?" To which Fraser added, "What?" When neither of us replied he continue in his narrative.

"Anyway Robert Zaehner turned their approaches down, opting for what he called a normal life. For a good many years he served in the CIA before becoming a director of the National Security Agency." I jumped in with both barrels loaded and the safety off.

"You never mentioned that little fact when I told you of the NSA signals yesterday. Did you have him send the one from Berlin? Is Harwood right in blaming you?"

"Is he like this when he's alone with you, Hannah? All pumped up and spitting dummies at everyone?"

230

"Well, not yet, sir, no," she said, looking at me before adding, "Perhaps it's the sight of a beautiful woman that's done it, Mr Ughert."

"Now you're fishing for compliments, young lady, and you have no need. Your speculation is obviously wrong as he casts his eyes on you every day, and your guesswork about Berlin is equally wrong, laddie. But I made some enquiries and I have a name for Berlin. That's for later. Let's resume with the Shorehams, shall we?"

I nodded yes to that, as Suzanna placed the tea tray on the table between us and Fraser, and I could smell the aromatic fragrance of gardenia. She sat herself down on the sofa where we were, requiring Hannah and me to move closer together. I was squashed tight against two beautiful women, but Hannah's words of not being able to avert my eyes from Suzanna were proving again to be correct. She had removed the towel from her head and her long black hair hung wet against her bare shoulders as she leant across and poured the tea into the four cups, her movement caused the towel wrapped around her body to pull apart exposing her bare leg and thigh which she pressed tightly against me.

"It would be best if you put a bathrobe on, Suzanna." Fraser never elaborated on his reasons for that request as he added milk to his own cup, and Suzanna never needed to ask for one as she and gardenia left the room. Once again Hannah felt the demand for a remark.

"One nil to me, I think," she said. Fraser smiled and so did I.

* * *

"Look Within Yourself To Find The Truth, the opening words to the *Sarah Mariah* file, is a code, Patrick. It's along the same lines as Razin's with his one-time pad, except this code has only letters and not numbers. The words Sarah Mariah are also a code. They relate to a family called Bingham from the southern state of Kentucky in America. They are whom Theodore Roosevelt referred to when he said there was an invisible source of government. They are still out there, Patrick. The branches of the family have spread out since the early parts of the last century, increasing their interests in media outlets across America and other nations where English is the chosen spoken language. They also have a controlling stock in no less than eighteen different railway companies in Africa. However, as I told you before, a code is no good if anyone can decipher it. There are many codes and symbols used within Freemasonry. The one about finding the truth is used in an early initiation, but within it lies the key to that inner circle of world control.

"Let's get back to Robert Zaehner and how he found the first two subjects covered in the file that Suzanna dealt with. He worked the code in such a way that it exposed a few companies that are legitimately owned but reasonably suspected of being under the control of one or more of the important eight. As you are aware, but perhaps Hannah is not, Suzanna…" His speech was halted by the lady in question as she entered the room dressed in a white transparent blouse and white skin-tight jeans. The flat was warm, but it wasn't that warm! Fraser looked at her then looked at me. I looked at Suzanna. Hannah coughed and I diverted my gaze to her.

"Yes, Hannah, Fraser was about to tell you how I killed both of those men but not before I surgically removed parts of them. Some I removed delicately whilst we engaged in a drug induced but coherent conversation, other parts not so delicately. I offered a quick death if I got what I wanted, which was the all-important truth. If it wasn't forthcoming then I indiscriminately hacked at bits of them. Big bits take longer and of course, the pain lasts longer. It requires great skill to level the methanol and the other drug I use. It is my own concoction a mixture of two potent agents, one is an animal tranquilliser and the other a surgical painkiller. The actual amounts I administer are variable depending on the agony I wish to inflict." It was then that she diverted her attention away from the pallid-faced Hannah to me.

"You see, I am not an object of sex you would like to bed, Mr West. I am a trained sadistic killer who one day may have to kill you." Her smile was not reassuring and nor was the severity of Fraser's admonishment.

"I cannot ever see the need for Patrick to become one of your victims, Suzanna, and I don't want any reference to personal feelings mentioned again. Okay?" Suzanna made no reply. It was Fraser who continued the narrative.

"Both those men copied to the *Sarah Mariah* file spoke of an English landed family with great wealth and tentacles inside Russia who owned chemical, engineering, oil extraction and refining companies throughout the globe. Robert Zaehner went back to the code again and it threw out Gilbert Shoreham. At best it was a calculated guess, as any decoding is ultimately. But with all that is happening and the approaching date of Henry Mayler's all-important thirty-third birthday ... " He caught Hannah's puzzled gaze.

"Hannah looks bemused. Please rectify that as soon as you can. To carry on; I judged it prudent to act without delay. Suzanna visited that home in Belgrave Square and killed them on my orders, laddie."

"What did you find out?" I asked, without hesitation or thoughts of rebuke. Hannah's colouring had returned to normal and I hoped she stayed that way.

"Gilbert Shoreham gave us another name, one that I suspected all along. He comes from a line of extraordinarily wealthy Israelis with business connections all over this planet of ours. For the Christmas holidays he's staying in Maine, New England, as a guest of another man we provisionally put on the list of the eight. Suzanna will be making arrangements to travel there later today. The estate is called The House of Cilicia, it's at a place named Jordan Pond, in Maine."

"Did Suzanna go to Berlin and send that signal for you, Fraser?"

"No she didn't, and we'll never know for sure who did, but it comes down to who you believe is telling the truth about taking something from the driver who chased Henry and Razin from Al Hasakeh about two weeks ago. If Razin took whatever it was, as Henry alleges, then our Russian friend has connections to the NSA that I never knew of. If Henry removed the damning evidence from the CIA agent then it follows that he had someone who could send the signal. And again, I never suspected that."

"It's a good job that little old me found out for you, then," Suzanna's sultry voice cut into the conversation.

"I bet this is when William B. Guerny II comes into this mix, eh? Hanging around with a gunshot wound outside the bazaar in Al Hasakeh waiting to be rescued when you just happened to be passing, Suzanna," I suggested.

"He was a very communicative guy, was William. Part of a three-man special reconnaissance team deployed near a town named Tal Afar waiting for fallouts between the local Sunni and Shia Muslims and taking advantage of what was left. At least that was his team's cover story if they ran into any other covert unit. The idea behind it was to blame the slaughter on Bashar al-Assad's government. The signal he received from Berlin gave map co-ordinates, times and the names and descriptions of the targets. One a Westerner; Henry Mayler, and the other his Arab driver, but here comes the bit that interested Fraser. His instructions from Berlin did not include any mention of a fire-fight. He and the team were ordered to observe and note. Not to shoot anyone. He said that came about because a big guy with the two they were sent to watch started firing at them. I insisted on more personal details than from a sterile radio signal, but unfortunately there was only one he could provide. He said he'd spoken to the man once before. He had a distinct Southern American accent.

"I pressed him for an opinion on that accent and he thought the man came from somewhere in Missouri. I asked him why he'd ruled out other southern states, settling on just the one. Apparently it's a colloquial thing. The man he spoke to used the word—dingnation: *Don't you three go making some dingnation of a mess over this one.* Guerny was certain that it was a word that Mark Twain had made up for a novel and a man from Missouri would know that. A learned man, was Guerny. Anyway, the matter these two had previously spoken of was the assassination of a Saudi Arabian general in the Gulf War conflict name of Imed Hamed Mohamed. The assassination was successful. Guerny and his two Delta Marine colleagues were to be paid a million dollars each, in ten equal instalments. By 2002 those payments had run out. I guess you can get used to having that kind of money available. Guerny told me it was the reason why they accepted another job."

"How did the dingnation man get in touch, Suzanna? Did you ask him that?" Hannah pitched in with a question.

"Oh, I thought you might have fainted, Hannah. Good to have you back. Oh yes, I asked him that. But I don't think you would like me to tell you what I was doing to him when I asked." She looked at Fraser, who returned her look with a stern shake of his head.

"He said the Missouri man simply telephoned. After the general job, Guerny took on a false name, moved north to Canada, and opened a bar named Busters in Ottawa. He kept in touch with the other two from a distance. Our mysterious dingnation man tracked him down, called the bar and left a message. Guerny rang him back and there we have it."

Chapter Twenty
Rebirth

"I have Mr Fraser Ughert on a direct landline, sir. Asked for you by Group name: Joseph." The voice came from the communications office in the Hub on the ground floor. It echoed from the open speaker in front on the desk as if it was an accusation from Hell. I cannot tell you of my expression, but the exhibition of shock conveyed by the three sitting the other side of my desk was reminiscent of Kerry, in Ireland, as she tried to remember how to breathe with the racing spasms of pain spreading through her body quicker than the blood trickled from it or the morphine could cope with. It was only in death that she found her peace. It was not necessary for Oliver Nathan, Sir Elliot and Sir John to die for their stupor to be eased away, all I had to do was take his call. Simple, eh? Anything but, was the truth.

If Monday was deemed a good enough day to start the week, then it should be equally good enough to allow a dead man to rise from the pathology lab where his body was supposed to be. Despite the approaching difficult ramifications of Fraser's miraculous return to life I had no alternative but accept his call.

"Put him through," I replied. The speaker went dead for a second and then I heard his Scottish intonation to the greeting, "Hello."

"As you requested, I have the Home Secretary and the Director Generals of MI5 and MI6 in front of me, Mr Ughert. I did not warn them of your resurrection."

It was then that the rehearsed excuses for his disappearance were recited verbatim to the script he and I had manufactured. What script? It was an imaginary one in our heads. No details or mentions were made to the murder of innocents. No specifics of operations were discussed. Some of what he said was factual, but most was pure conjecture albeit with a degree of justifications but conjecture all the same. Various points had to be covered first, but eventually he came to the fruity bits.

"Fyodor Nazarov Razin is much more than a lieutenant general in the Russian Federal Security Service, gentlemen. Spies or double-agents can be coerced by many forms of incentives, but not Razin, or Raynor if you prefer. He was to all intents and purposes born into our service. Razin has become Putin's closest counsellor since he became President of Russia two years ago. Whatever opinion Fyodor Nazarov Razin holds on Monday becomes Russian policy on Tuesday. Whilst he was my double he proved to be exceptionally valuable. For some considerable time it was my belief that he had become overwrought with the Rosicrucian-Freemasonry connection of Henry Mayler as set out before you by Director General West. Agitation overcame his sense of reasoning as Henry's thirty-third birthday on January third 2003 approached. I firmly believe that to be an important date, but Razin feared that date more than I. He seemed to think some monster would be released from Egypt. Mayler himself quoted an ancient Rosicrucian belief in a time referred to as Zep Tepi, a violent age seeking to establish a form of globalism. It was Razin's and my judgement that this globalism, although now well underway, would reach a crescendo near that January date and then stretching into 2003 and far beyond.

"Further apprehension began when I heard of Fyodor Nazarov Razin's appearance on the steps of the Russian Consulate after an altercation he and Mayler were involved in while in Syria. It was his way of goading me into disclosing the contents of the two American originated files; coded Gladio B, or as he would have liked me to believe, confirming their contents. When Razin learned that I had authorised the destruction of the first Gladio B file he was distraught, as, contrary to what he wanted me to believe, he had never seen inside the file. He had, as I suspected, lied on numerous occasions. When West, as Director General Group, cleverly told him of Henry Mayler's knowledge of the file he knew Henry Mayler would be his last chance to see inside it where he believes he will find the secret to this mystery. He cannot kill Mayler to achieve that because Mayler is pivotal to the future. No Mayler, no insight into what's to come. All of this was worked out between West and myself. My disappearance was essential to draw Fyodor Nazarov Razin into the open, gentlemen.

"Apart from Mrs Ughert there were four other people who knew of my simulated death, but not one of those was made aware of why that was necessary. It is possible to work without Mayler to uncover the extent of the present globalism, we already have a degree of penetration. The problem of finding Razin and Mayler is better left to the police rather than diverting our scarce resources."

"If I may, Mr Ughert." It was the Home Secretary who spoke first.

"By all means, Minister."

"According to the documentation the Director of Group here has provided, it says that we have, by that I guess it means you have, access to the second file. Am I correct in that assumption?"

"You are, Minister."

"And this Fyodor Nazarov Razin has no information from that file?"

"Again you are correct, sir. In Director Group's report he mentions the meeting he had with Razin at the Savoy Hotel where he said that he'd seen inside the second file. However, that plainly is not true. If it was then he would never have shown his hand by abducting Mayler. He's banking on Mayler seeing a code, a reference, directions or just plain instructions on how to access the second file and to decipher what's inside. The problem with that lies in the fact that Mayler has not seen inside the file and if he had, there is no magic formula to point to what it means. It was extremely difficult and challenging to get inside, Minister."

"What precisely is in that second file, Fraser?" This time it was Sir John Scarlett who asked.

"I'm afraid I cannot divulge that information, Sir John. First disclosure must be for the Prime Minister's eyes only. Then I would imagine it will go before the Chairman of the Defence Committee and on to the Privy Council. It is mind-boggling, gentlemen."

"Be that as it may, there're somethings I need to know now, Mr Ughert. In your opinion is any asset of ours threatened by what's included?" Oliver Nathan wasted no time.

"I'm not fully acquainted with our exact military status across the globe, Home Secretary. I've been out of the ring so to speak for some time and positions change so quickly, but from what I do know then, yes, I believe we are compromised. However, I must add a caveat to that observation. I am no expert on military weaponry, nor the effects of toxic gases, etc. That side of things would require qualified examination in greater detail than I can supply."

"Fine! Comment noted. Go on, please." Fraser had passed the first stage of his renaissance board.

"In that case I'll move on and address the Berlin question. Next number on the sheets, gentlemen, number twelve of the dossier."

"Before you do, allow me to say that I want your talents back in some capacity, Ughert. To work alongside the Director Group, or as he now is, chairman of JIC. He's doing a fine job in extremely difficult conditions. If you can do that, then I know I speak for my colleagues here; we will all be a lot happier."

Hear, hear was the call. No hats were thrown into the air nor was my back being slapped by congratulatory hands, but Fraser had won the day. I had the thought of Geraldine entertaining me in a few days' times to look forward to, and Molly had two chairs occupied that might otherwise have been empty. Which left the question of where was Jordan Pond and when would Suzanna be back?

* * *

I met with Fraser later that Sunday afternoon at his busy home. He had been there about an hour before I arrived. Molly's brother, the one I had seen on Thursday was there, as was Molly's older sister and her daughter, husband and two children, all with happy smiles on their faces. Fraser's brother with wife from Canada had landed at Heathrow and were in the back of a cab on way to Chearsley, probably totally confused, needing explanations on arrival. Molly had laughed and then praised my performance as if it was I and not her who deserved the Oscar. Affairs of state were blamed and we all moved on.

I had precious few moments with him to expand on the Berlin theory he had not told the audience at the Hole. The story he'd told the Home Secretary and the two heads of the UK's intelligence relied on a fanciful rogue NSA agent that he and Robert Zaehner were in the process of tracking, whereas his actual theory he had hurriedly explained to me.

According to Robert, the Doctor, Zaehner, the Berlin NSA station was more often than not unmanned than manned. It was merely a listening and organising post, segregating the most important signals from the dross. It wasn't an open door office, neither was it a fortress. In the Doctor's words, if you were in the business of knowing where it was you were halfway through the door. At 17:07 on Saturday 3rd of December, as part of a routine inspection, the steel door into the communications room was found by an agent sent from the American Embassy to have been forced by using an abandoned hydraulic device. The CIA swept the place but found nothing. Fraser worked along the lines of Hadad, Mayler's driver, telling of Karabakh the day before Henry said he was told. Hadad had been re-questioned over the date, but was uncertain. Maybe because of that, or in spite of it, Fraser's argument rested on his suspicion that Mayler knew Arnold and it was he, or an agent of his, who had used the Berlin station to signal Guerny. To prove his point he wanted to start with that Saudi Arabian general named Imed Hamed Mohamed and find why an American wanted an ally in the Gulf War of 1991 murdered.

* * *

Spencer Morrell was my way into the CIA's background on the Desert Shield liberation of Kuwait and any information regarding why General Imed Hamed Mohamed was murdered. I invited him to dinner that Sunday evening at Scott's Restaurant, in Mayfair. I invited Hannah as well.

I had been thankful that she had not left my side that whole day. The remoteness I felt when sitting next to her in her car on our journey away from Chearsley, only a few days past, seemed a huge distance away from how I felt about her now. The risk of being alone at the Hole on Saturday night with me had not stopped her coming up to the flat and although I fell asleep, nothing felt contrived or artificial. She had grown on me without me noticing and perhaps the same applied to her. I did not want her to accompany me to dinner as my personal assistant. I wanted her there as my companion, not to satisfy a part of me I did not want to reopen. I had no more room for Kerrys or Fiannas but plenty for Geraldines and her liking of casualness. My indecisive private life was bordering on a pathological disorder. Neither Fraser nor Molly had need to know that side of me.

Spencer and I were already there when she arrived dressed in an orange coloured chiffon, three-quarter-length dress which without the coat she had left in the lobby with the cloakroom attendant she would have frozen to death in. As I stood to greet her I struggled to remember we were here on business and not in my Canary Wharf apartment on the verge of becoming better acquainted. My resolve did not last long.

"Ahem! My, my, Patrick, you English do have some beautiful women," Spencer proclaimed.

"We do, don't we," I replied as I kissed Hannah on both cheeks adding quietly so only she could hear, "If I was a younger man I don't think my intentions tonight would be completely honourable, Hannah." She didn't reply.

According to Morrell the general was suspected by the CIA based in Saudi Arabia of being in Saddam Hussein's pay, deliberately misinterpreting Iraqi signal traffic and failing to update the coalitions control centre. He was questioned, but simply passed the blame downwards, citing various officers not informing him of important changes to events. Without undeniable evidence it was impossible to have him removed as he was not only a hugely popular senior officer within the participating Saudi army group, he was also a powerful voice on the permanent Army Council. At the end of the war a secret American led commission was organised to examine the causes of General Imed Hamed Mohamed and his entire staff of eleven other

Saudi officers being killed on a site to the rear of the battle of Khafji. The enquiry was concluded within a few hours with the blame being laid on a team of Iraqi commandos known to have been operating in the area.

An investigating team of CIA staff drawn from another location looked further into the decision the commission had reached, mainly because of those initial suspicions that the General and the raiding commandos were on the same side. They were looking for an Iraqi agent still inside the Saudi military who was trying to divert accusing eyes away from themselves. One was never found but one thing the investigating agency did turn up. Two of the general's brothers owned an oil exploration and drilling company which was in competition with Exxon Oil, as it was known in those days, over what was called the Sakhalin Project. Sakhalin is an island off the coast of Eastern Russia where eight years earlier a Russian interceptor was launched with orders to shoot down a Korean airliner which had strayed into Soviet airspace. It did shoot it down, killing all 269 passengers. The Russians said the Korean plane was on a spying mission. The CIA had become interested in Sakhalin Island from that day onwards, but after they found out about the dead general's brothers that interest widened.

"What exactly did they find out about Sakhalin, Spencer?" It was Hannah who asked the question and started the ball to roll down a hill that I thought might never end.

Chapter Twenty-One
Too Late

"It was a long time ago that I heard the name of Sakhalin Island from Razin. I would have to look it up, but I have it somewhere, laddie. What did your CIA chum tell you of it?" Fraser Ughert asked.

"He was okay to start with, as sparkling as the wine we were drinking with information, but when it came closer to what's happening there today, he was unsure of himself. Not hesitant to share, just unsure of what was going on. According to him it was dropped from any file five years ago in 1997. He's very sure on the date as he was in South Korea, attached to a Senate delegation visiting the country. It was his Korean counterpart who told him."

"We have a stand-down notice on the whole area around Sakhalin Island. It came from someone high up in the CIA. Our files were closed on Flight number 007, so what's going on, Spencer?"

"Spencer told him the truth and he didn't know. He told me that on his return he tucked his hands under his bum and left it alone. Added he was surprised I'd brought it up. But do you know what, Fraser, I don't think he was surprised at all."

It was a little after eleven o'clock that Sunday night when I'd spoken to Fraser from the public phone box at the opposite end of Mount Street to the restaurant. Frank had inquired if all was well and despite my reassurance that it was, he walked behind me and then waited as I made the call. I knew Fraser would still be up. From what Spencer had told me it was obvious that another visit to the Ughert residence was required and there was some urgency to it. One part of me didn't want to put Hannah through another late night whilst the selfish half didn't want to be parted from her. By the time I returned the situation had been decided for me. Hannah was in the lobby with Spencer standing behind helping her into the protective, warming coat with a smile on her face as welcoming as a log fire would be on a cold night such as this.

"I wish I had a PA half as good as yours, Patrick. Not only stunning to look at but, ahem, pays the bill as well. Maybe it was the oysters that did it."

"No, Spencer, it wasn't them. She has always been that beautiful and her generosity is legendary."

"Oh I don't know, sir. It could have been the oysters. Perhaps they got me too excited to be prudent." I fought hard not exchange a glance with Spencer who I knew was looking straight at me waiting for a ribald reply, but I had none, or at least none I wished to share.

"I'm afraid I can't add to any lack of prudence, Hannah. It's either dropping you off at home or an extended night listening to stories of Russian Islands."

"I'm up for the island tour, Mr West, in fact I'm quite looking forward to it." We left as Spencer sighed at the moon.

* * *

Molly opened the door with both a word of warning about keeping her husband up late and complimentary remarks about Hannah's appearance. She ushered Jimmy and Frank into her kitchen to await her refreshments then waved Hannah off towards Fraser's office. "He's expecting you, dear. I'll only keep Patrick for a few seconds."

She'd heard from Geraldine. In a conspiratorial voice she told how a letter from her younger sister had arrived on Saturday in which she explained how her life had suddenly changed. She'd become engaged three weeks prior to the letter and was bringing her fiancé for Christmas. Apparently there was a separate letter inside addressed to me.

"Sorry, Patrick, but with all the toing and froing I clean forgot to mention it." She passed a plain white sealed envelope to me, looking around for spying eyes. I popped my head around Fraser's office door, making an excuse to use the bathroom and went to read her note. Three minutes later my personal life was left bankrupt of Christmas partnerships. Geraldine had found love and relinquished casual sex.

'Could you be a real sweetie and pay no special attention to me, Patrick? Elliot is a really observant man.'

* * *

Fraser had found Razin's first mention of Sakhalin Island dated February 1992, however that was not the only time he'd seen it.

"It cropped up in general conversation over the Soviet mindset leading to the break up the previous year. I asked about boundary changes and if other countries who had vied with the Soviet Union would press their claims on territory reform. Japan and the islands in the Sea of Okhotsk, including Sakhalin and the Kuril Islands came to mind. Razin reminded me of the overflying Korean airliner and I asked if there were any installations worth spying on. He reminded me that it was a US spy plane high above the airliner that rattled the radar installations and scrambled the fighters in the first place. Ronald Reagan was pushing hard against the outer beacons of the USSR, testing their defences, making the old guard belligerent and worried at the same time. This was an example of the panic in the air. Things were electric around the intelligence communities of NATO countries. A nuclear war would not have been a surprise."

Fraser had Hannah and me on the edge of our seats listening to his account of the 80s of Reagan and Thatcher with their combined aggressive stance against Communism. A NATO military nuclear release exercise had been pre-planned, but on the day it was launched with coded messages that the Soviets were unable to read and significant movement of essential military, commanders and politicians caused the cracks in the Russian resolve to begin to open.

"The Soviet Politburo issued statement after statement exonerating the radar commander of blame, citing international law and failure of the Korean airliner to take notice of the attack aircraft when warned to alter course. They published what they said was radio traffic between the ground station and both aircraft, but at best it was confusing and at worst it was a total shambles. A US senator was on that flight, which didn't help to calm Reagan or the American war machine. We will never know how far the American led, but with huge support by Margaret Thatcher and the British military provocation would have gone. I remember it well as it's the only time I have seen the Defence readiness Condition DEFCON at One, its highest position. For some reason, I'm unaware of, the stand-down signal was issued and we all sighed in relief.

"In 1992, when I questioned Razin about the area around Sakhalin, he was of a lesser rank, of course, than he is now, so his specific knowledge was of an equally lower level, in spite of that he knew of two concealed submarine installations on the island of Kurilsky, east of Sakhalin and one of the Kuril Islands. In ordinary circumstances those secret facilities would be enough for the Politburo alarm and nervousness, just the same, it didn't finish there. Slightly further inland from the coast, near a nature reserve, lies a town called Ukhta, on the Amur River. That navigable river flows into the northern part of the Strait of Tartary which separates the mainland from Sakhalin and from there lies the open sea. When the Korean airline was shot down Razin suspected that Ukhta was a naval support base. The depth of the river is sufficient for warships. But I won't ask you to guess what goes on in that town nowadays, because that would be totally unfair of me, laddie. I only found out recently and by accident."

He wasn't looking at me, he was looking at Hannah, but it was the same—*I know something you don't, but if you are good I tell you*—look plastered across his face that I'd seen so many times.

"A short time ago I told you of an attachment to the Gladio B second file that I could not access. Well, that is not the case any longer. Suzanna carried the code for it when she arrived. I think we are now getting very close to infiltrating that inner circle of eight. Nowadays there is a chemical factory at Ukhta that has lost its Russian military classification. Because of that declassification there is no registration of it at Moscow Centre, nor in any files at Razin's Federal Security Service. There is no reason why anyone would take an interest in its existence, which the impenetrable surrounding forest only helps to aid.

"How do you know that it's a chemical factory, Fraser, or is that just a guess?"

"Patrick! You've given me another opportunity to shine in front of your lovely personal assistant."

"More chances than you gave me when you had Heavenly Helen as your PA at Whitehall, Fraser," I replied smiling thinking of the beautiful dark-skinned assistant that I'd met in the corridor leading to the office Fraser occupied as Chairman of the Joint Intelligence Committee. My smile disappeared almost immediately I stopped speaking. Would I have to work within those oppressive walls? It was Hannah who was the first to reply.

"I'm flattered by you both. But to be honest, I'd rather listen to the story as it unfolds." Suitably scolded, Fraser continued, and I stopped daydreaming.

"Martin Lennox of Armenia fame remember him, laddie? Communications director of the South Caucasus region of Eurasia? He was being taken through the history of his past postings by the boys at Cranleigh when he happened to mention that whilst stationed in Thailand he heard rumours of deformed births and unexplained deaths amongst farmers in Thailand, Burma, and Bangladesh who were buying insecticides from a distribution agent based in Bangkok. After doing what communications officers do to gather intelligence, he paid a visit to Laem Chabang, the largest port in Thailand and checked the manifests of ships unloading pesticides and fertilisers. He found a cargo ship that docked the previous day having apparently left Vladivostok, on Russia's eastern coastline. I've no idea how he did it but he checked and found a separate page in the ship's log noting Ukhta as its port of origin. Needless to say, before he was persuaded to tell us of it he passed the information he'd collected to Razin.

"Christopher Irons got close to the place. He has the same stoical look of the Russians surrendering to their fate. I got him in close but not right in, the security was too intense, however, he found a talkative woman in a nearby town on the banks of Lake Udyl who told of her husband dying because of the factory and she knew scores of other women who had lost husbands or sons in there. Her description of his death suggested some sort of poisoning, but without exhuming the bodies we have no idea what poison he could have ingested. As I was thinking of abandoning it all we had a piece of sheer luck. A freighter exiting the Amur River was spotted and identified by one of Hardball's AIS satellites. The satellite took a thermal image of the area, and lo and behold there was a huge trace of sulphuric acid. The scientific analysis was that the proportion of measured sulphuric gas in the atmosphere could mean only one thing; the manufacture of pesticides and fertilisers.

"Hardball's lot at Greenwich did not stop there. They traced the boat's registration, then its manifest and finally its destination. The same port it had used for six years. That ship and seven others who used the port were registered to the same company. That company's name was SanMonto. The port involved was Santos in Brazil and the listed cargo on arrival was Pesticides and Fertilisers manufactured by SanMonto. The British Embassy in Bangkok ran a trace on all shipping listed as leaving Ukhta or Vladivostok owned by SanMonto carrying pesticides and fertilisers and do you know what?"

"Not one was listed as leaving Ukhta," I replied.

"You're right. According to the manifests all of them sailed from Vladivostok carrying agricultural parts."

"Did they manage to question the distributor about points of manufacture?"

"They did, and surprise, surprise, he knew nothing of the whereabouts of the factory. Perhaps the owners of SanMonto could be in our top eight, laddie?"

"Plural, Fraser? More than one owner of the company?"

"More than one company under the same umbrella, dear boy, producing more than two products. One of the listed board members is the Israeli chap about to have a visit from Suzanna. By the way, laddie, did you manage to find out what happened to General Imed Hamed Mohamed's brothers' company of oil exploration and drilling services that were in competition over the Sakhalin project with Exxon Oil?"

"Spencer never mentioned the outcome, Fraser. Hannah did some research before we met tonight. They pulled their bid the day after the general and his staff were found dead. Quite a coincidence, don't you think?"

"SanMonto and the giant ExxonMobil oil. It's getting interesting, Patrick."

It was late by the time we left, and my impulses said 'ask Hannah to stay' when Jimmy stopped outside number 67, Lavington Street, yet my captious side disapproved, arguing for the opposite. Would my invitation to stay be solely because there was no satisfaction to unpack on Christmas Day or any other day I was staying with the Ugherts? Was that such a wicked reason for an invitation? Did I have to be in love with Hannah to have sex with her and just have lechery in mind with Geraldine? Safety with Geraldine against the danger of attachment with Hannah? I wanted to give in to my primal instincts except that would mean Jimmy and Frank would know and I certainly didn't want that for her or me.

"Thank you for a wonderful evening, sir. You were great company." We were standing on the pavement beside the rear car door, it was open with my hand resting on it. I felt awkward in offering a goodnight handshake and more so a goodnight kiss. She took the initiative. She leant and kissed my cheek whispering, "I don't want this night to end, but I don't want my job to end either."

Chapter Twenty-Two
Desolation

Monday came and went without news of Henry Mayler or Razin. I managed to square everything away with Oliver Nathan about remaining at the Hole as Chairman of the Joint Intelligence Committee before moving my stuff into Whitehall. It was his suggestion that the offices at Whitehall could wait until this inquiry, as he put it, was finished. That, of course, suited me admirably. My mind wandered back to Fraser's times there and to his protective secretary, Mrs Janet Bayliss, beyond whom nobody entered without an appointment. The dream continued as the maelstrom became my normality.

Hannah already succeeded Heavenly Helen in every physical department within my imagination; at Whitehall I could elevate her to a heavenly status that would require only worship from one side of a desk and no more, but would that be enough? I didn't think so. I needed another approach, a separate plan, one where our night would never end and her job would not be at risk. It was impossible for me to separate my heart from my personal life and with both came the certainty of torment, yet what would life be without the pain of attachment, but for now, however, all I wanted to attach was Henry Mayler to Arnold and Arnold to Razin avoiding any screams in protest.

I drew lines on blank sheets of foolscap paper from places I knew Henry had been to dates where Razin could be in the same area. I had the first Gladio B file open on the computer and referenced the known facts on there to the points where Razin and Mayer's paths might have crossed, but nothing corresponded. The only thing going for the theory that Henry Mayler was Arnold was Robert Zaehner's drop-off at the Medical Mission in Yerevan, and Henry being in Armenia at the same time. As for Razin, the possibility of him being the mysterious missing link was his failure to say where Henry Mayler went to when he flew into New York in November. With both him and Henry missing I had no chance to ask either to expand on that.

I spent hours delving into everything I could find on a Christian Rosenkreuz, who was said to be the legendary founder of the Rosicrucian, or Rosey Cross Order. According to some researchers, Christian Rosenkreuz was the last descendant of a German family named Germelshausen which flourished in the 13th century. The Germelshausen castle stood in a forest not that far away from Magdeburg, the hometown of Henry Mayler's grandfather Arek. The whole Germelshausen family, except for the youngest son who was only five years old, were put to death by the same Konrad von Marburg that Razin had quoted at Henry Mayler in the café in Kabul after the suicide bomber was arrested. The youngest Germelshausen son was carried away secretly by a monk who placed the child in a monastery in France, where he was educated and made the acquaintance of the four other brothers who were later to be associated with him in the founding of the Rosicrucian Brotherhood.

The myth surrounding Germelshausen tells how the castle and village of the same name was swallowed by the ground when cursed by Konrad von Marburg. The legend went on to say that the son, Arnold, set out on a never-ending path to find his home. Then one day the Germelshausen castle rose from the earth and on the battlement stood the beautiful Gertrude who Arnold immediately fell in love with. Once every hundred years it's said that event takes place with Gertrude disappearing and Arnold left to walk this life alone. Did Henry see himself as the mythical Arnold waiting for a certain time and had Bernard Higgins been his Gertrude?

I also read of a religion known as Zoroastrianism, closely connected to the fraternity of the Rosey Cross or Rosicrucianism. It is the belief of a single god in a world balanced by good and evil, but goes on to predict the destruction of evil. It is ascribed to the teachings of the Iranian prophet named Zoroaster who exalted his beliefs of judgment after death, Heaven, hell, and free will. Following on from the Damascus Spring uprising and the arrival of the Islamic theocracy in Iran, Zoroastrianism is having a strong revival amongst many Iranians who want to express discontent towards the dictatorial regime in both Syria and Iran. To me everything I read pointed towards Henry Mayler having a significant influence on what was contained in that second Gladio B file. Unrest within the Sunni Kurds was widespread and the world was already witnessing violent clashes with the Turkish administration as well as those in Syria, Iraq and Iran. It wouldn't take much to ignite a war on several fronts that would desolate the Middle East. I needed to see what was contained in the second Gladio B and we all needed to find Henry.

* * *

Fraser had a provisional appointment with the Prime Minister set for Tuesday at 11am and I was expected to be there with him. For that to happen without me appearing to look a complete fool, he would have to open both Gladio B files. I didn't trust computers then and I don't now. Face to face in a secure environment was my first choice for any revelations approaching this magnitude. Another journey to Chearsley on another freezing afternoon was called for. This time I took Michael Simmons with me, but before we left together I told Hannah that I was placing her in charge of Group. There were no arcing of eyebrows or the gaping mouth and lashing of arms and legs of a child in surprise, instead there was a steady probing stare from those once remote eyes that now shone with pride. In my professional opinion she would make a top-class Joseph, and for my personal life that would make things very easy for the two of us to explore parts that were presently hidden; in all senses of the imagination.

* * *

Despite Molly being her normal hospitable self, she was perturbed about Geraldine's letter and Hannah's absence. I reassured her on both counts, hoping my voice conveyed sufficient conviction to allay her worries. Seemingly I had succeeded as her attention turned towards Michael, who she escorted off to her spicy smelling kitchen where her brother and sister-in-law were helping with the preparations. Fraser's brother's family were braving the outside elements walking through the adjoining woods. As for myself I was searching for the solution to the puzzle that was engrained in my mind. Could it be solved in Fraser's office?

"I've been thinking about that place where the agricultural chemicals are being shipped from Ukhta, Fraser. And I'm wondering if it is really our job to hunt down discreditable companies, or is that something best left to environmentalists and the like?"

"If it was just that to consider then yes, you're right, more for the Department for the Environment or even the UN to police and prosecute. But we're looking at the intentions of a few that will affect millions of others, including all in the UK in one way or another. That's where my concern lies. My interests fade at our coastline."

"That brings me nicely to the Gladio B files. I want to be able to speak with confidence about any threat to this country at Number 10, Fraser. I want those files opened and shown to me, please."

"As your new position now dictates, laddie, and I should apologise for not showing you sooner. I will also drop that form of address, although I've only ever used it in a paternal sense, never in a derogative fashion."

He was obviously uncomfortable and I assumed that was because theoretically I outranked him. He gave me his chair at the computer screen as he saw to the whisky pouring ritual, retiring to the fireside to enjoy his comfort.

* * *

The first file carried the distinctive stamp of the military on its opening pages. In total there were over three hundred listed interferences in sovereign nations' affairs by covertly funded incursions. The minority were carried out by various American specialist forces, however the majority were local insurrections funded through numbered bank accounts predominately in Panama City. Appendages to the file were added against most of the bank accounts listing information from the Drug Enforcement Agency correlating drug cartels to the same accounts. It was of course all history and although controversial, nothing could be done to change the results. It was the second file that damned the future. An invasion of Iraq was planned in detail starting off in March next year. In the short term that would mean the stationing of American Air Command and military in Saudi Arabia. However, despite some withdrawal at the end of the operation others would remain for the long term, to be further garrisoned when other ambitions were imminent. It spelled out in detail the reasons for that decision and I could understand why only a Prime Minister would be allowed to read those details. It was shockingly obvious to even the insane!

Afghanistan was at the centre of all the proposed expansionist operations and they were not confined to appease American home grown expansionism. Russian, British and Israeli corresponding interests were documented in what amounted to a world dominated by ideals of profit. There were no specifics. No names, no specified military units. Nevertheless, monetary amounts to coded destinations were itemised along with the dates of local participation and what results could be expected. The names of local insurgent leaders as at 2003 were also itemised. The simplicity was astounding. There was no single point of reliance. All was minutely configured for a period of prolonged disruption over an initial twenty-six years. The cut-off point for completion to Part One was the year 2028. Once again, a number divisible by the magic 3! The ancient aims of the mythical Zep Tepi were quoted and broken down into targets of present and future dates of attainable degrees of what was labelled Democratic Emancipation.

That phrase carried a translation for every spoken language on the globe.

As well as heavily funded localised rebellion in the name of freedom from tyranny and undemocratic exploitation, there were page after page on proposed change to worldwide acceptance of certain practices; notably the monetary rates of exchange between countries would be centrally controlled. The sale of government bonds and treasury notes would be conducted from one centralised bank. That bank would be in London. World business would effectively be conducted from this London financial axis made up from four existing private banking houses that would be merged without compensation into a single resource, that would buy and sell governments, people, and beliefs. The stability of a united Europe would gradually be eroded away by the instability caused by aggression in the Middle East. Economic and humane migration would begin to overwhelm European governments' social spending ability. The economic file went on to paint a vivid picture of the unrest between immigrants from the warring countries in the Middle East and the indigenous people of Europe, with an inevitable devaluation of all European currency. Stock exchanges worldwide would experience the selling of government stocks on a scale that could never be imagined, making the Great Depressions of previous eras seem no more than mere blips on unemployment figures.

Culmination of global financial meltdown came after several terrorist attacks on prominent targets. Violent civil disturbances were planned to erupt throughout Germany, France and northern Europe by 2024, southern Europe the following year. The United Kingdom would be the last to witness massive street and city destruction along with prodigious casualty figures.

The economic situations that would exist in Greece, Italy and Spain by 2021 would have bankrupted the World Bank five years later in 2026. The centralised private financial institute flourishing with funds in London would then decide where insurrection would be financed and who would get the contracts to continue the destruction, and which companies were awarded the enormously valuable contracts to rebuild the shattered infrastructure of the isolated nations of a once rich Europe. In North America the reasons for the migration would be different, but the outcome would be the same. Mexico, the whole of Central America and most of South America will be infertile wastelands by the year 2027. Economic migration for health reasons from those areas would flood the defences of the United States, forcing their reliance on firepower to dissuade the migrants from leaving their homelands. Millions would die from starvation in the Americas and millions more in Asia where crops would fail in six successive years.

Agriculture in North America, Canada, China and the increasing boundaries of Russia would govern world market prices for the hugely reduced human population. Property values worldwide would collapse as choices of location widened and availability broadened hugely. The workforce available to the remaining centralised industry would also be reduced by starvation, the wastage of war, automation, and technical developments. Worldwide employment would gradually be consolidated into self-governing regions. The time scale for that completion of these aims was extended to 2034.

Away from the carnage of battlefields, falling stock markets, allied with agricultural decline, power provided by oil and gas were the main objectives for integration, but nuclear power had not been overlooked. Within the energy programme lay most of the forthcoming immediate desolation. Two precise references to dates were mentioned with a third concerning the allocation of money to achieve a political objective. Both dates were in March 2003, within six days of each other and divisible by three! The first date was the 19th of March. Alongside this was the following citation—19th Pathfinders. I believed this to be the time and military unit for first entry into Iraq.

The second date was 25th March 2003. Here the instructions were explicit. The 173rd Airborne Brigade were to be airdropped near the northern city of Kirkuk. The unit would joined forces with Kurdish rebels and fight several actions together against the Iraqi Army to secure the northern part of the country. Meanwhile the drop-zone for the nuclear target at Kirkuk would have been marked and neutralised for the19th Pathfinders who would facilitate the173rd Airborne deployment to capture and destroy.

The allocation notice of money again contained explicit information. Funds were to pass through a named Jordanian company destined for a jihadist terrorist organisation controlled by a man known as Abu Musab al-Zarqawi. I knew of Zarqawi. His name appeared on a United States list of most wanted Al-Qaeda terrorists still at large in early 2002. It was stated in open draft what the money was intended to do—turn the forthcoming uprising in Iraq against United States troops into a Shia-Sunni civil war in not only Iraq, but in Syria, Turkey and Iran, in fact aimed at completely enveloping what once was referred to as the four corners of the world, or the four corners of the compass, described within the great Assyrian Empire. In open draft Zarqawi was guaranteed further funding if he could provoke the invading American forces to attack Iran. It gave no reason for that.

I stared at the ending and imagined the scenario. If Russia supported Iran against an insurgence of either Shia Muslims or Sunni Muslims, and American not only sided with the Kurds but invaded Iran on their behalf, then the loss of civilian life would be a disaster that the world would turn their backs on as they tried to divert migration by erecting physical barriers or barriers of silence. It was only my opinion but I guessed the reason behind the financial incentive offered to Zarqawi to increase the level of insurgency in Iraq was to give the American military an excuse to strengthen their Saudi Arabian base. Couple that with the strategic base in Djibouti at the Horn of Africa and a solid footing in Afghanistan and the whole of the Middle East would become another territory awaiting statehood from the United States. When Russia withdrew its superficial show of support for the Iranian regime, the bolstered home support for American foreign policy in the region would result in the granting of a pipeline from the Russian oil fields to the north of the Caspian

Basin across Iran to the Persian Gulf. All would go unnoticed in the euphoria of an American victory.

According to Gladio B, that part of the Middle East along with Pakistan, India and Southeast Asia were destined to become a cesspit of human suffering for eight families' profit. The fundamentals to form a narrow controlling organisation being able to rule a whole planet was becoming a reality before my eyes. The intricacy of the jigsaw was to be respected and as far as the rationale was concerned, hadn't we all puzzled over world population and where the food to feed them would come from? Everything Fraser was fighting against was set out in cold black print on an icy white background of a computer file. Our need to find Mayler, Arnold and Razin was growing as every hour passed.

Chapter Twenty-Three
Tuesday AM

It's in the darkness that my breathing is impossible at times. It's the pain inside those unanswerable screams from unknown faces inside an exploding pub that stops the natural function of breathing for me. It's the uncertainty of life that causes the anxiety and worry, but it's also in the stable secure moments that fear has to be faced, and trust me; those can be as life-threatening as nails bouncing off hard surfaces and buzzing towards an unsuspecting victim.

I was lying down in the reclining chair in my dayroom with a blanket wrapped around my legs, my feet exposed as they always were, with shooting pains akin to bullets flying up and down my right leg from my foot to my abdomen with no respite other than a shot of self-administered morphine to restore my pride. I felt ill from lack of sleep, lack of food and the gentle companionship of a woman.

The future looked bleak on the last complaint that I suffered from, but it was my inability to breathe through the pain that troubled me most. I tried to stand and fell into a thrashing heap gasping for air and for a crutch to grab before I too was swallowed by fate, like Germelshausen. I'd had a nightmare believing I was outside the castle and then I aggravated my useless foot by trying to climb the walls to the imaginary battlements and rescue Fianna. My feelings for that woman just would not go away. It was 3 in the morning, I was sweating and I was cold.

For some peculiar reason that only a psychiatrist could diagnose I resented my night-duty Hannah and didn't want to call her for help. She was a substitute I wanted replaced, but in this moment of despair I needed her and a syringe filled with my morphine. I shouted, I screamed, I slammed the floor with my open palm and finally I dragged myself, painful leg movement over painful leg movement, for the full unmeasured distance from a dark forbidding dayroom to a white marble desk with the purity of relief a phone call away. I called. I passed out.

Nobody can be sure exactly how long I lay next to my desk but in the estimation of the blue and gold signet ring wearing physician who shook my hand holding only three of my fingers, it had not been long. However, not being able to leave a way of thinking without its justification, he added it could have been longer had he not been aware of my pain issues. He was apparently THE man in charge of the upper tier of the intelligence community. I had found respectability when I needed it the most. Nightduty Hannah was looking on with the oven-baked standard look of serious nonchalance. I instructed her to amend standing orders whereby everyone inside Group's location had a responsibility to list the medication they were taking long-term. Having done my good deed for the day I abandoned the idea of sleep, ordered a chicken sandwich and began to search through the files on Henry and Razin again. It was 04:32 by my desk clock. I noted the divisibility of the time by three.

I had withdrawn the file marked Raynor, when the oversized television screen burst into life. Through the desk speaker I heard an unfamiliar voice announce the after effects of a drone strike on a village in northern Syria. The target was said to be a wanted British national Al-Qaeda extremist named Arif Belmokhtar. An encrypted signal from GCHQ flashed pink on my desk monitor. I locked the office down, closed all communications and read it in the cipher *Pink Room:*—Time— 04:35 Eyes JIC chair only—The Al-Qaeda extremist named Arif Belmokhtar, (British name Paul Gardener. CPI number 7/237921/33 Last known British address 78 Nags Head Road Ponders End, Enfield EN14 5DD) killed at Ghmam, Northern Syria was identified target of asset code Antelope. Antelope is at the harbour awaiting tanker.

The message was signed by General Sir Douglas Walters. I was very much now part of top floor management. Why did this Arif Belmokhtar warrant a drone strike and what was in the tanker?

As I was rereading the signal and focusing on the name of Arif Belmokhtar Geoffrey Harwood's phone line lit up. I took the call.

"I thought I'd find you there, Patrick. You will have to start looking for a permanent home shortly. Love to recommend properties down this way but I don't know of any suitable at the moment. Rest assured, dear chap, when I do I'll let you know. By the by, you could do worse than ask your Scottish uncle about the apartments at his old office in Whitehall. I've never seen inside them, but they are yours to use. I guess being where you could be on top of things might be beneficial."

He sniggered and despite knowing why he did, I did not reply to his lewdness. That lack of response annoyed him as his voice sounded as though it was coming through clenched teeth when he continued.

"Although several words of the last signal from GCHQ are redacted at my end, I gather you're looking at the same scene as I am. Sir Elliot and Scarlett's Middle East people have pulled his record. They haven't come up with much so far. Hails from

Wolverhampton with no cross matching affiliations. It's going to be a long haul, I think. Elliot will need some facilities from Group. Now listen, old boy, this is entirely up to you. You can play with the big stuff that you and Ughert are working on, as well as deal with the unpredictability of your other life, or split them up now before you become bogged down by details. Not even you will be able to carry off duties as Chairman Joint Intel Committee and Director General Group indefinitely. You can submit two names through me to the Home Secretary as soon as you like and the selected nominee will officially take over on the day preceding your relocation to the Whitehall apartments. A one-day overlap will be fine. If this drone strike proves as complicated as it is looking then any time you have free now will disappear. I'm fully aware of the painful incident you've just suffered. It's flagged on the medical desk. That event did not instigate this call, Patrick, but I am not insensitive. I've said it before and I'll repeat myself here. I wanted you for Director Group and then Chair of Joint. I want you now to take up the Whitehall post in full. Your position demands it. If you don't you will kill yourself through overexposure. Two names, Patrick. Like you, I am now at my desk and won't leave until late tonight. You have my number."

* * *

I wanted Hannah, my daytime, teasing Hannah in that chair at Group. A Josephine to replace the senile old Joseph. But that couldn't happen. I had never heard of a biblical Josephine. Hannah couldn't remain Hannah. But Hannah was her birth name. How could a Hannah be a Joseph, and what would become of the two other Hannahs? I doubted my suggestion would pass Hardball's scrutiny. Geoffrey agreeing to a woman in a powerful position, and one who had little respect for him as well, no, that couldn't happen.

Could I play the wily diplomat role? Put Hannah's name forward as one of my choices knowing full well she wouldn't get it, but I might get something from her as a reward? Could I keep a straight face if I did that? Could I make love knowing I was a cheat? Yes, I could and I would have in the past, but I wasn't in the past. I was Chairman of the Joint Effing Intelligence Committee and acting like a dog on heat. Only give one suggestion—Michael Simmons, and be done with it. Enjoy the reflections from the glittering halo and get satisfaction from your virtuous behaviour. Nah! This was a 'me, myself and I' moment. Her name would go forward because I wanted her name to be considered alongside and equal to Michael's. Phone Hardballs and test his prejudice. Eventually sanity regained control and my weary mind clocked on for work.

* * *

I trolled through police reports from Saturday, looking for clues that may have been missed in trying to find Razin and Mayler. A red BMW car was sighted driving over Sparrowbill away from the Farm at Brightwalton, Berkshire, towards the B4494 in the direction of Farnborough, exactly within the time scale I'd been given—between 15:15 and 15:30. Three motorway cameras picked the car up heading west along the M4, but no more sightings were reported past the A419 north towards Gloucester or south towards Salisbury. Where would I go? If I was a fleeing Russian lieutenant general I would not drive near Hereford and the SAS. I would head south towards Southampton and Portsmouth or further west along the coastline looking for a ship's passage across the English Channel to France. Razin must have changed cars, as there was no red BMW on any road camera leading to those international ports. Poole to Cherbourg, that's how I'd go. I'd take the chance and go that way across the Channel to France.

If my guess was right then we were left with only facial recognition to find them. GCHQ hooked the station officer's lamp-burners room into the stored filming at the port from 15:30 onwards that Saturday when Razin and Mayler disappeared. It would have taken at least an hour if not more to Poole, but I wanted to be certain. There were three lamp-burners examining the port of Poole's tapes. I was at my desk when Fraser rang.

"The man I told you of as being in line to be selected as a Presidential nominee moved up a rung on the ladder to achieve that status in California last night. He's now first choice candidate for that state. That gives him twenty-one votes. His rival is trailing by eleven. Not many more to go, Patrick, before we know who will be one of the choices for the White House. How's it going with the files?" he asked lamely.

I told him how far I'd got and we spoke about my selections as Director Group. He was waiting to hear from Suzanna but as he said, it was too early to expect that. The only reason I could think of why he'd mentioned her was because he was worried, but I knew of no reason why he would show his concern with this mission rather than the one she executed with the Shorehams. Perhaps it was because Christmas is a time for memories.

Fraser and Molly had two sons, Gerry aged forty-three, and Hamish aged thirty-nine. Gerry lived in Australia with a wife and their three children and Hamish was in New Zealand, divorced and in a partnership. They would all be coming for the New Year. I wondered how they would take to Suzanna. Come to think of it, I had not asked Hannah what she was doing for the festive season. That could be remedied now as I heard her replacing my night time assistant, but before I could speak to her, the number two at the Home Projects desk at Sir Elliot Zerby's department wanted words. A British passport had been found in Bruges, in Belgium, and turned in to the local police. They in turn contacted Interpol who had contacted the top floor at MI5.

The name inside the passport was a one-time *Dark* name used by Henry Mayler. Belgium, no! I didn't buy it. My enquiry of the *burners* as to any luck they'd had drew a blank, but I stuck with my intuition and told them to run them again.

Hannah breezed into the office bearing coffee and a smile. I briefed her on the drone strike and as her hand was still resting on the Directorship of Group I left the gathering problems over Arif Belmokhtar's circle of associates with her. As the coffee breathed new life into my aching body I broached the selection process and the two names I would be putting forward. On hearing her position could be made permanent her jubilation was not difficult to see, wishing good luck to an absent Michael Simmons and heaping 'thank you' after 'thank you' upon me until I almost blushed. Despite the pleasure I could see on her face and the one I was anticipating on Michael's, I was not happy in this position of power in deciding on what could become someone's future. I think the irony of that stupidity focused my thoughts on the job in hand.

For the next hour I threw myself at inquiries of Special Branch and Interpol. I persisted in believing that Belgium was a blind alley and it was to France they had gone, but proving my suspicion was extremely hard. After two runs of the videos of the departure point at the port there was still no sign of Razin and Mayler leaving from Poole harbour. I backed my guess. I asked Interpol for the name of the person who handed in the passport. We ran that name through every computer we could use and half an hour later we had him and how the scam was run. Henry Mayler had freelanced for the same magazine our concerned citizen in Belgium worked for. He lived at a place just off the A419, heading south outside of Swindon, called Chiseldon. 'Yes', said his wife, he was home Saturday evening when a colleague knocked. 'Yes', she said again when asked if he was working in Belgium. 'Around Bruges was it?' the police officer inquired. 'Yes, it is', she replied, asking if everything was alright with her husband. My hunch had proved to be correct, but not always do the spoils come with victory.

Mayler had clearly travelled with Razin voluntarily and set up his disappearance without help. At first glance it would seem as though it had been planned some time in advance, but how? If my maths were right Henry had been at the farm for more than fifteen days, how would he know this other reporter was going abroad? My mind was in overdrive yet again, ploughing through the possibilities and running into brick walls. One possibility was the pair of them were still in England. But if that was correct where would they go, and why? The theory that Fraser held about Razin abducting Mayler because he needed to get inside the Gladio files was lying in tatters, so why did Razin jump and how did Mayler persuade him? That question had to wait as my burner phone that I'd almost forgotten about resonated in my pocket. It was Razin!

Chapter Twenty-Four
Cyanide

"I took a call from Geoffrey Harwood on Saturday morning saying that signal traffic emanating from the Americans in London would identify me as an agent of British intelligence later that night. He didn't tell me how he knew, but he said he wanted to give me a head start. Loved Russian spies, I guess. Said he was doing it to cover Ughert's arse. Didn't want it to blow up around Whitehall whilst he, Harwood, was briefing a Minister of the Government. I asked if he was sure it wasn't to cover his own arse and he just laughed at me. Told me he wanted Henry Mayler out of the country and far away. He could find room for me to go too, he said. *You can start a new life in North America*, he suggested.

"He said I should contact Henry Mayler at his location at a farm and scurry him away somewhere until it was safe for him, Harwood, to arrange transport for us both. Henry Mayler expected my call. He had it off to a tee. Times of camera sweeps, guards' patrols and even the fact of an arrival that Saturday afternoon that would require the attention of most of the staff to be looking elsewhere than at his hut. You will love this, he even told me where he would end up living—Springfield, Missouri. But then he killed himself! He took a cyanide tablet after apparently speaking to Arnold on his mobile telephone. I've got no idea what about."

The widow's son was dead.

Razin's voice was shaky and sounded far from composed, but given the circumstances of having a poisoned British asset lying at his feet in a part of the country he knew nothing of, quite understandable. His command of the English language was brilliant, as was his tradecraft, so I had no worries about him tripping over Henry's body and throwing himself in the arms of a local bobby by mistake, but he was in over his head with only me as his back-up. The secret relationship that Fraser and Fyodor Nazarov Razin had was always going to be difficult to conceal forever, but for it to be leaked beyond our intelligence service would require someone inside betraying it. Razin had no idea where Henry had got his phone. On my first visit to Brightwalton Farm I distinctly remembered seeing a telephone listed on the inventory I'd signed for. All his personal property that remained with him was recorded, but phones were prohibited in huts whilst under our protection. It would not have been easy to conceal a cyanide tablet either. There was no way a phone and a tablet could have remained in Henry's possession in that hut.

It is possible for any fool to make things more complex by loading the problem with unnecessary detail. Geoffrey Harwood was many things, but I never marked him down as a fool. However, although I'd left my analytical mind on my daybed anaesthetised by morphine, even in the state I was in I could see no rational reason why, if it was Geoffrey, he would be so obvious. Mayler could only have got a phone and a cyanide tablet from him whilst I was in the commander's office at Brightwalton signing the transfer forms on my first day as Director General Group. If that was not enough evidence to convict Harwood then how about the warning to Razin about the radio traffic from

Grosvenor Square hours before it was transmitted? As much as I could make a case for him shielding Razin from being exposed and caught in the open, I could not explain how Harwood knew of those signals.

"Tell me about the last call Henry Mayler took, General."

"He knew it was from Arnold before he answered it. How he knew that I've no idea as when I checked his phone all calls were deleted. There were no messages in his message box either. Whatever Arnold said it did not require much comment from Mayler. He never really spoke. All he did was shake his head and mumble 'yes', 'no', and 'I didn't know' a few times. You've met him and know that he wasn't a healthy athlete by any standard, but as he stood and took that call I truly thought his tiny legs would give way and he would topple over and fall. Within two or three minutes of him putting the phone into his coat pocket he was dead. I wasn't expecting cyanide. How could I know?

"Whoever told Harwood that the Americans would expose me has my balls in his vice. I don't like that. I don't trust any of you, including Ughert. You tell him that. The phones we are using are good, mine can't have been traced and nor can yours, if they had been then we would both be behind bars, but we will have to keep our contact down to the minimum. I cannot come back to London," he added in a sad voice.

When I agreed he carried on in a less hurried fashion. There was a side of me that couldn't stop feeling sorry for him. My professional side agreed with Fraser's synopsis, to leave him hanging, but I shared a kind of empathy with him. I'd faced some of the dangers he had. I feared the loneliness of street life and the constant risk of unmasking every time I raised my head on operational duties. It was always that way.

"I shall move on from here and keep moving until you can find a way out for me. I cannot go to Russia. Mayler told me you were thinking of sending him to Canada. I can go in his place. I think you owe me that for all the information I've given you and Ughert. I can get a passport. We have a man who can do them. I will need money though and you will need a way of getting it to me. Any ideas, Mr West?"

"Where are you?" I asked to which he replied that he wouldn't say, adding rather chillingly that he didn't fully trust me but had no option but to call. He did, however, tell me where Henry's body lay. He was in a house in the hamlet of Draycot Foliat, not far from the Cotswold Flying School.

Perhaps that was his escape route. I suggested that Sir Elliot's operational command send a team to scrub the place crystal clean and Special Branch liaise with the local police when questioning the pilots at the flying school. One section of our skill-laden intelligence service would be cleaning away a mess in Draycot Foliat, whilst another section, skilled in the art, would be telling the village gossips and the press that attended a completely different story than the one that had happened. Black arts they called it, but black magic may have been a better description.

* * *

I repeatedly tried to call Geoffrey on both his private numbers, but had no luck. In confidence I asked Peter, Group's head of control in the communications Hub, if there was any way heads of departments could be contacted or traced, if unreachable by telephone.

"Oh most certainly there is, sir. I would have thought you knew of it." Obviously I didn't, otherwise there would no need to ask, but I figured it would serve no purpose to point that fact out.

"It was Mr Harwood's suggestion some, oh I'm not sure exactly how long ago, but I could look up the exact date if you wish, sir?" He looked at me, expecting a reply. I had every reason to want to know the exact date and every reason I could think of for not being bored by gratuitous detail.

"When you find the date send it through to Hannah, please, Peter. For now just a rough guess will do."

"It was when he was developing the facilities at Greenwich. He intended his project there to have simply every surveillance device that could be supplied. One of them was what he christened the clucked box. I thought Mr Harwood was making a sardonic joke, sir." Oh dear, a Geoffrey Harwood joke and I would have to ask what a clucked box was.

I did ask, and I was pleased I did. Someone in one of our pipeline department had invented a device that protected the integrity of a minister's car, or those who used it in our name. It eradicated the effectiveness of fixed positioning bugs applied by foreign agents and at the same time indicated the precise location of each car on which it had been installed to a central point. I successfully skated around the nuances of clucked boxes and discovered Geoffrey's whereabouts. I tried his private mobile phone again. He answered.

"Good morning again, Patrick! I've had some things to do and I'm out of the office for a while, but I'll be on my way back shortly. If you're calling about your selections could you fax them over, please? It would be much easier that way."

"It wasn't about them, Geoffrey. Something more serious cropped up. Why is your location not logged?"

"Why the bloody hell should it be? That standing order is redundant. You really must find time to read departmental memos and updated protocols. Perhaps you could study them after the festivities at the Ugherts', as I understand you might have plenty of time on your hands. I was sorry to hear that Geraldine has company this year, dear boy."

It was true to say that his first spirited response to my question had disarmed me, and for a moment it was my reasoning that I doubted rather than him. But then came his normal unmerited comment which spiralled my intolerance level beyond where it should have been.

"We have you at a private address in Wimbledon Village, Geoffrey, a house belonging to a Giles and Paige Wilmington. A crew from D Department at Millbank should be outside this Wilmington person's front door any second. You are to be detained for questioning. I'm afraid you didn't cover your tracks well enough. I had the garage log of your car looked at. You removed the clucked box your department developed on the day it was fitted. Unfortunately you never told fitters of that contraption that you that didn't want it refitted. They were doing a routine roll call of departmental cars when they found yours without one. The one you took off was replaced three hours later."

I heard a muffled 'What?' coinciding with the crashing sound of a door being smashed open. There were sounds of heavy boots running up stairs and the pathetic voices of a female and a man that I did not recognise pleading to be left alone and allowed to dress. Then Geoffrey spoke on the still open phone link to me. "I hope you have enough to justify this intrusion into my privacy, West. Because if not you will be spending the rest of your life regretting you and I ever met."

* * *

It was just approaching 8am when I telephoned Oliver Nathan at his home before informing department heads of Geoffrey's detention. The Home Secretary was clearly disturbed by the news but after hearing a brief outline of what I considered to be the justifications of it, he agreed that I had no other choice. With that vindication in my back pocket I actuated one of the only protocols I was aware of; the one that goes—

We have a mole. Secure all sections of the service until further notice. Issued by Director General Joint Intelligence.

It was Oliver Nathan who reminded me that I had the responsibility of telling the Prime Minister. "What do I say?" I asked, as if I was to see the headmaster and beg for forgiveness after breaking a window on the quad?

"Tell him as it is, Patrick. You're the one in charge now. You will need a new Director General Group and I will need a new liaison officer. You concentrate on Group and my chief civil servant can do here. Do you have the scramble line for Number 10 where you are now, or shall I patch you across?"

I ducked out of appointing Hannah as Director General Group. I officially appointed Michael Simmons to replace me at Group, sending coded notification to that effect to those who needed to know. Having told the PM of my deeds it seemed easy to inform Hannah of her demotion, but it was anything but. To sweeten the bitter pill of disappointment I offered her the job as my new personal assistant at the Joint Intelligence offices in Whitehall. The position came with a significant wage increase along with the grandiose title of Steward to the Privy Council. The possibility of both changes did not immediately overcome her despondency, but as the day wore on, and the demands on our combined resources were ever increasing, she grew into her role as my right hand. The offices that came with the job were on the third floor of the Foreign and Commonwealth Building in Whitehall. Their operational status was immediate with both the Director's desk and the Steward's desk fully functioning within a matter of minutes and both adjoining apartments were made ready within a couple of hours. Until someone was appointed, Frank, with two other principal protection officers became my own version of Fraser's Mrs. Bayliss, but mine were wearing trousers and carried shoulder holstered side-arms.

With Frank in front and Hannah, also armed, beside me, off we went to meet with Fraser Ughert, but it wasn't to Chearsley, in Buckinghamshire, this time.

Chapter Twenty-Five
Prime Minister

By the time Fraser and I had exchanged the formal documents of occupation of the suites at the Foreign and Commonwealth building Geoffrey Harwood had been secured at the interrogation holding centre in the New Forest at Beaulieu, in Hampshire for some considerable time. He was in the same block as Martin Lennox, but they couldn't see nor hear each other. It was a lonely place at the best of times and in a cold winter a place for hardy creatures only. I had told Fraser of the morning's events leading to Geoffrey's incarceration, but even allowing for that prior warning the sorrow on his harrowed face when we met was unmistakable and genuine. Mayler's death had hit him hard, and now he had to contend with Harwood's arrest.

The opening reports of Geoffrey's emphatic protestations of innocence, when the evidence pointed in the opposite direction, were compelling, and as more questions were put and his answers forwarded on to me, credible, but I could not allow any doubts to affect my performance in front of the Prime Minister. There I had to be confident and composed. Fraser had carried this responsibility for years and none of it was as daunting to him as it was to me.

It was not the cold that caused me to shiver on the short walk from the car to the black glossy painted door and then the continuation along the thick carpeted hallway, it was, I believe, excitement. I had travelled a long way since being a young know-nothing, adrenaline-driven detective in London in the early 70s to the head of intelligence in this country in a relatively short time. It crossed my mind whether I would be able to remain in the job after the Harwood investigation and that enveloping world dominating business alongside Henry Mayler's Rosicrucians.

According to the floor indicator in the mirrored lift we plunged six floors from ground level to reach our destination. Hannah had stayed with the car with Jimmy and Frank, so it was Fraser and I who were escorted to combat against the establishment, except we weren't fighting them, we were warning them. The comparison to the Hub was obvious but the single fact of both being underground was where that similarity ended. The Hub was filled with vivid changing colour and activity motivated personnel with a mild buzz of quiet conversation in the air. Here the wide straight, carpeted corridor was brightly lit from overhead, lined its full length by a maroon coloured padded covering, and as silent as the British Library would be when closed to the outside world. There was a uniformed porter on the door which was opening as we approached. My breathing was normal, but I could see that Fraser was getting a little breathless. I asked if he was okay and he replied it was merely the nerves of an actor about to give a farewell performance in front of royalty.

There were no Royals to face in the room with its continuation of maroon decor and silent ambiance, but the braid of the distinguished crest of rank was impressive just the same. We were introduced to the other man in the room by a short, charismatic woman aged around forty plus, with blonde hair and a soft reassuring voice. Her name was Margaret and he was Air Chief Marshal Sir Graham Overton. He was, Margaret told me, Chief of the Defence Staff. We remained standing, staring at each other until the Prime Minister arrived through a door that was hidden in the far wall. As he sat, the wall to our left became one massive cinematographic screen. I wondered if Harwood had copied the idea but then I thought it unlikely he had ever been in this room. My ego was getting ahead of me. It wasn't long before Geoffrey's name was mentioned. The PM and Sir Graham had been notified of his detention and Fyodor Nazarov Razin's disappearance. Henry's death and the Masonic connection was briefly commented on.

A note was passed by Margaret to the Prime Minister, who then required an update on the drone strike that killed Arif Belmokhtar in Syria. He looked at me for that answer. Most of all he wanted elucidation on the role that Belmokhtar was suspected of playing within Al-Qaeda.

"I know he's a British citizen but Syria is not exactly Sussex, is it. We need to smooth the diplomatic waters, Mr West, and quickly. We can't allow a situation to develop in that part of the world at present. It's hostile enough."

I told him what I knew, which amounted to very little, adding that all was in hand at Group. He looked puzzled, but a smiling, nodding Margaret seemed to satisfy him.

The gigantic screen at the end of the room became split maps of the Middle East and Sir Graham was pointing to the British military bases that could be under threat by weapons aimed at them from Iraq if the information in the pages of Fraser's case study was correct. That was when Razin's credentials were questioned.

'Is the intelligence still current? Can we trust it now he's absconded? Was he spinning us a lie from the start? Where is he hiding and when will he be found?' I said nothing about the arrangements Razin and I were to make regarding his escape, in fact I had not even mentioned it to Fraser or anyone else. Our meeting lasted about an hour with Margaret taking shorthand notes and occasionally speaking into the PM's ear. His questions were astute and appeared to be welcomed by the Chief of the Defence Staff. He asked for our views on the threat the world at large faced from the weaponised anthrax and any long-term feasibility of the aims contained within the Gladio B file which he had read in parts. He asked me first.

I have always had a confrontational side to my character, never missing out on a chance for an argument or worse, but there was something hauling that side of me into order as I looked at him in search of a reasoned answer. Not so long ago I might well have answered, kick in a few doors, smash a few kneecaps, and pick the bones up later. I didn't offer that as my advice. Instead I tactfully suggested he speak with allies and decide a combined approach to both the immediate threat and the ones laid out in chronological order, up to and including the year 2028 and in some cases extending to 2034 and perhaps beyond. I felt a tingle of satisfaction as he looked at me and without the need of a spoken word, bowed his head in my direction.

"If you ever get fed up with the intelligence service, Patrick, I reckon you would get a recommendation from him for the diplomatic corps." Fraser was in his best complimentary mood as we returned to daylight and an awaiting ray of sunshine on Hannah's face.

"Who is this Arif Belmokhtar, that the PM knew of but I didn't, Patrick?" Fraser asked as soon as we were back in the car and exiting Downing Street through the flashes of cameras held by tourists and Christmas shoppers. If there were any press photographers I imagined snaps of us three would leave them perplexed.

"He was spotted by Liam Catlin, Fraser. His real name was Paul Gardener from somewhere called Ponders End."

"Paul Gardener? I know that name," he replied poignantly.

We were driving through the mournful suburbs of south west of London when it started to rain. That dismal damp rain of winter that just spreads the grime further than most festive spirits can cope with. I was bordering on the doldrums when Fraser broke the silence in the car.

"So what have we with this Wilmington chap, Patrick?"

"Michael Simmons is working that, Fraser, but at the moment all we have is that Giles Wilmington and his wife Paige are joint owners of a private sex club just off Putney Heath. Michael Simmons and his burners are sifting through the membership. As of yet we have found no other managers or upper level names, but he has found a Russian. Apparently, a property developer living in Cheam, near Sutton. Simmons is looking for connections. It's going to be a slow laborious job for a while."

"Did you get to look at Geoffrey's log at AIS, Patrick, after we were speaking of the Hands Off notice that seemed to originate from there?"

"I did, yes, and I've had him interviewed him about it." I looked at Hannah, who reached inside her briefcase and withdrew a small tape recorder.

"Hannah has it recorded, Fraser." She passed the machine across to him with the earphones attached. Her perfume was more intense as she leant across me.

"Where are you spending Christmas, Hannah?" I asked secretively as Fraser was listening to Harwood's explanation.

"I'm undecided, sir. My aunt is going to her sister's home in Wales. She's leaving tonight in order to miss the great exodus for the holidays. I have an open invitation to my brother's home.

I have the one brother and one sister. She will be going to his, as she is unmarried like me. He has three adorable children who still believe in the magic of Christmas. Will you still be going to Chearsley, sir?"

I wish I'd had an answer to that but I didn't. Things were happening by the hour that changed the whole perception of the problems that lay ahead, one of which we were on our way to see.

"What did you make of Harwood's reply, Patrick? He's a man of fine words, I must say." Fraser had finished the tape which he handed back to Hannah, saving me from supplying an answer to her question.

"I skimmed past the flowing rhetoric as quickly as I could. As you say, he's good at that. I found the logged signal from the US Libreville outpost in Gabon that he cites as the source, and my contact in the CIA over here confirms that Libreville is on their index. It's got a heavy occupation unit for reasons he never elaborated upon. I never knew but the Americans and the French have strong likings for the place. That could be because it's one of the most prosperous countries in Sub-Saharan Africa with loads of oil and raw materials, but hey, who am I to speculate. It's also got a corrupt government with advancing Russian devotees. Razin being in that part of world in '86/7 was confirmed, but why would a Hands Off signal emanate from such a faraway post? Why not from London? He was after all in London and not in Gabon."

"I can't answer that, Patrick, but if it's not on the level then why leave a trace back to Greenwich and his AIS? I was never his most ardent admirer but I never marked him down as stupid either. That bit doesn't make sense to me. Another thing that's eating away is why give Henry Mayler, who he had never met and only read scraps of, a phone and for goodness sake a cyanide tablet? A bit 'Cold War drama', don't you think?"

"I do, yes, but where else did Henry get them? I'm thinking he's trying to obscure certain things by being obvious about others. Goading us into thinking that he couldn't be that stupid."

The rain was getting heavier and the clouds lower as we drove ever south towards the New Forest and the grounds surrounding Palace House, Beaulieu, the ancestral home of the Montagu family. It served many purposes of the intelligence services, one perhaps best kept a long, long way from the public domain.

* * *

Geoffrey was inconsolable in his anguish. The bruising to his torso and upper legs were ugly in their colouration of merging blues, yellows, whites and mauves. He was naked, shivering, and sopping wet. It wouldn't take the brains of a medically trained observer to tell you that he was a broken man on the point of catching pneumonia. There was no bed in the room he was kept in. No blanket or stool either. No toilet, no hand basin. A room without dignity, just full of fetid air that held no promise of salvation. A stone floor and stone walls make an uncomfortable place to stay when naked, shivering, and wet. I had no power to arrest Harwood. Nobody in the intelligence services had that power. Not even the director and Chairman of the Joint Intelligence committee can arrest a British or foreign subject.

But we can detain those we suspect of spying, or of treason. Our method of compiling evidence is the same as an investigative police inquiry. Generally we apply patience, diligence and great care in arriving at a decision on someone's guilt. Notwithstanding that similarity, our methods of getting at the truth vary greatly from the gentle questioning in police stations to what we do at Beaulieu. I'm not made of steel. His condition upset me. I am acutely aware that those who are employed to extract what their victims do not want to give up must use a variety of methods in persuasion. However, although the methods practised at

Beaulieu have been adopted by most other peacekeeping agencies, and some who have no regard to peace, they can only be described as barbaric.

"Get him cleaned up and give him his glasses. Get him clothed and fetch him to an interview room, please."

* * *

There was Geoffrey and me in the room and one other person. Geoffrey winced when he saw him. Fraser and Hannah were in the observation room where the televisions and audio recorders were and the staff who understood them. They had fairly comfortable surroundings, whereas interviewing rooms had bare wooden scrubbed tables with manacles bolted to them and three hard chairs. Geoffrey was sitting in one, handcuffed to the table with his bare feet secured to the stone floor. I was standing, hands resting on the table top.

"I'm going to start at the beginning, Geoffrey, and please keep up. How many times did you meet with the Russian, Fyodor Nazarov Razin, from the time he appeared on Monday to when I took over at Group? That would be up to and including Friday morning?"

"I never met with him."

"There are no entries in your log for three hours on Tuesday, and another three hours the following day, Wednesday 8th December, here take a look." I passed the blue ministry personal log impressed with his name at the top across the table and the page opened on the date.

"Was Tuesday your first meeting and Wednesday the day he handed you the briefcase full of money?"

"I never met him," he replied without looking down.

I reached across the table and turned the page in the log to Thursday. The hours between 10:30 and 15:00 were blank.

"Did this meeting constitute the formal signing-on ceremony with a list of requirements handed over by our code named Raynor?" A shake of the head this time was the answer to my question.

"Let me recap on a question you have been asked whilst you have been here but could not answer. I will show you something that had me puzzled for some time, Geoffrey. Perhaps now you can shine more light on it for me. This is a British Transport photograph taken by the station camera at the exit to Charing Cross station on Thursday 9th December at 11:27." I passed it across the table. "It clearly shows Fyodor Nazarov Razin on the up escalator. What's puzzling is the man shielded behind him. It's as if he's trying to hide. It was one of Simmons' staffers who noticed an irregularity in the shot, sending it to the technical lab to have it enlarged. I know this is the first time you're seeing it, but I'm sure you will find it exciting. It's the ceremonial ring that caught you out. I believe it's your regiment's ring. The eyes of the young, eh, Geoffrey?"

"There were a few thousand men in my regiment, West. Circumstantial, nothing else. Have you got a good lawyer, because you're going to need one!"

"I seem to remember asking you why there was a rush to install me at Group on a Friday when an introduction tour that day would have been a better policy, leaving the whole weekend for acclimatisation ready for the normal Monday morning take-over. Do you remember your reply when I said as much to you, Geoffrey?"

"No, I do not."

"You said you had to take up your new position with Oliver Nathan on the following Monday, and had no time other than Friday for me. Remember now?"

"Did I? I don't remember."

"Oliver has a different take on that. According to him, and the official invitation he sent to you some eleven days prior to my appointment, the post was not urgent, having no cut-off date at all."

The dark circles under his eyes grew larger as he began to give way to the sleep he so desperately needed. Through my headphones I asked for coffee and cigarettes. I had forgotten mine on purpose, as I was trying to give them up, but this wasn't the place for me to feel uncomfortable. I put questions about the Hands Off signal to him again only for that standard answer of 'I don't know' to be repeated. The coffee and my brand of cigarettes arrived. I smiled at Hannah's thoughtfulness as I lit one and inhaled.

"Did you arrange for the civil police to turn out in numbers if the alarm sounded at Brightwalton in order to cover the tracks of an escaping project, or merely to slow our own investigations down, Geoffrey?"

His eyes flickered in response but there was no reply. I picked up his log book and slammed it noisily into the table in front of him.

"Keep awake, old boy, or I'll send you back with our friend here." I waited for his eyes to fully open.

"Let's go to the Farm at Brightwalton and refresh our memories. There we were together playing happy parents with the CO and a few others when all of a sudden you remembered something you had to sort out with our project. What was that something?"

"I don't remember."

"You gave him a phone and a cyanide tablet, didn't you? He took that pill this morning, Geoffrey. You could face a murder charge if we ever let you out." That's when the room exploded.

"He did what! I never gave Henry a pill. Why would I do that?" He was pulling at the chains attached to the table and when he went to stand the colossus standing beside him simply leant on his shoulder and forced him to sit.

"Ah, are we making progress at long last? You only gave him a phone. Is that what you're saying?"

"I'd fallen in love with him, yes. I'd never kill him and anyway why would he want to kill himself? He had the world to live. Fraser gave him over to me when they were housing him in the Rathbone Hotel near Lord's cricket ground. Told me to take him north to the farm so I did. He was the most beautiful thing I'd ever seen. I sat beside him in the car and just fell instantly in love with him. I could tell he liked what I liked just by listening to him. We were two song birds together in two separate cages. I had no phone I could give then and it was awkward for me to travel there with no legitimate reason. I saw an opportunity when Oliver wanted me to change direction and become his liaison officer. Yes, West, I gave him a phone. But I would never have given him a cyanide tablet. What reason would I have to kill such a rarity as him? If I knew where to get a cyanide pill I would probably have carried one myself. Of course I used you. I wanted to know what you and Fraser were going to do with him. Fraser would never have told me. He despised me. Perhaps he guessed what I was. Who knows? But yes, I thought you might divulge what was in store for Henry. If that's my crime then hang me now, dear boy, don't waste more of this animal's energy. I have to tell you, West, that if this is all you've got on me then it amounts to a bag of shite."

"How about your reasons for ringing Razin and telling him he was to be outed by the Americans? Was that just kind-heartedness on your part?"

"I can't remember doing that."

"I shall not keep you from the more detailed interrogation from our friend here much longer, Geoffrey, so please concentrate. What you say now will decide your treatment when I leave. Do you recall I mentioned seven men taken from a small village in Djibouti and trained as soldiers to fight alongside the mujahideen in Afghanistan against the coalition forces and how the surviving three were captured and interrogated at Kabul? Yes, you do? Good, I thought this might get your attention. That transcript, where they identified American motorised transport seen in camp as the same type of vehicle used to abduct them, was only meant for seven pairs of eyes, Geoffrey. Yours as Director Group was one. The others I can vouch for. How do you think dear old Razin got to hear of it?"

"Just maybe your Uncle Fraser gave him a peek, or failing that the Americans let it slide. I don't know. Go ask them, West."

"I did, Geoffrey, and guess what. They never got the copy you said you forwarded on to them. Did you put the wrong address on the envelope, do you think? Now's the time to tell us who flipped you, Geoffrey. It could save a lot of your suffering if you did."

"You put your questions so eloquently don't you, West. I was not flipped. What sort of word is that? Did you read it in a comic book? I got sick of the illusion I had to maintain. I'm queer. That's the strength of it. I no longer wanted the hired escort girl on my arm at functions pretending I was the playboy type and acting out what you lot perceive as the norm. I was no longer prepared to bow to the prejudice and heterosexism so prevalent in the social order of things within a regime that's blind to its own faults. There is too much vested interest in the status quo and it won't change. When I met with Henry Mayler I envied his openness. I wanted to be like him, live like him and be with him. I wanted to be honest with myself."

* * *

"What are you going to do with him, Patrick?"

It was Fraser who asked the question as we drew away under the gloomy sky and the gloominess of dejection. However, it was Hannah's eyes that bored holes into my soul. I should have held on to my childish annoyance, but either I hadn't learned enough of the subtle Whitehall mannerisms or I was just plain tired; whatever it was I gave her a mouthful of abuse.

"I'm beginning to doubt your suitability for this end of our business, Hannah. We are not the James Bonds of movie excitement, nor are we priests in civilian clothes offering salvation to the sinners. We are like Suzanna. Bastards dealing with bigger bastards who would willing chop our hands off to break free. We make sure it's their hands, feet, head and anything else we fancy that gets chopped off and fed to the pigs on the farm. We are not nice. I am not nice. I don't want you thinking any different."

Chapter Twenty-Six
Tuesday Early Evening

The rain, sleeting snow and the inevitable Christmas traffic had delayed our journey by at least an hour, and to start with the atmosphere I had created by chiding Hannah hung heavily over us all. My attention was diverted by calls from seemingly everywhere asking about Harwood, Mayler and Razin and then the drone strike. It was Hannah who broke our chains.

"I hadn't intended to say anything until we were alone, sir, but you are so busy that I doubted when that time would occur. I was not criticising the methods at Beaulieu, nor would I ever. I was expressing my concern for you as my boss. I thought the treatment of Mr Harwood alienated something inside of you. Whatever it was, it was pulling you apart, sir. I must reiterate that I'm not advocating a softer approach. I am trying to know you better and if I'm able to do that then I will be able to look after you better. When you're head of a company you don't have to clean the toilets, do you? The nasty things should be left to the nasty people. If we have cause to speak to Mr Harwood again why don't I request a television link where you can address him without having close contact? He can be dressed and presented in a more favourable and dignified manner. It would save that side of you that is being pulled under from further harm. That's what I meant by the look I gave you. It's my role to make your role easier, sir."

"Bloody hell, laddie, you have some PA there, boy, and no mistake. It will be wise to listen to her, Patrick, and to keep her close."

* * *

After making small talk with the ensemble gathered in Molly's dining room and exchanging Christmas pleasantries, Hannah and I answered Fraser's summons to his office. He had Christopher Irons on hold.

"I have Patrick West here with me, Christopher, along with his PA, both of whom you know. Patrick is the new Chairman of the JIC. I'm going to put you on loudspeaker so we all can hear. Hold on a sec. They we are. You're on."

From the little I knew, Christopher was a slow, deliberate speaker, a person who gave lengthy deliberation on each and every detail including the number of bran flakes he ate at breakfast, if breakfast was relevant. He was a good agent and luckily, bran flakes were not included in his agenda. His deliverance was quicker than I envisaged. When summoned I had just that moment driven my fork into Molly's roasted brisket of beef. As I rose to leave I lovingly looked at the crispy golden potatoes and the shredded beef that filled one side of my plate. It would have been my first cooked meal since I could remember.

"Don't worry, I'll put your plates in the oven to keep warm with Fraser's," Molly offered and I pictured the warmed crispy potatoes tasting like rubber. But there were other more crucial disappointments to overcome after Irons' succinct exposition.

* * *

"We had made base camp on Swan's Island in Jericho Bay earlier that evening but because of the conditions we were forced to wait longer than we planned. It became a bad night for visibility but eventually a good night for Suzanna to ride the swell in and out of where we were and where she was going. According to the satellite map the target was six clicks from the shoreline in a well concealed house, cleverly cut into a clearing of the forest below the Bubbles Mountains. When she came back she was shot up bad. By the time I tracked her radio beacon she must have lost four or five pints of blood and was clinging to life by a hair from a horse's tail. One wound had found an artery in her leg. There was nothing I could do other than run. By then there were three boats in the bay coming out of Mount Desert Island with searchlights buzzing over every ripple of water. I put her out of her misery, stuffed the pressurised tubes in the inflatable with rocks, tied her and boat together and towed her out towards Rockland where we had left a rental car. Ten kilometres out I sank the boat with Suzanna's body. I'm sorry, but there really was no alternative."

"When was all this, Christopher?" I asked as Fraser poured himself and me two large glasses of the obligatory whisky. Hannah preferred to pour her own.

"Suzanna set off, local time, Monday 22:40. We had a cloud clearing warning for around midnight for fifteen minutes that we had to avoid, Patrick. The weather was dreadful, as I said. She was back at base 23:21." As he finished speaking I checked my watch. I made it just past midday Eastern Standard Time.

"Why did it take so long to call it in?" I asked.

"I had to dump the rental, clean the motel room and then I backtracked to Canada before calling you and going *light* again. I had good cause to suspect it would not have been left uninvestigated by the aggrieved party. There was nothing I could do for Suzanna but I risked exposure if I wasn't careful. There was a hell of a lot of firepower on that island, sir. The noise of it travelled to where I was."

"Did Suzanna manage to say anything, Christopher?" At last Fraser was in the conversation.

"Bits and pieces, yes. She said she got a shot off at a man answering the description she had of the Israeli who was on the terrace overlooking the garden. It wasn't the plan to go hard on Monday night. She must have been spooked. Her idea was to gain entry and lay up until the house was quiet, then take one subject at a time, nice and quietly. Finish them when she'd done with them, and hog it out of there. There was never mention of any long range stuff. Her handgun was packed purely for defence."

"Are you on your way back, Christopher?" Fraser asked without any sign of emotion.

"Yes, I am, sir."

"Good, I'm pleased. Get yourself out of there as quickly as you can and contact me as soon as reach home soil. I have a far less dangerous job for you."

That's how I ended the call and closed the connection. I then turned my attention towards Fraser. He seemed okay physically but I had no idea what was happening inside his mind. It wasn't just another life lost in the ever-playing game of world domination. Suzanna was Fraser's link to his active participation in the past. All those years in the field play a tremendous role in shaping who it is that orders the possible death of others. Fraser had been a great champion for truth in his duties both on the ground and in his various sedentary positions, but it was my belief, which I did not share with anyone, Suzanna had been sacrificed in a cause that was not ours to meddle in. We could have, and should have, stood off and watched as the commercial situation unfolded. Our primary concern lay with the hardware somewhere on the ground facing either American forces or our own.

"I have an opinion to air," I stated, fighting back the emotions I felt. "I reckon this inner circle of yours, Fraser, pushed an alarm bell when the Shorehams were murdered. The Israeli guy had surrounded himself with protection. I doubt you will get that close to any of them again."

* * *

After our warmed-through dinner we were seated in Fraser's inviting office with our feet up and three glasses of the golden nectar to warm ourselves with, as he recited one of his many tales of entrapment which should have relaxed our profound mood. It didn't, but first he asked what should have been an innocent question.

"What did the message say about Belmokhtar, Patrick?"

He had not told Molly of Suzanna's death. Perhaps that was because of the company around the table that now awaited Geraldine and her fiancé's imminent addition to their number. It was not my place to comment on what he told her and what he did not. I ignored his grief and waded on.

"Usual intro from GCHQ then the identity of source; Antelope and the message that Antelope is at the harbour awaiting tanker, Fraser."

"Fine, okay! Let me tell you a story about the target of that drone strike. I first came across Arif Belmokhtar as Paul Gardener over twenty-five years ago when he was newly qualified and teaching about the transfer of wealth at the London School of Economics in London's Aldwych. He was a completely dedicated trouble-making Communist using the German philosopher Karl Marx as his spiritual guru. He had the ability to turn those innocent, inquiring minds into robots following a path to nothing more than defeatism. At that time in his life he was a middle roader in the Communist Party of Great Britain and a trophy in the Labour Party who cared nothing of his other religious convictions. I got him early by dangling sex in his face. Literarily I bumped into him on a winter's night similar to those of late. He was walking past the Waldorf on his way home when my companion, a beautiful young girl name of Sally, shoved him quite hard into the side of a stationary bus. You and she, Hannah, would have stopped the traffic in Trafalgar Square. All those cab drivers would have got out their cabs to worship you both. Anyway, less of my romantic notions and more of the solid stuff.

"She apologised of course, said she thought he was a friend of a girlfriend who abused her with his fists. He was all bulging eyes and horny thoughts, it didn't take much for me to persuade him to share my room in the hotel with her, with me looking on. The economics of a thousand-pound cash sweetener was too inviting for him to refuse. She was good at her job. I installed her in a nice flat near where he and his wife with their three-month-old son lived and he couldn't resist. Came visiting several times, filling reels of photographs for me to catalogue. I used her several times in fact. It was a sad loss to the service when she got herself arrested for extortion. Somewhat ironic that, considering extortion is a branch of our trade.

"I threatened to show the juiciest photos to his employers and his wife. I told him I'd keep the negatives for someone to show to his son when he grew up if he didn't do as he was told. He was mine from then on. He used his brains and got an invitation to join the Fabian Society. Once there he marked a few cards with the gold sickle and hammer, told his comrades of like thinking pinkos in British politics, and lo and behold I had the makings of a Labour Party unit leaning nicely to the far left that I manipulated now and again. Unfortunately for me, he found jingoistic Islamists spouting their ideology and he jumped ship and country.

"I gave Gardener to Razin for us both to share by promising that Russia would not punish his wife and son for his imprudent lack of respect towards her secrets. Razin paid nothing for

Gardener's agreement to sign the transfer papers and he duly joined the Russian side in the great game. He left his family, his job, everything including his razor. Travelling with the clothes he stood up in with his curriculum vitae detailing actions as a British spy against the Soviet Union, he became part of a Maoist group calling themselves the Afghanistan Liberation Organisation. He worked both sides of the war. Working with the mujahideen against the Afghan government then moving on to work for the Russian army the next day and vice versa. He was a prolific liar, winning the hearts of many. Now you two are wondering what on earth all that has to do with what's going on now, aren't you?"

I said I was and refilled all our glasses in anticipation of what was to come.

"Let's cross the T's and dot the I's then. Before going to Afghanistan, Gardener spent time in Pakistan at a compound, or commune, which may be a more accurate description of the place which was the home of the man Razin told you of when you met in the Savoy Hotel, Patrick—Ayman al-Zawahiri. It was partially Paul Gardener's intel of Ayman al-Zawahiri that allowed Fyodor Nazarov Razin's Federal Security Service to track all the CIA flight traffic to Turkey and Baku, in Azerbaijan. Henry Mayler met with him once in Peshawar, and as I understand things Liam Catlin was in the background of that meeting and the subsequent one when Gardener was introduced to Razin. But there are inconsistencies with that GCHQ signal. Catlin never uses Antelope in message traffic. He decided that, not I. He said it was a mindless piece of crap having an agent in the field using his trade code name also as his signal code. If the trade one was found, he or she would be easily exposed. He hated anyone at Centre being able to track him by any signals he had to send. The other consideration is that ending of Antelope is at the harbour awaiting tanker. *At the harbour awaiting tanker* was Razin's back pocket cry for help, Patrick." The room fell silent with just the odd crack of a burning log spitting out its disgust. It was Hannah who spoke first.

"Why am I thinking that the death of a known terrorist in Syria is directly tied to Suzanna's death in America and Razin asking for help? Ordinarily it wouldn't make sense, but if news of what happened at Jordan Pond filtered down and rocked Razin so much that he wanted out he could well have fingered Gardener as his ticket."

"Possibly, yes, Hannah, that could be the case. But if it is then he would have to expose himself to get Paul Gardener killed. And why risk that?" I answered as Molly entered carrying plates of mince pies and cream.

"Freshly made today. We have heaps more, Patrick, so please make sure you and Hannah eat them all and keep Fraser away from them. He will be allowed one on Christmas Eve and no more. They are no good for his diabetes, or his heart. But my husband has no willpower. Which is obvious because you've heard me tell him about his pipe and his drinking too often to remember."

As the door closed behind her he lit his pipe in defiance, topping up the three glasses with more of his whisky. Hannah tried to refuse but he ignored her protests and added only a small drop to her glass. The low-level table lamp lighting could not cast sufficient shadow to hide the evidence of the whisky-induced reddish glow that tinged her high-lined cheekbones above the full lips that I longed to kiss. It was more than my service position that stopped me. The ability that some are endowed with to refrain from an overindulgence in what harms them has never been my blessing. I fought against the image of our lips together and the height of ecstasy that would follow. I was winning the battle inside myself and I would not jeopardise the outcome by adding another memory to eat me alive. Maybe it was because I never showed enough love to the subjects of my memories that now they hated me and needed to destroy whatever it was they felt for me. It was as I gave in to another addiction and lit a cigarette that Molly's word of willpower unzipped my memory.

"I have one possible answer to the why kill Arif question, but although it's a long shot I think it's worth mentioning. When I met with Razin at the Savoy Hotel, he got himself into a showing off mode. Russian flowery bits about how important he was inside the Federal Security Service. He gave the full 'admire and fall in love with me' bit. After he was satisfied he had my attention he tells me an allegorical story of a garden which was full of weeds but the weeds kept growing no matter what he did. He said he loved the garden and could put up with the weeds because of the colour it gave him and his friends. Then he added what I imagined was a warning for me to stay at arm's length. He said: *'I will abandon that garden if I feel my friends are laughing at my lack of control. I will kill the flowers and leave the weeds if I feel one drop of rain, Mr West.'*

"If his fictional garden was Paul Gardener, who we know he knew, then his *lack of control* could mean he's in too deep and can't get out. The main fault with my idea is he never mentioned any of that when he called. Now I wonder why that would be?"

"Maybe because Henry Mayler's suicide had lifted some pressure?" Hannah answered, pushing her glass towards me. My eyes were filled by the vision of me as a smiling fool dressed in a clown's circus outfit.

"I've been had like the fool I am," I shouted, almost knocking over the table that held our glasses.

* * *

The house at Draycot Foliat had been scrubbed clean and the body taken to the pathology laboratory in Swindon, about five miles away. It was late when we arrived, and specially opened for us. The Chief Constable of Wiltshire Police met me at the door and led Hannah and me to the body. It was as I had eventually suspected, the body of Fyodor Nazarov Razin and not Henry Mayler. I had swallowed his impersonation without one thought of it not being Razin. Henry's story of his own death had bought himself more time to escape. Heathrow was only an hour away by car, giving him a huge time advantage in the search for his whereabouts.

Chapter Twenty-Seven
Whitehall

That Tuesday night I picked up some of my clothes from Lavington Street and moved into one of the two huge apartments that came with the post of Chair of the JIC. I missed the Hub and the Hole as soon as I did. Perhaps it was the mood of the place with the spilling-over energy and togetherness that I found the hardest to let go of, but I was determined to turn my new accommodation into my permanent home. I left a message for the man at Acquisitions and Disposals sections of the Audit Office that Harwood had given me, asking him to put my Canary Wharf apartment up for sale.

Before taking advantage of the bed in my new palatial surroundings I contacted the Commander of the British attachment to the Joint Task Force Southwest Asia, based in Saudi Arabia. He set in motion the mechanism to track down the origin of the drone strike that killed Arif Belmokhtar. The military use of drones was a relatively new concept in warfare against terrorists. The strike capabilities they delivered was still being assessed and evaluated. The strike against Belmokhtar had been clinical and error-free and would, I suspected, rate highly within American Joint Command. I pulled every mention I could find on Arif Belmokhtar when plainly known as Paul Gardener, settling down to one of the privileges of my new position; a bottle of

40-year-old Isle of Jura single malt whisky drunk from a crystal glass thistle tumbler. The cupboards, fridge and even the freezer were all well stocked as was, according to the cellar book, the whisky allocation. The only thing missing was someone to use the space with, and to share the bed.

I was in the throes of welcoming the bonus of sleep when an almighty buzzing sounded from somewhere in part of the offices. I found my way there and watched the fax machine spewing out a message from Geoffrey's old AIS installation at Greenwich in code. It had landed simultaneously with me and the ninth floor at Vauxhall. It was sent direct from Moscow Central to Baku, in Azerbaijan.

Date: Wed Dec22. Time: 02:14. Intercepted signal traffic from Islamabad to Kirkuk recipient name unknown, quotes— TEAM 6 states Iraqi military base KI neutralised. Target code MACHINE. Yellow/9 Bubble.

I called the Directorate on the ninth floor. At such an hour I was surprised to hear Sir John Scarlett himself answer my call.

"We have Baku, Azerbaijan down as a Black-Ops Rumsfeld site. By that we mean it's financed through illicit redirected military funding. We have it marked as part of the trillions missing from Pentagon budgets that Rumsfeld highlighted. We were waiting for a signal such as this one. Our overall analysis is that the President in the White House intends to bypass the UN and obliterate Iraq's nuclear power project at Kirkuk. We had that pinned as a blue project. We use the same colour codes as everyone else, so we weren't overanxious, but it seems to have notched up to yellow overnight which means it's imminent. The problem we have, is how much of this is genuine White House policy and how much of it comes from outside influence?

"Aides at Downing Street are clamming up on this, Patrick. They say he's undecided on which picture to believe. It's my personal judgement that he will jump on the American wagon. The consensus from the Middle East department is the same, as is the Russia desk who are currently examining the bigger picture. The overall view is that it's a done deal with or without confirmation, nevertheless, I'd like to know who is controlling it."

"Yes, Sir John, so would I. Is there any way we can firm up the details that my Russian gave us without using him?"

"Are we to assume that his synopsis of the situation is to be questioned, Patrick? Is Ughert of the same opinion?"

"I'm always suspicious, Sir John. I would like second and third confirmations if that's possible. I have an appointment with the PM tomorrow and I hope to be able to put something new on the table." Nobody beyond our triangle knew that Razin was dead and I was not about to invite newcomers.

I was under no illusion that MI6 would strain themselves to help in this direction. I was hoping for information from Joint Task Force Southwest Asia plus something either I or Michael Simmons at Group could discover about Paul Gardener to place in front of the Prime Minister. I fell asleep and woke just after five-thirty that Wednesday morning to the humming sound of a vacuum cleaner in the office suite.

There were four rooms to my new little empire. The communications room, where amongst many other contraptions the fax, coding and decoding machines were situated. The secretaries' room. Apparently I had three of them, all of whom started the working day at 8:30am and would be at their desks until midday this coming Friday. Then there was my office that I already described as palatial. It was also sumptuous in every detail of old-fashioned styling. Lastly there was my Personal Assistant's, or Steward's office, as large and magnificent as my own. The corridor where I had met the formidable Mrs Bayliss when Fraser had the tenure of these fine rooms, was now manned by another shift of principal protection officers. I was bedding in nicely.

For me it was a slow realisation of the immensity of being the sole arbitrator on what the UK considered to be our *at risk* status. It was my role to evaluate what intelligence could be shared with friendly agencies, also what was passed on at Privy Council meetings and told to individual Ministers of State. It was me to whom the heads the intelligence services of this country passed on their current status of alert, current state of worldwide ongoing operations, along with any counter-intelligence techniques being employed. I was expected to tell Chancellors what budget was needed to protect our interests at home and abroad, and it was I who had the responsibilities of overseeing not only our military commitments but how much they were told of our ultimate aims. GCHQ, AIS and all Yellow Gate, Electronic Support Measures, fell under my jurisdiction. The only person I had a duty to tell the truth to was the Prime Minster, but what version of truth could he accept? I had no trouble with any of that, other than I never knew the full truth of Mayler's importance and I had enormous trouble managing my own life without sorting all that out.

There was nobody else I wanted other than Hannah. I called her, and her constantly turned on telephone woke her. My sales pitch for the accommodation must have been good because she accepted my proposal of moving in the moment I stopped speaking. Jimmy drove her in a little over an hour from the time we spoke, and a ministerial van was dispatched from the transport pool to carry her belongings to the King Charles Street entrance of her new fully appointed apartment. We started our working relationship over breakfast overlooking Horse Guards Parade.

Midmorning Air Commodore Phillip Moon, from Joint Task Force Southwest Asia was on a secure line from an American aircraft carrier in the Mediterranean. It was one of his Nimrod aircraft that had sighted the drone on its route to kill. He was emphatic that it was not a Joint Task Force strike.

A radar calibration aircraft plotted the Predator B drone flight path from the launching site bordering the town of Antakya, southern Turkey. The hellfire missile was fired from an altitude of 1,100 feet when 800 yards from its target. We then tracked it back to its landing strip in the desert. The UAV was loaded onto a trailer unit and towed away by a US army Oshkosh tractor towards the Syrian border. The Nimrod aircraft then resumed its patrol.

This was one hell of an expensive kill operation, not the type of weapon to find in the normal arsenal of a local Taliban warlord. The last recorded location for Narak Vanlian was in Antakya, right on top of the launch site. Coincidence I'm sure, as was the fact that he knew Simon Ratcliffe, executive officer for Venery Munitions Ltd, the first choice Ministry of Defence shipping company for untraceable weapons used to unseat unfashionable governments or maybe kill no longer wanted terrorists. But why go to all that expense to kill one person?

* * *

I would have loved to have traced Henry Mayler's footsteps away from Draycot Foliat and Fyodor Nazarov Razin's body, but nothing had come from the notification bulletin Special Branch had passed on to all airports and ports and as of yet no sighting had materialised. It was with only the drone update that I and Hannah travelled a novel way to the appointment with the PM.

This time we met in the Cabinet Room on the ground floor at number 10 Downing Street. With Hannah beside me I sat opposite the PM and his media spokesperson, along with the serving Lord Chief Justice who I'd met when sworn in again on taking the chair at the Joint Intelligence Committee. The questions this time regarding the Gladio B files felt more tilted towards the legality of how the information was come by and how accurate I thought it to be, rather than any analysis Fraser and I could put on it. Mention was made of the anthrax and phosphorus ammunition, and the PM asked if it was possible that both could be in Iraq. I answered a straightforward and honest *I have no knowledge on that, Prime Minister* which was greeted by three all-knowing, nodding heads.

The meeting lasted an hour with no real interest shown towards the drone's launch site. The only one present to speak of it was the media spokesman, who suggested I left it alone for the Syrian government to take up if they wanted. My palate for advice was not stronger at this meeting than any other. I forgot about it and him as soon as we left by the same way we had come; an electric motorised underground tunnel that Fraser had never spoken of.

* * *

Apart from a hastily grabbed lunch prepared by a delightful, smiling, Welsh housekeeper, I occupied myself with the victim of the drone strike for most of the day. Paul Gardener's name was filed twice, once as a British operative and once as a Russian agent who ran nine agents in three Afghan cells. When I was in Ireland I had a total of thirty-one informants supplying me with secrets about the IRA, but I had only two cells, or units of more than one operative. Working one-to-one in the collection of intelligence is in total contrast to working a group of people who oppose the doctrine of another group, but have different solutions to the problem. In that scenario, it's the responsibility of the one in charge of those groups to supervise their independent actions and responses with regard to the safety of the other individuals and groups.

To supervise any collection of individuals with different motives and targets is a dangerous game, even for the most skilled agent. I wasn't the most skilled, but the effects of the nail bomb in the

Erin Arms of Derry constantly reminded me of the stupidity of espionage when it becomes personal until the close connection can be conclusively removed. Although there was never enough evidence to convict the perpetrator for that bombing I knew who it was; a tall red-haired Irishman with an assumed name and part of a cell I called The Camels. He disappeared and never showed on a security screen again. I could take you to where I shot him but there are no remains to prove what I say is the truth. Personal disputes can end in disaster of one kind or another.

According to a report filed by Fraser, originating from Fyodor Nazarov Razin, Gardener had requested one hundred thousand dollars in 1981 when part of the Afghan Liberation Organisation to foster new informants and, in his words, 'regulate' those he had. Razin wanted the names, particularly those Gardener wanted to regulate and details on how it would be done, but he never specified whether the names came before the *regulating* was applied or after. Bombs can never be a pure sanitary method of killing a single target if that target stays in a crowd. Paul Gardener's problem amounted to that. The target he wanted to *regulate* was an Afghan government minister who no longer wanted to betray his fellow ministers and was close to betraying Gardener. Unfortunately for all concerned, the minister worked and slept in a government building always guarded by Russian troops in the centre of Kabul. He was never alone. He knew his worth. The rocket-propelled grenade not only killed the man it was intended for, it also obliterated two Russian troops; one a Captain Anton Valescov, eldest son of Bohdan Dimitriyevich Valescov, one of the powerful elite of the Soviet Union. Bohdan could afford a drone, the logistics required for the launch along with the missiles and guidance system, and if I knew anything of Russians, he had long arms when it came to revenge.

There was one other part of my investigations I disclosed to Hannah as we held an impromptu meeting in my Persian-carpeted office with us sitting either side of my walnut inlaid mahogany desk drinking good coffee. The person who Henry Mayler met in New York back in November, on the Saturday after leaving Razin in Kabul and taking the flight from Damascus was Bohdan Dimitriyevich Valescov.

"How the hell do you know all that, Patrick?" she asked, the *sir* now only to be used when necessary.

"Because Henry made a mistake and either Fraser never looked far enough or he's holding it back."

* * *

It snowed in central London on Wednesday night and for a while it settled. We were walking beside the Mall towards the Palace, as the tiny flakes blew into our eyes, nestling into our coats then melting away from view. I was wondering what kind of trick Henry had played on Razin to be able to kill him, whilst at the same time I was visualising Razin playing with his flame and knife as a captivated Henry Mayler looked on. Were the gentle falling snowflakes playing the same tricks as his flame? And would the memory I was creating with Hannah be another that must be forgotten to ease the passage of my soul into the afterlife?

Questions, questions and then more questions. Why did Razin have to be murdered? Henry had enough information to effect his escape without Fyodor Nazarov Razin along for a car ride, he also had the phone from Harwood to arrange everything he needed. Again, why Razin? Neither snow nor Hannah's perfume mingling with the crisp air could pull my mind away from that engaging riddle. I had been invited to dinner by Sir Elliot Zenby at his club in St James's Street. The truth was I'd fished for an invitation when I learned that he was staying on in London until the Thursday before Christmas Eve. I had let it be known in the corridors surrounding my office and over the courtyard into the Home Office that I wanted a reputable London club within walking distance, where I could get away from the afflictions of Whitehall to sit and dream without being unnecessarily disturbed. Sir Elliot had offered Brooks's as his recommendation. Not unnaturally Zenby wanted to know more of Geoffrey Harwood and if his department had been breached in any way, and I wanted to know if he had more insight on the Prime Minister's thinking than Sir John Scarlett. It was a probing expedition by both of us but I figured that Hannah's presence might just swing the outcome more my way than his.

Have you ever been in a situation where talking about nothing takes as long as if you had some really important things to say? Yes? Well, that was me with my evaluation of Harwood; it lacked any substance as did the meal I ate. However, his appraisal of the PM's thoughts was shrewd and comprehensive.

"The Americans don't need allies in what will be their invasion of Iraq. They are the same as Russia in that respect. Neither need allies to back them in anything they wish to do. But both have interests to serve. Saudi Arabia is one the Americans have to consider; but not for too many years to come, I fancy. America is the biggest user of oil in the world, but as of yet the business interests that drive American politics cannot get their greedy hands on the wells or the refined petroleum Saudi Arabia produce. The House of Saud is too prosperous and too powerful for them on a financial front. Next to China, the Saudis hold the most American government issued bonds. If they were to cash them in it would cause a slow meltdown of the continent of the United States as we know it. I don't believe that's in the interests of whoever is driving American foreign policy. With Kuwait firmly ensconced in the American oil gathering basket, then next year Iraq and a few years down the line Iran and Syria, oil from Saudi will not be as important to America as it is now. Russia, of course, will have a say in how the oil from the Middle East will be divided, but ultimately it will be divided. The rest of us would normally have to sit by and cross our fingers.

"However, there is another player at the OPEC table which will eventually supersede them all and it's on America's doorstep. Venezuela will be at the top of the production tree in the not too far off future. At present there is one problem to harmonise American interest. Venezuela's president—Hugo Rafael Chávez Frías, or more commonly known as Chávez. It's the view of most economists that there's just too much oil, and therefore money for him to handle. Left on his own he will squander it on social reform that will be without sustainable foundations. Our Prime Minister has his eye set on a different goal than just achieving distinction in politics or as a sidekick of President Bush. He wants universal power, Patrick, and what's more he thinks he is clever enough to get it. He and two of his aides have met with Chávez and his policy makers several times. According to the intelligence I have seen from a very reliable source inside the FBI, our socialite PM believes the American President shares the same ideals as he does. His thinking goes along the lines of, if I help you then you will help me."

He laughed and Hannah laughed with him. I carried on wishing I was eating Molly Ughert's roast potatoes instead of the thinly sliced garlic potatoes on my plate.

"If, as seems highly likely, Bush goes into Iraq, we will follow. That's Scarlett's opinion as well as my own. What our boss will do then is anyone's guess, but if I was a betting man then I'd back him to leave domestic politics and jump on the business wagon giving weight to a selected few in the pharmaceutical and energy industries. It wouldn't surprise me to see him on TV endorsing a Russian car in the future. My FBI friend tells me that the PM is trying to wheedle his way into becoming the political media spokesman for Hugo Rafael Chávez Frías when he leaves Number 10. Provided of course the Americans haven't invaded or persuaded Chavez to offer his black gold to them at a discount. But ultimately, if there is a war in the Middle East, my bet is he quickly jumps ship and goes to where the remuneration is the highest, cleansing his soul in it."

Chapter Twenty-Eight
Repercussions

As Suzanna pulled her inflatable boat across the pebbles and smooth sand of Mount Desert Island and hid it under the low branches of a pine tree near the water's edge, the blustery dampness of the night kept the fragrance of pine low in the air invading her nose without complaint.

Akhtala in Armenia had its fair share of pine trees under which she had played as a young child, wondering why her mother had left her until eventually she was told her beautiful mother had died. But what did that mean? she wanted to ask, not daring to in case to die was something bad that came to you in the night and swept you away. She remembered being picked up in some person's arms and gazing at a figure dressed in a white veil lying down inside a wooden box that people were gathered around crying over, but not she.

After climbing the steep hill towards the crest she was able to look down to Jordan Pond and recall how she had never cried in all the thirty-seven years of her life. Then she started to remember the names of the ones she had given cause to cry, or scream as her methods of inflicting pain had become more terrifying as she had grown into the game she played. It was the same on any mission. Remember those that have gone, so they might not be so unforgiving when you all meet up in Hell.

Ten feet from the crest she knelt and checked her equipment. Today she had both poisons, scopolamine and methanol she had brought a lighter as well to see how much pain lighting the methanol and dripping it into an eye socket could cause. At the top of the hill she fell. Nobody could suspect trip-wires that far from the house. During the daylight hours, when she and Irons had trekked part of the island, they hadn't ventured this high in case of being noticed, but the forest was a national park with trekking paths, so surely people wandered away from a path, she thought as she awkwardly bumped into a tree. She hadn't fallen far. Feet more than yards, but the wire had done the damage. A cosmic proportion of lights lit the night sky and swept the banking hillside where she stood against the trunk of the tree that had halted her fall.

Two figures appeared on one of the many balconies of the house below and she could vaguely hear them shouting and pointing in her direction. Smack, like an angry hand slapping flesh, the trunk of the tree above her head absorbed a shot. It was followed quickly by a series of smacks as bullets from an automatic weapon found nearby trees. The ground near her feet sounded as though waves were crashing onto a rocky shore as bullets tore at them.

Nothing like this had ever happened to her. She was a close-in killer, not a commando in a raiding party. In a window above the balcony where the accusing fingers were pointed at her, stood a shortish, bald-headed man with a grey beard dressed in a white shirt wearing black-rimmed glasses. White was the target's favourite colour and the rest of him fitted his description. She took aim with the Glock pistol she carried, gently squeezed the trigger twice and a head shot killed the Israeli.

A smack didn't hit a tree. It went through her boot and into her leg just above the ankle bone. Hobbling and reaching out to trees for balance she made it to her boat without the next bullet. With immense strength she dragged the dingy into the water, fired the motor and steered for the lights on Swan's Island. The boat took a line of shells luckily all above the waterline but unluckily three hit Suzanna. The first two in her arm, upper and lower but the third broke a rib on entry and passed through a lung on exiting. The next one to hit was of a heavier calibre. It lodged in her liver causing massive internal and external loss of blood. Nearing her base camp she managed to zig-zag the boat away from the searching lights of the pursuers. With every pain-driving lurch over the choppy waters of the bay her hopes of survival increased. That wasn't the case for long. Breathing hard as she climbing out over the one remaining inflated tube, two stray rounds from a light automatic weapon hit her body. One in the femoral artery and the other in the widow maker artery on the left side of her heart. She was aware of Christopher Irons kneeling over her but not the first stab of morphine nor the next. By the time Irons had shot his whole pack of pain-relieving morphine into her bloodstream she had died, but it was from her wounds, not his overmedication as was his unenviable intention.

* * *

Searches began in earnest the following morning, beginning at the Israeli Embassy in Washington D. C. Later that day Michael Simmons passed on the GCHQ notification to Group and AIS of 'unusual activities' attributed to agents of Mossad in and around Mount Desert Island, Maine. The FBI were contacted by the Maine State police department and started inquiries of their own. Early on Thursday morning Al Jazeera announced that Tamimi-Dayut, the chief financial fund raiser of the Palestine Liberation Organisation had been found murdered in his hotel room in Paris, France. He had been dead for at least thirty-six hours. About an hour later Eastern Standard Time, the FBI found a rented open-backed Chevrolet abandoned in the trailer park north of Rockland, in Maine. Against the car registration number in the rental book was the name of Tamimi-Dayut, along with the requisite details from his passport. The agent of the rental company was asked to give a description of the man who had rented the Chevrolet; it matched Tamimi-Dayut to a tee. The black magic art of disguise Christopher Irons learned at Beaulieu was never a waste of time.

* * *

My guest at breakfast that morning in Claridge's Hotel was less despondent than when I'd left him.

"Not all was in vain, it seems," Fraser announced. "Moshe Gabbai and Tamimi-Dayut both dead should make the world a safer place in the long run. Overall Christopher made a good job of it. Inside I'm devastated about Suzanna, but what can I do. There was always an out for her but it was the life she chose. We both knew she wouldn't never make old bones," he announced solemnly, then added,

"It's always sad when one of ours cops it. How goes the Venery Munitions Ltd file, Patrick? Any luck on your UAV?"

Fraser and Molly were staying in the hotel in the room kept by the Acquisition and Disposals on a renewable annual retainer. He had suggested they stay in the second apartment at his ex-office that was now mine in Whitehall; however, it was easier to explain that Hannah had moved in there whereas the truth was that she shared my rooms now.

"There's nothing showing on the Venery books that Ratcliffe keeps, and there's nobody at the Pentagon who will comment on UAVs. However, I did manage to get some information. In February this year two US army Oshkosh tractor and trailers were purchased by a Syrian registered company from an American approved supplier. In the same month two USAF C-17 took off from Kabul landing at Antakya with unspecified cargo. Simmons at Group did a normal sweep. The company doesn't exist. The address is a shop front in Damascus."

"When you told me the name of one of Paul Gardener's victims it rang bells in my head, Patrick. Is Henry Mayler's November visit to New York what you wanted to discuss this morning?"

"Yes, Fraser, it is. There was a meeting of International Master Freemasons at the Four Seasons Hotel in New York on the Saturday following Razin and Mayler's exchange of words in Kabul. That's where I believe Henry met Arnold. The FBI were out in numbers that weekend along with ex-President's protection details, and special forces were on high alert. The FBI had several specific targets to watch. One of them was the next presidential candidate from the Democratic Party, Tucker Stoneman, another was the Russian oligarch Bohdan Dimitriyevich Valescov. I used a contact in the CIA to profile all they had listed on Valescov. I tried to get them to give me all they had on Stoneman, but they wouldn't budge on that one. Did you know Valescov is of the same Rosicrucian order as Henry?" Fraser shook his head.

"I traced their affiliations to a founding lodge in Zaragoza in Spain. Do you know of that lodge, Fraser?"

"I've heard of it, laddie, yes. And I did the same research as you but I hadn't had all the information on Gardener that you had. Be that as it may, laddie, William Guerny II said the man he spoke to had an American accent, not Russian."

"I know that, Fraser, but I doubt Arnold uses the phone to speak to the likes of William Guerny II. I played around with the theory that Valescov may have mentioned his son to Mayler at some time and Henry may well have told Valescov of Razin. Now where Gardener comes into it I'm not sure, but if his name was mentioned, then Mayler could have twisted Razin's arm for a location and Valescov could have killed him."

"Then why the—*Antelope is at the harbour awaiting tanker?*"

"That's what's confusing me, Fraser, and what I want to work on. Hannah is tracing the original message and will have it worked back to cover all transmitting possibilities. I've put AIS under Simmons' direct control and he's weighing in with them as well. I want to keep Sir John Scarlett out of the mix at the moment. Too many eyes at Vauxhall. When the signal about Gardener's execution pinged up it went to Geoffrey Harwood with the Antelope in the harbour bit redacted, but it did show Arif's name and—*identified target of asset code Antelope.* Would Geoffrey have known Liam's code as Antelope, Fraser?" He turned his head away from the table and fixed his gaze to floor. After several seconds he said three simple words that contained a complexity of meanings. "Yes, he did!"

* * *

The Arif Belmokhtar flashed signal, at 04:14 on Tuesday, had originated from the same NSA relay station in Erbil, Iraq, only this time there was no NSA footprint.

"It can't have come from Razin as he's dead. So someone else is using his 'Help Me' card in the harbour thing. Maybe Geoffrey knew Razin's code and told Henry Mayler just as small talk or worse. He could even had told Henry Liam Catlin's code name. But neither of them would be aware of Catlin's preference of not using it," Hannah emphatically declared.

"It also means one of them knew how to lock into the NSA signal networking system. I would put my money on Geoffrey knowing about that sort of thing after all the hardware inserted at his Greenwich AIS. I want you to call Spencer Morrell, Hannah. He might have gone home for the Christmas holidays, but if he's still in his offices he'll meet you, whereas if it's me calling I won't get past his PA. Ask him if he has any ideas. We're looking for any kind of fingerprint that could have been left. I'm scratching away in the dark on this. I need to fix a name to whoever dispatched it and then match that sender to Bohdan Dimitriyevich Valescov."

Spencer was still at work and, so he told Hannah, could be there until the New Year. His department had been tasked to find the same target as us, but he was hampered by not knowing that Razin was dead and our project was on the loose looking to meet up with Arnold. All he had was an IT location address in Wiltshire, England. After a shared coffee in a reception room with Spencer, Hannah decided he was of no further use to us and returned empty-handed.

I contacted Peter, back at the Hub, and he was more useful. I sent him the signal with all mention of Antelope removed and he promised to do his best with it. Around 2pm that Thursday he had news.

"I had to get through a variety of firewalls on the NSA sites and interestingly some highly sophisticated Russian data filters as well. They really were top-notch, but not as good as ours at plugging leakage. You see, sir, a mobile phone will always give you a location, but as the signal was sent some days ago the likelihood of the dispatcher still being there is very low so I looked further. The other thing one can get from a phone signal, if one knows how to look, is its number. That's the tricky part where filters play their role. I got through them all, sir. I have the number." I could visualise him jumping up and down as he told me. It was not Razin's phone. It was the one given to Mayler by Geoffrey Harwood.

"You have done it. You've just confirmed a conclusive connection between Arnold and Henry's phone. Do you think it's possible that Geoffrey Harwood had that phone tweaked in some way, Patrick?"

"I thought you disapproved of me getting my hands dirty with that side of things?"

"I've come around to your way of doing things a lot. Haven't you noticed?" she answered, seductively sweeping her long black her away from her sculptured face.

Chapter Twenty-Nine
Christmas Eve

The first gathering of solid intelligence that had any connection to Henry Mayler and Razin to land in my hands came from an ExxonMobil employee via Christopher Irons on the Friday of Christmas Eve. I had declined to spend the holiday period with the Ugherts, citing the operational state as the cause, but it wasn't only that. One part of me wanted the semi-permanence of company, the warmth that a close friendship of others would give, but the stronger part wanted the same isolated life I had some two weeks or so before when in my old flat at Canary Wharf doing whatever I wanted, because with that separation or self-inflicted quarantine came the excitement of no responsibility, nobody to consider before jumping into an adventure that could end badly. Hannah had become a slight impediment to that, all the same, provided I never allowed the comfort of sex and a warm firm body to lie against to amplify into anything else, then there would be no sense of duty to obstruct my inclinations. Despite all those considerations the furtive business I was in was paramount.

Allowing for a few who had nobody to share Christmas with, everyone who was anyone in my line of work was packed up and headed for home or places to stay for the holidays by Friday lunchtime at the latest. Certainly at the time of night I had arranged for our meeting there would be no one of significance left in town.

Jimmy and Frank had three days' leave and although the two special protection officers assigned to me were as amiable as one could hope, the conversation we had on the walk through St James's Park that night under a cloudless sky and full moon lacked the synthesis that people who know details of each other have. I left them both waiting in the hotel foyer looking as unobtrusive as possible, whilst I went searching for illumination on a member of the Rosicrucian order whose ideology could fill a room with toxic garbage.

My educator was waiting in the Martini Bar of Duke's Hotel. It was busy. Josh Polish, Christopher Irons' man within ExxonMobil, was a tall, confident man of medium build and on whom the expensive clothes he wore hung well and naturally. He spoke in a cultured English accent that had been nurtured at an early age on his family's estate in Gloucestershire before he had settled in America and made his fortune. His bearing and pose belied his age of seventy-one. He wasn't doing any of this for money, he had plenty of that, I'd seen his bank accounts, neither was he doing this as a penance to offset the damage his company may have caused throughout his forty-plus years as company treasurer and chief negotiator. His reason was one of plain and simple revenge for being passed over in the upper echelon of business life.

"If you carry a stone in your shoe for any distance, Mr West, it either becomes part of your foot or part of your shoe. I can afford as many pairs of shoes as I want, but I only have one pair of feet to carry me until I've left this life. Now's the time to care for my feet and ditch the stone in the shoe. In these documents you have all you need to blow Tucker Stoneman's presidential candidacy as high as the moon. It will make a gigantic splash across America that will drown many like him. He is an evil man who stupid-minded people admire and look up to. The kind of paganism this man privately preaches becomes dangerous when they are more disciples in his tent than critics. I do realise the people you represent will use the information contained in here to your country's advantage, better that than no action at all, which would happen in the States. I'm on a private jet out of here in three hours' time. I have a heart condition which the doctors say will allow me to live for at least eighteen months. For the remaining time I have, I want a peaceful life alone with my wife. We never had children, neither of us wanted them. We have no living relatives either. No ties, Mr West. Just plain, ordinary creatures that fell in love with each other and are now joined at the waist."

"Could I ask you one question before you leave for that idyllic life Mr Polish? Have you ever heard this Tucker Stoneman use the word 'dingnation' at all? I believe it's used as an expression of surprise. I also believe it hails from Missouri. Would he have any connection to that state?"

"He doesn't, no. Comes from sunny California, does Tucker. But I know a man in his inner circle who comes from Missouri and uses that word often. His name is Calvin Zunkel. He's one of Stoneman's heavies. If it ever leaks out that you got all this information from me it could be Zunkel who pulls the trigger and kills me."

I had briefly glanced at the written sheets of papers and pocketed the memory stick after Polish left, leaving me to finish my drink alone. From what I saw it was every bit as good as I'd hoped. I was certainly not about blow Tucker Stoneman's political career to the moon and back. That was never part of my agenda.

* * *

That night, as I lay beside Hannah, my mind was on what Josh Polish had said about no ties. He had a wife but he never thought of her as a burden. I lay there probing everything I had experienced to discover why that would be, but the truth he found in his marriage would not shine on me.

* * *

As far as I could see, Harwood giving Mayler a phone had greatly complicated the investigation and left himself wide open. Mayler had made his decision to escape from the farm when it was obvious to him we were not flying him straight to Canada. He had enough on Razin to be able to find him and rightly suspected he had followed him to London. Getting hold of a phone would have been no problem for Henry, and for all I knew he could have had one concealed on his body and bribed a guard to let him keep it. The important thing was Fyodor Nazarov Razin was destined to die as soon as Paul Gardener, as Arif Belmokhtar, murdered Bohdan Dimitriyevich Valescov's eldest son.

From what I had deduced it was obvious that Tucker Stoneman was the mysterious Arnold taking advice from people such as Valescov and the like, but they were not my immediate worries. They could be left in the Pending file to use at a later date, or unveiled to either their own governments or the United Nations to regulate and oversee. My job was to safeguard the British population, including overseas military personnel, and then propel GB Ltd forward riding on the information I had.

* * *

Narak Vanlian met with the Sunni Kurdish followers of Alaz Karabakh in the mountains beyond Antakya over the weekend before the Christmas weekend. The UAV and hellfire missiles were transported through friendly territory under their supervision and launched, guided and fired by USAF personnel paid for by transferred funds from Panama. The payment to Sunni Kurds for the assassination of Arif Belmokhtar was not paid in money. It came in the back of the five trucks piled full with a variety of weapons that Narak and his team had brought from the Venery warehouses, further north in Turkey at Gaziantep. From the information I gathered that drone and remaining projectiles were returned to Kabul under political cover provided by the company who sold the transporters to the Kurds; Springfield Munitions, part owned by Calvin Zunkel. Was it not Springfield that Henry Mayler, posing as Razin, declared to be his destination?

The fact that Christmas Day was celebrated in Britain and America at the same time helped Michael Simmons at Group to provide the invaluable intelligence he was doing partially through the state-of-the-art technology that Geoffrey Harwood had installed at AIS in Greenwich. GCHQ had worked wonders on intercepting CIA and NSA messaging, having electronically inserted listening devices on Zunkel's main fixed telephone line and fixed a signal from his mobile phone along with another electronic inserted bug installed in Stoneman's campaign headquarters. But that wasn't enough. Peter at Group had tracked the actual instructions from inside the Pentagon to Narak Vanlian regarding the coordinates for the UAV and its launch requirements. I was on my own in the silence of the Whitehall office, hearing the footfalls of the two protection officers patrolling the outside corridor, puzzling over Liam Catlin and had he played a role in all of this.

It wasn't long before Liam took second place to an announcement on the CNN news channel. The US Agency for International Development (USAID) had awarded a multi-million-dollar restructuring contract to a company based in the Netherlands named Barrow & Martin Investment Group. I had researched this company before finding it to have several operational constituency elements involved in Eastern European emerging markets. Some were preparing feasibility studies on the privatisation of mining rights in Uzbekistan and others financing drilling operations in a region of the Caspian Sea. According to the news reporter, a part of Barrow & Martin's, calling itself B&M Regrowth had gained a reputation for doing economic project work in post-conflict regions of the Middle East. As its company emblem it had an eight-pointed red opened rose above a traditional four-pointed cardinal cross in gold and a four pointed ordinal cross in silver. It was an exact replica of Mayler's tattoo. Could there be a better day than Christmas Day to let slip a news bulletin that was anything but straightforward? I found the home telephone number of the Minister for Trade and Industry. Using the power of my official title and office I set him to work on running down all he could find on the company.

Once again it was the sophistication of the AIS networks that Michael Simmons employed to locate Liam Catlin in a town not far from Al Hasakah, almost on top of the Iraqi border. According to the satellite overfly Michael ordered, several thousand heavily armed Kurdish warriors were amassed nearby with American artillery pieces and rocket launchers. On closer inspection of the photographs provided it was plainly evident they had surface-to-air capability. I passed on this information to the ninth floor at Vauxhall and to the CIA in Grosvenor Square in London, and to Langley in the US. I also notified Fraser by coded fax. Within minutes he was on the phone to me.

"Can we get any intel out of Iraq regarding Razin's missing anthrax, Patrick? Once this intelligence gets to the Defence Staff and the PM they will want confirmation of that. I would like us to have it before the Americans. Did Fyodor have any idea where it might end up?"

"No, none! The only place he knew of was where the Russian colonel should have been, in Dagestan. His son was killed in Kohe Belandtarin where there was a mujahideen presence. I had Hannah ferret around listings of mujahideen known to be in the area when that incident occurred and she found a group calling themselves the Hizbul Mujahideen now in northern Afghanistan. She sent that information to the American military who were supposed to have sent troops into the area with biological tracing equipment, but I've heard nothing back and my contact in the CIA won't say a word. I can't see the two hundred or so Hizbul Mujahideen carrying artillery shells filled with phosphorous and anthrax from Afghanistan to Iraq, can you, Fraser?"

"No, I can't, laddie, but if this conspiracy goes as deep as you and I suspect then military air transport is not out of the question, is it? What about this supergun that Razin spoke of?"

"There was no evidence on the probes we did."

"Have you added that to the signal you have sent to the PM, Patrick?"

"I have, Fraser, but he asked for a breakdown on Iraqi nuclear potential and I told him the UN inspectors have not had full access to it and it cannot be completely surveyed from the air. He told me that wasn't good enough and he needed firm evidence of strike capabilities. I told him nothing of how we know there is an American Black-Ops agent there now and we know of a proposed landing by paratroopers near the end of March next year. Neither did I tell him of the December 22nd signal saying an Iraqi military base near Kirkuk has been neutralised. I can only assume it's referring to Iraqi retaliation when the nuclear power station is attacked. I've asked at the Ministry of Defence and they confirm it is possible to lay remote-time-controlled mines around a target to nullify it at a future date. Stars war to me, Fraser, but there we have it; no confirmation before March next year. I would be willing to bet that the reference in the second

Gladio B file to the 19th Pathfinders on the 19th March is the date that the first high value targets will be acquired."

* * *

I wished him and Molly the season's salutations and spoke briefly to Geraldine wishing her a happy future. I had never spent a Christmas Day on my own. In Ireland I may have been operating alone but had others closely around at all times. Here in lifeless Whitehall I was feeling lonely for the first time I could remember. Hannah was having Christmas lunch with her brother and sister, having left around ten that morning promising to return by six that night. That was hours away, as was the reservation for dinner I'd made for us at the Connaught Hotel at 8pm, a favoured haunt of the American secret brigade and in consequence attracting free-loaders.

Chapter Thirty
Miller the Killer

"Well, well, Patrick West, as I live and breathe! How are you, old man? I must say you are looking rather good for your age. Aren't you the same age as myself, fifty-two? Whatever line of work you're in it's positively keeping you in shape, West."

I recognised him as soon as we entered and wished I had booked somewhere else. If it wasn't Christmas night I would not have removed my coat, just turned away and walked on, but I had no choice if I wanted a hot meal. He had been at Oxford with me, studying the same subjects of analytical chemistry and the science of psychology. I had heard he was an expensive psychologist with a practice in Los Angles, California and another one in New York. At university he was a bore of outstanding proportions, but I'm ashamed to say he had something I had not, money, and that overcame my aversion to him. Along with other friends I attended his wedding reception some twenty-five years ago, and even allowing for plastic surgery along with pints of anti-aging serum, the woman at his table was far too young to be his wife.

"Is this delightful lady your wife, West, because if so you have divine appreciation of the female of the species?" he drooled on.

"She is a close friend, Malcolm, and if you'll excuse us we have a table in the corner. Good evening to you both." I offered my hand across their table to his blonde, twenty-something attractive guest, with a strapless dress that revealed almost all of her ample bosom. She took my hand and I added, "Enjoy your meal," just as I placed my hand in the small of Hannah's back inviting her to walk in front, but her feet were stuck to the carpet.

"I think I've seen you on television?" Hannah announced to the blonde woman.

"Most probably, yes," she replied, "I'm Roxanne Miller of the infamous *Miller the Killer* chat show on morning television."

"Don't put yourself down so much, darling," Malcolm Turnbull came to her aid. "Your show is not infamous at all, it's the opposite. The guest speakers tell their version of the truth and then you try to drag more out of them. It's highly entertaining with a really top-class A list. Have you seen it, West?" he asked.

There was nowhere the three of us, plus my security detail, could stand other than to block the walk-through between the tables and as such we were impossible to ignore. Again I suggested we move, however this time the restaurant manager was beside me when I did and Hannah complied. I never answered his question.

"What a polite man and an attractive woman. She looks as sexy in real life as she does on the TV. Have you not seen her before, Patrick?" Hannah quietly asked.

I replied that I hadn't, and was addressing the wine waiter when a man dressed in a scruffy dark blue Barbour type jacket and wearing a grey and blue chequered flat cap entered the restaurant and made straight to the table where my two protection officers had sat. I saw them both put their hands to their handguns, loudly telling him to stop where he was. He did, by which time most heads were turned in his and their direction.

The man stood with his hands in the air whilst one PPO searched him thoroughly and the other personal protection officer had his holstered gun exposed with his hand firmly on it.

When they were happy that he wasn't dangerous to anyone they brought him over to our table. By now we had the whole restaurant diners enthralled.

"I'm a cab driver, guv. That's my badge hanging round my neck. I was on the rank at the Hilton when a guy gives me an envelope and says to bring it here and give to the two men sitting just inside the door. He added they will look like bouncers and I couldn't mistake them. He gave me fifty quid and said he'd know if I didn't do it."

I took the sealed envelope from him and passed it to Hannah who recognised the Egyptian Arabic on the envelope:

27th December movement on Tiran Island. Look it up and keep watching.
Look Within Yourself To Find The Truth.

As the shaken taxi driver left I saw Roxanne Miller replace her mobile phone into her handbag. Although it was just another one of those coincidences in life that seem to be happening more and more, I thought the last number dialled would be worth a look. In spite of it not being her role nor had she trained for it, I asked Hannah to do her best to get a look at the phone. Immediately after placing her food order she left our table.

"Have you got a second, Miss Miller? Only I would love to have a private word with you about that show of yours," she said to Turnbull's guest on her way to the Ladies room. Ten minutes later she returned without the number.

"She asked me who you were to have two bodyguards. She thought you were important and might be a drug dealer. I said I had no idea what you did for sure, but thought you were in property and you were just someone I'd met who treats me well. However, I said I knew Cherie Blair and I thought I might be able to get her to appear on her television show. I asked to use her phone and call her there and then, and ask. She flatly denied having a phone. But when we came in, and you and her companion were speaking, I saw her with one. I think we should call whoever is staffing the Hub and see if calls from here can be traced back. Worth a try I think, sir."

The Hub found the number Roxanne had dialled and it was being traced by Special Branch as Hannah told her that Cherie was on holiday until the latter part of January and suggested she make contact with her through her barristers' chambers in the Temple. Luckily, to save further embarrassment, Turnbull and Miller left with just a cursory wave in our direction. Once outside they were stopped and searched by armed police officers who found confirmation of Roxanne's called number on her phone. When questions were put to them both, it appeared that Roxanne had been asked by a former boyfriend to suggest that she and Turnbull eat at the Connaught that night because I had a booking there. Her former friend was an Egyptian businessman by the name of Zoser Antar. It was he who she telephoned from the restaurant. He was still at large by the time we returned to the apartment at the Foreign and Commonwealth building. The identity of whoever told Antar of my reservation was a mystery, as the knowledge of that was not secret within the secretaries' room at my Whitehall offices. That loose end needed to be looked into.

Hannah and I spent the remainder of Christmas night making up for our day-long separation and for the inactivity of the night before. A fax arrived in the early hours from a police inspector at West End Central police station saying that a Thomas Maitland, a London taxi driver, had been questioned about delivering an envelope to the Connaught Hotel. The fax went on to say he had responded well with the facial composite, but although the man who hired him was Middle Eastern in appearance he had not recognise any photograph of the man Roxanne had named. A few minutes later I read another fax. An Egyptian by the name of Zoser Antar had been found dead in his apartment opposite Battersea Park. Apparently, the police were not looking for anyone in connection with this sudden death.

* * *

Tiran Island was in the middle of the Straits of Tiran, which connects the Red Sea to the Gulf of Aqaba giving access from Suez to the ports of Aqaba in Jordan and Eilat in Israel. The Israelis briefly took over the Island during the Suez Crisis and again from 1967 to 1982 following the Six-Day War. According to what I read the government of Saudi Arabia had made claims on the island but at present it was protected by military personnel from Egypt. What sort of movement would call for a message to be delivered in such a convoluted fashion?

Fraser was awake and in his office when I rang well before breakfast on Boxing Day morning. When I told him of the incident in the Connaught he too was at a loss to explain it. He asked if anything had been flagged and I replied that it hadn't. I had been in touch with MI6 and even though they had skeleton staffing levels, their exhaustive search had found nothing more about Tiran Island other than what I'd found. All my contacts in America were of little use being beyond reach for the festive season. Downing Street was closed as far as returning signals were concerned and I was left floundering, wondering where to go for information. As a shot in the dark I called Robert Zaehner, the Doctor. It was three in the morning in New York but he was awake!

"In 1981 Israel were in talks with the newly elected Egyptian president Hosni Mubarak over the Island. Anwar el-Sadat had just been assassinated and Egypt was thrown into political turmoil. I was heading up the small CIA station in Cairo and stayed there until '87. That was my last posting for the CIA. When I was recalled home I was offered a role on the quieter side of life in the

National Security Agency. I took the job. Anyhow, Menachem Begin wanted rid of the island and Mubarak didn't want it back to pay for garrison troops on it forever. He sold it to the Saudis for oil, but soon enough the Saudis found out they had a bum steer. It was just somewhere their money melted away. They struck a deal and it's stood to this day. Good luck to them, I say. I've no idea why there's interest in it now, but it is in a handy place if you want to disrupt the sea traffic from the Red Sea up the Suez Canal and from the main ports of Jordan and Israel."

* * *

Liam Catlin was found in Tartus, a city on the Mediterranean coast of Syria whose main claim to fame in all that was going on was that many centuries ago it was one of the last strongholds of the Knights Templar; one of the Masonic orders that Fraser belonged to. I woke Hannah.

"Pack a bag, Hannah, and book two tickets to Damascus in Syria. We're going on holiday for a few days. I'll call the embassy and arrange to be met."

Chapter Thirty-One
Island of Tiran

We arrived in the cold city of Damascus early on the morning of the 27th with as yet no sign of movement on the Island of Tiran, but that serenity did not last long. Liam was with the ambassador when we arrived at the embassy; he looked well but older than I imagined he should. We all exchanged the welcoming handshakes, comments on health and admiration of my travelling companion and after that it was down to business matters in the safe-room of the residency. I needed first to know about Narak Vanlian and his role in the drone strike.

"Fraser gave Narak Vanlian and me the responsibly of raising a Kurdish resistance capable of withstanding a short but bloody battle with a disciplined, but disorganised and disheartened Iraqi army fleeing from an invading American and British force. Narak stayed in the region longer than I, teaching them radio procedures in their own coding. We had the weapons shipped in from Turkey, most via Ratcliffe's Venery Ltd but some through an Israeli company registered in Eilat. Narak never told me of a drone and catapult launcher nor the transport, Patrick. I'm blind on that one and I've no idea of what was behind it."

Unless he had metamorphosed into Richard Nixon declaring *I'm not a crook*, when out of my sight, I believed he had no knowledge of Vanlian and the drone strike. I did not interrupt him.

"Our initial plan was that the Kurds would be split into two groups by March next year, one to assemble north near al-Malikiyah for a combined attack on Mosel alongside a US parachute regiment, and the second to assemble in the desert area of Ar Rutba on the highway into Bagdad. It's along that route they will form a barrier against retreating Iraqis, holding them until the Mosel grouping arrived. It's going to be a slaughter, Patrick, but I guess that's what the coalition will want."

"Was it Fraser who told you all of this, Liam, and if so, when?"

"The foundations were laid a long time ago, Patrick. Over ten years I reckon. But we met in the middle of last year in London, when he spelled out the big picture to me as he called it. Agencies within the US would invade Iraq on the march to bag all the oil in the Middle East. Those were the words he used before he added that Great Britain needed to have a say in who was to control the oil if only to nullify the American use of excess force."

I was thinking about that answer and how far Fraser would go in his reaction to a situation that would require delicate manipulation when Hannah read aloud an incoming signal.

Chair Joint Intelligence Committee:

Island of Tiran taken unopposed by small unnamed forces 09:56 GMT 27/12/02. Occupying garrison withdrawn towards the Red Sea. No reported casualties. Purpose of occupation unknown. See attached images.

The satellite photographs showed a dignified exchange between the occupying Egyptian officer in charge of the eighteen army personnel and nine naval officers and the commander of the seizing group of eleven men wearing different coloured keffiahs and black and white thawbs. After a few formal salutes the twenty-seven military officers who formed the garrison on the island took to the two attack boats flying the Egyptian flag and made off towards the Royal Saudi Naval Western Fleet in the

Red Sea. By way of standing protocol the Foreign and Commonwealth Office in Whitehall had notification of the same signal I'd received, and it was a message from them that Hannah summarised.

"The Minister of State for Foreign Affairs wants to know if it's anything to worry about, sir."

I wasn't sure if there was anything to worry about, but I was certainly worried. In particular I was worried about what was in the five large oblong boxes that were lifted ashore and placed under hastily erected camouflage netting beside three field artillery pieces. I instructed Hannah to send a *Watching* signal in reply. With half a smile on his face Liam suggested the two of us take a Land Rover and drive the six hundred odd kilometres, take a boat to the island and see for ourselves what was in the mysterious boxes. It held appeal if only to get more from him on what Fraser planned for the future.

"If I was going on my own I'd go through Jordan and stay well clear of Israel. You can get lost in Jordan whereas in Israel there's someone every mile wanting to see your papers and check you're not a Hezbollah terrorist. I'd go as far south as Saudi Arabia, hire a fishing boat and then work out how to get on the island." It was Hannah who replied as I sat contemplating his suggestion.

"It sounds a little stupid to go all the way there without having a plan of how to land on the island. Surely it would be tons better to have a couple of ideas how that could be accomplished."

"She's got a point, Liam," I expressed in agreement.

"She has, but more to the point have you still got the balls, Webby, or is your bum glued to a chair nowadays?" Liam asked with a huge smile plastered across his face.

"I saw the name Jack Webb on the passport you gave me when I ordered the flight tickets, sir, and wondered who he was."

"Someone I thought I'd left in Ireland, Hannah."

"I don't think you should go, sir. I think we will all better served come the third of January if you are reading the situation from Whitehall, not here in the middle of it."

"What's the third of January got to do with anything, Webby?" Liam replied.

"I'll tell you when you're driving me across the desert. Could you ask our smiling friend here to write you up a list of supplies he'll think we will need to get us to that port in Saudi Arabia, Hannah, and then ask the ambassador to find a Land Rover with some suspension for my aged bum, please? I'm off to Tiran."

* * *

Fraser must have been reading my mind as it was his call I received on one of the satellite phones. We also carried three handguns, although I would have been the first to admit that if I was caught in a fire-fight I did not believe I would have fared well, but as I was often told in more circumstances than I care to recall—some precaution is better than none. A good many years had passed since I had come to know of Fraser's connection to Egypt. How he had studied Egyptology at Oxford and then, after he joined the Special Operations Branch of a fledgling MI6, spent time behind the Egyptian military lines during the Suez Crisis in 1957. He and three others were what remained of the British legation in Cairo from 1958 onwards until things became more regulated in the 60s. Fraser had expressed his dislike of how the American government had pressurised Great Britain to end the Suez Crises by blocking oil from the region and imposing a threat of bankrupting the Bank of England by selling British government stocks. It was his view that the British, French and Israeli attempt to seize the Canal was justified and should have been permitted to continue to completion. If not, then the three allies would have been vindicated in invading Qatar and Kuwait to safeguard their oil supplies. He said Eisenhower had *bottled it* when Khrushchev threatened a nuclear attack that would never have happened. Must I take his jaundiced opinion on America into consideration with the current circumstances?

"The American support of her NATO allies during those times was non-existent, laddie, and believe me had it come to a real dogfight with the Russians the Americans would have stayed at home."

I had listened avidly to his description of events in Egypt during the Suez Crises and at no time in my memory had he openly condemned the president of Egypt, Gamal Abdel Nasser's decision to privatise it, even though he thought we had a just claim. He praised Nasser for his courage of conviction. Fraser was similar in that respect; a man of firm beliefs.

His original reason for calling me was he wanted advice as to whether to take a flight to Boston and drive closer to Mount Desert Island to pay his respects to Suzanna, but when he found out I was in Syria he put that aside, wanting to know why I was not in Whitehall. I advised him not to go to America whilst at the same time admitting my hypocrisy in wanting to put myself in danger, but I argued that it would not be the FBI staring at me and recognising my face. Mine would belong to just be another European poking his nose around in Arabia.

"I'm coming with you," Hannah announced as I was speaking to Fraser. "I've looked on a map and I have the semblance of a plan." I put the phone on speaker.

"We will want some diving equipment to be loaded and we won't need to beg, steal, or borrow a boat. We'll take our own inflatable and then you and I, sir, can pose as a couple taking a winter's break to go coral diving. I'm a diving instructor, you see. I've dived all over the world, sir."

"I told you she was a special personal assistant, Patrick, just don't let her die the same way as Suzanna." The connection was lost from his end.

* * *

As the winter night closed in on Damascus we left the city with the specialist supplies Hannah had requested tied conspicuously to the roof. We carried cans of spare fuel, two spare tyres along with a suitable amount of grub to eat with what would pass as Arab cooking utensils. The idea was to resemble just another pair of Western tourists on a diving expedition in the Mediterranean with Liam as our Bedouin guide.

Once into Jordan, Catlin drove across desert tracks to avoid the metalled roads around the capital of Amman then once clear he re-joined the main highway due south to Saudi Arabia. Taking full advantage of the conditions we made good headway on a calm but cold night. As the sun was coming up we skirted a small settlement at a place called Hamid to find a deserted coastline bordering the Gulf of Aqaba about 8 kilometres from the island. Roughly twenty-four hours after taking possession of the Island of Tiran the occupying forces were met by a different personality; me dressed in a scuba diving wetsuit.

In our rubber inflatable boat we pulled alongside the same jetty from where the Egyptian military had vacated the island and with the Arabic shouted invitation of the sentry ringing in my ears I disembarked, leaving a much curvier Hannah than myself as the visual entertainment for the nine soldiers gathered around us. The shabbily dressed sentry took me to a hut where his equally unkempt commander was. In broken English he asked what I was doing on his island. I told him we hoped to dive the coral and having seen the signs announcing the island's military status had come to ask permission. He was as loud and obnoxious as his sentry had been, telling me to take our boat as far away as possible and not to return. As I started the boat's engine it seemed to me that Hannah's departing wave to the men on the wooden jetty appeared to have more expressiveness than simply a gesture of goodbye. I wasn't wrong.

"Were you successful, Jack Webb?" she asked, her eyes as large as saucers and a smile a country-mile wide as soon as we were a fair distance away.

"Are you being cheeky for the sake of it, Hannah, or are you flirting with me with a particular motive in mind?"

For some time we could hear the crude remarks from the bawdy soldiers as the boat rose and fell across the waves with the rudder secured and our naked bodies engaged under the warm sun. For those pleasurable moments in time my mind was totally removed from the scene on Tiran Island, and as much as I wished pleasure could last for an eternity I was not powerful enough to ensure that truth could be concealed for long.

* * *

Over coffee that our Bedouin Liam Catlin poured in the cool shade of the towering cliffs, I told how I had seen one of the oblong boxes stencilled with gas mask symbols on the sides, and on another of the blue spray painted boxes I made out the undeniable outline of a skull and crossbones not fully camouflaged by the paint. The boxes could, in my opinion, contain artillery ammunition to fit the howitzers pointing out to sea, but I was not an expert. For the late Razin's scenario of exploding anthrax shells I needed analysis of what calibre those howitzers on the island were. If they were capable of firing the missing Russian M107 shells where was the target? Tuesday night whilst I lay beside Hannah in the apartment in Whitehall, the officer commanding the Marines from the Special Boat Service despatched from Cyprus confirmed my worst fears; the guns were American ex-army artillery of the correct calibre to fire the shells.

Chapter Thirty-Two
The Levant

"Okay, if I may I will start with a huge thank you to our new Director in the chair of the JIC on finding the anthrax shells. However, that leaves the phosphorous ammunition. We need the location of those shells fast, Mr Chairman." It was Air Chief Marshal Sir Graham Overton who spoke first after I had finished giving my findings on the Island of Tiran to the three representatives from the Defence Staff in the lounge area of my office in Whitehall. It was he who continued—

"The Prime Minister is to meet the President in Washington tomorrow afternoon on a flying visit and Iraq is on the agenda. He has a two-hour turn around. My estimation of the situation has not changed. He will sign on with Bush if, as seems highly likely, Bush ignores the UN and cranks it up into invasion mode. But, and it's a big but, our PM is after any crumb to justify Britain being loyal to an ally who can handle an invasion perfectly well themselves. Yes, it's true, we would provide vital support to ease their way in if he gives the order, but candidly I think the PM's backbone is aching under his own prevarication. He needs us, Mr Chairman, to provide the basis to start the train in motion.

"The guns were originally positioned on the Island to defend the Straits of Tiran from the Israeli navy threatening the Red Sea coastline of Egypt. It's true the guns could be targeted on parts of Egypt and Saudi Arabia, but they could not reach Israel, which surely would be the target of a terrorist aggressor? Therefore I for one can't see the point of weaponised anthrax being used from that position," Overton continued.

"What's our political policy towards neutralising the weapons on the Island?" This time it was Field Marshal Sir James Phillips who asked me.

"There is none, gentlemen, and nor will there be for the foreseeable future. The political situations is delicate at best with neither Egypt nor Saudi Arabia recognised as sovereign owners of the Island of Tiran. Plus I have advised the Prime Minister that is not in the UK's interest to alert either of those nations to our surveillance capabilities in their region. I have conveyed my thoughts to him and he is in complete agreement that for the time being our knowledge of a possible attack is not to be shared. We are maintaining satellite imaging and I have a contingent of Special Boat Service Marines nearby."

"Are you sure it was a global hazard symbol that you saw, Mr Chairman? Could it possibly have been something else?"

"I only wish it could have been, but I'm afraid it could not, Admiral. It is the anthrax that our Russian source mentioned."

"Then what is the target?" he asked.

I had one possible answer but if I was right then now was not time to reveal it. I needed time to further Britain's ascendancy in the clandestine world which was my home. I played for time.

"From what my people have gathered we're saying that it's likely to be an attack on the resort of Sharm el-Sheikh, or the Mosque at Nebk further north along the Egyptian coastline. If either of those targets are correct it will set tourism back a hundred years in that part of the world."

* * *

"Why did you not mention Henry Mayler's birth date being what you consider to be the axis around which any action in the area will take place, Patrick?" Hannah asked when we were alone.

"Because if I'd said anything about that to the Prime Minister or the Defence Chiefs then I think I would have been marched to the nearest lunatic asylum. That's something we only discuss with Fraser Ughert."

* * *

Within the not so secret government compound that is named Fort Halstead, near Sevenoaks in Kent, there were several areas of rocket and projectile technology, which although dealing with some secrets of value were allowed to be known to exist. However, under the original defensive structure there are miles of underground connecting tunnels, most of which go to extremely sensitive areas dealing with top secret developments in specialist fields of explosives. When I'd heard of Razin's missing ordinance it was to the experts in the tunnels of the fort that I first turned and tasked them with finding the Russian phosphorous shells. Those experts, working with the Middle East desk at the Vauxhall Box of MI6 who had protected assets inside the Ba'ath Party, were instructed to find Colonel Antolov Puskin, the escapee from Dagestan who had a violent dislike of American tourists near his home town of Listvyanka in the mountains of Siberia. By various means far beyond my mental capacity, along with the expertise of two covert Special Air Service soldiers from B Squadron, both targets were to be found in a place called Paprok, in the north-east corner of Afghanistan near the border with Pakistan. As of Christmas Day further members from B Squadron, 21st Artist Regiment, arrived in Kabul and started to monitor the camp at Paprok. Three members of the team penetrated the camp and found the ten cases of M549 phosphorous shells reported as missing from the Aral Sea depot. The cases were divided between the two well concealed American army M114 155mm howitzers pointed at a town called Kamdeish where a heavy concentration from an American Army Rangers Regiment were stationed. Colonel Antolov Puskin had been seen in the camp but on the night it was penetrated by the SAS he was in Islamabad drinking vodka with a Pakistani lieutenant general at the headquarters of the Pakistani Inter-Services Intelligence.

* * *

I received that information on my return from Syria and added it to the file I placed on the Prime Minister's desk at the meeting I shared with him and his three aides. As far as I was concerned the matter of Razin's banned, unaccountable ammunition had been solved and was no longer my responsibility. I had loaded it onto the shoulders of others to deal with. But Fraser wanted to know more when he phoned.

"Did he not say he would forward your report on to the United Nations, laddie? Both the anthrax and the phosphorous shell are in direct violation of the Hague Convention, which prohibited the use of poison gas or poisoned weapons in warfare."

"The trouble with that is that they have not been used in any war, Fraser. One could make a case for both being in the hands of suspicious organisations, but again we have no knowledge who controls them. Do we tell the Russian we know where the biological weaponry they lost from the Aral Sea is? Because if we do we run the risk of exposing some agents to their Federal Security Services, don't we? I did not advise the PM to do that. It's an internal problem for whoever is in charge in Dagestan or some other region inside Russia. It is not my concern whilst sitting here in Whitehall supping a gorgeous Jura whisky chatting on the telephone with an old friend. The same argument about the onus of responsibility applies to the anthrax shells on Tiran.

We own up to the Saudis or to the Egyptians and it will get back to Moscow Central quicker than a camel can lick its arse."

"What a very picturesque scene you do paint, Patrick. So appropriate for the Christmas period. Did you find that one in a cracker? I can never remember the quotes or jokes in them." At least for a while he forgot about my earlier meeting with the PM.

"Have you any news on Henry Mayler?" he asked.

"Not yet, no, but I'm forever the optimist, Fraser."

"Bring Hannah with you and get here around seven, Patrick. I'll ask Molly to lay on some cold bites. We can have a chat about one thing or another and you never know, I might be of some help in that direction."

* * *

"Our understanding of the world today is of states and countries defined by manmade borders and lines drawn on maps, but that was not always so, and in some people's minds it will never be again. Not all ancient races, along with their religions, are archaic in the sense that they no longer exist. Some do exist, Patrick. Please, enjoy your drinks and my short story of the Levant and how that impacts on what we are dealing with."

And that was Fraser's opening address to Hannah and me when we were once again seated around his log fire, awaiting yet another of his tales of yesteryear delivered in his fine Scottish brogue enlivened by his fine Scottish whisky. As strange as it may sound I was positively looking forward to relaxing in his company, thinking of nothing else than a story of the past.

"Let me get one simple thing out of the way before I begin with my main story." It was my experience that whatever was to follow that throw-away remark of simplicity would be far from straightforward and simple.

"All I have told you of Henry Mayler is true, however, he has a strong connection to the Levant that I have told you nothing of. That now being said I can begin."

I could feel the hair on the back of neck stand on end as a rush of adrenaline hit me at the same time as I caught Hannah staring at me in disbelief, of what I wasn't sure. Perhaps she knew what the Levant was, because I had no idea and what's more I was thinking I was about to regret the word existed.

"To understand all that I'm going to tell you we must have a small amount of knowledge on what predates recorded history, but fear not, I'll keep that bit short. The earliest evidence of civilisation in Lebanon dates back more than seven thousand years. The region came under the rule of the Roman Empire, and eventually became one of the Empire's leading centres of Christianity. However other faiths and religions were born in and around that area, one being what was called the Druze faith. Its followers were an esoteric group originating from the east of Lebanon, who identified themselves as Unitarians. Another faith was the Maronite Church with followers who later identified themselves with the Roman Catholic Church in Rome. Next door to where all this was happening, in Syria, the Roman occupation was ended by the Arab Muslim conquest. From the outward spreading of these different religions came a church named The Church of The East and it's to this faith and following that Henry Mayler is affiliated within his Rosicrucian fellowship. I hope you are awake and following me, as there is more to come and I can assure you it will tie everything you know and have been told together, Patrick. Henry is following his interpretation of the Hebrew word—Jahbulon. To him it means freedom for his Rosicrucian fellowship and his Druze religion.

"The disciples of the Druze religion maintain a lifestyle of isolation where no conversion is allowed, either out of, or into, the religion. When Druze live among people of other religions, they try to blend in, in order to protect their religion and their own safety. They can pray as Muslims, or as Christians, depending on where they are.

"Under the terms of an unwritten agreement known as the National Pact between the various political and religious leaders of Lebanon, the Chief of the General Military Staff must be a Druze. In August last year the head of the Maronite Catholic Church met with the Druze leader of the General Staff, Walid Jumblatt and the two of them reconciled the differences between their denominations after the bloody war they fought against each other in the early 80s. After extensive discussions with a highly respected Egyptian American journalist based in New York who shares Mayler's Druze faith and his Rosicrucian morality, it has become Henry Mayler's objective to take what he considers to be his ancestral race of people, the Assyrians, to a higher and more materialistic plain assisted by the Chief of the General Military Staff of Lebanon. And if I can have your attention for a little while longer I will try to explain how he means to accomplish that and where we fit in."

His last sentence left me with an ominous foreboding feeling but coupled with a sense of relief, as I think I always knew we, the intelligence service of GB, would have a hand in the unveiling.

"In the 1830s, Armenians who occupied high diplomatic posts within their country joined masonic lodges during their trips to Europe and did not conceal this fact. The motive for that was to use close ties with the European intellectuals in order to solve various issues of concern for the Armenians inside the Ottoman Empire. In fact, during those years it was common practice for Armenians to form their own Masonic Lodges as a protest against the Turkish rule. At around the time of this happening an English company called The Levant Company was trading in many cities and on many fronts within the Ottoman Empire. Not only was it concerned with commercial trade, it was used as an instrument of the British government to spread its gospel throughout the region. As far back as the collapse of the Ottoman Empire it was this country's policy to establish itself in Azerbaijan as well as Armenia. Our policy advocated that all of what is now known as Karabakh should be part of Azerbaijan until the boundaries could be decided upon peacefully. Surrounding regions listened to us. It was that kind of brawn that forced Great Britain's foot inside the Armenian Masonic Lodges and one of the reasons why the intelligence services of this country became home for Henry Mayler.

"It is difficult and perhaps even impossible to find Henry's connection to Assyria. He was a great student of history when at Oxford so it could have started in those hallowed libraries, but the only certain place I can point to where it may have gained a foothold in his mind was when he first met and worked with the journalist in New York that I've already mentioned. At this point of time I will not name her. It's not necessary, and it may influence your opinion as I believe you have some damaging information on the presidential candidate, Tucker Stoneman, who is a personal friend of hers. She backs Stoneman's campaign using a trust fund from the Cayman Islands. It is her husband's money. He is a leading Assyrian in the Assyrian Democratic Movement who has been a target of the Saddam Hussein Iraqi Ba'ath regime for many years. He is also one of those I suspect to be in the circle of eight. Here is an opportunity to add another hypothesis—perhaps this Assyrian funding could be one reason to explain the current President of America's thinking towards Iraq. After all, the Bush family are certainly not far removed from my inner circle by their accumulated wealth. By now, Patrick, you can see part of the complexity of this international defining affair.

"The policies of Hussein's Bathists have long been mirrored in Turkey, whose governments have refused to acknowledge the

Assyrians as an ethnic group and have attempted to Turkify the Assyrians living inside Turkey's borders by calling them Semitic Turks and forcing them to adopt Turkic names. In Syria too, the Assyrian/Syriac Christians have faced enormous pressure to identify as Arab Christians and not Assyrian Christians for centuries. It could be that Henry formed an affinity to those being persecuted through the books that he read, and it was in Oxford that he began to focus on forming an autonomous area known as the Republic of Nagorno-Karabakh for Armenians and Assyrians alike."

"It's the second time you have mentioned it and I know that name of Karabakh. Henry was sent to Syria to follow a man by that name, was he not?"

"Not quite, no, Patrick. That was the name he gave you and Hardballs before you, but that was not the man's name. Karabakh was just another sign or semiotics integrated into Rosicrucian symbolism. And as you should know by now all branches of Freemasonry has a myriad of symbolism, some old some new. And then we come to biggest symbol of all; the nucleus of worldwide Masonic Fraternity—

We speak unto you by parables, but would willingly bring you to the right, simple, easy and ingenuous exposition, understanding, declaration, and knowledge of all secrets.

"What the bloody hell does that load of tosh actually mean, Fraser?" I asked, feeling the effects of the drink more than I would normally.

"That's where we are heading, laddie. Be assured of that."

"How do you know all this?"

"I'm just a good listener, Patrick, haven't you noticed?"

Chapter Thirty-Three
The First Third of The Finale

The Henry Mayler Story

Henry Mayler drove the knife through Fyodor Nazarov Razin's left eye and into his brain whilst the Russian slept. There was no spark of suspicion in Fyodor's mind that Mayler harboured vicious thoughts towards him; after all had he not answered his Rosco's friend's call for help in escaping from the English? Why should he be wary? But fate has a way of playing the cards that are hiding from the view of mortals, slamming them down onto the baize to win the hand.

Razin's withdrawal from the game was going to end this way ever since Henry saw the murderous stiletto blade shimmering in the dancing flame at the press corps camp when Fyodor pretended to be Oban Raikkonen from Finland. Razin had been good at keeping his identity unknown to Mayler up till that point. He had to be good as nobody knew then what Henry's true convictions were when it came to politics. Henry was unsure of them himself. He was aware that he was different from others around him from the time he began to form a memory. One of his first recollections was always being surrounded by older people rather than children of his own age, whom he was seldom allowed to mix with. His education came in the shape of elders teaching him the meaning behind images for the construction of his body, mind and soul. The triangular threefold that God is one God, but three coeternal consubstantial persons of the Father, the Son, and the Holy Spirit was the uppermost teaching in his education.

If that was not enough to concentrate on, there was the mystical ideas preached by a fraternity called Rosicrucians who stood and applauded when a Rosey Cross was tattooed on his hand. His embryonic inspiration was drawn from the simple symbols of the tools of stonemasons—the square and compasses, the level and plumb rule, the trowel, and others on a mesmerising list. A moral lesson was attached to each of these tools and the meaning behind the symbols was continually taught and explored through the Masonic rituals and levels. Numbers were coated in divinity only to be mentioned in a solemn voice with respect etched on each multiple of three.

An image of a skull with crossed bones underneath was not the representation of toxic waste it became, it was Henry's symbol of mortality and his very own hourglass pointing to the brevity of his mortal existence. Bread and water indicated simplicity to his mortal soul. And a painted rooster standing proud above them all, symbolised the alchemical principle to the philosopher's stone which represented the other trinity of faith, hope and charity. These lessons had to be learned before tackling anything of an academic nature. Henry's only understanding of the word groomed, was in regard to clothing. However, his tutors understood a different meaning, one where it was their choice of his fate.

* * *

Oxford became his place of adjustment from a follower of the mystical to a devotee of an ancient faith and the Egyptian teachings of an age called Zep Tipi. So were sown the first seeds of the madness that remained fertile inside Henry Mayler's mind, waiting to be saturated by more demonic visions of massacres shown to him in a superlative fashion which turned words into pictures and pictures into destiny. The roots of Henry Mayler's genesis lay in the holocaust of Armenians by the Turks and the genocide of Assyrians by Turks allied to Arab nations, learned not just from the prosaic history books in Oxford libraries, but later from the lyrics of a Lebanese journalist his preordained path was designed to meet.

* * *

Henry signed with British Intelligence because it seemed to be the easiest of ways for him to obtain more knowledge and secrets of the outside world. He liked Fraser Ughert and he especially liked Bernard Higgins. Lovely Bernard with his colourful braces and spotty bow ties. He was almost blind without those beefy spectacles of his and he was cheap. Ate like a mouse, did Bernard, and as he visualised his ex-lover, Bernard began to resemble one.

'Funny that,' he thought. 'It never occurred to me when he was alive. Mind you, mouse or not, I had no trust in Bernard from the start. I knew he had a Russian contact whom he was feeding the stuff I meant for Ughert only, but what the hell. I liked him, and after all the Russian fought against the Ottoman Empire in the war and protected the Armenians after it finished. I owe them something. But Bernard had no loyalty. Along comes a husky American Afrikaner and Bernard jumps into his bed as soon as say whistle. Yes, I'm pleased I told the Americans about Bernard and, what's more, I have no regrets about them both being dead. Had I known that Bernard's Russian was the same Fyodor Nazarov Razin I ran into when he was pretending to be a Finnish war correspondent, then maybe things might have been different had it not been his bullet that slammed into my leg at

Al Hasakeh. Yes, I knew it was he who shot me. And I knew from that day that I would have to kill him.

'I made up the story I told to the English because I wanted to see where the Russian would lead me and where the English would abandon me. The Russian told me that he could have killed me either inside the bazaar or outside in the streets of Al Hasakeh, but didn't feel like it. Shot me as a warning, he said. But I think it was because I fell over just as he fired. He'd said he could have let the suicide bomber deliver the bomb and blow me to kingdom come that day in Khost, but he added he didn't want to—*it was a bad vibes day*. Said he might kill me later, the arrogant fool. It was always, *later, little Rosco*, with him. But later never arrives for fools. He had served his usefulness to me by the time I killed him. I knew what he wanted, and once you know what a fool wants you can string him along until you've had enough fun. He knew I had a friend in America who was a candidate to become President and he knew I had a journalist friend whose husband supported that American. He also knew I had heard of a secret file named Gladio B.

'I hadn't been told by London to follow a man named Karabakh when I arrived in Syria. The name I had was Abel Hassad. I substituted the name of Karabakh to see who out of the two British Josephs I saw knew the significance of the word. The first Joseph, the English queer, did not take much to entice and once I had him I simply dangled sex in his face to get the phone I wanted and everything else he could provide. He was easy, but Elijah was not. I could tell he knew the name of Karabakh. The second Joseph was not a man to turn. That too was obvious. With him there was no way I was going to leave England peaceably. He was one of those who cuts open the toothpaste tube to scrape it all out.

'Fydo, the Russian, came as fast as the car he had would go when I phoned him. He was tripping over his waggling tongue on the way to where I knew a photographer lived and I needed to buy time. Tell me this, tell me that, tell me it all, little Rosco, and I'll put you in the first-class seat next to me on the plane to Canada. Why would I want to go to freezing Canada? Why would I want to go with a Russian bear like him? That was just another story for a pair of Josephs to believe and an Elijah to know better. No, I wanted the warmth found in revenge. The new era for Assyrians and Armenians, they would be the receivers of the world my friendship with the watchers would build.'

* * *

Over the years of the association Henry enjoyed with his Lebanese, American born and New York based war correspondent, the pictures she planted in Henry's mind were the ones he used as his cornerstone of his own Solomon's Temple to the Rosicrucian fraternity. The concentration she evolved inside Henry's psyche towards the cruelty of the Ottoman Empire was swayed by her references to newspaper reports of the English fight against the oppressor whilst the Americans sat in their consulates in Turkey looking on and complaining of the slaughter of one and half million Armenian Christians but lifting not one finger to alter the course of history. Worse was to follow in her rhetoric. Some ambassadorial Germans who watched the atrocities made notes to use when butchering Jews in a similar, barbarous way twenty odd years on. Surely someone had to pay? he asked of the wise and influentially placed newswoman who responded with her interpretation of the meaning to the Masonic word Vitriol—

Look within yourself to find the truth my little Rosicrucian.

He peered deep inside, inviting the Unitarian side of his ancient Druze faith to take control of his earthly soul, turning inwards to construct his conviction towards the persecuted Assyrians and fellow Armenians not recognised by other countries.

Henry Mayler may have found the temporal home for the purpose to his life from the tools and drawings his journalist mentor provided to solve the puzzle that racked his brain and ate at his soul, but they came with a heavy price. Her husband supported a rival to the incumbent President of the country he hated; however her husband was a wanted man by a mad dictator of another country. But, said our worldwide journalist, if Henry Mayler was to align with her husband, it would be his money that built the bricks to the visionary Elysium field that Henry dreamt of for his displaced Assyrians. Before he could deliver the final part required for an invasion and death to the pretender's enemy, Mayler's teachings told him he needed a Russian out of the way.

* * *

Tucker Stoneman was the man with access to the Panamanian bank accounts waiting to oust the incumbent and sit behind the White House desk, unfolding the pages of Gladio B as did so. The opening page of Tucker's version was entitled Iraq, and there Henry would find the oil on which the green pastures of Nagorno-Karabakh would be founded.

* * *

Henry caught a flight to Istanbul then one to Erbil. From there he was escorted to the Iraqi Kurdish village of Sharanish, close to the border of south-eastern Turkey.
"I will remain here in the Church of The East until they all come to celebrate with me as I receive the truth of the thirty-third degree next month on the third day when all the numbers fall into place."

The Second Third
Fraser Ughert's Story

"Two meetings in New York were the turning point for Henry Mayler. I'm going to start at the second one. The one at the Four Seasons Hotel in New York on the Saturday following Razin and Mayler's exchange of words in Kabul. This was where he met up again with Tucker Stoneman, but met the Russian oligarch Bohdan Dimitriyevich Valescov for the first time. It was from them he received the assurances he wanted for the formation of his version of paradise, his Nagorno-Karabakh. That idea had been planted in his mind ever since he worked on a journalistic assignment as the cameraman to Judith Simonin, a native New Yorker with an Egyptian background who was married to an ambitious Lebanese Assyrian before any of them had a real significance on the world we live in.

"For reasons unclear to me Aaron Simonin, Judith's husband, denounced Saddam Hussein when he return to Iraq in 1963 after a failed assassination attempt on the previous leader of the country. That leader's death prompted Saddam to return whereupon he was arrested because of Simonin's testament. Despite his imprisonment Saddam's stay in prison led to his subsequent rise in fortune and position, but when he emerged he had not forgotten whose indictment had put him behind bars.

"Judith Simonin's effect on Henry was immense. They worked together on six projects until his last meeting with her on the same weekend as he'd met Valescov and Stoneman. Her husband, Aaron, was present at both meetings. It was he who brokered the deal for the stolen Russian munitions between the Shariat Jamaat group, the militant followers of Zep Tepi in Egypt, and with the Hizbul Mujahideen in Afghanistan. It was through his wife's influence within the journalistic world that rumours of Iraqi weapons of mass destruction first started to circulate in the year 2001, following on closely from the whispers she generated about the nuclear ambitions of the Saddam Hussein regime.

"Under the combined influence of the three men Henry Mayler met in New York that fateful weekend, the plan to decimate what we currently know as this world was unrolled, but remember these were only three of the Circle of Eight I've mentioned. Razin referred to twenty names and they too all played a role.

"Do you recall the name the House of Cilicia; the place that Suzanna paid a visit to before she died? That house where she shot Moshe Gabbai dead belongs to one of Razin's outer circle of twenty. It's far from important that we know his name, that is retrievable anytime we need it, what is of importance is the name he chose for the estate. You, or anyone else for that matter, may think Cilicia to be a woman's name, it would make a beautiful one if it was, but in this case it's not. It was an area in southeastern Turkey that was once ruled by the Kings of Egypt and before them it formed part of the Assyrian Kingdom. It would not have much connection to Henry if it wasn't for the fact that it also formed part of what became the Armenian Empire.

"Henry's plans intertwine with those of the Circle of Eight; his to start a war to rebuild his lost empire, theirs to build an even bigger empire. Mayler intends to use the munitions on Tiran Island and those in the north-east of Afghanistan to amount to his declaration. You know of the targets, Patricks. The problem you have is when to disclose them and how much of what you and I know to disclose. The clue will come from Lebanon. Yes, as we both know, Henry's target will be American, but sometime before an American-led coalition attacks Iraq, Lebanon and Syria will sign an agreement to formally recognise the Assyrians as an ethnic race deserving of a home. The endorsed home they will advocate will be based on the anachronistic region of Cilicia and, of course, Turkey will never agree to such demands.

"Any alliance that acknowledges Assyrians as an ethnic group will antagonise Turkey so much so that a war will be the inevitable result. Russia has recently ratified and signed a defence treaty with both Lebanon and Syria. If either of the two nations are attacked by Turkish forces then Russia will be required to come to its aid. If that aid amounts to the death of Turkish troops, or destruction of its lands or equipment then it will instigate its own defence treaty with NATO and call on its support. As you can see if the plan that the three devised in New York is made manifest, then we have the start of the meltdown process the second Gladio B file predicted."

The Third And Final Part Of Chapter Thirty-Three
Patrick's Explanation

I had the restricted counselling that only the Chairman of the Joint Intelligence Committee was privy to. I also had the information that dammed Geoffrey Harwood to a life of degradation and contempt. Both those pieces of seemingly unconnected knowledge were all I had to save parts of civilisation from a calamitous event of huge proportions, but in consequence, allow a smaller one to take place. The American Fifth Fleet were due to sail through the Suez Canal in the early morning hours of the third day of January 2003. The first ships would be clearing the Island of Tiran around midday on that date. The company of American Rangers in Kamdeish, Afghanistan, were unaware of the threat of the phosphorous barrage that awaited them and would still be ensconced in their camp at the same time.

The anthrax and the phosphorous ammunition posed a problem, but not one that was unsolvable, whereas Henry Mayler had too much data sensitive material on too many important people to be allowed to remain alive. There was also the matter regarding the weapons of mass destruction that the US incumbent along with the Prime Minister of this country believed to be in Iraq. I could allow them to think that the anthrax and phosphorous were all part of a sinister plan of Saddam's, or wipe the board clean and tell of Mayler's mysterious Rosicrucians.

Mysticism and the reality of the political pursuit of a holy grail are not a mixture that would fuse together amicably. To apologise for the mistaken belief that an autocrat wished to destroy all that he did not own, could not be considered and blamed on a fanciful Circle of Eight of which there was little proof. In times of peace governments required excuses to invade, and anthrax and phosphorous shells provided those excuses.

* * *

To get close to wherever Mayler may be I needed Geoffrey Harwood's cooperation as he was the only man I knew who might have that information. I feared that I would have to prise it from him. As regards the remaining members of Fraser's Circle of Eight, I judged that could wait until more pressing worries had been sealed in a box and buried somewhere safe. I knew I was gambling, but the whereabouts of Henry Mayler took precedence over all things until that American fleet neared Port Said and the mouth of the Canal.

I finalised the arrangements to visit Beaulieu that I'd discussed with Hannah on the Thursday before Christmas. As we were preparing to leave I received the standard notification from the Foreign Office that would arrive on my desk whenever senior ministers of state of foreign counties met one another. This message told of the Lebanese Foreign Minister announcing that a meeting was to take place in Damascus on the third day of January next year with his Syrian opposite number. Pieces of the jigsaw were falling into place. I was trying to think of ways to make them fall as softly as possible. Neither Jimmy nor Frank were scheduled to return to their duties until New Year's Day but I knew that as both were single the boredom of freedom was probably wearing thin by now so I gave it a try in recalling them. Both agreed! In the purgatorial state I was in I didn't know whether to conduct a carol service on the drive to see Geoffrey Harwood or to weep over the bodies that lay in the path of a speeding juggernaut.

Geoffrey had been told of Henry Mayler's resurrection and of Razin's demise. I had used that as an opportunity to lever more information from him. I had sent prepared questions to put by those at Beaulieu asking of Bohdan Dimitriyevich Valescov's son's death, Liam Catlin's coded name being Antelope and Fyodor Nazarov Razin's *get me out of here* card. All were met with full cooperation and a confession of his participation. I had offered incentives for that information but only if he was also to collaborate with me whenever we were to meet. That moment was drawing ever more close as the unexacting journey passed quickly under clear skies and a low sun. Harwood was fully dressed and expecting me.

"I wish I could say you're looking well, Geoffrey, but sadly I can't as you don't. You look decidedly out of sorts and missing a good old Christmas roast with a few glasses of brandy to wash it down. All things considered I've had a great time and I know you've had a lousy one. I believe you've been told of a possible present in the post that may change your future. Let's see it can be delivered.

"I have nothing but praise for your performance in the confessional, and I'm hoping for all our sakes we can look forward to concluding our business today, thereby starting the New Year afresh. I have the power to grant you freedom from prosecution and the willingness to resettle you in Australia with all pension rights if you tell me where Henry Mayler can be found. If, at the back of your mind, you hold some far-off fantasy of rekindling your affection for Mayler when in a new place of freedom then, yes, that may be a possibility, but only if we can tell Henry of your new address, Geoffrey. You can see that, can't you? Another thing to bear in mind is that Henry has made some powerful enemies. It will be in his, and your, best interests if we find him first. Do you agree?"

"What I think is not important, West. The only thing that is important to me is getting out of here. The chances of you allowing me to see Henry Mayler again are zero even if he did live, and you and I both know that may be impossible to achieve. Henry has sort of dropped me in it, hasn't he. He hasn't thought of my well-being in the least. Why should I consider his? My one consideration is how can I be sure you will honour your word regarding my avoidance of prosecution? But don't trouble yourself, dear boy, in answering. I know there is no guarantee you can give me. I'm going to take your word, West, because funnily enough I believe you to be an honourable person.

"It's my belief that Henry is at a place called Sharanish, an Assyrian village located close to the borders of south-eastern Turkey, in Iraq Kurdistan. Henry told me of a religious connection he'd found there to the Armenian Kingdom of Cilicia. He spoke often of it when we shared moments on the phone together. Another thing he mentioned was of a straight friendship he has with a Lebanese Assyrian billionaire who has promised Henry astronomical amounts of money to rebuild the village and contribute to Henry's ultimate aim of a place for what he calls his people. I'll add this for what it's worth, and then leave it there, Patrick. Henry expressed serious worries about a genocide of Assyrian Christians by the Iraqis after any invasion by the US. I doubt there's anything that can be done about it but it eases my conscience now I've told you and made you aware."

"Two final questions before I go and confirm your story, Geoffrey. How did you have the telephone you gave Henry Mayler configured into NSA signal trafficking?"

"Knowledge is not only confined to what you know, dear boy. It's where to go to find the answers to what you don't know that's important. I had those around me who could do such things."

"And why did you include Razin's 'Help Me Escape' code in the signal that bounced from Erbil about Arif Belmokhtar's death?"

"Yes, that was an overplayed hand of mine, wasn't it? I haven't a real answer on that one other than I wanted to prove how important I was in knowing things above my pay grade, old boy!"

Needless to say, Geoffrey never made it to Australia, nor did he expect to, but part of me admired the way he accepted his end; perhaps he even welcomed it.

* * *

In the early hours of the morning of December 30th, three boats containing twelve members of 6th Marine Corps, Special Boat Squadron, landed on the Island of Tiran, took control after a short fire-fight capturing the whole garrison and then decommissioned the American manufactured howitzers. The anthrax shells were loaded into the naval vessels the terrorists had arrived in and sailed off towards Port Tawfiq, Egypt where I had a team of expert scientists from QinetiQ at Fort Halstead waiting to disarm the biological weapons. The occupying garrison was left unarmed on the island for the Saudi military, who I'd notified after the raid, to deal with.

At precisely the same time as the successful raid on Tiran, three teams from B Squadron, 21st Artist Regiment, Special Air Service, took over the site at Paprok and dealt with the camp peaceably, decommissioning the M114, 155mm artillery pieces in a similar fashion as their colleagues on Tiran had done. Once again this mission was concluded without casualties on either side. The banned artillery ammunition was loaded onto an American helicopter and flown to Kabul.

* * *

By mid-afternoon that day Great Britain's position as number one in the espionage charts had been underlined by every nation who in any way had been put in danger several times over. Our diplomatic standing ratcheted-up tenfold, with the telephone lines at the Foreign and Commonwealth Office in danger of exploding from the workload. I was flown to a secret location in Italy where the Prime Minister was spending his Christmas, to be present when he spoke with President Bush on the telephone. The conversation ranged from complimentary to one of passive acceptance of the inevitable. Iraq was still to be invaded. President Bush allowed Group the use of a US satellite to pinpoint Henry Mayler's precise location. In the cinema room of the Italian multi-millionaire's home the PM and I watched images relayed from the monitors in the Hub of a hellfire missile fired from a US drone that killed Henry Mayler as he walked towards the picturesque waterfall at Sharanish. He was alone when he died.

I was not alone when my future was discussed. It was midday on New Year's Eve. Hannah and I had been invited to the home of the American Ambassador in Regent's Park that evening to see in the New Year with a grateful ally, as he'd put it. I could wait no longer. One thing I try hard not to advertise is my desire for power. In order to achieve that prize I have come to learn that the investigation into those that become close to me should be undertaken at an early date and not a late one. I had learned of Hannah's secret three days after accepting the Directorship at Group. Her ancestry went back centuries to an old European dynasty called the House of Hesse. The family's history could be easily traced back as far as 1264, but it was a more recent date that had impacted on my life. I had discovered that all three of Hannah's godparents were related in one way or another to the famous, and previously mentioned, Rothschild family. She and her two siblings had wanted a life where they controlled its outcome, not one lived within the shadow of their godparents' reputable name. There was no animosity towards anyone, just a simple wish to manage their own destiny.

As I have plainly said before in this narrative, I did not consider the fate of the commercial world as my direct responsibility. I have seen governments come and go and do nothing other than line their own pockets with influence or shower its potential on their supporters. None have been different. Why would any future government decide to tackle those that supply their financial needs? I was not about to start a fight I could not win, however if I was close to the centre of the decision-making machinery then maybe, just perhaps, I could steer it in a way to benefit this country.

* * *

"I have confirmation back from Samuel Rothschild that he will organise the meeting you've asked for, Patrick. What is it you propose to do?" she asked on returning to the bed in which we lay together sharing a bottle of champagne. Fraser had asked the same thing when I told him of my intentions on the telephone after I'd told him of my wish to involve Samuel Rothschild.

"I will not be joining any fraternity to do with Freemasonry, not because I believe them to be evil in any way, because I don't believe that at all. It's just because I hate all that numerical rubbish and the idea of not being in charge of it. I'm looking everywhere now for the number 3. It's ridiculous. What I do want to do is stop this Tucker Stoneman achieving the aims of Gladio B, along with whatever the ambitions of Bohdan Dimitriyevich

Valescov are. I can't prevent this coming war in Iraq or any others likely to arise as an outcome of it. But I can try to stop a war between Turkey and Lebanon and Syria.

"I want to meet with the head of the Rothschild family along with Aaron Simonin. The three of us can discuss how we could create a safe haven for displaced Armenians and Assyrians by utilising the assets that will be freed up when Iraq is defeated. I will raise the levels of awareness within the United Nations and the World Health Council of the practices of SanMonto and I will give their representatives the responsibilities of finding a resolution. On a world stage that is all I can do, but I change things on a personal front."

That is how I ended my declaration of intent to Fraser Ughert, however I went a stage further in my explanation to Hannah when I joined her in a relaxing bath.

On the first day of 2003 Jimmy, with Frank sitting beside him, drove Hannah and me to the Ugherts' home in welcoming sunlit Chearsley, where I announced my engagement to Hannah Sofia Rachel Landgft. We married in June 2004 at St Margaret's Church, next to Westminster Abbey, within walking distance of our apartments at the Foreign and Commonwealth building in Whitehall. In the pews on my side of the church sat Molly with Fraser Ughert and a few faces from the intelligence community who happened to be in town. On Hannah's side was her aunt from Bermondsey and her sister and brother with his family. We had both wanted a quiet affair with little fuss and even less trappings of grandeur. Despite our request and the small circle of friends we had informed, we were presented with the keys to a small mansion in Sussex as a gift from an anonymous benefactor. The only pointer to whoever that was were the words engraved on the box that contained the keys; From the Home of Cilicia.

***

Some three years after our marriage I received an invitation from Fraser to meet with him and a friend who he declined to name at that stage, only telling me that I may have something in common with him. He said it was my interest in the analytical sciences that might be *piqued,* as he put it. I was intrigued. We met at my London Club; Brooks's in St James's Street.

Fraser's guest was aged around sixty, tallish, grey thinning hair, with nothing aesthetically remarkable about him at all. His English was impeccable, but his accent was unmistakably Russian and his sense of dress both fashionable and expensive. Over drinks and a light lunch, he told a story of how of the head of a department reading American signals, inside Moscow Centre, had deciphered some NSA reports of what the Americans called Data Mining. This internal surveillance allowed Washington to spy on millions of emails, web histories, phone records and other personal data directly from telephone companies and internet firms around the world. Apparently, the aim behind the *Data Mining* was to create a programme whereby global hacking of international countries, both friendly or not, was both feasible and operational. He told me how the same person was willing to supply the intelligence community of this country with the ability to hack into the mobile phones of several international leaders. In exchange for the knowledge he asked for one thing; that the department head who discovered all this be allowed to live in England. As travel between Russia and the outside world was seldom restricted, I asked why he could not make the move himself. He was not a he!

"She is under the influence of a highly placed political leader in the Russian Government who will never allow her to leave the country. She is aware of too much. No, she must be helped to escape." He offered photographs of her. Work addresses and those of her home, as well as written details of her life that he said were authentic and true.

"I am Nikita Sergeyovitch Kudashov, her grandfather. I have been a friend of Fraser's for years," he told me before adding her name.

"She is known as Cilicia Kudashov. Our surname derives from the Armenian word of kudo, meaning home," he innocently added as I racked my brain trying to recall that surname and his face from an earlier time. But I couldn't. I simply replicated Fraser's phlegmatic smile and wondered where this adventure would take me.

The End

About the Author

Danny Kemp, ex-London police officer, mini-cab business owner, pub tenant and licensed London taxi driver, never planned to be a writer, but after his first novel —The Desolate Garden — was under a paid option to become a $30 million film for five years until distribution became an insurmountable problem for the production company what else could he do?

Nowadays he is a prolific storyteller, and although it's true to say that he mainly concentrates on what he knows most about; murders laced by the intrigue involving spies, his diverse experience of life shows in the short stories he compiles both for adults and children.

He is the recipient of rave reviews from a prestigious Manhattan publication, been described as —the new Graham Green — by a managerial employee of Waterstones Books, for whom he did a countrywide tour of signing events, and he has appeared on 'live' nationwide television.

http://www-thedesolategarden-com.co.uk/

Lightning Source UK Ltd.
Milton Keynes UK
UKHW021557191120
373696UK00004B/527

9 781715 802714